Vivian Conroy is a multi
contracted titles. Away
crafting and spending too
can connect with her under @VivWrites.

Also by Vivian Conroy

Miss Ashford Investigates Mysteries

Mystery in Provence

Cornish Castle Mysteries

Rubies in the Roses

Death Plays a Part

Country Gift Shop Mysteries

Written into the Grave

Grand Prize: Murder!

Dead to Begin With

Lady Alkmene Callender Mysteries

Fatal Masquerade

Deadly Treasures

Diamonds of Death

A Proposal to Die For

Merriweather and Royston Mysteries

Death Comes to Dartmoor

The Butterfly Conspiracy

Murder Will Follow Mysteries

An Exhibition of Murder

Under the Guise of Death

Honeymoon With Death

A Testament to Murder

LAST SEEN IN SANTORINI

Miss Ashford Investigates

VIVIAN CONROY

One More Chapter
a division of HarperCollins*Publishers*
1 London Bridge Street
London SE1 9GF
www.harpercollins.co.uk
HarperCollins*Publishers*
Macken House, 39/40 Mayor Street Upper,
Dublin 1, D01 C9W8

This paperback edition 2022
1
First published in Great Britain in ebook format
by HarperCollins*Publishers* 2023
Copyright © Vivian Conroy 2023
Vivian Conroy asserts the moral right to be identified
as the author of this work

A catalogue record of this book is available from the British Library

ISBN: 978-0-00-854927-5

Printed and bound in the UK using 100% Renewable Electricity
by CPI Group (UK) Ltd

Chapter One

Miss Atalanta Ashford couldn't quite believe she was casting her eye across the *laguna* of Venice. The water moved in countless shades of blue and green and the sun made everything sparkle: the bright colours of the boats that took tourists across to Murano, the famous glass island; the spires of Venice's many churches in the distance and closer to her, the lemons in twined baskets on the dock waiting to be transported.

There was an air of expectancy, with everyone bustling to do some task, make the best use of this beautiful day. New arrivals discussed where to go first: to a workshop or the museum. A man with a hat askew on his rich dark curls carried a large canvas that he wanted to place in the best possible spot to paint the sights. And local women offered flowers and freshly baked sweet treats. From where she stood, Atalanta could smell the butter and sugar worked into them. It seemed as if she was the only one standing still, not pushing to the nearby café to occupy the table with the best *laguna* view, or going to explore Murano's first-rate glassware created by true artists with the blowpipe. She was like a statue in the midst of a crowd rushing to and fro, caught in the moment, unable to move away from a sense of disbelief that this could actually be her life now.

It was so hard to grasp that only a few weeks ago her daily routine had consisted of giving lessons to pupils at an exclusive Swiss boarding school. A strict schedule of teaching French and music, having meals and correcting essays and tests, with barely half an hour to herself to take a little walk down into the picturesque village with its wooden houses and decorated balconies, or further up the mountain to the ruins of the old burg overlooking the lush valley where the river wound its way between the snow-capped mountains.

It had been her favourite leisure-time activity: to walk and fantasize that she was elsewhere, in some remote, possibly exotic destination, seeing the wonders of the world. She knew the sights only from books and postcards her students sent her during summer holidays. But they had come alive in her imagination: the Parthenon rising above her in white marble columns or the sleepy sunlit villages of the Italian countryside amongst vineyards and olive groves. She had pretended to hear other languages and bitten into her simple bread-and-cheese sandwich lunch as if it were calzone. But with all the mental power in the world, she had never been able to guess that her dreams were about to come true, far beyond what she had imagined.

All because of her dear grandfather.

His death had left her with a fortune, houses in various places, cars and stocks, more money than she could ever spend. And a rare vocation: to follow in his footsteps and do his life's work: sleuth discreetly in the highest circles. Her very first case had taken her to a lush estate in the glorious lavender fields of Provence where a company of rich and famous people had gathered for the wedding of the Comte de Surmonne. The sights had been breath-taking – the whitewashed manor house with sleek turrets, the rich gardens full of roses, dahlias and an amazing shell grotto – but she had not been able to fully enjoy them with the strain of unravelling clues and facing a cunning killer who stopped at nothing to keep their secret safe. So, after a successful conclusion of the case, she had decided it was time for a little holiday. Some days spent far away from crime and the complicated thought process that came with assessing if perfectly normal-looking people might be cold-blooded murderers.

With her unlimited funds Atalanta could go wherever her heart desired, and she had retrieved her box of cut-out magazine articles and postcards that students had sent her. Her box of places she had wanted to go to, long before she had come into money. The box of her hopes and dreams that had carried her through the most difficult times after her father had died and she had been all alone in the world, with a load of debts on her shoulders. Now that everything was so much better, that box was still like an old friend and opening it made her heart flutter.

She had closed her eyes and rummaged through it and pulled out a postcard. She had waited a few moments, fingering the card, and then opened her eyes to see where she was travelling to for her holiday.

Venice.

The mere name on the card, printed in a dark yellow almost like gold, had taken her breath away. It had to be a magical city with canals instead of streets, with countless elegant bridges across the ever-present water, with so much romantic history attached. A city of gondolas, delicious food, a language that sounded like poetry and memories to be made.

She had asked her butler Renard to book her passage and a hotel. Of course he had managed to get her a room in one of the most illustrious hotels which had received famous writers and artists from all over the world. Their photographs hung on the walls of the high lobby with its stuccoed ceiling full of lions, the iconic animal ever present in the floating city.

The very efficient and resourceful Renard was a treasure with global contacts that came in very useful when she was investigating. But the trip to Venice would be about pleasure only, about spending time in a beautiful place, far away from intrigue and murder.

Ah yes. With a sigh of satisfaction Atalanta turned her back on the dazzling *laguna* view and started to walk, slowly, savouring every step, every sight around her. She inhaled the scents of a hot summer day deep into her lungs: citrus fruit, sun-drenched cobbles, flowery perfumes…

Her gaze brushed past ladies in colourful dresses and large sunhats, one with a small, white lapdog on her arm that barked ferociously at everyone in sight. The buildings had fronts full of white stone arches and pillars. At first glance they were all alike but when one looked closer, there were details on all of them: some round like beads, others carved like flowers.

On the corner of a tall apricot-coloured house a man stood in a light suit. A Panama hat was pulled over his eyes, hiding his face. But for a moment, when she caught sight of him, her breathing stopped and she involuntarily started forward.

Raoul!

Raoul Lemont, the race car driver she had met on Bellevue in Provence, during her first case. He had been a guest at the wedding of Eugénie Frontenac and the Comte de Surmonne, the grand feast where Atalanta had discreetly conducted her investigation into the question whether the Comte had murdered his first wife, Mathilde. Raoul had been an old friend of Mathilde and at one point even a suspect, to her mind. But she had realized later she had never wanted him to be a suspect because...

Stop it. She shook her head with an impatient movement. That man wasn't Raoul. He only bore a superficial likeness to him. She had to stop thinking about him. He was far away from here, preparing for some race.

As a driver of fast sports cars in those daring races that had gained popularity all across Europe, he risked his life on a daily basis, something Atalanta couldn't understand or condone. In general, Raoul was impulsive, irreverent, opinionated and proud. Character traits that made him her polar opposite. Atalanta liked to look before she leaped and assess a matter from several sides before coming to a conclusion. Raoul had even blamed her for being too rational and not allowing herself to feel. But feelings were deceptive and led one astray. It was much better to look at the world with a clear analytical mind and judge facts without allowing emotion to overshadow everything.

She smiled at her own inner dialogue with Raoul, as if he was indeed here by her side, and she needed to defend herself, and her opinions, against him. But he was leading his life full of adventure and risk, and she was on Murano enjoying a well-earned holiday.

And if she didn't want to think of murder, she shouldn't

think of Raoul as well, as he had been so closely tied to her case and its dangerous resolution. She had to fully focus on the enchanting views and living the dream of actually walking here, instead of merely imagining it and having to return to her duties at the school. She did miss her students, their eagerness when they learned French by listening to *chansons*, their sulks when there was a test forthcoming. Moments where they confided in her and she felt more like an older sister to them than a teacher. But the strict director had made sure she could never get close to any of them. For the better, perhaps, but it had been a lonely life.

"Buy flowers?" An old woman touched her arm and held out a large twined basket holding several single roses in bright colours: red, pink, yellow. Their stems had been wrapped with cloth and a pin was attached so the flower could be worn like a brooch.

Atalanta's gaze travelled the flowers, admiring the silky smoothness of the petals. They had been grown with loving care. But she shook her head at the woman and walked on. It felt odd buying a rose for herself. It was something adoring fiancés or husbands should do. There were plenty of couples around among the tourists, and many more coming later today. The old woman wouldn't have trouble finding takers for her floral offerings.

I'm here for glass. Atalanta halted at a table bending under the weight of vases, vessels and jugs. The sun conjured rainbows in the facets and made the pieces look even more magnificent than they were because of the craftsmanship put into them, skills handed down the generations for as long as Murano had existed. She wanted to buy something, but she had to think carefully about what to get. She'd have to take it home with her and it shouldn't get broken on the journey.

Perhaps a large solid piece is better than those smaller delicate champagne glasses?

But the four-piece set did look lovely, and she could see herself drinking from such a glass at home and remembering this beautiful sun-soaked day and tasting the unlimited freedom her grandfather's inheritance had brought her.

She took several items into her hands, turned them over, ran her finger round the perfectly smooth rim. The seller behind the table tried to explain how good it was in broken English, falling back on Italian every third word. Atalanta tried to follow along as best she could. The exclusive school where she had worked had often housed Italian girls from elite families and she knew a fair bit of the language. But it was special to hear it now on soil where it had been spoken for many centuries. At times she had to pinch herself to make sure she wasn't dreaming.

She said she'd be back later and wanted to look around more first. He kept shouting after her how good his wares were while she walked to the next table and the next seller eager to impress upon her that *he* sold the best wares of the entire island.

The tourists that had been on the boat with her had filed out and were standing at various stalls or ducking through low doors into the buildings to see more inside. It had to be deliciously cool in there, away from the summer sun that burned down mercilessly on everything around. Atalanta felt sweat drip across her neck and slip down under her light dress. On the boat she had already put her white lace gloves in her purse. They might be elegant, and a lady should aspire to dress her best on any occasion, but under the Mediterranean sun they were a burden sooner. Perhaps she should have sat down for a cool drink? There was no rush to buy anything right away. She could take the entire day to explore, returning to Venice on the last boat.

Again she caught a glimpse of the man in the light suit with the Panama hat. He seemed to be alone. Perhaps that wasn't odd, as she herself was here without a companion. But most people had come either as couples or with friends, and his lone figure drew her attention. He wasn't haggling to get a good deal on glass or admiring the architecture. It felt almost as if…

He was watching her?

A cold shiver crept across her spine. Her grandfather had made it clear when he had explained his work to her in a letter written before his death that it was not without risks. That, in the pursuit of justice, one might also make enemies.

And Renard had told her on several occasions to be wary of everyone, not to take things at face value, not to trust even the stories of her own clients. Perhaps all this mention of having to be careful and expect dangers lurking had made her a touch overcautious?

Even paranoid?

She was on holiday here, there was really nothing to fear.

Still, a sense of unease accompanied her as she continued her search for the perfect glass souvenir, and she caught herself looking over her shoulder at various occasions. The man in the light suit was nowhere to be seen. Happy voices rang out around her, laughter and the tinkle of glass exchanging hands. One couple had bought a man-sized mirror and watched as the seller put it in a crate filled with straw for safe transportation.

Three boys balanced on the stone railing of a bridge,

singing an aria from *The Merchant of Venice* at tourists in a gondola which approached the bridge. The gondolier shouted abuse at them and warnings that they might fall and land on his boat. Some of the tourists laughed at the antics but a lady in a pink dress ducked and covered her head as if to ward off a boy avalanche.

The three suddenly jumped down the railing and fled when a man in a dark suit pursued them for a few yards, then leaned into the wall of a blue house, gasping for breath and pulling out his handkerchief to wipe the sweat off his brow. A disgruntled father? A private teacher landed with the task of guarding these unruly charges on an outing?

Atalanta smiled to herself. Those were the kind of innocent deductions she had to focus on. Why ruin a beautiful day with worries about her safety?

She fell into a conversation with an English lady who explained to her that she had visited Murano every summer when her husband had still been alive, and this was her first time here without him. "It's like he's still here," she confided. "I can hear his voice and I can see him walk beside me. My children were afraid the trip here would make me sad, but it only makes me happy. We've spent so many wonderful years here which I will cherish forever."

"I'm glad for you." Atalanta adjusted her sun hat. From the corner of her eye she caught sight of a woman in black with a veil over her face. Her dark clothes stood out among the colourfully dressed tourists and Atalanta wondered if she was a local widow. But her dress looked too expensive and the veil was attached to an elegant little hat that could have come straight from a Parisian boutique. Who was she, what was she doing here?

Questions you will most likely never get an answer to, she chided herself.

"There's a special place here," the English woman by her side explained, "a little courtyard down that street. You can freely enter it, no one will stop you. You can walk to a waist-high white fence on the other side of that courtyard and you have a lovely view of the water with Venice in the distance. My husband and I used to stand there for quite some time and admire it. There's always something new to see. It's a perfect day for it too, sunny and bright. We have also been here when it rained and it's not quite so cheery then." She touched Atalanta's arm a moment. "Enjoy your stay here, my dear."

Atalanta thanked her and walked down the street. The voices of the people died down behind her. It was much quieter here, without the bustle of sellers. Scents drifting from open windows suggested lunches were being prepared with fresh herbs and garlic. *Lots of garlic.*

Atalanta drew a relieved breath, realizing she wasn't really a person who enjoyed crowds. Suddenly, in the silence, she could hear herself think again.

She laughed softly and entered the courtyard the English lady had directed her to. It had uneven greyish cobbles that led to a white wooden fence on the other side.

An olive tree threw meagre shade, and from a wire cage against the wall small songbirds chirped at her, flying nervously from one perch to another. She leaned her hands on the fence. The wood had become warm in the sun and the cracked paint felt comfortingly real under her fingertips. Sometimes this new wealthy life was like an elaborate dream, carrying her from one day of wonder into the next, but always with the realization it had to end somehow. She wasn't truly rich, she wasn't really able to do anything she wanted. She would wake up in her small room at the school and then the stern housekeeper would be pounding on her door to tell her she was late for class.

A shadow fell over her. She noticed it in the last instant, caught in her thoughts and turned sharply, her hand up to push away whoever was so close to her.

She gasped, staring up into the deep brown eyes of the man she had thought about half an hour ago. "Raoul," she whispered, her eyes taking in the frown over his eyes, the lines around his mouth, the tightness in his lips. "I thought I saw you earlier, but … surely you wouldn't be here? What…?" She barely had breath to continue. Perhaps it was the fact that they had conquered evil together that made her heart race and her mouth go dry.

He said, "You shouldn't wander away from the crowd, Miss Ashford. It may not be safe."

That he called her Miss Ashford cleared her mind. She flushed at her own mistake, using his first name as if they were that familiar. They may have stopped a murderer together, but they had never become actual friends.

At least, she didn't think so.

Her doubts as to what their relationship amounted to annoyed her. She prided herself on her ability to work out difficult problems, but she couldn't qualify what it was that connected this infuriating man and herself. She forced a smile, gesturing around her. "I think it's perfectly safe here. I'm on holiday."

"I know." He kept looking at her, his eyes searching her expression as if he was trying to find something there. Had she changed that much? She had her hair done before she had left for Venice, thinking she needed to have a little polish for the grand hotel's revered rooms, but she had kept makeup to a minimum this morning, and while her dress was fashionable enough, her shoes were chosen to allow for comfortable wandering rather than elegance. He still had to be able to recognize the rather unconventional woman he had met at Bellevue.

His insistence in studying her face had to be connected with something else.

Suddenly it clicked into place. Him being here, seeking her out away from others. "Has something happened?" she asked. "Do you need my help?" She knew with a breath-taking intensity that she would do anything, travel anywhere, if Raoul asked her to. Perhaps he had a sister who was in trouble? She knew so little of his personal life. Only that he had a French father and a Spanish mother. Nothing about siblings, personal ties. There were so many blanks she wanted to fill in, to get to understand him better.

Raoul smiled, that slow smile she knew so well. The smile he used to keep people at a distance, because it was a little haughty and always made her feel like he was enjoying himself at her expense. Had she drawn a wrong conclusion? Or jumped at a bait he had consciously laid out for her?

"I don't need your help," he said in a low voice, "but you might need mine. You're being watched."

Chapter Two

"Watched?" Atalanta echoed. She had believed *he* was watching her, from under his Panama hat. But if it had not been him, then who?

And why?

"Hush, not so loud," Raoul urged, leaning closer to her. "Pretend you're looking at the view again."

Obediently, Atalanta turned and studied the boats crossing the water, but without really seeing much of the *laguna*'s glory. Her heart raced, and it echoed in her mind: *I was right, something was wrong here, I felt it, I sensed it. My instincts were right.*

Part of her was pleased that she could rely on her gut feeling – something that could prove invaluable in her new line of work – but at the same time she realized that this meant innocent time, away from sleuthing, might be hard to come by. Was it even possible to separate her work from her personal life? Had she now suddenly become a person of interest wherever she went? Like a movie star who couldn't get around without people pointing and whispering or wanting autographs?

Did she now have money and opportunity but no way of enjoying it because of the tasks that had come, inevitably, with it?

Raoul said, "I was in Paris and telephoned to invite you to dinner but your butler informed me you had left for Venice. He was kind enough to give me the address of your hotel. Venice has some of the best seafood, so I decided on a whim to come over for a few days and ask you on a little tour of the city if you felt like it. I wouldn't bore you with the Piazza San Marco but take you to lesser-known places that are just as beautiful, or even more so. A friend of mine lives in a doge's palace. You have to see all the rooms there, relive the grandeur of old. And I know all the best restaurants. You cannot leave Venice without having tried some of the local dishes. *Sarde in saor* and *risotto*."

Atalanta gripped the wooden fence again. A tour of Venice, in a gondola with Raoul beside her, listening to him as he spoke Italian with the gondolier. The words would sound even more poetic coming from him. Perhaps because he loved this country so much?

The experience would be utterly … romantic?

She almost laughed at the word choice. Knowing Raoul's ideas about relationships, she could deduce that romance was the last thing on his mind and he probably felt it was his duty to show her around the country that was almost like a motherland to him because he had taken part in so many races here. He had told her earlier she could always reach him by writing to the Hotel Benvenuto in Rome.

Raoul continued, "This morning on my way to surprise you I saw you leave the hotel and before I could go across and address you, I saw a woman following you. She was dressed in black, wearing a veil."

Atalanta narrowed her eyes. The description sounded familiar. "A woman in black with a veil? She is on Murano now. I saw her just before I walked to this place."

"And she saw you go here." Raoul's tone was grim. "I followed you quickly to prevent her from coming after you and…" He fell silent.

"Do you think she wants to harm me?" The peace of this quiet courtyard was so at odds with the idea of someone following her with bad intentions. Which was exactly why this location could be perfect for an attack on someone. Lulled by the birdsong and rustle of the breeze in the branches of the olive tree, the potential victim would be totally unsuspecting.

Images whirled through her mind of a blade hidden under that black outfit and a quick stab in passing. No one would notice anything and by the time the alarm was raised, the culprit would be long gone, and her dead body would be carried away.

But wasn't that overly dramatic? Why would an unknown woman in black want to harm her? What point was there in injuring or even killing her? She had done no one any injustice.

No, but she had exposed a killer and ensured that person was imprisoned, awaiting trial and the death penalty. A life was forfeited because of her investigation. Could relatives be out for revenge? Was she a target now?

Raoul said, "Initially, I only wanted to show you Venice and ensure you had a better experience than the average tourist who follows the trodden path to all the advertised sites. But perhaps, having spotted this woman trailing you, I should offer you my assistance to keep you safe." It didn't sound like a suggestion, but more like a conclusion.

"I'm not certain you're seeing this in the correct light." Atalanta tried to sound strong. "You saw me leaving my hotel and a woman in black took the same route and is now also on this island. She may be another tourist wanting to buy glass souvenirs. We are far from the only two women here. Can't her presence be a coincidence?"

"Of course. But do you really want to find out the hard way?"

Atalanta drew breath slowly. What did she want? It wasn't like her to indulge in a dramatic fantasy that her life was in danger, but she also didn't intend to take unnecessary risks. She had only just started out in her new profession and intended to continue in good health.

She relaxed her hands on the fence and inquired practically, "What do you suggest?"

"I can accompany you for the rest of the day here on the island. Once you've finished shopping for glass" – it sounded ironic, as if he thought enough time had been spent on that already – "we go back together and I show you Venice and we have dinner. We can see if the same woman in black keeps following us or if she relents as soon as she realizes you're no longer alone and vulnerable."

The word 'vulnerable' stung. Yes, she was a woman on her own, but that was a fact of life. She couldn't change it and she couldn't depend on Raoul's presence all the time.

She asked softly, "How long are you going to accompany me?"

"How long?" he echoed, as if not understanding.

"Yes. A day? A week? Forever? If that woman is after something, she won't give up just because I have a companion for the day."

"Is that an invitation?" Raoul's voice held a hint of amusement.

"It's realism. You can't protect me against people with bad intentions." She took a deep breath, trying to imprint that reality on her mind. She had accepted her grandfather's vocation as her own and now had to deal with the consequences. "And we haven't even established that this woman does have something sinister in mind." She didn't want to accept so easily that she could never have time to herself and sightsee without looking over her shoulder. She wagered her grandfather hadn't let his life be ruined by a fear of vengeful enemies.

"Very well." Raoul stepped back.

Atalanta suddenly felt a coldness on her arms. Why had she turned him away so brusquely? Was she afraid of how she might feel, spending time in his company? That the relaxed atmosphere of sightseeing together would pull down her usual guard and make her more susceptible to his charms?

Was she, in fact, more afraid of Raoul's nearness than of the mysterious woman in black?

Raoul said in a whisper, "I'll act as if I'm saying goodbye and leaving, while you stay to browse. I will, however, be near to come to your aid if the woman does something. Be on your guard all the time." Out loud he said, "Then we'll see each other tomorrow. I look forward to it. Until then, goodbye." He made an ostentatious bow and walked away.

Atalanta thought wryly that this act wouldn't fool anyone who knew Raoul well, but the woman in black was probably a perfect stranger who would take him for a dandy who flirted with a lady and tried to win her by offering her a tour of the city, or a dinner, or whatever they might be meeting for the next day.

She raised a hand to her flushed face. She had to look totally happy and unaware of any threats to her safety. She forced a smile, gave the stunning *laguna* view one last loving glance and then left the small courtyard.

For the next hour Atalanta ambled past workshops where the craftsmen wielded their blowpipes, the tips red-hot orange from the heat of the furnaces as they shaped the fabled glass. At stalls bending down under the weight of souvenirs, she checked aventurine carafes, pier mirrors and chandeliers, haggled with sellers and eventually agreed to buy a set of six glasses that were to be wrapped and sent to her hotel by courier later that day. She felt relieved that her task of selecting a memorable keepsake was accomplished and at the same time oddly disappointed that nothing mysterious had happened. Had Raoul been wrong about someone following her?

Had he exaggerated the threat the elusive woman in black might pose to explain why she should accept his invitation to spend time together? Perhaps he had sensed her reluctance and believed he needed an extra inducement to get her to agree?

Why had she not played along and accepted his offer of

protection, regardless of whether there truly was any imminent danger or not?

She could have spent a delightful afternoon with him in an elegant gondola gliding through the countless canals and touring the doge's palace he had mentioned, then eating a dinner of fresh seafood in an intimate little restaurant. The memories of carefree moments with a friend would mean far more than the precious glassware she had now acquired.

Shaking her head about her bad judgement, Atalanta turned into a side street that led back to the dock. At least she thought it did, but walking down its uneven cobbles, she realized she was leaving the bustle of the glassblowers' workshops behind and entering a quieter area of private houses. Earthenware pots with flowers and herbs flanked the simple wooden front doors. Two small children who had been throwing pebbles to see whose would go further ran away at her approach, leaving the pebbles behind. A metal gate closed with a bang. A dog barked somewhere on the other side of the house.

As its sharp yaps died down, Atalanta caught the echo of a more subdued sound. Footfalls behind her.

Her mouth went dry and her hand closed into a fist. If only she carried something to defend herself with... Her eyes sought for a suitable object in the vicinity: a thick branch, a loose rock, but there was nothing there but the ridiculously small pebbles. Not even loose sand to gather and throw in an attacker's eyes.

You should have listened to Raoul.

The footfalls became louder as if the person behind her was closing in. Should she keep walking or turn around to see who it was? Perhaps it was an inhabitant about his business, something perfectly harmless.

She glanced over her shoulder. A tall figure, all in black…

She lengthened her stride. Where was Raoul? Was he still watching? Or had her disbelieving response driven him away, thinking she didn't need his help?

A wooden door stood open on her left hand. Inside was a dim space lit by candles. She caught a glimpse of gold-embroidered wall coverings and a saint's statue in a niche. On impulse she entered, hoping this was a church of some kind and there would be people praying.

Or a priest? Any form of company means protection.

But there was no one inside. The scent of candle wax was heavy in the air. The flickering flames lit the saint's marble features. Atalanta had no idea who this female figure represented.

Behind her something shuffled. She knew before she turned that it was the woman in black. Now standing close to her, Atalanta noticed the woman was her own height and build. Because of the veil she couldn't see any features or determine her age, but the woman exuded strength and agility. It was definitely not an old island widow.

"You've been following me all morning," Atalanta said, to take charge of the moment. "You might as well tell me right away why."

"I was waiting for the right moment to speak to you." The voice was low and whispery, almost out of breath. "I asked myself several times whether I should. When the man approached you, I was certain he would invite you to look at the island together and my chance would be gone. I hated myself for the relief I felt. The idea that I needn't act at all."

Atalanta tilted her head. The woman didn't seem hostile or intent on harming her. Instead, she sounded … uncertain and even afraid.

"How may I help you?" Atalanta asked.

"I know that you are the heiress of Clarence Ashford."

Atalanta drew breath sharply at the mention of her grandfather's name.

The woman said, "I can't explain how I knew him. It would require giving details about a time of my life I'd rather forget. But he did something for me that I can never repay him for. He saved everything I had, everything I was." She was silent a moment as if reflecting on that time. "He told me that should I ever need him again, I should contact him."

She laughed softly. "I was certain that would never be the case. I had learned my lesson. I would stay away from risk. And yet, here I am, asking you for help."

"What is wrong?" Atalanta asked.

The woman hesitated. "What I am about to tell you is what I believe, not what I know for a fact. It's based on my intuition. My instincts as a mother."

Atalanta waited. The cool in this room was pleasant, as was the quiet company of the saint's statue. Perhaps a mother as well?

The woman said, "I'm a member of an old Venetian family. We came to the city when it was first built and have always lived here. We traded and we travelled. We believed we owned the world." There was a hint of pride in her voice. "We built houses and burgs everywhere we went, along the Silk Road."

Atalanta felt a rush of excitement at the mention of that old trading route leading into the heart of China.

"There are old Venetian burgs on the Greek isle of

Santorini. Some of my distant family still live there. At the start of this summer" – her voice caught a moment – "my daughter Letitia travelled there to be a companion to an elderly lady. She was to read to her, fetch her things, walk with her. It was a comfortable arrangement for both parties, as the old woman wanted someone around and my daughter would have time to explore the island when the old lady slept or rested. She had always been a wild child wanting to see the world."

Atalanta said with a smile, "I was like that, growing up."

The woman barely seemed to hear. She continued slowly, "My daughter went to Santorini. I got a few letters. They sounded happy and full of plans. She had taken her camera and was taking pictures of beautiful places: the red and black beaches, the picturesque fishermen going about their business. She wanted to be a photographer. My husband was very much against it. He thinks women should marry and be mothers. But Titia was still so young. Only nineteen."

With a shock Atalanta realized that the woman was constantly referring to the girl in the past tense. Did that mean…?

The woman said, "Last week we got word that…" She swallowed hard. "That Titia died. She fell off some cliffs into the sea. She … suffered from vertigo, and we had told her before she went not to look through her camera whilst standing on cliff edges, as she would get dizzy and might fall. We had told her not to risk anything by…" Her voice broke.

Atalanta reached out and put a hand on her arm. "I'm so very sorry."

The woman continued, her voice strangled with tears, "I can't believe she's dead. I lie awake at night thinking it must all be some mistake. That she will come back home. She has to."

She sobbed, and tears leaked out from under her veil. Atalanta squeezed the woman's arm, knowing nothing she could say now would truly help.

The woman took a deep breath and pushed on, "I can't believe she's dead. But I also can't believe she had an accident. I think … she was murdered."

Chapter Three

"Murdered?" Atalanta repeated, perplexed. "Why would you think so?"

"Because of her last letter. She wrote that she would have news for us soon. Shocking news." The woman made a hand gesture. "I thought that she might have met some young man or someone who fired her desire to be a photographer. That she would startle her father and me by getting married or leaving for New York to work there for a newspaper, or something else silly girls do." She sniffed. "But now I'm certain she meant that she had discovered a dangerous secret and that someone killed her to keep it hidden. It must be so."

Atalanta carefully considered her response to this. She didn't want to hurt the woman's feelings by dismissing her suggestion in a careless manner, but at the same time she couldn't quite embrace a direct link between a veiled statement in a letter and someone's sudden, apparently accidental death. Didn't people examine innocent events in a different light once they had convinced themselves something must be amiss? She said softly, "You don't know that. What huge secret could your daughter have discovered if she lived with an elderly lady?"

"The elderly lady in question is only staying at the burg. She doesn't own it." The woman rushed to explain her theory, her voice husky with urgency. "The burg belongs to her nephew Pietro Bucardi. He is a successful businessman. He and his wife Victoria often invite guests to the burg so he can impress them with the splendour of the place. I heard before that he gets people to invest in plans he has. What if those plans are somehow faulty and my daughter found out?"

"Then you think he would have her killed? To protect his secret?"

"If money is involved, people are capable of anything. Anything!" The woman's voice was determined. "You must find out what happened. I can't live with the idea my girl was murdered and her killer will go scot free."

"I understand that, but … how could I possibly discover something like that?"

"The elderly aunt needs a new companion. Because the Bucardis were so happy with Letitia, I said I'd ask around for a replacement. I can recommend you. I can make up some references to get you accepted. Please go there and investigate. Put my mind at ease." The woman grasped Atalanta's hand and squeezed. "I don't want to believe she was murdered. Honestly. I would rather accept it was an accident and I have to live with the knowledge she will never come home. I can then start to work through my grief. If one can ever do such a thing. But I must first have certainty about how Letitia died. That it was indeed an accident while she was alone on the cliffs. That there was no one with her who pushed her over the edge. If you go there and can see things for yourself, you can work out what happened. Her things are still there. Victoria promised to pack them and send them to us but she hasn't done so yet. Letitia took many photos and made albums of them. Find out what Letitia photographed. If she made a discovery that way. Perhaps you can even find proof of what secret she uncovered and who might have felt threatened by her."

Atalanta took a deep breath. The photos might hold a clue.

But even if they did... The task seemed enormous and impossible to complete for an outsider who would have to pose as the new companion. She might show some polite interest in her predecessor but nothing major. That would draw unwanted attention and frustrate her purpose. "Why don't you go yourself? You're family and can ask more questions."

"I can't be objective. I would betray myself or jump to conclusions. I need someone who is not personally involved who can look at things with an open mind. You are capable and you're admirably suited to play a companion. You look sophisticated enough to satisfy their demands for someone with taste and breeding. But you won't outclass them."

Atalanta didn't know whether to be flattered or insulted by this assessment of her person.

The woman continued, "As companion you'll be in a position to blend into the background but still see and hear everything." She pressed Atalanta's hand with urgency and warmth. "I owe so much to your grandfather. He restored life to me. Now I need you to do the same and set my mind at ease. Please consider my request. I'll reward you handsomely." The latter words were added almost as an afterthought.

"I don't need a rich reward." Atalanta said it quickly. "My

grandfather always believed in helping people, in solving cases, because it was a moral obligation if one has the skills for it."

"Then at least let me arrange for your trip to Santorini. I'll send details to your hotel. Once there on the island, you'll work for the Bucardi family and have the income they pay you."

Atalanta felt rather awkward accepting money for a position she hadn't earned, as she was hardly a qualified companion, but she could always set that straight later. She did want to see Santorini. She knew but little of it and longed to experience island life for herself, to explore the walkways along the cliffs and stare across the endless sea views, realizing that these islands had been part of the huge Greek empire that she had read about as a little girl, devouring the history and myths about the Trojan war and all the Greek heroes and heroines. She was even named after one: Atalanta, the huntress. A name chosen for her at birth, long before she had been asked to follow in her grandfather's footsteps and hunt killers.

Atalanta nodded at the woman opposite her. Her mind was made up. Apparently, it was time, despite her holiday, to hunt a killer once again.

If there was indeed a murderer, she reminded herself, and this poor grieving mother wasn't deluded in thinking her daughter couldn't have been snatched away from her by some meaningless accident.

"I can't promise you results," she warned.

"I understand that. I only want to have tried. For my little girl." The woman fought new tears. "I wasn't ready to let her go into the world, to allow her to work in America or marry. And now I have to let her go for good. How can I endure it?"

Atalanta lowered her head and stared at the floor while the woman wept. It was impossible to say something uplifting. The mother's heart was broken. And it would never mend again. The loss of her child would remain a crack running through her life forever.

All Atalanta could offer her was to seek the truth, to reassure her that it had indeed been an accident, or...

She wet her lips. The idea that it had *not* been an accident was startling. Not just for the mother who would have to face that heartbreak on top of her grief, but for Atalanta herself as well. If she went to Santorini to take the place of someone who had been murdered, possibly for a discovery made at the burg, inside that household ... would she be in danger as well?

She'd have to be extremely careful, to protect her cover and hide her true purpose as long as possible.

She said, "If you arrange for the introductions ... You can reach me at my hotel. I will be staying there for a few more days. I had intended to travel on to Florence but that will have to wait."

"Thank you." The woman stepped back, almost stumbling. "Thank you. I'll get everything ready and let you know." She left the room quickly, her dark figure blotting out the sunlight for a moment.

Dressed all in black because she was in mourning for her daughter. And Raoul had thought she was some vengeful assassin...

But although this idea was now dismissed, her situation still required thought. She had accepted a huge assignment which had come with very little information. Just that a nineteen-year-old girl had died, falling off the cliffs. Where to start?

Atalanta pressed a hand to her face. How to tackle the task ahead? Who to talk to? And most of all, how to ever deduce something useful without drawing attention to herself? For if her interest in her predecessor's death was noticed, it might become her own undoing.

A new shadow darkened the entrance. Was the woman coming back? Atalanta stood rigid, all her senses alert as she stared at the figure who entered. Tall, broad, light suit and hat.

Raoul.

Despite the weak light of the candles she could see the shadows in his eyes. "Why did you agree to this?" he asked in a low voice. "I couldn't overhear everything from the outside, but I got the general idea. You are to put yourself at risk to find out what happened to that girl."

"She is a devastated mother. I could hardly turn her away. Besides, I've always wanted to see Santorini."

Raoul shook his head. "You make light of it, Atalanta. But you know as well as I do what it entails. Pursuing the truth is never free. It comes at a price. And you know precious little."

"I knew precious little when I took Eugénie Frontenac's request in Paris to look into the anonymous letter she had received, accusing her husband-to-be of murder. I dived in without much thought, accompanying her to Provence, and it worked out."

She realized how careless it sounded and added hurriedly, "Also because of your help, of course."

Raoul gave her a cynical smile. "And who will help you now? You will be all alone in that household. Members of the family could be involved, or someone lurking among the staff.

30

I've met the Bucardis. They are a charming couple when they host a society dinner, but they both come from powerful families and like to have things their way." It seemed he was about to add more details, and Atalanta waited with eager anticipation to start forming an idea about the family circle she was stepping into. Perhaps he had also met the elderly lady she'd be working for and could tell her if she'd be very demanding. She would need to have some time to herself to sleuth. Or could she learn a lot by simply being present in the household, at dinner or other moments where the family gathered, to sense tensions and read the dynamics?

Raoul said, exasperated, "Why put yourself in danger because a woman who doesn't even show her face asks you to? Her entire story could be a fabrication."

"To what end? You just said you know the Bucardis."

"From races."

Meaning he had never exchanged more than a few polite words with them? "But you could find out if they have a burg on Santorini, couldn't you? And if Mr Bucardi has an elderly aunt who needs a companion because the previous one died in an unfortunate accident. Then we'll know those details are true. Besides, the woman in black promised me an introduction to the family. The Bucardis asked her to find a new companion. Doesn't that support her story?"

"It seems so. And the Bucardis do have a burg on Santorini where they stay during the summer."

"There, it all fits." Atalanta felt a rush of relief that she hadn't been lied to. Raoul thought she was so naïve that she believed every word that was said to her, but she'd prove otherwise. She put a reassuring hand on his arm. "I'll ask Renard to do some additional research. He's very thorough, usually. But I'm quite sure her story will prove to be the truth where her daughter's employment at the Bucardi burg is concerned. Of course, we won't know if Letitia was indeed pushed. That's merely what her mother thinks. Can't she have concluded it must be foul play merely because she can't accept that death snatches a young girl? A death like that seems so unthinkable, there must then be another reason. A hand behind it, someone who actively decided to do it. But it need not be so. If I can prove it was truly an accident, it can put her mind at ease. Or else she'll keep wondering for the rest of her life."

"I see what you mean." He thought a moment, a heavy frown over his eyes. "But you can't make a judgement from here," he gestured around him, "about what happened on an island far away. You must go there to find out, and then you might be in danger. A burg like that has high watchtowers and deep, dark, damp cellars; a terrace overlooking the sea with just a low stone wall between you and the ocean below. One push between the shoulder blades while you're admiring the view…"

Atalanta could almost feel the sudden shove in her back, tipping her over, sending her body sprawling into the waters below. She gasped for breath. But he was merely testing her to see if she had thought it through. "Surely if there is a murderer, they won't be stupid enough to kill again so soon? One accident might be acceptable, but two in a row?"

Raoul shook his head. "That's not the point. You must consider what you are setting yourself up for." After a few moments he added, "You needn't do it alone."

Atalanta stared at him. Did he mean what she thought he did?

She had said no to him earlier today and had regretted it soon after. She shouldn't make the same mistake again. Still, why would he offer this? "Would you really come along if I asked you to? Or are you only eager for an invitation so you can tell me that you don't have the time?" She was feeling for his reasons to insert himself in her case – a case he had just berated her about, considering her ready acceptance too great a risk. She had to ask questions, knowing at the same time that Raoul was far too clever and too guarded to ever give much away.

Raoul held her gaze. "I only want to know if you think my presence was helpful last time."

Helpful and confusing, infuriating and distracting, all at the same time. He challenged her to look at the case but also at herself, her motivations, thoughts and feelings. "Yes," she said hesitantly.

Raoul chuckled. "That doesn't sound very convincing."

"Yes, it was, you know it was," she said impatiently. "I could never have captured the killer without your actual assistance."

"That is what I wanted to hear. If I change my schedule to dive into this matter, I want to know I'm actually a valuable asset. An equal partner. Not just someone who must lend his muscles when the killer has been cornered by your brilliant deductions."

Atalanta bit her lip. She tried to look as if she was genuinely torn. "An equal partner? I don't know if you contributed that much last time. You were constantly putting me on the wrong track."

Raoul looked piqued. "I was testing your theories, throwing up valid questions. You need someone who

33

challenges you, and doesn't follow meekly whatever you suggest."

She had to admit he was right, but would never tell him to his face. Instead she asked, "What do you mean by changing your schedule? Aren't you committed to racing?"

"Actually, I have two weeks off. I intended to use them to go and see some sponsors, but I also promised to look in on the possibility of doing an island race comparable to the one on Crete. And Santorini came up as an option. I have no idea if there are actual possibilities for a good route, so I could travel there allegedly to investigate the opportunities to do an island race, while in reality I look into the girl's death with you." His brown eyes sparkled. "What do you think?"

"That sounds like a brilliant idea." Atalanta suppressed the surge of joy at the idea of seeing more of Raoul. She shouldn't overestimate the advantages of working together. He would probably just irritate her with his remarks and the ways in which he wanted to approach the matter.

"Good, that's agreed then." Raoul turned away.

Atalanta said hurriedly, "I bought my glassware. If you still want to go and see Venice, your friend's doge palace, and then have dinner tonight…"

Raoul stopped. For a moment she was certain she could hear him laugh softly. "I'm afraid I can't," he said. "You see, if I have to leave in the next few days, to go to Santorini, to help you out, I need to wrap up my business here before I go. And that means I must keep my promise to take another lady to dinner. Tonight."

Atalanta hated the flush creeping up in her cheeks. He always did that. Say one thing, mean another. Spin her in circles and leave her wondering what had just happened. "I'm sorry," she said. "I didn't mean to impose on you." Silly of her to remind him of his earlier offer.

Raoul said, "Don't worry. We'll be seeing enough of each other soon."

"It doesn't sound as if you are looking forward to it," she called after him as he stepped outside.

He disappeared from her view and then returned to stick his head in and say, "Speak for yourself, Miss Ashford. I look forward to Santorini, because it's an amazing island. And whether you will enjoy my company or not, mostly depends on you."

And there he did it again, Atalanta thought, half annoyed, half amused. *He leaves me to ponder what on earth he means by that last remark. Must I simply let go of my expectations of him and see what this cooperation can bring?*

It had certainly changed the perspective of her holiday. She'd be leaving Venice soon and heading for a gorgeous Greek island to dig into a young woman's accidental death.

A new case and a new chance to test her skills on a complicated puzzle.

Chapter Four

*A*nd one more step to dry land. Atalanta gingerly left the rickety plank, clutching her suitcase in her hand. The sunshine reflected off the white houses that seemed pasted on against the rock face. Having just left behind the opulence of Venice where every house had several storeys with extended balconies and elaborate decorations, the houses here were surprisingly alike: modest in size, square with a flat roof and narrow windows. Here and there were bright-blue doors and window frames, the occasional domed roof. Bushes that seemed to grow from on high, dripping down from the tops of the buildings, unfolded clouds of scarlet blooms. Stepping up to study them closer, she realized it was bougainvillaea.

The whole was stunning in its simplicity: a tranquil habitable world in the midst of a vast expanse of deep-blue sea.

The water filled the air with a tangy saltiness and there was the constant murmur of waves lapping against the volcanic rock. She was cut off from the mainland, as only experienced seamen could navigate here. She could see for herself how dangerous it would be to try and land, with those unforgiving cliffs everywhere.

"Miss Renard?" A male voice addressed her from her right. She saw a man in his thirties stepping up to her. With his olive skin, thick black hair and brown eyes, he was handsome, like most Mediterranean men, and flirtatious. His gaze travelled down her light-yellow travel ensemble with relish and his lips broke into a smile of appreciation. He reached out a hand to take her suitcase from her. "I'm Andreas Papoudopolis. I work for the Bucardi family. I was asked to meet you here and escort you to the burg. It's quite a walk up there, but I see you are dressed for the occasion." He nodded at her sturdy shoes. "Are you perhaps familiar with Santorini?"

"I'm afraid not. I've always been stationed in France." She knew the details of her cover by heart: she had adopted the name of her faithful butler and passed as a Frenchwoman. Having taught French for years at the Swiss boarding school, she spoke the language fluently. Allegedly, she had worked as a companion for several rich families in Paris and Nice. There was even a telephone number her new employers could call to speak to a lady who was very satisfied with her services, while she had in reality never even met Atalanta. All arranged by Renard, who had told her that if one assumed a cover, one should make it as perfect as could be.

Especially if one was to step into the company of a murderer.

"That's a shame," Andreas said. He smiled again, baring his perfect white teeth. "Greece is very beautiful." He gestured to steps to their left. "Shall we?"

Atalanta saw that these hewn steps led up between the

houses. It wasn't a broad path but they could walk side by side. Andreas said, "I'm prejudiced, of course, because I'm Greek, but it truly is an exceptional land. A land of myths and heroes."

"I'm a huge fan of Greek mythology," Atalanta enthused. At least she need not pretend that. "My parents even named me after a Greek heroine. Atalanta." On her previous case she had also kept her own first name and it had worked well, so she had decided to do the same here.

Andreas gave her a sideways glance. "Your parents also loved mythology, then?"

"My mother did." Atalanta tried to find a good pace to climb the steps without getting out of breath too quickly. "Unfortunately, she's no longer alive. But she left me a beautiful book of myths I regularly read."

Andreas nodded. His expression was serious when he said, "Your predecessor also loved our old stories. I explained about a few of them while we explored the island."

Atalanta's heart skipped a beat. Here was her first chance to speak about the deceased girl and learn more about her life here. "I understood that the vacancy came up rather suddenly because my predecessor passed away." She glanced at him. "I was surprised, as she was quite young. Young people normally don't..."

"Just die?" Andreas supplied. He put her suitcase down to pick it up again with his other hand. Atalanta had the impression he was consciously stalling. A fit man like him would have no problems carrying a case that size. And if he went up and down these steps all the time, he couldn't be winded either.

After securing the handle in his palm with painstaking

care, he rose to his full height again and said, "She had an accident. I warned her several times about the walk along the cliffs. They are steep and the path is narrow, with slivers of stone one can slip on, especially after rain. It's easy to miss a step and fall."

Rain in the Mediterranean summer? She had always thought it was very hot and dry on these islands. But perhaps she was mistaken. A local would know such things better than she. "But she didn't listen to your advice?" she asked, tilting her head as she studied him.

Andreas smiled again, but softer. He continued to walk. "She was a wild girl. She wanted to do whatever she put her mind to. She always had a little camera with her and loved to explore the island. It's a comfort to know people died while doing something they loved."

Atalanta thought this was a rather peculiar observation, but she said, "So you knew her fairly well?"

Again there was a pause before he replied, "What is fairly well? We talked a few times. She told me it was her dream to work as a photographer, but her parents weren't in favour of it. That was about all she ever said. We were both just employees, you must remember. We were here to serve, not to enjoy ourselves."

"I know very well what that is like." Atalanta looked about her. A fig tree leaned over a fence between two houses, and an old woman sat on a stool with an earthenware bowl in her lap. Her wrinkled hands were kneading dough. She hummed a tune that hovered in the air.

With a smile Atalanta observed, "Still, being just an employee is much more bearable in nice surroundings. And this island looks gorgeous. So authentic."

"It is beautiful now in summer. In autumn and winter it's different. The sea can be wild and when the skies are grey, even the white of the houses doesn't cheer up the view. Life on an island is always lonely. It is isolated from the mainland."

Thus the perfect place to commit a crime, Atalanta mused. Had someone followed the girl here to kill her, far away from Venice? It was a possibility. One that made her task all the harder. For if the killer had come to Santorini, posing as a tourist, had pushed the girl off the cliffs and vanished again on the next boat, they would be impossible to find. The assignment given to her started from the assumption that someone still present knew more about the death, and she could find out who that was and what had happened.

They came to an open space, much like a small village square, where several dark-clad men sat at a rickety table moving pieces across a board. One of them gave a disgruntled cry while the other smacked his hand on the table in a gesture of victory. "It looks like backgammon," Atalanta said to Andreas.

He smiled. "We call it *tavli*. It's the favourite pastime here for those who don't have to work." He threw the men a half-envious, half-resigned look. "They have nothing better to do all day long than sit, drink coffee and play *tavli*. Well, at least in the afternoons it's coffee. Later at night it might be something stronger."

"Like *ouzo*?" Atalanta asked.

Andreas laughed out loud. "I wouldn't advise you to try it. It's very strong, especially when you're only used to wine. But you must taste our other local specialties, like *spanakopita*."

"*Spanakopita*," Atalanta repeated, tasting the syllables. She knew some Greek words from her mythology reading but couldn't make head nor tail of this word. "What is that?"

"Pastry made with spinach and goat's cheese. It's usually shaped like a discus, but we have an island variety where it is more of a half-moon." With his free hand he drew the shape in the air. "Resembling a fisherman's boat, perhaps, or referring to Selene."

"Goddess of the moon." Atalanta nodded. "She must have been important to fishermen, as the moon influences the tides. Are those old beliefs still very much alive here?"

"Oh, the people are certainly superstitious. Every fisherman can tell you some strange story about a creature he saw when out at sea. They take all kinds of precautions to protect themselves against evil influences. And they don't like outsiders." He pointed ahead. "Those burgs have lasted longer than they should have."

Atalanta cast her eye across the extensive stone building rising up above the village. It dwarfed the houses with its imposing walls and high flat tower topped with merlons. It had a medieval sturdiness about it, as if it had been built for protection of the houses below when invading forces had come across the sea or pirates had attempted to take whatever valuables the inlanders might have. Goats and donkeys they depended on for their livelihood, or silver candlesticks and altar pieces from the churches?

But Andreas's tone made it clear that the locals didn't look up at those walls with admiration and a sense of gratitude for the safety the fortress had most likely provided throughout the island's turbulent history. No, instead they regarded them with hostility.

She cast him a curious look. "How do you mean?"

"Just that other remnants of settlement have been vanquished. Do you see Roman arenas here or Byzantine warehouses? No. Those intruders have vanished and their remnants are insignificant, only to be found if you search hard for them. But those *castelli* persist, high and mighty, flaunting their presence in our faces. Tokens of the Venetian power over this region."

"Ah, perhaps as a proud Greek you see them as symbols of foreign conquerors? Are they offensive to you?" She asked it with a smile as if it was a light-hearted question, but the possible answer did intrigue her. What if Andreas disliked his Venetian employers? Could that provide a clue in the case of Letitia's sudden death?

The girl had also been Venetian, after all.

Renard had established for her that Letitia came from a well-to-do family of silk merchants who were distant relations of the Bucardis. They had offered Letitia the chance to become a companion to Pietro Bucardi's elderly aunt, Delilah, who lived at the burg with them. Letitia's sudden death had created quite a stir in Venice's upper circles, although no one seemed to think of foul play. There was merely a sense of shock and compassion for the poor parents who were devastated by the loss.

Andreas seemed taken aback by her question. Perhaps it was a little forward, as they had barely met and had only shared this hot walk up to the burg. Atalanta's calves ached with the strain of climbing, step by step by step, and sweat beaded on her brow. And she wasn't even carrying the luggage!

"I can imagine," she said quickly to explain her question,

43

"that if I lived here, as a Greek person, I might also have liked those burgs to be Greek rather than Venetian."

"Oh, that." Andreas's features relaxed. "One cannot change the past. The Venetians were here, as they were everywhere in the Mediterranean. They were a people who liked to extend their power. Over land, over seas. But nowadays the Italian families who still populate the burgs are weak and spoiled by their riches, indulging in too much food and wine. They are mere shadows of their illustrious ancestors." It sounded deprecating. "I don't fight shadows."

Atalanta nodded. "Have you worked for them long? And what exactly do you do in the household? I know very little about the Bucardi family, and it would be helpful to prepare for my arrival."

"You'll be serving the old Mrs Bucardi. She is an aunt of the master of the house. She never married and she considers herself entitled to meddle in everyone's affairs. She has a sharp tongue and an even sharper mind. But because she is sometimes forgetful of small matters – where she put her glasses or what day of the week it is – her nephew treats her like an invalid. He doesn't take her seriously. Hey!"

Adding a few Greek words, Andreas lifted the suitcase high as a group of half-clad children ran past them, chasing a football made of rags and string. Their excited cries mixed with the sounds of the gulls soaring overhead.

Andreas shook his head. "Little rascals. When they're playing, they don't look where they're going. Now, where was I?"

"Mr Bucardi doesn't take his aunt very seriously."

"Oh, yes. Mr Bucardi believes himself to be master of the

house, but his wife Victoria determines everything. She's a beautiful woman and she knows it."

There was a strange tone to Andreas's voice. Before Atalanta could tune into the underlying emotion, he was already continuing, "She spends a lot of money on clothes and furniture. Nothing made on this island is good enough for her. It must be brought in from Italy. She also refuses to serve Greek food at the table. It must always be Italian dishes. Or what she believes to be Italian dishes. As if her ancestors personally invented everything."

He threw up a hand in an exaggerated gesture of feigned despair.

Atalanta said, "Aren't all people proud of their heritage? And if they live abroad, they often like to cling to something that reminds them of home."

"You're too understanding," Andreas scoffed. He glanced at her as if he contemplated adding another remark about her attitude, but then he continued telling her about the family, saying, "They have one child. A boy." He laughed softly. "I would almost say: a boy, *naturally*. Bucardi is the type of man who wants an heir and gets it, with a snap of his fingers. They both adore the child who is consequently horribly spoiled. You'll soon have to dance to his tunes as well."

Atalanta didn't feel the need to defend herself. Instead she focused on something that struck her. "You speak English very well," she said. "Perhaps you studied in England?"

"Oxford." Andreas cast her a look. "I'm sorry I don't speak French. That is your native tongue, isn't it?" His gaze grew probing. "Or is it English? You too speak it so very well."

Atalanta felt a flush come up at this flaw in her presentation as Mademoiselle Renard, the quintessential French companion.

"I was raised bilingual," she explained quickly. "My mother was English."

"I see. Where were we? Oh yes, the spoiled little boy." Andreas gestured over his shoulder to the local children who ran after their makeshift ball. Their laughter echoed against the walls of the houses. "He doesn't have playmates like they do. He's not allowed to have contact with the island children, as Mrs Bucardi thinks they are dirty and a bad influence on her little darling. He has a room full of beautiful toys but no one to play with. I pity little Luca."

"Are you Mr Bucardi's secretary, perhaps?" Atalanta hazarded a guess. "You could help him with all his international business correspondence."

"He mainly does business with Italians and my Italian isn't very good. No, I'm just a jack of all trades. I repair things, run errands ... pick up the new companion."

Atalanta tilted her head again. Things didn't quite add up in her mind. "It seems unusual for someone educated at Oxford to accept manual labour." She added after a moment, "Especially as you don't seem to like Venetians."

Andreas stiffened noticeably. "I needed the job," he snapped. He lengthened his stride to get ahead of her, taking two steps at a time.

Atalanta wondered if she had touched a sore spot. Did he have financial problems which had forced him to seek employment with someone he would normally have avoided? There couldn't be many well-paid jobs on the island. She imagined most of these people were fishermen, or had other age-old professions such as baker, weaver or wood carver. Tourism might start to bring in some money but she didn't see many souvenir shops here, as she had in Venice. Had Andreas felt compelled to go to the burg and work for a family he loathed for their 'occupation' of the island?

As if he followed her thinking, Andreas halted allowing for her to catch up. He said, "There are many other islanders working in the burg. It has a lot of rooms and there's always work to do. Mr Bucardi has his own staff: a manservant, secretary… And Mrs Bucardi has a maid and a nanny for the little boy. You'll get to know all of them. Or do you feel above other staff?"

Atalanta shook her head. "Most certainly not. In my earlier positions I had pleasant relations with the other staff. It's true that a companion is usually considered more part of the family than one of the servants, but I never saw it that way. I work for my money, and I keep that in mind."

"That's sensible." Andreas's jaw tightened. "Others before you made the mistake of thinking they were indeed part of the family."

"What a cryptic remark." Atalanta tried to sound light. "Do you mean the girl who passed away recently, or others before her?"

"It was a common problem, I believe. But I assume you're too sensible to fall victim to something like that. Just watch out that you're never alone in a room with Mr Bucardi."

The last sentence was added in a lower voice, with a warning tone.

Atalanta felt a shiver crawl across her spine. "What are you trying to tell me?"

"You're not a naïve schoolgirl, you can work it out for yourself. We're almost at the entrance of the burg."

They passed a house with a laundry line spanning beside it. But the pink items suspended weren't clothes. Atalanta blinked to ensure she was seeing this correctly. Long tentacles waved in the wind. "Are those octopuses?" she asked.

"Oh yes, it's the perfect time of year to fish for them. The tentacles get cut off and fried. With a slice of lemon it's a real treat."

Atalanta shivered at the idea of putting a thing with suckers on it into her mouth. That was one local speciality she wasn't eager to try. Perhaps it was a good thing Mrs Bucardi didn't allow Greek food at the burg. If something like that was served at dinner, it would be almost impossible to refuse to eat it.

Andreas led the way up the final set of steps to a large wooden gate. In the enormous door was a smaller door that stood open. "In here." He went ahead of her, leading her into a cobbled courtyard. There were high walls around with narrow windows. Behind one of those she saw a figure move, stepping back hastily, to avoid being seen.

Atalanta's heart was beating fast from the exertion of the steep walk uphill, but also the conversation with Andreas. Perhaps it was natural to share a little gossip about the employers to make friends with the new arrival, but she had the distinct impression Andreas had been very forthcoming with his information.

With the information he wanted her to have, of course, she realized. For what purpose?

A blonde woman in her late twenties came up to them, in a dramatic dress that was red on the shoulders, running into orange across the chest and then turning yellow in the skirt. She held a large sunhat in her left hand. When she saw Andreas, she slapped at him with the sunhat. "You liar. You said you'd show me around and there you are, with another victim of your charms."

"I was merely performing a task for Mr Bucardi. This is the new companion for the old Mrs Bucardi. Miss Renard. Or perhaps we should say Mademoiselle Renard, as she is French."

"Oh." The woman's light-brown eyes turned cool and she ignored Atalanta as if she had suddenly turned into a piece of furniture. "Then deliver her to the butler and come with me. I've been waiting far too long."

"Yes, my lady." Andreas made a fake bow and said to Atalanta, "You can go in through that door…" He pointed ahead to a door that was left open. "And find the butler, Lemusier. He is also French so he will be pleased to have someone to talk to. He struggles with Italian and his Greek is non-existent." Andreas sounded deprecating. "He'll show you to your room where you can unpack." He handed her the suitcase.

"If Aunt Delilah doesn't want to see her sooner," the woman said. "She must make haste."

Atalanta was annoyed by the woman's way of instructing her without even directly addressing her, but she said to Andreas, "Thank you for your help. We'll see each other again later." She walked away and heard the woman say, "The nerve, to appropriate you like that. She is nothing but a hired hand."

And so is Andreas, Atalanta thought. But the woman didn't seem to mind that. How odd.

She entered through the open door and stood in a large hallway with purple coverings on the walls and heraldic shields with gold leaf. A carpeted staircase led upwards, splitting halfway. Usually in the centre of such a split stairway at a grand home, flowers stood or a work of art, but here it was a large marble statue of a woman dressed in an exquisite robe. Only the robe wasn't carved out of marble, it was made of real fabric and draped on her as if she were a mannequin in a very fashionable shop on the boulevards of Paris. Was it a silk dress, an echo of old when the Bucardis had earned their money trading along the Silk Road?

It was very silent in here, all sounds being drowned out by the thick walls. After the heat outside the cool was delicious on her skin. Finally, the sweat on her face and neck could evaporate.

She put her suitcase down and looked around her. There were several closed doors. Most of them had doorknobs, but one had a large metal ring attached to a metal plate. It probably led to the tall flat tower she had seen from the outside. It was like a sturdy watchtower. She wondered if there was a great view of the sea from up there. Something to explore some time, she supposed. If she was even allowed to.

Raoul's voice whispered in her head that those Venetian burgs were dangerous, with high watchtowers and cellars and a stone terrace where only a low stone wall stood on the edge of the cliff, protecting one against the sheer drop to the ocean below.

"Paula! Paula!" A thin voice echoed from above. After a few moments a little boy in white trousers and a blue shirt appeared at the top of the stairs. He peered down. "Is that you, Paula?" He spoke Italian.

Drawing on her boarding school experience communicating with Italian pupils, Atalanta replied, "No, I'm Atalanta. I have come to live here."

"How come?" Holding the railing, he came down. He was

50

just four years old, she supposed when she saw him better. He shouldn't be walking about unattended. *Where's his nanny?*

"How come you live here?" the boy demanded. "This is Papa's house."

"I work here. There are many people working here. We all work for your father."

"Where's Paula? She said she'd play with me."

"Is Paula your nanny?"

The little boy sank down on the last step of the stairs and began to sob. "She said she'd play with me."

"I can play with you," Atalanta suggested. Andreas's snide remark that she would soon be dancing to the boy's tunes came back to her, but she did think his crying was so sad. She never knew what to do with little children. Her experience at the boarding school had been with ages twelve and up.

The boy looked up, tears on his cheek. "Promise?"

"Promise. What shall we do? How about you show me your toys? I heard you have a lot of beautiful toys."

But the little boy had already run past her out the door. "Hide and seek. You look for me."

"Wait!" She ran after him, worried he would go through the other open door and wander away from the burg. Her heart beat fast. How careless, to throw herself into a task she wasn't engaged for. If she made a mistake, that could be the end of her position here, before she had even begun her investigation into Letitia's death!

The boy called, "You have to count to ten before you come looking. Count to ten!"

He sounded so excited, she didn't want to disappoint him. Andreas had told her on the way up that the children from the village could play together, but Luca was always alone.

Atalanta took his arm before he could run off and said emphatically, "I'll count to ten, if you promise me you won't go outside the courtyard."

He looked up at her. "I'll stay around, I promise. Count to ten now. With your eyes closed."

Atalanta closed her eyes but kept peeking through her lashes. He ran across the courtyard and for a moment she was certain he would slip out of the door and she'd have to chase him down all those steps. At the thought her leg muscles hurt even more. But he turned left and hid behind a few stacked crates. She smiled to herself and called out, "*Otto, nove, dieci!* Coming!"

Although there were precious few hiding places in the exposed courtyard, she started to walk around looking and calling for him, "Little boy! Where are you?"

"What are you doing?" a cool female voice inquired.

Atalanta halted and turned around. A woman in a beautiful blue dress with golden floral patterns stood in the door of the burg. Her dark hair was pulled back and secured with golden pins, giving her an elegant but stern appearance. She could have been a medieval lady of the manor as she stood there, gazing out across her property. She bore herself with a natural grace as she walked out and called, "Luca! Come to Mama."

The little boy didn't show.

"Where is Luca? And why are you concerning yourself with him?" the woman demanded.

Atalanta switched to English and explained, "I'm Atalanta Renard. I've just arrived to become Mrs Bucardi's companion."

"I don't need a companion. Oh … you mean Aunt Delilah? I suppose she requested someone new after…" She fell silent a moment, her fine brows drawing together.

Atalanta wondered if she would refer to the death. It was indelicate, she supposed, and Mrs Bucardi looked like a woman who valued correct behaviour.

Her hostess said, "My husband didn't inform me he had arranged for it already."

"I'm sorry if this is unexpected. I ran into your little boy and he was crying because his nanny promised to play with him but she isn't around. I offered to play a game of hide and seek merely to distract him." Atalanta flushed as she explained herself. As an experienced companion she should have known better than to interfere with a task that was not hers to perform. She had simply felt sorry for the crying child, but this faux pas didn't endear her to her new employer.

"I suppose you meant well. But I don't want an old woman's companion to play with my child." Mrs Bucardi sounded cold, her features marble, like the statue in her stairway. From a distance, judging by her regal bearing, Atalanta had estimated her at over forty, but up close she looked younger. Did she feel she had to be distant, to assert her position here?

Mrs Bucardi asked, "Where's Paula?"

"I have no idea. I don't even know what she looks like."

Mrs Bucardi smiled suddenly. "You'll soon find out. Paula isn't a person one overlooks or forgets."

Atalanta tried to determine what her tone implied. Venom? Envy? Or admiration?

"You have to look for me," a voice resounded from behind the crates. "Not talk."

"Mama knows where you are. Come out now. I'll take you up to the nursery and get you milk and apricots. Come, now."

The little boy appeared and ran for his mother. He hugged

her legs and tried to climb onto her. She didn't make a movement to lift him. "Come with me." She turned and walked away. He hung his head and followed her slowly, dragging his feet.

Atalanta released her breath. She shouldn't judge a woman she had met only briefly. She couldn't know whether she was a good mother or not. A small interaction with a child was no measure for that. Still, Mrs Bucardi's response to the little boy's affection had been very aloof. Chilly, almost unfeeling.

And Andreas said that both parents adore the child and spoil him. But I've seen no proof of that as yet. What a strange household this is.

Atalanta went back inside where she found a man in a butler's uniform waiting beside her suitcase. His dark hair was combed back from his long face which had deep-set dark eyes. "Mademoiselle Renard?" he said in a pleasant baritone voice. "A pleasure to meet you. My name is Lemusier. I'm also French."

"How nice to make your acquaintance," Atalanta replied, relieved that knowledge of French wasn't a pretend part of the role she played, but was a skill she actually possessed. If she had lied about her aptitude in the language, she would have been in deep water indeed. "This is a beautiful burg. It must be very old."

"It dates back to the fifteenth century, when the Venetians first came here to use the island on their way to the east to trade. Many parts of the burg are still authentic, such as the watchtower."

"Oh yes, it's most impressive and must offer a gorgeous view of the surroundings. Is that the door leading into it?" She pointed to the door with the metal ring.

Lemusier nodded. "Yes. An internal stairwell leads up to

the top. One can also enter this stairwell via a door on the first floor. That ring…" he gestured to the metal ring in the door, "must be pushed in and twisted to open the door. It is an old mechanism, I understand, but it is very convenient now, as it ensures the little boy can't open it. He is not allowed to go up there. It would be too dangerous."

"I see. It must be a challenge to live in a building this old."

"Well, it's not all authentic anymore. Parts have been added to it and rooms have been modernized so guests can have all the amenities. Mr Bucardi is quite proud of his heritage and is intent on preserving it for the generations to come. If you'll follow me to your room? It has a very nice sea view. I trust you'll like it."

"Oh, I'm sure I will. I feel quite lucky to be working here." Atalanta walked after him up the stairs. He carried her case.

She said, "The only shadow on my happiness is the death of the girl who came before me."

The butler released the grip on the handle of her case and it fell down the stairs with a clatter as it struck step after step after step before reaching the ground with a deafening bang. The sound echoed back from the high ceiling.

"*Cosa c'è?*" A man with a red face appeared at the top of the stairs. "I thought we were under attack."

"No, Signor Bucardi. I'm sorry. Mademoiselle Renard's case got caught in the carpet and slipped from my grasp." The butler rushed down to retrieve it.

"Mademoiselle Renard, ah yes. Welcome." Bucardi came down the stairs smiling at Atalanta. He was a handsome man of about forty with deep-set brown eyes, a generous mouth and thick black hair that fell over his forehead and in the back brushed his collar. It gave him a bit of a roguish appearance, as of someone who didn't care much for the demands of society.

The warmth in his approach surprised her after the other members of the household had been so distant. He reached out a hand to her. She put her hand in his and he squeezed, holding her gaze with that smile. "Welcome to the Bucardi *castello*. We've been living here for many centuries." His English had a charming Italian accent. "I have houses in Rome and Florence, Monaco, on the Riviera..." He made a careless hand gesture. "But this feels like home. This is the place where my ancestors laid the foundation for our fortune. They were all very hard-working men."

He pointed at the marble statue dressed in the rich silk robe. "That was their main trade. All the way to China for the silkworm. They stopped at nothing: distance, heat, deserts or robbers waylaying them. I suppose they wouldn't have approved of modern appliances like the telephone which make life so easy. From a leather chair behind a desk one can order goods from far away, without travelling a mile or shedding a drop of sweat. They did things in person. Trade, fight... court."

Atalanta felt uncomfortable under his persistent look. "I doubt people court each other over the telephone," she said curtly.

Bucardi laughed. "You don't know my wife's best friend. She is constantly calling young men or the young men are calling her. It's all very complicated. I wager that we might even hear of a duel one of these days. All those hot-headed Italians and Greeks vying for her affections. And she even encourages them. Women like to feel they are wanted." He said the latter words with a little smile, holding her gaze as if to see if she understood his meaning.

A discreet cough resounded, and Atalanta looked up to see Mrs Bucardi standing higher on the stairs. Her expression was unreadable, but her posture was tight, as if she was displeased with what she saw.

And I can understand that. This is not the way to start my working position here. Atalanta quickly removed her hand from Mr Bucardi's grasp.

The butler had returned to them with the suitcase. It had taken a few dents from contact with the staircase.

Bucardi said, "You'll have that repaired, Lemusier, and I'll deduct the costs from your wages. You must be more careful with my property." He cast Atalanta a look from under his thick, dark lashes.

The idea that he considered her suitcase *his* property was unpleasant.

Or did he even infer that she was his property now?

Chapter Five

Mrs Bucardi said, "I'll show Miss Renard to her room, dear. I wish you had told me this morning that she was coming. I would have asked the maid to put some flowers on the nightstand. It's always nice to feel welcome." Although her tone was perfectly friendly as she spoke, the look in her eyes belied that she had truly wanted to accommodate the new companion. Atalanta wondered if perhaps Mrs Bucardi disliked her husband's aunt and, by association, anyone who worked for her. Was the elderly lady's presence at the burg perhaps a decision Bucardi had made without asking for his wife's opinion?

"Didn't I mention it?" Bucardi frowned hard as if he was searching his memory. "I did intend to. Oh well, I have a lot on my mind. You see to the new arrival." And he walked back up, avoiding meeting his wife by turning right.

Mrs Bucardi's cheeks flushed a little at this clear sign of disrespect. Her eyes sparked as she gestured to Atalanta to follow her. The berated butler trotted after them with the battered suitcase.

Upstairs, Mrs Bucardi led the way to a large room with a four-poster bed. The dressing table with chair and large wardrobe were all white with blue accents, echoing the colours of the island. On the windowsill was a jar with small stones and bits of black rock, resting on a copy of *Jane Eyre*. Atalanta wondered if these stones had been collected by the unfortunate Letitia during her explorations of the island. Were there other things of hers left in this room? Her camera perhaps? Photographs she had taken? Could these provide clues as to how she had lived here, spent her days, met her untimely end?

Mrs Bucardi said, "I had initially decided against this, but I've changed my mind." She looked at the butler who had put the case beside the bed. His hands were shaking as he stepped back to the door. Was he calculating how much the repairs were going to cost him?

Or was his heart still hammering because Atalanta had referred to the death of her predecessor? What did Lemusier know about that?

Atalanta was itching to find out but Mrs Bucardi told the man, "You can leave now."

He bowed his head and quit the room, leaving the door open.

Atalanta looked at it, torn as to whether she should close it. Was the butler hovering outside, trying to listen in? What did he think Mrs Bucardi wanted to discuss with her? Her husband's behaviour?

Andreas Papoudopolis had warned Atalanta never to be alone with Bucardi and Mrs Bucardi had seen her husband holding Atalanta's hand. Would she feel obliged to comment?

Mrs Bucardi went over to the open door with quick steps, looked out, waited a few moments and then closed it. She turned to Atalanta, pulling back her shoulders as if to make herself taller. "I must address this topic directly. No matter how painful it is to me."

Atalanta straightened up. She assumed that Mrs Bucardi would explain to her that her husband was flirtatious with women, and that it didn't mean anything, and she shouldn't think he was serious and get ideas into her head. Or something worded more subtly, leaving the conclusions to Atalanta's own intelligence.

Either way, she prepared herself for a conversation that would be awkward, requiring a lot of tact on her part.

Mrs Bucardi said, "You're here to be the companion to my husband's aunt. Delilah is the elder sister of his father and already advanced in age. Her mind is not as clear as it used to be. My husband doesn't want to see it and he would strongly object to me telling you this, which is why I ask of you not to reveal this to him, ever. But while you must, of course, care for the old lady with all your strength, you mustn't believe anything she says."

Atalanta blinked at this decided statement. She had heard before of people who became a little forgetful and should be indulged, as they sometimes said things that were out of the ordinary, but to simply state that she shouldn't believe anything the old lady told her was very extreme.

Was Mr Bucardi blind to his aunt's condition and was Mrs Bucardi trying to warn Atalanta in advance against the old woman's fanciful stories?

Or did she have another reason for wanting to convince Atalanta, even before she had met her charge, that she couldn't be trusted and shouldn't be believed?

Mrs Bucardi continued with a sad little smile, "She's often confused and making things up. She believes people steal from her, rummage through her things, that someone skulks through the house at night, looking in rooms... She's a very light sleeper and every time she wakes up she thinks she hears a burglar or a prowler."

Mrs Bucardi spread her hands in an apologetic gesture. "At breakfast she treats us to all kinds of stories about what she saw and heard, and whom she believes is behind it. You mustn't mind her at all. Just listen politely and forget about it as soon as you can."

"But of course. I can assure you I'll be very discreet about it." Atalanta was relieved that Mrs Bucardi wasn't addressing her husband's forward behaviour. She already understood without any explanation what kind of man he was and would be careful that she was...

Never alone in a room with him? Andreas had said as much. Why had he warned her? Kindness? Loathing for the man who showed this sort of behaviour?

Or some other reason she wasn't able to work out yet?

Mrs Bucardi said, "I hope you don't feel as if you accepted a position with a patient, Mademoiselle Renard. For I can assure you that my husband's aunt isn't ... mentally unstable in any way. She's just very fanciful. I suppose one gets that way when one is locked up inside too much."

"Perhaps I can take her out?" Atalanta suggested. "A short walk to see the view and a bit of sunshine on her face. Early in the morning when it is still nice and cool? I'm certain she would appreciate staying in touch with daily life on the island.

Seeing the fishermen come in or sit on the dock busy cleaning their nets…"

Mrs Bucardi pursed her lips. "We try not to encourage outings. She can get very excited and it's bad for her heart. Not that she has a heart condition or anything. She's just old and … easily tires."

Atalanta nodded. "I understand. I'll take good care of her."

"I do understand you're not a nurse, Mademoiselle Renard. Nor does Delilah need one. Just company to keep her from getting morose thoughts. I'll now take you to her. She'll be eager to see you."

Now? Atalanta was surprised, having hoped for an hour to get settled in and rest up after her journey. An hour also to inspect her room and find traces that proved Letitia had lived there before her. Perhaps there was something left in the room that could give her a clue as to why Letitia had to die?

If her death was more than a mere accident, Atalanta added to herself. She had to keep that caveat in mind.

But there was no way she could ignore her employer's wishes or claim an hour for herself. Here she was a hired hand again, as she had been at the boarding school, and if she wanted to stay in everyone's good graces and get information, she had to comply.

"Of course." With a smile she nodded, leaned down to the mirror briefly to check on her hair, and then followed Mrs Bucardi who led her to a room down the corridor.

Inside, an elderly lady sat at an open window overlooking the sea. She had some knitting lying in her lap, but her hands were folded and she seemed to be close to dozing off. Mrs Bucardi tiptoed to her and said, "Are you awake?"

The elderly lady turned flashing dark eyes on her. "I am now. Why do you come sneaking into my room like a thief?" She spoke rapid Italian. The next few sentences were lost on Atalanta, who could only make out "frighten to death" and "trying to kill me".

It seemed that this was indeed a highly strung lady who expressed herself vocally when something wasn't to her liking.

"This is your new companion. Mademoiselle Renard. You can speak French with her if you want."

Mrs Bucardi looked at Atalanta. "Why?" she barked in Italian. "Can't she speak our own tongue? Why not ask a nice Italian girl like the last one? Oh, I still cry because she is dead. Murdered."

Atalanta froze. Had she understood the last word correctly? Yes of course. There was no mistaking the word *assassinata*.

Mrs Bucardi didn't show any sign of shock. "You'll have to make do, Aunt Delilah. I'm now leaving you two to get acquainted. Mademoiselle Renard can pour you your tea."

"I would rather have some prosecco," Delilah lamented.

Mrs Bucardi snorted and left the room.

Delilah said to Atalanta, "I'm an old woman. Nobody takes me seriously. They want me to drink tea all day long and take my pills."

"You take pills?" Atalanta asked curiously. Mrs Bucardi had just emphasized repeatedly that her husband's aunt was *not* a patient.

"Sleeping pills. I hear things at night and I talk about them. They don't want me to, so they give me pills to make me sleep deeper. But I never take them. I hide them away. They can't make me swallow them."

"They can't." Atalanta came to her. "I do speak some

Italian. But not much. We can try and talk but you must forgive me the mistakes I will make."

"I'll not listen to you mutilate the language," the old woman said, in surprisingly good French. "I went to a fancy boarding school, I speak French. I read French novels to ensure I don't forget."

"You speak it excellently. I'm very happy we can speak freely without me having to look for words all of the time."

"Why did you apply to work with an Italian family on a Greek island if you only speak French? Is France not large enough for you to find a position?"

"Someone pointed out the opening to me and it seemed like a wonderful chance. I have never been to Santorini before."

"What is it with this island?" the old woman scoffed. "It doesn't have grand doges' palaces as Venice does. Merely small fishermen's huts. Everything stinks of fish." She pulled a disgusted face.

Atalanta had to admit that the sight of the octopuses on the line hadn't been very appetizing. But learning about different cultures came with new experiences, opening the mind beyond acquired ideas and tastes. If everything was the same here as it had been in Venice, what would have been the point of coming?

Delilah continued, "They play atrocious music. I can't sleep at night because of the music. I think they worship the sea. But Pietro assures me they have saints just like we do. Well, I can't imagine that the saints I pray to are anything like theirs. Still everyone wants to see this island. This barren rock battered by the sea. The girl who came before you…" She fell silent, her eyes turning pensive. She looked up and said, "She was murdered, you know."

"I heard she had an accident. She fell down the rocks."

"She didn't fall. She was pushed. She knew that someone was stealing. Like I do." The old woman's expression turned fearful. "Will I be next? Will someone murder me? Shove me into the sea?"

Atalanta guessed that if the woman felt that way, she had better not suggest taking a walk, or she would be accused of having come to personally push the old woman over the edge. Still, what she said was interesting in the light of Atalanta's investigations here. "Why would you think she was pushed?" she asked, sitting down beside the woman.

Delilah looked her over with a sharp look. "Did I invite you to sit down? No, no, don't get up, it's fine. Why do I think she was murdered? Because she was too curious for her own good. She was constantly looking into things. Even my nephew's desk."

"His desk?"

"Yes. Someone was in his study in the middle of the night. I heard the sounds of rummaging. I got out of bed and opened my door. I saw the shadow of a young woman, tall and slim, sneaking back to her room."

"But you didn't see her actually leave your nephew's study?"

"I can't see the study door from here." Delilah looked at her as if she was stupid not to get that right away. "I saw the girl come back to her room and put two and two together."

"But two and two don't always make four." Atalanta smiled at her kindly. "Do you have other reasons to think she was murdered?"

"Why would you care? You don't seem shocked that it might have been murder. Most people are disgusted at the mere idea. It can't happen here on this beautiful island. Why would you believe it can?"

"Because I'm a realist. People die everywhere, even in the most idyllic places. And it is odd that a young girl died suddenly. There must be some reason."

"I know that there are people prowling at night. Perhaps she caught them and they killed her."

Atalanta bit her lip. The first idea to come to mind was that Mr Bucardi had figured out the companion was going through his things and he had done something about it. But could he not have dismissed her, sent her away? Why murder someone? It seemed such a drastic measure, and perilous too, if he got caught out.

"Go to my dressing table and open the lower drawer," Delilah said.

Atalanta did what she asked. Inside the drawer were folded stockings.

"Feel under the left stack," the old woman ordered.

Atalanta did so and retrieved a bottle of prosecco and two glasses.

Delilah cackled, "We must drink to your arrival."

Atalanta carried the bottle and glasses to the small table beside the old woman's chair. She opened the bottle and poured. The bubbles spritzed against her hands. She gave Delilah a glass and raised the other herself. "To my arrival."

"May you have a happier stay here than poor Letitia."

Atalanta was about to take her first sip, but the remark turned the drink sour. Could she discover anything? Would it help the grieving mother or only make it worse? And how could she protect herself?

Delilah said, "Come, come, drink up. You can't convince

me that I, a woman on the brink of death, like champagne better than you do. You have your life ahead of you. Tell me … are you in love?"

Atalanta almost choked on her drink and coughed.

Delilah cackled again. "You look all prim and confused. Letitia was in love. She hid it from the others but not from me. She hummed and sang all day. I never asked her who it was, though. I despise the Greek men with their coarse ways."

"So it was a local man?" *Interesting.*

"Yes, but not a fisherman, I'm sure. Letitia hated the smell of fish as much as I do. It must have been someone better."

Andreas? Atalanta said cheerfully, "Well, falling in love is usually a good thing. It's nice to know she was so happy…" *Before she died.*

Hadn't Andreas said it was better if people died doing things they loved? Had he been with her when Letitia took the fatal fall? Had it been an accident, and had Andreas thought it better no one knew he had been there, but unable to prevent it? Did he perhaps even feel a bit guilty and tried to convince himself that at least she had died happy?

Or was Delilah consciously leading her astray? Setting up the idea of a local man Letitia had been in love with to lead attention away from the burg? While in reality … Mr Bucardi had flirted with Letitia and Mrs Bucardi had wanted to end it by shoving the unwanted companion into the sea? Did Delilah suspect her nephew's wife? Judging by their interaction, there was no love lost between them.

Which could also mean that Delilah merely *wanted* to suspect Mrs Bucardi, without having any actual proof of her involvement in Letitia's death.

Atalanta rubbed her forehead with her free hand. This was going to get very complicated. How to work out all of the relationships and determine who had had the best motive for murder.

Chapter Six

Atalanta spent the afternoon reading to Delilah and helping her with various tasks. She soon discovered the elderly lady liked to make a fuss about everything. First, her wool was missing, but the instant it was found she didn't want to knit anymore. Then she wanted a particular book of poetry. As soon as it was fetched, she was tired and needed a nap. But only if her legs were covered with a particular silk shawl. And so the hunt for the shawl began.

Atalanta maintained a pleasant attitude throughout, as she was conscious of her position as subservient to this woman, and she didn't want to ruin her stay here on the very first day. It did sting a bit. At the boarding school in Switzerland, she had been an employee but people had still treated her with some respect. Especially the pupils. Here Delilah determined what she did, where she was, every minute of the day. She hoped it would leave her some time for actual sleuthing.

When they came downstairs for dinner, the old lady leaning on Atalanta's arm, they found Mr Bucardi already seated at the head of the table. He looked distracted and was flicking through a small leather-bound notebook. Mrs Bucardi had just entered before them and strode up to sit at her husband's right-hand side. But Delilah suddenly let go of Atalanta, overtook her nephew's wife with a few quick paces and took the seat before she could. "I've explained to you before," she said sharply, "that this is *my* place."

"It's not," Mrs Bucardi protested. "I'm the mistress of this house."

"If you really think so, you're even more pitiful than I imagined." Delilah focused on her nephew. "Put away that business book and make some conversation. You are able to be so charming, I hear, but you rarely display that quality at home."

Now both spouses were livid, judging by their high colour and the way in which Mrs Bucardi's nostrils had widened, as if she were a horse gearing up to rear.

Atalanta said for distraction, "Can someone please tell me where I may sit? I don't know if we are expecting more people…" She glanced around the long table with the many set places.

Mr Bucardi said, "Paula and Luca will be here in a minute."

At her surprised look he explained, "I know it's customary in other households for the children to eat in the nursery with their nanny. But we Italians strongly believe in family. A child should be with its parents. Luca eats with us. Paula sees to it that he behaves."

"Or not," Mrs Bucardi said, just loud enough to be heard.

Her husband shot her an irritated look. Then he started a conversation in rapid Italian with Delilah.

Atalanta realized she still didn't know where she should sit.

The door was pushed open so wide it hit the wall with a bang and Luca stormed in. "Papa, Papa," he called, "look what I've got." He ran for his father, holding something in his hand.

Upon spying it Mrs Bucardi gave a scream. "It's a live animal. Take it away."

"It's only a crab," her son said impatiently. "I found it by the water."

"You know you're not allowed near the water. You could fall in and drown."

Luca looked up at his mother. "Titia drowned, didn't she?" His young face was serious, his brows drawing together. "But she didn't like water. I don't understand why she went near it. She never wanted to play on the beach with me."

Atalanta held her breath. Was this an important clue? The young woman having a fear of water, and still falling down rocks and drowning? Who had lured her there? With what strong inducement?

Mrs Bucardi said, "Don't talk such nonsense." She threw Atalanta a quick look. "Letitia loved water. She even asked me several times where you could swim around the island. I told her it might be dangerous as the tide could be strong and the rocks are unforgiving. But she had a mind of her own."

"She was a headstrong girl," Delilah agreed. She shook her head. "It's regrettable that people have to pay so dearly for a single mistake."

Atalanta narrowed her eyes. The elderly lady had told her that the girl in her employ had been murdered. Now she acted like it had indeed been an accident. After all, that was what she meant by paying for a mistake, didn't she? That the girl had gone near water despite warnings and…

Or was she misreading Delilah's words? Was there more to them than she could fathom right now?

The butler appeared in the doorway and announced, "Miss Calista is here to see you."

Mrs Bucardi turned with a ready smile. "Calista? How wonderful. I had no idea she was coming to the island this month. You?" She glanced at her husband who shrugged while flicking through the notebook again.

Mrs Bucardi left the room with feather-light steps and was back in an instant ushering a stunning woman in her mid-thirties with raven-black hair that hung down her back in dramatic curls. Her pale face was dominated by huge brown eyes framed by thick lashes. She wore a long sea-blue gown with turquoise lace fluttering down from her waist like strands of seaweed. In all, she looked like a mermaid who had been washed up on the shore.

Luca ran for her. "Look, Calista. It's a crab."

She leaned down and admired the little creature. "That's very beautiful. But you must not keep him, Luca, or he'll die. He needs the sea. Shall we put him back, you and I?"

Luca nodded. "Can I?" he asked his mother.

Mrs Bucardi nodded with an indulgent smile. "But don't stay away too long. Dinner is about to be served."

A female voice said, "Shall I go along to ensure Luca isn't too wild?" In the doorway stood the blonde young woman who had left the burg with Andreas after Atalanta had arrived. She had changed out of the red, orange and yellow dress into a dark-green garment that was more of a uniform, with its white collar. But nothing about her vibrant face had changed. She tilted her chin up as if daring Mrs Bucardi to say no.

Mrs Bucardi met her gaze with a blank look. "That won't be

necessary, Paula. Sit down and have dinner with us. You may sit there…" She pointed to a seat down the table. "Opposite the new companion."

Paula threw Atalanta a curious look as if they had never met before. "The new companion? So shortly after Titia died … It was quite sensational, you know."

Atalanta held the gaze of the young woman who was apparently Luca's nanny. A member of the staff who simply left the burg as she pleased, forgetting about her charge.

"We need not discuss it over dinner," Mrs Bucardi said. She took a seat at her husband's left hand, leaving Delilah in the place she had demanded for herself.

Atalanta sat down opposite Paula, sensing the deliberate insult in placing both of them away from the family much further down the long table. Admittedly, they were not guests here, but employees. Still, all the empty seats in between seemed to smirk at her that she was now degraded in the world, no longer part of the circles she had moved in as a new heiress.

Something struck her foot under the table. She looked up at Paula. Earlier she had believed her to be in her late twenties, but right now, as she could study her features better, she concluded she had to be younger. Around Letitia's age? Had the two of them been friends? Could she learn more about Letitia's death from Paula?

The girl mouthed to her, "Need to talk to you. After dinner."

Atalanta didn't commit to anything, by keeping her features neutral, but as she focused on her plate, the foot under the table made contact with her ankle. She looked up and nodded briefly to acknowledge she had understood the girl. Else she'd keep prodding her all during dinner.

Paula's behaviour now showed a marked change to her distant and almost haughty approach earlier, in the presence of Andreas Papoudopolis. Was Paula enamoured with the handsome Greek and had she therefore ignored a potential rival?

Or had Andreas told her something that had convinced her she needed to befriend Atalanta, as soon as possible?

What had the two of them been up to, away from the burg?

The list of questions in Atalanta's mind became longer and longer, and this was only her first day here.

It took Calista and Luca until dessert to return. Not much of interest had been said, although Mrs Bucardi attempted to draw her husband into conversation about something called the festival of saints. Atalanta didn't know what it was but it seemed to be important and it also seemed the Bucardis played some part in it, as Mrs Bucardi mentioned preparations of the courtyard and the acquisition of candles, seafood and flowers.

When Luca stormed into the room, his dark hair was dishevelled and there was a smudge on his cheek. Mrs Bucardi half rose from her chair. "What happened? Did you fall?"

"When releasing the crab, he almost fell into the water but I managed to grab him by the shoulder and nothing disastrous happened." Calista laughed. "You know I would never let any harm come to him."

Mrs Bucardi shook her head. "I wish you wouldn't indulge his wild side."

"He is a little boy. He needs to have a wild side, or I would wonder if he was ill." She turned to Luca. "Now sit down and eat your dinner. We're so late already. And I don't want to hear you don't like it. Eat whatever is served."

Luca nodded earnestly and climbed on his chair as the butler began to serve the soup.

Calista stood there with her curls scattered across her shoulders, her dress darker in places. Atalanta looked closer and deduced it had been wetted. Mrs Bucardi said, "I can't believe you take chances with such a beautiful dress. It deserves better treatment."

"I designed it to live in it, not to hide it away in a closet where nothing can happen to it," Calista replied carelessly. She stretched her arms up to the ceiling. "It's such a beautiful evening and you're all sitting indoors."

"We're having dinner, like normal people are wont to do," Bucardi replied with a shake of the head. "Every time you appear at the *castello*, things get stirred up."

"Perhaps they need a bit of stirring," Calista said with a firm nod. She walked over to Delilah and said, "How are you, Aunt Delilah?"

Delilah barely gave her a glance. "I'm not your aunt. And I'm fine, thank you. Please sit down and be quiet, or leave the room so we may eat in peace."

Calista blinked a moment, then she burst out in heartfelt laughter. "*Si, Signora.*" She darted from the room.

Mrs Bucardi caught Atalanta's befuddled look and explained, "Calista is a dear friend of mine. We met when we were children. We attended the same boarding school and had our debut together. Calista has a Greek father and an Italian mother. She is at home in both cultures. In fact, I think she feels at home almost anywhere. She travels a lot."

"Because she makes wonderful clothes," Luca enthused. "She made her own dress. Isn't that clever?"

Atalanta nodded. "Very clever."

After this outburst of enthusiasm about her friend Mrs Bucardi returned to her dessert of caramelized fruit with zabaglione, and silence hung in the room. No one seemed to find it painful. Only Paula tried to draw Atalanta's attention again, making faces at her to convey how idiotic she thought all of this was.

Atalanta was determined not to be pulled into confidence with the nanny, who was obviously more forward than was appropriate. If she wanted to accomplish anything here, she had to stay on a good footing with most people around her. *If that means that Paula thinks me dull, all the better.*

After dessert was finished, Mrs Bucardi invited everyone to have coffee on the terrace. Atalanta discovered it was a beautiful wooden structure built beside the burg on an outcrop of the rocks and full of potted palms and blossoming plants. The steps leading up to it made Atalanta's tender calves ache once more.

Calista was there already, lounging in a deck chair. She jumped to her feet when she saw them coming and exclaimed, "I have some wonderful news. Can you guess who will be celebrating the festival of the saints with us tomorrow? I met him on my way over here. Yes, it's a male."

"With you it's always a male," Delilah said in a mocking tone.

Calista didn't reply. She kept her gaze on Mrs Bucardi as she said, "Go on, guess. You'll never be able to work it out."

"Then why should she guess?" Bucardi said, half rebuking, half amused.

Atalanta recalled Bucardi had mentioned a best friend of his wife's who was courted by men on the telephone. He had even mentioned the possibility of duels. It had struck her as over-dramatic, but having seen beautiful, lively Calista now, the potential for drama became more viable.

Calista came closer to Mrs Bucardi. "You'd never think he'd come here. He'd sooner avoid it."

Mrs Bucardi looked alarmed now. Atalanta sensed it by her stance, the way she clasped her hands together and then relaxed them again with an effort.

Calista said, "Last time we met we were all in Monaco. For the races."

Mrs Bucardi turned pale. She walked to the railing and looked out over the sea. Her shoulders seemed to quiver with tension. "Is it Fernando Guitarez?" she asked.

Atalanta had the impression she was choosing the first name that came to mind, to buy time to compose herself or to divert attention, instead of mentioning the person she was really thinking of. And clearly anxious about.

"No." Calista waved a dismissive hand. "You know better than to mention him. He behaved terribly on that occasion."

"He was dead drunk," Mr Bucardi said with loathing in his voice. He had extracted a cigarette and a golden lighter but was watching his wife too intently to complete the gesture of lighting it.

"Well, you did say we'd never guess he would show his face here again," Paula interjected. "So it could be this Signor Guitarez, couldn't it?" Her eyes were alive with curiosity.

Mrs Bucardi said, "Please take Luca to bed, Paula."

"No, Calista is going to do that," the little boy protested. "She promised me when we set the crab free."

"Take Luca to bed, Paula." Mrs Bucardi turned around, her eyes flashing at the nanny.

Paula said, "Luca, come," and held out her hand.

Luca shook his head, sticking out his chin.

"Luca …" His mother's tone was warning now.

"Luca, do what your mother says," Bucardi snapped, his hand up to insert the cigarette between his lips and light it.

But Luca threw himself on the floor and yelled, "I won't go to bed. Calista must take me. She promised."

"Luca," Bucardi warned, taking two steps to his squirming son.

"I'll go along," Calista said, walking to Luca who immediately jumped to his feet and put his hand in hers. "Promises must be kept." At the steps down from the terrace she said to Mrs Bucardi, almost as an afterthought, "It's Raoul who is coming tomorrow."

Mrs Bucardi's already pale face didn't move a muscle. Only her eyes flickered a moment with something Atalanta could not quite define. Was it fear?

Or anxiety?

"Raoul Lemont?" Bucardi asked. "That daredevil race car driver who's always risking his life? I didn't know he cared for religious festivals. Not that he can't use the protection of a few saints…" He laughed ruefully before taking a deep inhale from the cigarette.

"Paula," Mrs Bucardi said to the nanny. "Go with Calista and Luca."

Paula stood with her back to the company, staring out across the island. She didn't respond to the order.

"Paula…" Mrs Bucardi said again.

The girl turned around reluctantly. "I was just looking to see if I could spot the red rocks from here."

"Red rocks?" Mrs Bucardi frowned. "I do know we have a red beach here, but it's on the other side of the island. You certainly can't see it from here. Now, don't stall, and get on with your duties."

"I wonder if they're visible from the tower," Paula said in a dreamy voice. "I love the view from up there. Especially when it's clear, you can see across the entire island." She held her hands up to her face, her fingers curled into tubes, as if to mime looking through binoculars.

"Paula…" Mr Bucardi shook his head at her. "At times you can be worse than Luca, making up stories when he doesn't want to go to bed."

"I never make up stories," Paula said with a dazzling smile. "But if you don't know where the red rocks are exactly, I'll have to ask Andreas. He knows this island like the back of his hand."

"I thought he wasn't a native," Mrs Bucardi said. "He must have told you some tale to make himself interesting."

Paula seemed to want to protest, but Mrs Bucardi said sharply, "I know you left the burg this afternoon to dally with that man. And I don't want you to do that again. You're employed to take care of Luca, and I expect you to take that seriously."

Paula just laughed and darted down the steps after Calista and Luca.

Atalanta wondered if the forward nanny was a family relation of the Bucardis. She didn't behave like a servant at all and even tried to stay with the company for the after-dinner coffee. Was it just because of the beautiful evening that she didn't want to sit indoors in the nursery?

Or had she been attuned to the tension and wanted to know what the arrival of Raoul Lemont truly meant?

Atalanta had known he would be coming and he would somehow place himself in her path, but it also surprised her. Not because he was so brazen as to come here to the burg instead of settling on the island and waiting for her to reach out to him, but because it seemed all these people knew him. Not as in knew of him, of his name or his racing, but it felt as if they had some history with him.

Raoul hadn't mentioned that to her at all when they had made plans for this trip. He had said he knew the Bucardis, knew that they had a burg on Santorini, and she had assumed he had heard about it. But now she recalled how he had described the burg to her in detail, even mentioning this very terrace with the low stone wall and the steep drop to the sea.

At the time she had believed it to have been a general description of such a *castello*, not of a place he had actually been to. Why hadn't he said he had visited the burg before? And wouldn't he have been able to deduce something about the Bucardis' personal life if he had indeed stayed here? Atalanta had been here for mere hours and already she knew that the marriage was fraught with tension, Bucardi liked to flirt with other women, his wife was remarkably cool to their son, and Calista...

Did Raoul also know the beautiful Calista?

Atalanta's mind whirled. The way in which Raoul had tried to dissuade her from taking the case now gained new meaning. He had to have known more about the risks she might run here. Because of Mr Bucardi's flirtatious antics?

Mrs Bucardi's jealousy? Or something else she didn't know about yet?

Why had he been so reticent? He had seemed worried about her well-being and the danger she might be in at the burg. There seemed only one conclusion possible. His loyalty to the Bucardis was somehow greater than his inclination to protect her. Did Bucardi sponsor races? Was Raoul keen to stay on a good footing with him?

But he could have told her a few personal details and she would have been discreet about them, making certain Bucardi never found out who had shared with her.

She frowned hard. If Raoul hadn't been honest with her about whatever personal tie connected him to the Bucardis – the very employers of the girl who had died – could she even trust him to help her with an open mind?

Her heart was heavy as she stood beside Mrs Bucardi looking at the gorgeous view. Mrs Bucardi said in a forced cheerful tone, "You must wonder, Mademoiselle Renard, what festival it is we're all so excited about. It is called the festival of saints and is celebrated on Santorini in August. The island's people gather to share food and play sea-themed games that have connections with the local saints who protect the fishermen and the community. My husband's grandfather created a new tradition of inviting the villagers to the burg for the day, where there are celebrations and games of archery with prizes, and at the end of the day a meal together in the courtyard. At first people were reluctant to come because we aren't Greek, but many years of wonderful festivities have changed the mood. Now everyone is looking forward to it."

"Everyone but the person who sent the note," Delilah's voice said behind them.

Mrs Bucardi turned round. Her features had become livelier as she had spoken to Atalanta, but now they turned still again and watchful, suspicion flickering in her eyes. "What do you mean?"

"The note," the elderly lady said with apparent glee. "A note was delivered yesterday saying the sea took one Venetian as sacrifice, and it will take more. To make us pay for usurping the island which isn't ours."

Mrs Bucardi's pale cheeks flushed fiery. "What nonsense. Who'd write such a thing? Are you making this up? Yes, I guess you are. Just out of spite." She threw in a few Italian words which Atalanta didn't know but supposed weren't too flattering.

Delilah didn't flinch. "It was a warning. Perhaps even kindly meant? The sea did take a Venetian. Letitia."

"She had an accident. The sea didn't take her. All these superstitious mutterings…"

"Still you celebrate the festival of saints tomorrow. You burn candles for saints who are not your own. You pray to them for another child. Is that not superstition?"

Mrs Bucardi was crimson now. "I don't feel too well," she muttered. "I must lie down." And she left the terrace in a hurry.

Delilah looked after her with a dispassionate look. "For many years," she said to Atalanta, "my nephew and Victoria hoped for a child that didn't come. They had about given up hope when Luca was born."

Atalanta glanced past the elderly lady at Mr Bucardi who sat on a deck chair, looking in his notebook again. It didn't seem like he cared that his wife had just fled the terrace because of his aunt's derogatory treatment. At dinner he had also not corrected Delilah when she had taken Mrs Bucardi's seat.

Delilah said, "She is very worried about him all the time that something will happen to him and her happiness will be snatched away from her. That's why she wants another child. As insurance."

"I believe she loves Luca very much," Atalanta said, although it struck her as odd that if the child had been so wanted, the mother would treat him so coldly at times. But perhaps her focus on producing an heir had changed her personality and made her less open and unguarded than others might be who had not had the same experience? Atalanta didn't know her well and didn't want to judge her harshly.

No, she had to understand people better first, their dynamics and the undertows of their relationships.

And also find out how Raoul fitted in, before she carelessly shared details of her discoveries with him.

Chapter Seven

Atalanta was in her room getting ready for bed when a rap sounded on the door. Without waiting for a reply, the door swung open and Paula burst in. She shut the door and leaned against it. "Finally I can catch you alone." She blew a lock of loose blonde hair away from her hot face. "In this household you have to be on your feet from dawn to dusk."

"But Luca is a little dear, isn't he?" Atalanta said, to provoke her.

Paula rolled her eyes. "A manipulative little monster, you mean. He knows exactly when to smile and be nice, or to break out into a terrible temper. You saw him on the terrace. That's how he gets his way."

"Aren't all young children like that?"

"I wouldn't know. This is my first time working as a nanny. I only wanted to get away from my mother and have a change of scenery." Paula stretched her arms and walked about the room. "Your room is bigger than mine. But I guess you are higher in rank, as you serve the *grande dame*." She burst out laughing. "A woman who can't remember what she had for dinner two days ago, and still we all have to kiss her feet."

Atalanta sat on the edge of her bed, watching the girl's lively face. Paula was outspoken and at times even spiteful, but Atalanta had often noticed this behaviour among her pupils and knew it could cover insecurity and a need to be loved. Did that also explain Paula's strange metamorphosis from a distinguished lady of the world who went walking with the handsome Papoudopolis, to a carefree schoolgirl who now freely shared her thoughts?

Or did it suggest that Paula was anything but carefree and sharing her thoughts?

Was this a role she had assumed with Atalanta to play into her sense of superiority and gain her confidence? Was she suddenly acting like she was much younger and more naïve, to ensure that Atalanta didn't think her capable of subterfuge?

Capable of … murder?

Atalanta felt her spine stiffen at the idea of facing Letitia's killer right now, but she assumed a light conversational tone as she said, "How long have you been here?"

"Since spring. Luca had a string of nannies before that. None of them wanted to stay. It isn't him, I guess. He isn't too bad if you just do what he wants you to. But his mother is a disaster. She's always unhappy about something. You can never do anything right for her."

She stopped and eyed Atalanta. "Don't you worry that you're cast to replace a dead girl?"

The direct reference to the death surprised Atalanta. Surely, if Paula was involved, she would be more circumspect? Or did she want to ascertain if Atalanta believed the accident story and her guilty secret would be safe?

"I thought she died by accident?" Atalanta asked. "Why would that bother me?"

"I don't know." Paula rubbed her arms. "Sometimes there's this heavy atmosphere of gloom and doom at this burg. Perhaps it's cursed?"

"Cursed?" Atalanta echoed, thinking of the threatening note Delilah had mentioned on the terrace. A Venetian sacrifice. Andreas had said the islanders were superstitious. Had one of them been involved in Letitia's death? Perhaps also because of her infatuation with a local man? Something the islanders didn't like because of their strained relationship with the Venetian 'usurpers' at the *castello*?

Paula rolled her eyes. "Well, not literally of course. I don't think there's some evil power destroying whoever lives here. But the people are all so ... morose and unhappy. They are, themselves, the curse on this place."

"I see what you mean." This conclusion was quite perceptive and suggested that Paula was anything but the superficial, loud girl she pretended to be.

Was the girl's behaviour intentional or was she just young and candid, without guile?

Let's see if we can find out. Atalanta stretched her legs and asked casually, "Did you know the deceased girl well?"

"We had talked a few times. But Titia was awfully timid. She was terrified of Mrs Bucardi. As soon as I said something not too nice about her, she would tell me to shut up. She seemed afraid someone would overhear and report us."

"Who would do such a thing?" Atalanta asked, widening her eyes as if the prospect worried her. "Lemusier, perhaps? Butlers can be so controlling."

"Not him. He trembles like a reed when Mrs Bucardi

chastises him." Paula pursed her lips. "Of course, Mrs Bucardi would like to have spies everywhere to know what everyone is doing. Especially her husband. He's not exactly faithful to her. He only married her because his family wanted him to. She is from an old Venetian house, like he is, and money must marry money. Titles must be connected and property must stay together. That kind of story. He never loved her and she certainly doesn't love him." Paula fell silent.

Atalanta asked, "Does she love someone else?"

Paula looked at her. "It's your first night here and you ask a question like that? Men are allowed to have affairs, but not their respectable wives."

Atalanta shrugged. "I'm French. We aren't easily shocked by affairs, whoever is having them. If you tell me that theirs is a loveless match, I assume that they have others in their lives."

Paula's eyes lit up. "I can talk to you. Yes, I think she's in love with someone else. She keeps it hidden very well. He can be more open about his affairs. I mean, a rich man with good looks is more or less expected to have affairs, isn't he? As long as he doesn't flaunt the other woman, and his wife isn't humiliated by his behaviour, he can do what he wants. She, on the other hand... If Bucardi ever found out she was unfaithful, he'd..."

"Divorce her?" Atalanta suggested.

"He'd sooner kill her. He has a terrible temper. I once saw him get angry with a local who had sold him something that wasn't up to par, and he grabbed a knife and waved it at the man. The fisherman ran and Bucardi even chased him with the knife." She leaned over closer. "I wouldn't like to get into trouble with him."

"Thanks for the warning, I appreciate it." Atalanta

wondered how to tread from here. She could obviously learn a lot from the talkative Paula but she shouldn't alert her to an unusual interest in the household. For she was certain that Paula would also discuss her behaviour with other people and she didn't want to draw special attention to herself.

"I have some nougat in my luggage. Do you want some?"

Paula shook her head. "I don't have a sweet tooth." She walked to the window and looked out. "You can make it easy for yourself by being nice to the old lady. If you talk along with her and nod to everything she claims, she may give you money or things."

"Things?" Atalanta asked.

"Yes. She gave me a gold necklace. Told me never to tell a soul as Mrs Bucardi would be livid that she gave it away. But it is hers to do with as she pleases. I hid it among my clothes. Once I can get away from here, I'll sell it and have a nice holiday. My mother never gave me any money of my own so I have to fend for myself."

Paula turned to Atalanta and added, "I don't intend to work as a nanny until I'm as old as you are."

Atalanta wanted to protest she wasn't that old, but Paula didn't give her the chance. "I want to make something of my life," she said passionately, "while I have good looks and can snare a rich man. My sister said it was cold-hearted to think that way, and I'd be sorry if I was older and no one loved me, but I think money is just wonderful. It can buy you so many beautiful things." She nodded at the white-and-blue dressing table where Atalanta had put two perfume bottles and a modest jewellery box. "Luxurious scents, gorgeous necklaces and bracelets, the best dresses … I want it all. And I'm going to get it." She smiled, a self-confident triumphant smile.

"I suppose you don't earn all that much here," Atalanta said. "And how much can that gold necklace Delilah gave you be worth?"

"That's not the point. I have" – Paula seemed to hesitate, as if she was torn between a desire to share and doubt whether this was a sensible thing to do – "a little business. It'll soon take off and then I'm rich. I'll never have to take orders again. Certainly not from *her*." Paula seemed overjoyed at the prospect, staring into the distance as if she could already see a glorious future unrolling in front of her. Then she snapped out of it and said to Atalanta, "At least tomorrow we have a day off from chores for the festival of saints. We can also dress up and mingle among the locals."

"What are we supposed to wear?" Atalanta asked, genuinely interested. Local traditions were fascinating and she intended to learn as much as possible about them.

"White clothes and flowers in your hair. Mrs Bucardi said a few days ago it makes all of us into brides. But some are definitely better-looking brides than others." Paula sniggered as she went to the door. She halted with her hand on the doorknob and asked, "Oh, did you hear Raoul Lemont will also be here? I've never seen him in real life, only in newspaper pictures, and he looks very handsome. I want to get his autograph." She opened the door and stepped into the corridor, adding with a little titter of laughter, "And who knows what else I might get?"

The door shut. Atalanta blinked to herself. Here was a young woman who wasn't ashamed to criticize her employer, accept gifts from a confused elderly lady, chase handsome men… That seemed to be a recipe for disaster.

But it wasn't Paula who had fallen down the cliffs in a supposed accident.

No. It had been the quieter and more subdued Letitia, who hadn't wanted to upset Mrs Bucardi by gossiping and had tried to please everyone. Why?

The more Atalanta thought about it, the less sense it made.

Chapter Eight

Atalanta awoke to the sound of voices in the corridor. Excited voices. And even music in the distance. Oh yes, it was the festival day. The entire island would be gearing up for a long day of eating, drinking, singing, dancing and playing games at the burg. She slipped out of bed and walked to her window overlooking the sea. When she glanced straight down, it was a steep drop to the water. It almost felt as though the *castello* teetered precariously on the edge of the cliff and could fall over at any moment. But that was silly, of course. It had sat there for centuries, as steadfast as the rock it was built on. Still, Atalanta couldn't shed the sense of nervousness she felt as she cast her gaze across the endless water. Raoul was coming today. She had to tell him something useful about the case. But all she had learned so far were people's opinions, not solid facts.

She turned away from the window with a sigh, washed and dressed in a simple white dress with short sleeves. She pulled her hair together in a small bun on her neck so she could put in flowers or add a flower wreath on top of her head, whatever was required. She had never heard of this festival of saints before but was excited to experience first-hand how it was celebrated. She only hoped it didn't involve any octopus tasting.

As she came down the stairs, Mrs Bucardi was in the hallway in a gorgeous white lace dress with her hair piled on top of her head like a crown, adorned with white roses. She looked younger and less tense and even seemed to greet Atalanta with genuine kindness. "I have flowers in the other room for everyone in the household." She gestured to an open door. "If you go in now, you will have a choice before everyone takes the best ones."

"Thank you," Atalanta said, walking inside. On a table were several vases holding dahlias and other white flowers which Atalanta didn't immediately recognize. "Do these grow on the island?" she asked Mrs Bucardi.

"Some I had brought in from the mainland earlier. Others were provided by the local women who also prepared food for today. They grow flowers and herbs in pots on the roofs of their houses. And that orchid" – she gestured at a gorgeous large plant with a dozen flowers – "is from my own collection."

"It's almost a shame to pick a flower from it for just one day. It'll wilt quickly."

"Well, you might as well do it, as others will have no such qualms."

Atalanta realized she was right and selected two beautiful white orchid flowers for her hair. It reminded her of her mother who had loved growing orchids, and she smiled as she stood in front of the mirror to put the flowers in place.

Glancing in the reflection at Mrs Bucardi, she said, "You must have been very busy for weeks, preparing everything. And may I say, you look radiant in that dress?"

"Oh, thank you." Mrs Bucardi flushed. "I was quite uncertain what to wear today. I'm the hostess, of course, but it's a festival of humility and gratitude, so it doesn't seem appropriate to overdo it."

Atalanta wondered if someone had pointed this out to her on a previous occasion. After all, Mrs Bucardi had explained earlier that the celebrations at the burg had a long tradition, so she must have acted as hostess before. Had her husband reproached her that her dress was too ostentatious?

Or Delilah?

"Good morning." Calista breezed into the room. She wore a white dress embroidered with gold thread in an elaborate pattern of shells and waves. Her loose curls were entwined in white flowers that seemed to stick miraculously. Atalanta looked closer and realized they had been attached with thin black wire that was almost invisible against her hair.

Mrs Bucardi gave her a look that was half startled, half indulgent. She had just explained that it was important not to overdo things, but she probably also knew that her friend was like this: an exuberant, happy person who dived into everything she did with zeal.

"Good morning," Calista cried again. "I've already been to the terrace to overlook the sea. I don't believe in saints, but I do believe in the forces of nature, and the sea looks positively good-natured this morning. She can be such a cruel mistress when she wants to, but today she isn't hostile at all."

Atalanta was reminded of the note about the Venetian life

taken by the sea, and asked, "Are the locals very superstitious? Do they believe that the sea takes sacrifices?"

Mrs Bucardi's jaw set, but Calista gasped and said, "Human sacrifices, you mean? What a totally wild and inspirational idea." She looked down at her own dress. "I guess if it did, I am perfectly dressed to be the victim sacrificed. Don't you think?"

"Please don't say such gruesome things," Mrs Bucardi reproached her with fervour. "The sea doesn't take human lives, at least not in that manner. Of course, the occasional fisherman may drown…"

"And Delilah's companion did," Paula cried. She dashed in, wearing a very simple white dress and a wreath of small flowers on her head. She looked like a girl walking in front of a procession to a church. But there was nothing innocent about her as she looked at Mrs Bucardi and said, "Drowning is such a nasty death, don't you think? You probably have time to think about your life and how you wish someone would save you, but it's too late for that."

Her words seemed to carry some deeper meaning that eluded Atalanta. She only noticed how Mrs Bucardi stiffened.

Calista said, "I don't want to think about it. We all have to die someday, I suppose, but if I did pray to saints, I'd pray my death would be peaceful, in my own bed. Now shall we go and have a look at the courtyard? I assume the locals were up early to get everything ready."

Atalanta followed her, eager to see the festival preparations, but not without looking closely at both Paula and Mrs Bucardi. The girl was all smiles, but her eyes were cold and insistent, imprinting the message she had delivered by her cryptic words. Mrs Bucardi looked startled, but it was impossible to determine whether it was because she understood, or just disliked this sinister topic raised on a beautiful day.

In the courtyard women in long white dresses with flower headbands were putting earthenware dishes on long tables. The bowls were covered with coarse cloth to keep insects away. Children played with a dog in the corner and men in sleeveless garments put out wooden targets for a game. Would that be the aforementioned archery? It looked like it.

"There is Raoul!" Calista ran away from them to the main gate.

Atalanta's heart skipped a beat when she saw the familiar figure, casually dressed in a white linen shirt and trousers, his Panama hat in his hand. He grabbed Calista's hand and kissed it, saying something to her in her ear. She laughed and whispered back.

The intimacy of the little scene hurt a bit. Raoul obviously knew Calista a lot better than as a casual acquaintance. On the other hand, he might not have known she would show up here and hadn't seen the need to mention her. Once they had a moment to themselves, Atalanta had to ask him what he knew about the Bucardis that might help the case. She need not let on she was annoyed by his earlier reticence. She could merely observe that he seemed to know them fairly well and could really help her with his knowledge. Appealing to him that way would get her further than reproaches.

She did feel a bit nervous about that moment and to divert herself, Atalanta looked at Mrs Bucardi, intending to ask more about the festivities that day. But the expression on the woman's face struck her dumb. There was such a powerful feeling alive behind her eyes as she watched her best friend flirt with a handsome man.

Was it jealousy? Did she herself ache for a man's appreciation, as her husband didn't love her?

Or had she even had a brief affair with Raoul, but he had diverted his attentions to someone new now, and she could not bear to see him say to another the charming things that he had once said to her?

Was it something else altogether? Something related to the strange events here and to the atmosphere of impending doom that Paula had called a curse last night?

Raoul came over to them, Calista two paces ahead of him. "You know Raoul, Victoria," she said to Mrs Bucardi. "This is Paula, the nanny, and Mademoiselle Renard, the new companion of Aunt Delilah." She grinned. "She doesn't like me calling her Aunt, but I still do."

Raoul nodded at Atalanta. "Pleased to meet you." His gaze brushed past Paula without much interest. Atalanta guessed he avoided the adoration of girls who could only embarrass him with their schoolgirl infatuations. Was it even about him, or about the aura that clung to him because of his dangerous profession, the expensive cars he drove and the luxurious life he led?

"I'm dying for a smoke," Calista said and pulled Raoul along to the terrace. "We don't want to upset the locals who are getting things ready for the feast. They abhor women who smoke." Her voice died away in the bustle as she kept talking to Raoul while leading him up the stone steps to the terrace.

Atalanta stared after her. She'd give anything to have ten minutes with Raoul alone and discuss what she had learned so far, hear his opinion, not do this by herself. But Raoul could perhaps not be trusted. What was his connection here? Why had he not revealed to her that he knew the Bucardis more intimately and had been to the burg before?

Why had she ever let herself be talked into accepting the mysterious assignment from the veiled lady?

Because of a mother's broken heart, she told herself. *Grandfather would have approved.*

As she considered the words, she realized something with a sharp jolt of awareness. Yes, he might have approved of her taking the case – especially as the veiled lady had told her that her grandfather had helped her before, and had said he would always be there for her, should she need him again – but her grandfather would also have warned her not to take anything at face value and to guard her back at all times. *And to ask myself why Raoul Lemont offered to help me.*

According to his story, he had called Renard in Paris and had learned from him that she was in Venice. That was true, because Renard had asked her if she had managed to meet with Mr Lemont. So Raoul had wanted to meet her to show her around Venice and had then *accidentally* seen the woman in black following her.

But what if he hadn't told her the full truth? What if, upon arrival in Venice, Raoul had heard about Letitia's death at the Bucardi burg? What if he had known or at least suspected who the woman in black was, even before she had approached Atalanta with her request?

But if Raoul had inserted himself in her case on purpose, what could he possibly want to achieve? To be present as she investigated, to know in what direction her suspicions went?

Or to actually direct her to follow a certain line of argument?

Why had Calista thought Mrs Bucardi would never expect

Raoul to turn up here? Had they been lovers? Had it ended badly between them? But did Raoul still feel some kind of obligation towards Mrs Bucardi? Had he come to find out if she was involved in Letitia's death? Or to prevent Atalanta from even thinking in that direction?

Atalanta lifted a hand and rubbed her forehead. This was a complex case with many angles to keep in mind. Until she knew more about the personal relationships between all the players – Raoul included – she had to be very careful how she proceeded.

Mrs Bucardi said, "I must discuss a few last things with the women who take care of the food." She walked away and engaged in conversation with two women who placed more large earthenware bowls on the table. Atalanta wondered if goat's cheese would be among the treats offered. She had tasted it in Switzerland, but had heard the Greek variety was especially delicious.

Paula cast angry looks in the direction of the terrace. "Why must Calista usurp him like that?" she whispered to Atalanta in a hateful voice. "He is not hers. Or could they be involved? She is a very good-looking woman."

Calista. Could Raoul be interested in protecting her from involvement in a murder case? But Calista had appeared on the island last night. She hadn't been here when Letitia had died.

Or had she? That was something Atalanta had to ascertain.

Paula said in a vicious tone, "I wish I could tell him, though, that Calista's hardly faithful. I heard Mr Bucardi tell his wife that her best friend was a shameless flirt who wouldn't hesitate to seduce a man for a fortnight on his yacht or in his villa."

"That's quite enough," Atalanta said with determination. "We're here to celebrate a festive day. I would advise you not to be a fool and run after that race car driver all day long. He'll probably pay you no mind and you'll only ruin the fun you might have if you focus your attention elsewhere."

"You should say so! You practically lost both eyeballs ogling him," Paula chided. "But he has better picks here. By the dozen." She laughed spitefully and walked away.

For a moment Atalanta was tempted to go after her and tear the flower garland off her head. But that would be very childish. She was a grown woman, and on a case here. She shouldn't let her hurt feelings get the better of her.

Still, the remark stung in earnest. Had she been ogling Raoul? She had been eager to see him, of course, to discuss the case and…

And his good looks have nothing to do with it? she questioned herself with a half-smile. Paula wasn't so terribly wrong perhaps, which made her words all the more hurtful. Because there could be a kernel of truth in them. Raoul was a handsome man who had so many opportunities to meet the most beautiful women in the world: movie stars, singers, dancers, titled ladies. He could have his pick, choose a bride from among the most eligible ladies.

Still, he had told her he didn't believe in love, or in earnest relationships.

She almost shook her head in an attempt to dispel the thoughts. She wasn't here for Raoul. She wasn't here to analyse her complex feelings for him. She wanted to be friends with him, to have someone to support her on a case like this, but the realization that he had kept information from her had made it painfully clear that no one could be trusted. She couldn't afford the luxury of relying on another. She'd have to do this alone.

And in her life she had so often been alone that she could certainly do that. She had to concentrate on the case and on finding out what had happened to her predecessor.

"Enjoying yourself?" Raoul's voice was warm at her ear. Atalanta stood at the back of a crowd watching the archery. Men from the village with muscled bare arms were shooting at targets with homemade crossbows. The metal-tipped arrows pierced the boards with a thudding sound, drawing cries of admiration from the crowd. Andreas Papoudopolis kept the score on a large blackboard he had erected. He had written the names of the participants in Greek, and Atalanta tried to make out the letters. Foreign languages fascinated her, especially those written in letters other than the Roman alphabet.

When she heard Raoul's voice, she didn't turn her head but acted as if she was still completely engrossed in the archery. He was speaking softly and in French, which was something most local people wouldn't follow.

"It's nice to relax a little," she said softly. "The atmosphere has been tense since my arrival."

"Why?" he asked sharply.

She realized how happy she was to discuss things with someone, with him, with … a friend? But was he truly her friend if he had lied about knowing the people here personally? She couldn't imagine he had simply forgotten to mention that he had stayed with them before.

And she even suspected him now of having offered his

help with the case for an ulterior motive. Of having followed her to Murano exactly because the woman in black was intent on hiring her.

She needed to know why he had held back information before she shared anything important with him.

She looked around her to ascertain that none of the key players were anywhere near and could catch something they shouldn't. She discerned Mrs Bucardi's rose bun ahead, with Calista's wild-flower stream beside her. To their left, by one of the tables with food, Paula had Luca on her arm. He tried to pull at her flower wreath and she relented and let him wear it for a while. Bucardi and Andreas stood in front, overseeing the shooting. And the old lady was in her room resting. She wouldn't join all of the festivities as the entire programme was considered too taxing for her.

This should be perfectly safe.

Atalanta stepped back and drew Raoul into the shadows of a niche. Her heel struck a casket of wine that had been put there for later. The locals had also brought in large barrels of some other alcoholic drink that was produced on the island. *Ouzo* perhaps?

"You know Calista," she said to Raoul. It wasn't a question but a statement of fact.

He eyed her without understanding. "Yes, I've known her for quite some time. Is that important?"

It is, if you had an affair with her, and are here to keep her out of the murder case, Atalanta thought with a squeeze of her stomach. She could ask now, but she didn't. She wanted to appear unemotional and in charge. "And Mrs Bucardi knows you too. Something about a race in Monaco?"

Raoul waved a hand. "I meet dozens of influential people

at races. I know half of Venice through my work. Vaguely, that is. I told you I knew the Bucardis."

Yes, but he hadn't exactly expounded how well he knew them. And a gut feeling told her there was a reason for that. Something she should try to unearth before it led to trouble down the road.

She tried to fish carefully. "I felt like there was a little tension between people when your name was mentioned last night."

Raoul exhaled. "I wouldn't know why. There's certainly nothing I did to warrant it. Aren't you overthinking things?"

The easy way in which he dismissed her observations as imaginings stung. She was good at what she did. And she had to rely on her instincts. Her grandfather had told her that female intuition was second to none.

But perhaps some facts could induce him to share? "I heard from several sides that the match between the Bucardis was demanded by family and they don't love each other. That means they could be having affairs."

Raoul didn't respond.

Could she ask him outright if he had had an affair with Mrs Bucardi? A flirtation perhaps, nothing serious on his part, but something she might have liked to develop? Anything that would warrant her uneasiness in meeting Raoul again, at her home?

It would be quite brutal to suggest it, she supposed. If nothing had happened, Raoul might wonder if she had lost her mind. She could better phrase it in a general manner.

"Do you know of any such affairs that might be relevant to the case?" She tried to see the truth behind his dark-brown eyes, but his steadfast gaze betrayed nothing.

He said, "I know Bucardi is a ladies' man, but I know very little about her. She is fiercely loyal to her husband, it seems, because her marriage to him was exactly what her family wanted. They didn't have a child for many years and there were whispers about it, but the arrival of young Luca made the dark skies clear. They should be perfectly happy now."

"I doubt that they are." Atalanta took a deep breath. "I even wonder if Bucardi tried to start something with the girl who died. His aunt, Delilah, told me that Letitia was in love. Delilah believes it was a local man she was in love with, but … would Letitia, who wanted to travel, really settle for a Greek bound to this small island?"

"And you think she would have been interested in a married man?"

"Bucardi is very charming and he has houses everywhere. He told me so himself. Letitia might have felt flattered by his attentions and fantasized about a life with him after he had abandoned his wife for her."

Raoul whistled. "And you think Letitia was murdered to keep that fantasy from materializing? By Mrs Bucardi?"

Atalanta couldn't detect any shock in him at the idea that Mrs Bucardi was the murderer. In fact, his expression was perfectly neutral, as if they were discussing the nice tomatoes grown here on Santorini, which the locals had turned into salads for the festival meal.

"I'm not accusing anyone," she said. "That would be most unfair, as I've barely had a chance to look into matters. But it was strange that Mrs Bucardi said that the girl had asked about places to swim, and someone else said that she was afraid of water. That doesn't quite add up."

"So someone is lying." Raoul nodded pensively. A lock of

his dark hair fell over his forehead and he brushed it away with an impatient gesture.

"Do you think Mrs Bucardi would be capable of murder?" Atalanta asked outright. After all, he had just suggested that Mrs Bucardi might have killed Letitia because of an affair the girl might have had with her husband.

Raoul shrugged. "How can one tell? I just mentioned that Victoria is fiercely loyal to her husband. If she felt the perfect façade of her happy marriage was threatened... But then again, she is loyal to her friends as well. She and Calista are as thick as thieves. Years ago when Calista had a mental breakdown, Mrs Bucardi left her husband for months to care for her friend. He wasn't happy about that but she didn't take his opinion into account. She merely said Calista needed her. And I truly believe she might not have survived that time if she hadn't been cared for."

His tone was urgent, genuinely concerned. Atalanta studied his expression to discern more. He seemed so worried, mentioning Calista's problems. Had he once loved her?

Did he love her still?

Considering Calista's character – daring, wild, life-hungry and spontaneous – it made more sense to cast her as Raoul's secret love rather than Mrs Bucardi, who seemed a totally different personality. Was it not easier to imagine Calista as the one Raoul wanted to protect by involving himself in the case?

"Why would you think that Calista wouldn't have survived if Mrs Bucardi hadn't cared for her at the time?" she asked softly. If she kept him talking about Calista, she might learn more about his feelings.

"I saw Calista once, before she disappeared from public view. She was very pale and worn, she looked ready to collapse. Indeed, I heard from others she had fainted at a party. She was exhausted. Rumour had it there was a man involved whom she had lost her heart to and who had dropped her carelessly." He smiled sardonically. "With Calista it is one affair after another, and it's always 'the one' as long as it lasts. She has no reserve when she throws herself into a situation."

Atalanta couldn't quite determine if there was any jealousy on Raoul's part. Instead he sounded … tender? Indulgent?

Raoul continued, "Although after her breakdown she seemed changed. Calmer and more balanced somehow. As if she had decided that it was time to be a little more careful about herself. I can only applaud that."

Atalanta hesitated whether to put it into words. But she had to understand him better, his personal ties to the case, or else she couldn't work with him.

"You speak of her with kindness and understanding." Atalanta saw the warning flash in his eyes like he was gearing up to argue, and added quickly, "It seems that aside from Mrs Bucardi, she isn't much liked here. Would you know why?"

Raoul seemed to quieten down once he understood she merely wanted a general impression. He shrugged and said, "Bucardi never forgave his wife for leaving him for months to care for a friend. And the others must feel Calista is frivolous and a bad influence on her more sensible friend?" He leaned closer, lowering his voice. "Instead of asking me to speculate, you could try and find out for yourself, Mademoiselle Ashford. You are the one *inside* the household."

"Mademoiselle Renard, please. And I know what I should do. In fact, I feel I have seen and heard a lot already. There is enough high emotion to form a powerful mix."

"That could explode into murder?" Raoul asked.

Atalanta nodded. "I just don't see how I can separate half-truths and lies from what actually happened. Everyone seems to have an opinion about it and be equally vocal about expressing it."

"How odd." Raoul's eyes were pensive. "You'd think a death, even accidentally, would be hushed up. Unpleasant and all that. A stain on their perfect life here. Why would they want to discuss it? And especially with the person who arrived to replace the deceased party."

"Exactly. Which is why it is so odd that everyone I have met has mentioned Letitia's death or told me something about it. Freely. I didn't even need to ask." Atalanta pursed her lips. "Or people are all so accommodating, they want to make my investigation easy for me, or…"

"They want to influence your view of the situation," Raoul provided in a grim tone. His eyes were worried.

"Exactly. And I don't know why. They can't all be the killer, can they?"

Loud applause resounded as the archery demonstration came to an end and the crowd broke apart. Men surrounded the winner as a garland was placed on his head and cups of wine were handed around.

Raoul quickly stepped away from Atalanta before anyone they knew saw them together. He did manage to whisper, "Come to the cyclops rock later so we can talk more."

"The cyclops rock?"

"If you leave through that small wooden door in the courtyard…" He pointed it out to her. "Then you can follow a path that leads to an outcrop. I'll be waiting for you there, an hour from now."

Atalanta nodded and walked away from him, running into

Luca who held Paula's wreath in his hand and wanted to toss it away. Atalanta grabbed him by the shoulders and turned him round so he had to return the adornment to its irate owner. Paula put aside a cup of wine she had just emptied and huffed while putting the wreath back on her head. Her fiery-red fingernails contrasted sharply with the white of the flowers. "I went to a lot of trouble to weave that wretched thing with my own hands. I need another drink, my lips are parched. This is supposed to be a cheerful day of celebrating, and all I'm doing is running after this little bandit. Can't you watch Luca for half an hour, Atalanta? Please?"

Atalanta should have reproached her for using her first name, but she knew with Paula it wouldn't leave an impression. She merely nodded and Paula dashed away without even saying thank you. Paula picked up a cup of wine and took a few deep sips, before spying someone among the crowd. Clutching the cup, she began to move through the throng of people, apparently intent on meeting up with someone she knew. Atalanta wondered whether she should follow her, but she could hardly do so while Luca was with her, and she also caught Mrs Bucardi looking in her direction. She hoped she wouldn't get told off for taking on other people's duties while neglecting her own. But Delilah was comfortable in her room and had assured her she could celebrate if she wanted. This was a rare opportunity to enjoy some freedom and breathe the spirit of the island.

She took Luca along to see women dancing to the melancholy music of the bouzouki, their arms around each other's shoulders, weaving up and down the courtyard like waves of the sea. At times they gave a high-pitched cry that could be anything from a shout of joy to a call to battle. Luca hung against her, complaining he was thirsty. She brushed the hair away from his hot face and took him inside for a glass of milk and some biscuits.

Becoming lively again, he told her an entire story about a whale in the sea that had overturned a boat, and about people worshipping whales. He even said there was a saint for them but she doubted he had got that right. She did enjoy listening to his babbling and it eased some of the tension she had felt despite the enjoyable day. She shouldn't forget how she had always wanted to travel, to see different places and learn how the people lived, and today she was immersing herself in Greek island life.

Suddenly a male voice said, "Hidden away from the crowd?"

Andreas stepped closer. Like other local men, he wore a short-sleeved shirt, leaving his tanned, muscled arms bare. He smiled at Luca, but the boy immediately pushed himself against Atalanta, hiding his face.

"Children," Andreas scoffed. "One day they want to be friends with you, the next they're afraid."

"You go and play with your wooden sword for a bit," Atalanta said, sending Luca into the next room. She said to Andreas, "I thought you would take part in the archery."

"No, it's strictly a thing for the locals. It's a tradition that dates back across the centuries. I only oversee some parts of the festivities for Mr Bucardi."

"But you're Greek. Can't they make an exception for one of their own?"

Andreas laughed heartily. "There are all kinds of Greeks, my dear lady. They're all rivals. I grew up in a village where the boys would fight any boys from the neighbouring village who came to look at our girls. There was just five miles between the villages, but they were 'the others'. I guess we Greeks have always had a strange sense of what we consider pride. We don't give away what is ours."

Although his laughter suggested he was teasing her, the undertone of his words was very serious.

Atalanta looked him over. "Still, you're a Greek working for an Italian burg owner. Doesn't that hurt your sense of pride? To leave to a Venetian what is actually Greek?"

Andreas shrugged. "I didn't say I feel the same way as the poor, uneducated people from villages do. Times have changed. We must be realistic about that. This burg isn't going to come back to the Greek people just because we want it to. Certainly not after Bucardi had an heir."

Yes, Atalanta realized, that had been doubtful for many years, it seemed. Had the locals hoped that he would leave the burg to others? But certainly not to Greek people, then?

Andreas said, "Have you seen the women dance? They're so elegant in their white dresses with their flower headbands." He reached out a hand to her. "Would you like to learn a Greek dance?"

"I saw women dance with women and men with men." Atalanta frowned a moment. "Is it also acceptable to dance…"

"Acceptable? Does that matter? No one sees us in here. Let me teach you a few steps." He took her hand and held it up in the air. "Now step back and make a little bow in my direction."

She followed his instructions and enjoyed falling into the rhythm of the dance she had seen practised outside. It was lovely to move like a wave of the ocean, back and forth, increasing the pace until it was an intoxicating feeling of being one with the sea.

Andreas laughed out loud. "You could be Greek, you dance so well." He halted and they stood close together while he looked down on her, his smile lingering. "Pretty too," he muttered and leaned in to kiss her.

No, don't. Atalanta stepped back with a snap. "I didn't ask you to do that," she said sharply. Her breathing rasped.

Andreas pulled up a brow. "Yes, you did ask me. You asked me without words by dancing with me with that look in your eyes. You wanted me to kiss you."

"You misunderstood. I was enjoying the dance and not—"

"The dance partner?" His eyes grew dark. "You have a strange way of dealing with men. Attract first, then push away."

"I assure you I didn't…" Atalanta stuttered. She had little experience with men, but she refused to blame herself for this awkward situation. "You shouldn't simply assume things, but make sure before you act."

"Really? It's hardly my fault that you can't make up your mind. First lure me away from the crowd for a rendezvous and then tell me no."

Atalanta's cheeks were on fire. Lure him away from the crowd? Did he really believe she had gone inside to get him to follow her?

"During the archery you couldn't keep your eyes off me. But perhaps you feel you can do better?" He turned away in a jerk. "You should be more careful. Or someone might get the wrong idea and not be so gentlemanly about it." His footfalls reverberated against the walls as he stormed off, shutting the door with a bang.

During the archery you couldn't… She had simply watched the sport out of interest and had also been fascinated by the

Greek letters written on the blackboard. It had nothing to do with him.

How conceited could a man be?

Atalanta tried to control her breathing. Her legs were trembling, both with anger and shock at his latter words. Was he warning her against Bucardi? Or was he simply angry and uttering an empty...

Threat?

Gooseflesh formed on her arms. Had Letitia also made the mistake of being friendly to someone who had mistaken her intentions and had tried to force a kiss? Had she fought to free herself from an unwanted embrace and in that struggle fallen down the cliffs?

"Did he hurt you?" Luca stood in the doorway, looking at her earnestly. "He hurt Mama once. He was holding her arm and twisting it." His voice was high and brittle as if he were about to cry.

Atalanta drew in breath. "Andreas was twisting your mother's arm?" she asked softly.

Luca nodded. "I saw it. He saw me too. He said if I told Papa, Papa would be very angry, leave us and never come back. Is that true?" His frightened eyes begged her to assure him it wasn't.

"I think if you told Papa, he would be angry, but not at you." Atalanta smiled at the little boy, leaning down to brush through his hair. "Still, you mustn't tell your father right away. I'll first ask your mother if she's all right. I can help her. You understand?"

Luca nodded, visibly relieved. The worried frown between his brows disappeared and his entire face opened like a flower to the sun. He held his sword up and cried, "*En garde!*"

115

Chapter Nine

It was almost an hour after Paula had disappeared on her half-hour break, but Atalanta was too concerned about Luca's revelation to go and look for her yet. She left Luca in the care of Calista and went to find Mrs Bucardi. She didn't have to look for her for long. She found the woman on the terrace overlooking the sea. She stood at the low stone wall, seemingly lost in the view, but when Atalanta came up to her, she noticed her employer was panting as if she had walked fast to get here. Had she hurried to evade someone? Andreas?

"Such a lovely tranquil view," Atalanta said, coming to stand beside Mrs Bucardi. "But Andreas told me upon my arrival that the island may be beautiful in summer but can be quite lonely in winter. I don't know if I could stand that."

"You'll find out soon enough," Mrs Bucardi said. "Or will you be leaving again soon?" She threw her a quick probing look.

"No, I wasn't thinking about leaving at all. You've all made me feel so welcome. You even allowed me to use blooms from your personal orchid for my hair adornment today." Atalanta smiled. "Such kindness isn't normally shown to an employee."

To lure Mrs Bucardi into confidentiality, she had to emphasize her subservient status and continued, "I've slept in small rooms and been treated like a servant. You, however, have given me a beautiful bedroom and invited me to join in these festivities today. I feel I ... owe you for your kindness. I must tell you what I heard."

Mrs Bucardi froze, her fingers knotting. "Heard?" she repeated in a sharp tone.

"Yes, from your son. He witnessed an incident which is troubling him. He wanted to tell his father but I told him it might be better if he doesn't, that I would tell you."

Mrs Bucardi blinked nervously. Atalanta wondered what she was now thinking. Did she have something in mind that her son might have witnessed? A forbidden meeting perhaps, kisses exchanged? Mrs Bucardi and Raoul?

"Luca is a child with a wild imagination," Mrs Bucardi said. "He thinks he's a knight or a pirate. You shouldn't believe everything he says."

Odd. Mrs Bucardi had said the same thing about Delilah. Why was she so eager to convince Atalanta that what the others at the burg saw or heard was just make-believe, not reality?

Atalanta said, "Your son was upset because he saw Andreas Papoudopolis twisting your arm and hurting you. Andreas later threatened Luca that if he told his father, his father would leave and never come back. I think it's a terrible thing to say to a child."

"Indeed." Mrs Bucardi's eyes flashed. "He should know

better than to come anywhere near my son." Her voice hissed with venom.

"Is he bothering you?" Atalanta asked. "I myself was almost forced into a kiss. I can assure you I had no intention of inviting him to any such intimacy."

"I guess it's because of Paula." Mrs Bucardi made a hand gesture. "She does flirt with men wherever she goes. It might give them the idea to try with others as well. Andreas is a very presumptuous man. He thought that ... I would welcome attention, as my husband is so busy with work. But I told him in no uncertain terms what I thought of his proposal. He was angry but…"

"Aren't you afraid of him? Shouldn't you ask your husband to dismiss him?"

"On what grounds? I would have to explain about the situation and that's infinitely painful to me. My husband has a terrible temper and he might hurt Andreas and cause all kinds of trouble for us here on the island. Andreas is Greek and ... well, those Greek people are fiercely protective of each other. We'd be hated. No, I told him what I thought and he won't approach me again."

Atalanta tilted her head. Things didn't quite add up. Andreas had told her that the islanders considered him an outsider and didn't even allow him to participate in their archery games. Now Mrs Bucardi said the locals would protect Andreas at all costs. Was that merely her interpretation or her personal fear, because she was a stranger to the Greek culture?

Or had Andreas consciously exaggerated the locals' loyalty to him?

And if he had, why?

Mrs Bucardi said, "I wouldn't worry about it,

Mademoiselle Renard. And Luca must certainly not worry about it."

"Perhaps you should tell him. He seems eager for your company."

"Not truly." Mrs Bucardi smiled sadly. "He enjoys wild games and…" She stared at the sea again. "I can never throw myself into life with carefree abandon like others can." It sounded wistful, as if she wanted things to be different, but had no idea how to achieve that.

"Still, you must try and win your little boy's heart. I believe he does want to be near you. Little children are open and warm, they don't carry a grudge. In fact, if you go now and spend some time with him today, telling him about the festival, the food…"

Mrs Bucardi stiffened and said, "I can't recall inviting your opinion about my son, Mademoiselle Renard. You are *not* his nanny. On the contrary, you were hired to look after another. Please go see to your duties. Delilah must want you for something."

Atalanta stepped back. "Please excuse me. But I only want your son to be happy."

As she spoke the words, she saw a flash of intense pain pass across Mrs Bucardi's features. Was it because she knew she wasn't the sort of woman who could make her son happy? Was it because others played with him in a way she never could?

"Think about it," Atalanta urged and then turned and walked away. She checked the time and realized that Delilah would want to get up in half an hour. She could still meet up with Raoul at the cyclops rock. Calista was looking after Luca and assured her she would do so until Paula resurfaced. "I wouldn't worry about her," she said with a ready smile. "It's easy to lose track of time when it's such a celebratory day."

Atalanta thanked her and went inside quickly. The sun was hot and the meeting place might be exposed, so she put her orchids in a bit of water in her room, put on a sunhat and started out. She recalled with a smile how she had once, back in Switzerland when she had still been a humble teacher, promised herself that if she ever got to see the Parthenon, a stylish sunhat would be an essential. Now she wasn't at the Parthenon, but she was in Greece, walking a cliff path where other feet had trodden for ages, where people had looked out over that clear blue sea, waiting for ships to pull in with riches or for wandering loved ones to come home. It was easy to feel like Penelope or Clytemnestra.

But in the latter case the return of the husband had led to bloodshed. The wife had murdered him. Had Mrs Bucardi contemplated murdering her husband for betraying her, but had not known how, as he was strong and agile? Had she decided to kill Letitia instead because it was easier and it removed the immediate threat of her husband leaving her? But surely she was intelligent enough to see that he would always find another pretty face to fall for, and she would never be truly safe from the humiliation of abandonment and divorce?

She glanced back at the burg and saw a bird of prey soaring high above it. A peregrine falcon perhaps? She hadn't expected to see any of those here on the island. Had they once been kept and trained to hunt with?

As Atalanta came to the spot where something vaguely like a large human head protruded over the sea, she saw that Raoul had arrived before her and was already sitting on a large rock beside the path. He held his face up to the sun and had closed his eyes. He looked younger and more approachable. Suddenly as she watched his profile, something nagged at the back of her brain. A resemblance.

Luca.

Could he be Raoul's son? Had Mrs Bucardi, caught in the hopelessness of a loveless marriage that stayed childless, had an affair? Had she then fallen pregnant and made her husband believe it was his child? Did she fear Bucardi would one day learn the truth and her marriage would fall apart? Had she therefore been shocked at the news that it was Raoul visiting the burg?

If she harboured such major secrets, it was logical she had said she couldn't enjoy life. There was a shadow hanging over her at all times, a sword of Damocles about to fall and destroy everything.

Atalanta's brain raced. Part of her refused to accept this theory as anything near the truth. But her logical mind couldn't deny that it fitted several of her observations. When Calista had asked Mrs Bucardi to guess who was coming to join them for the festivities, she had at once seemed tense. And the look on Mrs Bucardi's face this morning when Raoul had spoken intimately with Calista... Was she jealous because he didn't show that kind of attention to her anymore?

But if Raoul was Luca's father, why had he agreed to come here, risking that Bucardi would suddenly understand?

Or didn't Raoul know? Had Mrs Bucardi hidden the truth from him as well?

Her heartbeat stuttered as she walked closer. What had she done in involving him in her case? Or rather, in accepting his offer to help her with her investigation into the fears that Letitia had been murdered? In doing so, she could have unwittingly lit a fuse that was going to blow everything at the burg apart.

Raoul heard her footfalls and opened his eyes. He smiled at her. "There you are. I almost thought you weren't coming. That someone had found another task for you."

She held his gaze, wishing she could answer his smile without reluctance. But her insides were so cold. The idea that he had fathered a child touched her on a deeper level than just complicating the case. It involved Raoul and might make him vulnerable. If she didn't handle this right, he could be hurt. His career, his reputation, but also deeper than that … Their friendship could be ruined. She'd lose him forever.

But what if he did know?

Or suspect?

What if he had come on purpose, to protect the mother of his child?

If Mrs Bucardi was hiding such an explosive secret, it might have made her prepared to silence people who threatened to divulge it. What had the girl who died written to her mother? That she had made a sensational discovery.

Atalanta's breathing caught. Could it have been the fact that the long-awaited and fiercely adored Bucardi heir wasn't a true Bucardi at all?

"Deep in thought?" Raoul asked. "I can see the cogwheels of your brain churning. What did you see today? What did you deduce? Come and sit." He produced a large piece of linen cloth like the women had used to cover their bowls of food this morning. "I took it along especially for you." He covered the rock and made an inviting gesture. "There you are, mademoiselle. Your beautiful white dress shouldn't get dirty."

"*Merci.*" Atalanta came to sit beside him. Even through the cloth, she could feel the stone was warm from the sunshine. She so needed these quiet moments with him, a chance to speak freely instead of having to play a part. But she wasn't certain she could fully trust him. No matter how much she ached to let herself fall into a confidential atmosphere, she had to be on her guard and explore the situation better. "Why didn't you tell me earlier when I took the case that you knew all these people and had even been to the Bucardi burg?"

"You asked that before and I answered. If you keep coming back to the same issues, we'll never make progress," he chided her gently, but still it felt as if he was purposely evading the question.

"Raoul, it could be terribly important." She eyed him with a pleading expression. "Is there anything I should know?" She hoped that he realized how much rested on this for her. That if he didn't open up, she might ... lose confidence in him? Merely to think so hurt, but she had to consider her position here, the case and her own safety. If he wasn't honest, he could put her in danger, without even wanting to.

Or would there come a moment when he would have to make a conscious choice, between her interest and someone else's? What would he choose then?

What would it mean for their friendship?

Oh no. Why did I come here? Why did I agree to take this case?

Her heart hammered furiously as Raoul held her gaze. She thought for a moment he was gearing up for a confession. That he was looking for words to explain something that might be painful to him. She appreciated that it could be extremely difficult to share something personal and wanted to give him the room to do so.

But then he said brusquely, looking away, "There's nothing I can think of."

Nothing? Just like that?

She felt the urge to shake him. Didn't he see that it mattered? That he couldn't simply decide to conceal a major fact from her?

But what if Mrs Bucardi had fallen pregnant and had never told Raoul about it? Was Atalanta even allowed to suggest it? Mrs Bucardi was married and her husband apparently believed without question that the child was his. He was happy with his heir. Raoul was a man who valued freedom and would hardly be eager to hear of a son he possibly had. No one would benefit from the truth.

If it even is the truth, she reminded herself. *Perhaps you're connecting things that are not connected... But why did Raoul want to be involved in the case once he realized what the woman in black was after?*

Why is he really here, sitting beside me? For me, to help me, or for some other reason that might even obstruct everything I'm trying to achieve here?

Something green moved between the black rocks at her feet. A small creature that showed itself for a moment, sticking its head out from a crack. A little tongue flicked out of its mouth.

Atalanta sucked in air sharply. "A snake!" She jumped to her feet, looking at the rock she had just sat on.

Raoul laughed softly. "It's a lizard. Not a snake. You really must learn to tell your species apart." He patted the rock where she had sat. "You can safely sit down again. Those lizards are afraid of everything that moves and run if they see as much as a shadow falling over them. He won't bite you, let alone poison you."

"But Santorini does have snakes?" Atalanta queried as she carefully lowered herself beside him again. "I mean, snakes play such a prominent part in Greek myths that there must be serpents in Greece."

"I suppose it differs from place to place. If you really want to know, you must ask a local." Before she could respond, Raoul continued with a probing gaze, "Why are you so set on believing I kept something from you? Is the whole idea of the girl before you being murdered influencing your judgement? Or is it the whispers of that old woman Delilah that someone is rummaging through things and prowling the house at night?"

"How do you know about that?" Atalanta asked, surprised.

Raoul rolled his eyes. "The nanny, Paula. She wanted my autograph and almost threw herself at me. She explained that she has a terribly difficult life here and needs someone to offer her some distraction. I said it wasn't me and when I added an explanation of the type of woman I can get, she was insulted and ran off." He shrugged. "I fear I hurt her self-esteem. But that was intentional. I know her type. She sticks to a man like glue. Only harsh measures work. I trust that if you run into her later and she's still in tears, you'll tell her to cheer up? Older woman to young girl?"

I'm not that old! Atalanta wanted to protest but she said nothing.

Raoul continued, "I would listen carefully to your elderly charge, if I were you. People who spend a lot of time inside see everything that happens. Dear old Auntie Delilah could have important information for you about the murdered girl."

"What would really help is the motive for her murder,"

Atalanta said. "Delilah did say she suspected Letitia of having rummaged through her employer's desk in his workroom. Do you think Bucardi might be hiding something?"

Raoul shrugged. "He had this awkward little conversation with me, asking how I liked his burg, and if I was ever interested in settling somewhere ..."

"A sort of sale offer?" Atalanta queried, her head tilted. "How interesting. So he could be in debt and eager for money?"

"Well, I don't know if it was meant in earnest or not. Rumour has it he ached for an heir to take over all of his property, so why would he be eager to part with this burg?"

"Because he has enough other houses? He mentioned a ton of places to me. He did add that this is his favourite of all, so if he does need money, why not sell some other house and keep this?" Atalanta played with the long, blue ribbon dangling from her sunhat. "What do you think of Andreas Papoudopolis?"

"A little conceited perhaps. Not much else. How come?"

"He tried to kiss me." Atalanta glanced at Raoul to see how he took this.

Raoul's eyes glinted with amusement. "And? Did you smack him in the face?"

"Who says I didn't want him to kiss me?"

Raoul tilted his head. "Are you trying to fool me? You don't care one bit for that man. I mean, I would be hugely disappointed if you did. Such a self-centred, vain, smug—"

Atalanta burst out laughing. It felt good after all the tension. "Obviously you don't like him."

"And neither do you." Raoul's smile faded as he added, "Or do you? I must admit, there have been instances before where I was highly surprised by a lady's choice of man. But perhaps other considerations weigh in, then?"

Atalanta studied her hands. "I have no intention of getting entangled with anyone here. This is just a case to me and I must keep a clear head."

"So you told him no but secretly you're sorry?" Raoul moved a little closer to her. "You were never able to convince me before that you have no heart."

"A heart has very little to do with Andreas Papoudopolis's attempt to kiss me. He doesn't want a woman hanging around his neck expecting anything serious of him. Just a flirtation, a few kisses… I wonder if he ever tried with Paula." She bit her lip. "The day I arrived they went for a walk together. Paula was dressed like it was a real outing."

"Still Paula came after me to throw herself at me." Raoul's voice was too close for comfort. "She isn't in love with Papoudopolis or he with her."

"Or they both pretend they aren't to keep their relationship a secret. Can they be up to something here? Paula was so forthcoming with all kinds of suggestions about people who live here. And she even told me last night that she had some business going which would deliver money soon."

Raoul whistled softly. "What can she mean by that?"

"There are multiple options." Atalanta counted on her fingers. "She has an affair with Bucardi and she thinks he will divorce his wife for her. But I can't see her truly believing that. She's not that naïve, no matter what he might have said to her. Secondly, she might believe Delilah will give her more jewellery such as the gold necklace she already received. But surely the Bucardis won't let an aunt give away her entire fortune in jewels to a mere nanny? What else?"

"Blackmail?" Raoul suggested. "If she knows something about an affair Bucardi had, or his wife..." He waited a moment before adding, "She may even know something about the way in which Letitia died. If she saw something that day... Not the actual shove into the ocean but someone coming back from the walk in a hurry ... you get the idea..."

"Paula did mention the tower last night and being able to see all the island from there. So your suggestion that she saw something makes sense."

"There. She's blackmailing the killer with her knowledge."

"That could end badly for her." Suddenly uneasy, Atalanta rose to her feet. "She said she wanted to take a walk and I had to look after Luca for half an hour. But I haven't seen her since. It must be two hours already. As she does what she wants, I didn't think much of it, but ..."

Raoul looked up at her. "She asked you to look after the little boy because she wanted to spend time with me." He said it without satisfaction, merely as a statement of fact. "She ran off disappointed. I wager she's crying in her bedroom."

"For hours? That doesn't make sense. I'm going to see if she's there. And if not, I'm going to look for her."

"Why would you?"

"Because I want to know where she is. I didn't see her in the crowd."

"There are so many people there, how could you even have seen her?"

"Calista did say she was probably forgetting about the time..."

"Or she drank too much wine and went to lie down for a bit. Now come and sit with me again." He patted the linen cloth. "The nanny doesn't need a nanny."

Atalanta was undecided. Paula had been emptying cups of wine in quick succession. Perhaps she had overestimated her tolerance for the alcohol? Shouldn't someone look in on her? "Until I see Paula alive and well, I won't feel easy." She nodded with determination. "I'm already late to go to Delilah, but I'll ask a maid to tend to her needs. Paula might have acted like a self-centred little brat last night, but she shouldn't be at risk. One young woman has already died here…"

As she said it, a coldness touched her arms despite the hot sunshine. Had she made a terrible mistake not keeping a closer eye on Paula? The girl had threatened Mrs Bucardi with her odd words the previous evening. And what about the note saying the sea wanted another Venetian sacrifice?

"Atalanta…" Raoul stood up and caught her arm. "You've been here for only a few days and already you're so tense, jumping at shadows. Why? It is no different than the earlier case you did."

"Yes, it is." As Atalanta said it, her heart squeezed. The warmth of Raoul's fingers on her arm begged her to open herself to him and strengthen their bond. But a voice inside whispered he was hiding something.

"Why?" he asked again.

She looked into his deep-brown eyes. *Because Luca might be your son.*

She couldn't say that. It was a wild guess and it could ruin everything. Her co-operation with him, the potential friendship between them. Why couldn't she simply forget about the idea? She could investigate the case without knowing whose son Luca truly was.

Perhaps even without knowing if Raoul had come here on purpose or not?

She said with difficulty, "Because there's so much tension between all these people. And Paula is up to something. She made a very cryptic remark about drowning last night when we were all together on the terrace before she had to take Luca to bed. Mrs Bucardi seemed to understand what it referred to."

Atalanta thought of the moment earlier today when she had found her employer on the terrace at the low stone wall, completely out of breath. Had Mrs Bucardi hurried back from some place? From the rocks where she had … attacked and killed Paula?

As she had previously killed Letitia?

But surely, a woman with Mrs Bucardi's sharp wit would realize she couldn't just kill girls and believe it would be ascribed to accidents?

Once perhaps, but not two times in a row.

No, her worry was getting the better of her. There was nothing wrong. She repeated it a few times to herself to will it into her brain. *There is nothing wrong. Nothing.*

Still, she meant what she had said to Raoul. She wouldn't draw breath easily until she had found Paula recovering in her bedroom or seen her out and about, enjoying the feast.

Chapter Ten

"I haven't seen her," the butler said when Atalanta asked him, having come down from an idle knock on Paula's bedroom door. She had wanted to open the door to look inside, but it had been locked. She assumed, however, that if Paula had been in there, she would have responded to tell her to go away, leave her alone.

The butler asked, "Is something the matter, Mademoiselle?" A frown formed over his deep-set dark eyes.

"No, I had seen Paula rushing off after an altercation with a famous guest. I just wanted to know how she was."

"Well, she isn't inside."

Atalanta recalled how Lemusier had dropped her suitcase down the stairs when she had referred to Letitia's death on the day of her arrival. She said, "I'm worried about Paula if she took a walk along the cliffs. After all, Letitia died in a fall."

Lemusier stepped back, turning away from her. "I can't help you. I haven't seen Paula."

"Please, you're a fellow countryman." Atalanta tried to

sound a little desperate, to appeal to his compassion. "I feel so ... lost at this burg. The people are cold and distant and ... the idea that my predecessor met such a gruesome end ..."

"If you're truly afraid," Lemusier said in a whisper, "then stay away from the Greek."

"Andreas?" Atalanta asked in the same low tone.

Lemusier's eyes flashed. "Andreas? Is it that already? Women are all the same, enchanted by a handsome face. But that man is ruthless when it comes to getting what he wants. He only used Letitia. And when she had become redundant..."

"How do you mean? What did he do to her?"

Lemusier shook his head. "I can't talk about it. But stay away from the Greek." And he hurried off.

Atalanta wanted to go after him but realized that he was headed for the kitchens where other staff would be present. The chance to learn more had passed. She had to look for another opportunity later.

Redundant... It was a terrible word to use for a human life.

She stepped out into the courtyard where the locals were passing around roasted meat drizzled with honey and meatballs covered in pomegranate seeds. The buzz of their excited voices seemed to interfere with her ability to think logically.

Or was it her fear for the girl's safety? Paula might have been insolent, gossipy and snide, but she didn't deserve to die for her faults.

She ran into Raoul who asked her if she had located the girl. Atalanta shook her head. "Where exactly did you last see her?" she asked him.

"I'll show you. Come along." He took her across the courtyard, through yet another wooden door into a small stone

134

passage that led to the back of the burg. There was another vantage point there with a few potted palms. A dove flew away when they approached.

Raoul pointed down a narrow path leading away from the vantage point. "She ran off in that direction."

"But there is nothing to go to there." Atalanta stared down the path that lay fully exposed across the rock face. She could follow it with her eyes until it led downwards. "Does it go to the sea? Is there a beach there?" Had Paula wanted to go for a swim?

"I don't know. I've never been that way."

"On the day of my arrival Luca and Paula were at the sea and caught a crab. He later took it back with Calista. Perhaps they went via this path?" Atalanta began to follow it. She went faster than was advisable in the heat, but she needed to look down and see Paula on the beach, alive and well. She would scold her for asking for half an hour off and then staying away for so long. She would bring her back to the burg and let her watch Luca again, while she herself could then go to Delilah and apologize for her absence, making up an excuse about being engrossed by the dancing and the delicious treats on offer.

Raoul came after her. "I don't want you out here alone," he said softly. "I think I saw someone watching you."

"Watching me?" Atalanta echoed.

"Yes, after you walked away from me to look for Paula, I decided I might as well help you. I followed you and saw an elderly man in dark clothes watching you. He seemed local. He chose a spot from where he could see the door into the house and waited until you came back out again. He is also watching us now. Don't look back. Trust me when I say he is."

"I don't understand. Why would a local man be interested in me? At least I assume he will be local?"

"Perhaps he is a Venetian spy?"

"Under whose orders?"

Raoul shrugged. "Perhaps Letitia's mother wanted someone here to keep an eye on you? She must realize the danger, after her daughter died."

"We still don't know how Letitia died." Atalanta kept her eyes on the path in front of her. It was narrow and uneven and the sound of the sea was too close for comfort. It seemed to be down there, waiting, lurking, slapping against the rock as if it wanted to break down this obstruction in its path. This entire island was nothing but a pebble in the vast ocean.

Where the path stopped and led down, she halted and looked over the ridge. There were steps hewn out in the cliff leading down to the sea. It would be treacherous to clamber down, especially the last few steps that were wet with the spray of the water. "I don't think Paula would have gone down here. Not in a long dress."

"But what is that?" Raoul pointed at something white on the bottom step.

Atalanta squinted. It was difficult to make out. "It could be a…" Her heart skipped a beat. "Little flower."

"From her wreath. So she did go down there. I'll follow." Raoul gently pushed past Atalanta and began to lower himself, placing his feet gingerly on the narrow hewn steps. "It's probably easier for a goat," he called. "Have you seen them clambering across the rocks? Light on their feet and never missing a step."

He continued down and then called, "There's an opening in the rock face here. Some sort of grotto. I think it was used as a

136

hiding place for someone. I can see some fabric inside. Perhaps Luca has a hut here?"

"It would hardly be safe for a four-year-old to climb down," Atalanta objected. "It can't be his hiding place." But whose was it then? Letitia's?

Raoul came to the bottom step and picked up the white object. "It's a flower, like you supposed," he called up to her. He put it in his pocket and looked to his left. "I can move along the ledge here to another opening. I can have a peek inside."

"Paula!" Atalanta called. "Paula! You have to come back to take care of Luca."

The wind scattered her words. Raoul stepped onto the ledge, his back to the rock face, and moved to get to the other opening. Atalanta held her breath. He disappeared from view. A few moments later he appeared again. "No one here. But there has been activity. Traces of a fire made."

He came back up to her, with more vigour, as if he had decided something, and stood beside her rubbing his hands. There were smudges on his white clothes. "We're wasting our time looking for the elusive Paula. She's probably back at the party enjoying herself, while we are out here, risking life and limb. We must get back to the burg. I really need a good glass of wine. Or something stronger."

Atalanta realized she had dragged him into this wild goose chase and said, "You go and have that wine. I want to follow the path in the other direction for a while."

"You really don't give up, do you?" Raoul sighed. "I'll accompany you. But only for a few minutes, then we go back."

They turned and Atalanta saw a dark shadow disappear into the wooden door they had emerged from. Who had been watching them? And why?

When they returned from their fruitless search, more food was handed out among the crowd: black olives, halves of fig and dates filled with a white paste. Chunks of flat bread were dipped in ground tomatoes mixed with basil. Everyone was laughing and shouting over the music that rose into a wild rhythm like the sea against the shore. Atalanta caught sight of Calista carrying Luca on her arm. He had pressed his cheek to hers and she was telling him a story, judging by his wide eyes.

Atalanta forced herself through the crowd in her direction and gestured for her to wait a moment. Calista seemed to see her but didn't wait, walking out of the courtyard, away from the burg towards the village. The evening sun made the gold embroidery on her dress sparkle like it was genuine gold.

"Calista!" Atalanta ran after her and caught her arm. "I want to talk to you."

Calista turned to her, her eyes wide with a feverish glow. "Hush," she said. "We are escaping."

"Escaping what?"

"The goddess of the sea. She wants human sacrifices. She especially loves little boys, because they have such soft white legs." Calista tickled Luca's calves and he giggled, squirming in her arms. "But don't you worry, little prince," Calista continued. "I'll save you. I know where I can hide you from the goddess of the sea. She need never have you. I'll hide you and we'll be together in a secret place."

Luca clutched her neck and hid his face against her shoulder. "Secret place," he echoed.

Calista winked at Atalanta while she continued, "No one

will ever find us. We can do what we want. Eat pudding all
day long and play games."

"And never go to bed on time," Luca muttered.

"Never," Calista confirmed. She cradled him in her arms
like a baby. To Atalanta she said, "Just let us play for a while.
No one is minding the time. This is a special day."

"I agree. I only wanted to ask if you've seen Paula. She
seems to be missing."

"Missing? I don't think so. I saw her half an hour ago."

"Really?" Atalanta's heavy heart grew lighter. "Where?"

"Why, in the courtyard. She was guzzling wine like it was
water. Or perhaps it was *ouzo*? Hard to see in those
earthenware cups. Anyway, she walked a bit unsteadily. I think
she might have gone inside to freshen up or lie down."

"I see." Atalanta felt slightly silly for her fears for the girl's
life. Paula had simply indulged in too much alcohol and stolen
off for a nap. Why did she allow the strange tension at the
castello to get to her? "Thank you."

Calista widened her eyes. "What do you have to thank me
for?" She suddenly seemed less carefree and said, "I saw you
with Raoul, Mademoiselle Renard. He seems to know you."

Atalanta's shoulders stiffened. Of course, in her role as
companion she should have been more careful about
approaching Raoul, who was socially higher placed than she
was. She was supposed to keep her distance from the guests.

"I'm sorry if I offended anyone. He came to the house of
one of the families where I previously worked, and as I was
allowed to sit at the dinner table there, I did happen to speak
with him. I … wanted to know how he was now. He told such
riveting stories of his races."

Calista's eyes sparked with a fire that Atalanta couldn't quite place. Was it jealousy? Was it possessiveness?

"There's one thing about Raoul you should never forget." Calista balanced Luca better on her arm. "Every time he steps into that race car of his, he could lose his life and he doesn't care. Because racing *is* his life. Outside of it, there is nothing."

Atalanta tilted her head. "What are you trying to tell me?"

"Did you know you can sometimes see dolphins around the islands? Not often, but sometimes." Calista looked away, her face touched by a tender smile. "They're so beautiful, especially when they jump out of the water. So free."

"What are you trying to tell me about Raoul?" Atalanta repeated. The day's events – Andreas's attempt to kiss her, the futile search for Paula – had worn her patience thin. If this woman had something to share, she should just say it.

Calista said, "Raoul is like a dolphin. He needs to be free." She turned away from Atalanta, carrying Luca in her arms.

Did Calista know Luca was Raoul's son? That he had refused to take responsibility and had forced Mrs Bucardi to continue in her loveless marriage with the child that was not her husband's? Did Calista blame Raoul for the havoc he had caused that way?

But she had seemed pleased to share the news that he was coming. If she knew of this painful affair and past events, she would have told Mrs Bucardi in private, surely?

Calista had probably just wanted to warn Atalanta off to ensure she could charm Raoul herself.

Luca cried out to Atalanta, "The goddess of the sea can catch you. Like she caught Titia."

Calista said something to him that sounded reproaching. Perhaps that he shouldn't say such nonsense? But why had she revived this goddess-of-the-sea tale? And was it related to the threatening note about one Venetian already having been swallowed by the sea? And another being next? Calista was not Venetian.

But Paula is.

Atalanta turned around and marched across the courtyard, determined to set her mind at ease now. She had spent so much precious time on this, ignoring her duties to Delilah. If Mrs Bucardi found out she had asked a maid to look after Delilah while she herself lingered at the party, her employer wouldn't like it. An explanation about Paula would get Paula into trouble. Atalanta had to find the girl and press upon her that she shouldn't disappear again for hours, having said she would only be taking a little walk.

She ran upstairs and knocked on Paula's door. No reply.

She tried the door handle. The door was still locked.

She found the butler Lemusier and told him that she needed the key to Paula's room. He spluttered, but she told him she knew he had keys to all the rooms and it was urgent, as Mrs Bucardi wanted Paula to come and look after Luca. "You will open the door *now* so I can talk to Paula."

Lemusier strode ahead of her in quiet indignation at being ordered about like that, but Atalanta had little time for his feelings. Her heart beat fast with anticipation. As soon as she saw Paula alive and well, she would have a little word with her about shirking her duties.

The butler knocked on Paula's door and called, "Signorina Paula? Are you in there? Mrs Bucardi wants you to come and look after Luca. Please open the door."

No reply. Atalanta gestured to him. "Open the door with your key."

141

He tried the handle but the door was still locked. Reluctantly he inserted a key from his key chain and turned it. The lock opened with a click. Atalanta pushed the door handle down and opened the door. Her heart beat even faster and her breathing came in rapid gulps.

Sunlight streamed into the room. On the bed Paula lay, dressed in her white dress with the flowers in her hair. Her eyes were closed and she seemed to be sleeping. Had she drunk so much, she had fallen asleep on her bed? It had to be a deep sleep if she hadn't heard the knocking on her door.

Atalanta entered the room and walked over. She leaned over the young woman. "Paula? Paula, wake up."

But Paula didn't move.

Atalanta touched her hand. It was cold. She gasped. "I think…"

The butler who hovered at the door asked, "Is she ill? Should I call a doctor?"

"Yes, please, call a doctor, quickly."

Alarmed by her tone, Lemusier turned and left in a hurry.

Atalanta stood and watched Paula's pretty face, so quiet as she lay there. So peaceful and still. There was no mark of violence on her body.

But Atalanta was certain that the doctor's help would come too late. The moment she had touched her hand, her earlier rush of relief had left her, and a dead weight had crushed her inside.

She had failed.

Paula was no longer alive.

As she stood there in the quiet room, looking down on the seemingly sleeping girl, a shiver crept up Atalanta's spine.

Paula had died in a locked room. Her body showed no marks of a physical struggle. How had she died?

Another accident, as with Letitia? A case of too much alcohol?

But Paula had told her she had some lucrative business set up, and she had spoken to Mrs Bucardi in cryptic words. Blackmail, as Raoul had assumed? Had the victim ensured that Paula could never tell what she knew?

Atalanta's gaze roamed the pretty face, the long lashes resting against the full cheeks, the lush blonde hair and the white flowers in it. A few were crushed and an empty spot seemed to indicate flowers had fallen. On her left hand one fingernail was very short, as if it had been torn off. And there were some vague abrasions on the wrist, as if her hand had been chafed in contact with something solid and uneven.

Had Paula clambered down to the secret grotto where Raoul had stood? Had she met someone there? Raoul had mentioned traces of fire made.

But Paula hadn't been murdered there. She had died here, in her own bedroom. Judging by the coldness of her hand, she had been dead for some time.

With another shiver Atalanta realized that when she had knocked on the door before and called for Paula, she had probably already been dead on this bed. Unable to answer.

But … if Paula had died hours ago, why had Calista told her she had seen her half an hour earlier, guzzling wine? Had Calista been mistaken?

Or had she consciously lied?

If so, why?

Footfalls resounded. Atalanta looked at the door, expecting the butler with a local doctor. But it was Delilah. She stood in the doorframe and looked at the bed with a strange expression on her face. "So young," she said, "and so wicked."

"Wicked?" Atalanta echoed.

"Yes. She stole from me. She denied it but I knew it. She went through my things and she stole from me."

"Paula told me you had given her a necklace."

"Why would I do that? I don't give my property to servants. Certainly not someone who is so forward all the time. No, she stole it from me. She shouldn't have done that."

Delilah looked at Paula's still form and smiled, adding softly, "She won't do that again."

Atalanta stared at the old woman. To someone just arriving on the scene, it had to look as if Paula was merely sleeping. How could Delilah be certain she was dead? Unless, of course…

"What is the matter, Aunt?" Mr Bucardi pushed past the elderly woman and looked at Atalanta.

"Paula isn't feeling well," Atalanta said. "I sent the butler to fetch a doctor."

"Not feeling well?" Delilah laughed softly. "She is not feeling anything. She is a heartless monster."

"Please, Aunt…" Mr Bucardi reached out to wrap an arm around her shoulders and lead her away, but the old lady stepped back, hissing, "Don't you touch me. You know very well what you did to feed that girl's vanity. Making her think she could become mistress of the burg."

Bucardi flushed crimson. "Aunt, you're not making sense."

Delilah stepped back with a look of disgust on her face. "I'm the only one making sense in this house. Good night." And she turned and walked off, her back straight.

Bucardi said to Atalanta, "You mustn't mind what she says. She's often confused. She must be thinking it's the middle of the night, and she caught me in the girl's bedroom and something improper is going on." He flashed an embarrassed smile. "She has no idea it's a festive day or that there are a hundred guests outside. It's pitiful, really. But we must be kind to her. She can't help it."

Yes, Mrs Bucardi had taken great pains to make it clear on the day of Atalanta's arrival here. Delilah was confused, she shouldn't be believed.

And Atalanta herself knew from experience that Delilah could be difficult to please, spiteful and demanding. But confused to the point where she simply told lies because she didn't know what the truth was? What reality was or where her own imaginings began?

No, Atalanta thought that solution was a little too easy. Delilah meant what she said and it remained to be seen how much of it was true. Had Paula received a gold necklace as a gift? Or had she stolen it, thinking no one would believe Delilah when she said it was missing? People would simply assume she had mislaid it.

"Poor girl," Mr Bucardi said. "Look at her arms. She was exposed to too much sun. Together with a liberal intake of wine or *ouzo*, it can be fatal." He shook his head. "I warned her earlier today not to drink so much. Especially not what these Greeks brew locally. It's so strong, it can knock out a man who weighs three times what Paula does. But Paula didn't listen. She never did."

Atalanta studied his features, as smooth and handsome as those of marble statues in ornamental gardens. But there was something about him she didn't like. Was this because of

Andreas's suggestion that she should never be alone in a room with Bucardi?

Now she was. Because the dead Paula hardly counted as company.

Gooseflesh crawled over her arms. Bucardi focused on her. "Are you cold?" He stepped closer, his gaze probing. "Or shocked because you found her? What prompted you to ask the butler to unlock the door?"

It was a logical question but Atalanta was cautious in her reply. "Mrs Bucardi wanted to know where Paula was," she lied. "I asked Calista, who said she had seen her half an hour ago, drinking a large quantity of wine. She suggested Paula might have gone to lie down in her room. I knocked but there was no reply, so I asked the butler to open the door so I could see if Paula was unwell. As you just said, sunburn and alcohol can cause illness."

Bucardi nodded slowly. Atalanta had the distinct impression he wasn't satisfied by her answer. Was it because he assumed Paula had been dead quite a while, and that didn't fit with Calista's statement that she had seen her alive and drinking wine half an hour earlier?

"Here's the doctor." The butler rushed in panting, followed by an elderly man in white. He wasn't carrying a doctor's bag and looked more like a local seller of fruit or fish than a doctor. He leaned over the girl and pulled up one of her eyelids. Then he felt for a heartbeat, first at the wrist, then the neck. "She's dead," he declared. "Her body is starting to cool." His English was broken and Bucardi fired some questions at him in Greek.

Atalanta couldn't follow everything but she did catch the word for "sun" and a repeated mention of *ouzo*. Apparently Bucardi asked the doctor to confirm his theory that exposure to heat and the intake of too much alcohol had caused the girl to collapse and die.

The doctor pointed at her arms and then at her feet. Atalanta looked and saw that her bare ankles were also sunburned. She also noticed that the leather of Paula's white shoes seemed abraded in spots.

The doctor said something and gestured with his hands. Bucardi shook his head. He ushered the man out of the room in deep discussion.

The butler said, "How can someone so young suddenly die? And this is the second girl within a few weeks."

"Letitia fell off the cliffs during a walk," Atalanta said.

The butler scoffed. "So they say."

"What do you think happened?" Atalanta asked softly. "Was Andreas involved?" Earlier he had warned her so earnestly to stay away from the Greek.

Lemusier didn't reply. He was staring at the dead girl in wide-eyed horror. Then he seemed to remember where he was and that he wasn't alone. He stood up straight and said, "Mrs Bucardi must be informed." He left the room.

Everybody seems to know more than they are letting on, Atalanta thought. She cast one last look at the body. Underneath Paula's left shoe, embedded in the sole, was a little shard of black rock. Atalanta touched it with her fingers. So Paula had been away from the burg, walking across the rocky paths. Had she been sunburned while waiting for someone? A rendezvous away from the festivities?

She looked around her at the simple wardrobe, the dressing table with drawers and the night table beside the bed. Her fingers itched to search everything and find some clue as to why Paula had to die. There was a photo stuck under the edge of the dressing table's gilded mirror. A view of Venice.

Had it been taken by Letitia? After all, she had been an avid photographer. Were there more photos of hers here? Had Paula appropriated them after Letitia's death and learned something important from them? Something she used for her little business?

So many clues could be hidden here. But Atalanta already heard footfalls coming in this direction and she didn't want to be caught rummaging through a dead girl's things. She could get dismissed for that, and she still had a lot of work to do here.

Not one murder to solve, but two.

Chapter Eleven

"Who says it was murder?" Raoul asked softly. He sat on the terrace's low stone wall, his back to the view, and toyed with his Panama hat. "Did you see any marks of violence on her body? Stab wounds, strangulation marks?"

"None."

"See? People have died of heat exhaustion before."

"Yes, but before they do, wouldn't they have symptoms like dizziness or a rapid heartbeat or whatever, and ask for help? If Paula felt unwell, why not say so to someone in the household? Why go to her room and lie on her bed and die quietly, away from everyone?"

"Perhaps she didn't feel well and thought lying down would help. Because of all the alcohol she imbibed, she fell into a deep sleep and, while sleeping, her heart gave out." Raoul rubbed his fingers together. "It can happen."

"You seem determined to make it anything but murder." Atalanta sat down on a deck chair near him. "But we were looking for her because we thought she might be in danger."

"*You* thought that." He seemed to want to argue more, then he merely smiled at her – a slow, almost sad smile. "I just don't want to accept it was murder. It makes it even more difficult for you."

His sympathy warmed her, but also made her feel another painful stab of failure. She had come here to look into a suspicious death, and now another young woman had died, under her very nose. It felt almost as if the killer had spited her to her face.

"I can handle myself." Atalanta sat up straighter. "There's so much here that intrigues me. Delilah and her alleged disturbed state of mind. Her viciousness in talking about the dead Paula, calling her wicked. Then the Bucardis and their unhappy marriage. Andreas, who twisted Mrs Bucardi's arm. All because she rejected his advances? Or was there much more to that incident? Everyone is up to something, and I can't quite make the puzzle pieces fit."

Raoul checked his watch. "It's late already. Perhaps we should get to bed. This happy day of celebrations ended in tragedy." He threw a look over his shoulder at the restless sea. "At least she didn't get her second sacrifice. Paula died in her bed, not in the water."

"But she might have been near water. One of her shoes had a shard of black rock embedded in the sole. And her flower wreath was damaged. Don't you remember the small white flower on the stone steps leading to the grottoes? She was away from the burg before she died. I wonder what happened there. And who might have been with her."

"Who says she's been near the grottoes? The flower could have come from someone else's wreath. All the local women wore them."

Atalanta pursed her lips. Luca had been playing with Paula's wreath. It could have been damaged then. It need not have happened at the grottoes. But Mrs Bucardi came to mind standing on the terrace, out of breath. Had she followed Paula to see what she was up to? Had there been an altercation?

But even if Mrs Bucardi and Paula had argued about Paula's negligence towards Luca, for instance, and Paula had gone to her bedroom after, where she had died, how could an action by Mrs Bucardi have led to Paula's death? There had been no marks on the body suggesting physical violence, such as a blow to the head, which might have caused internal damage that had killed Paula later, when she had been alone.

Raoul said, "We must first hear what the police have to say. The doctor was adamant that he had to inform them. Bucardi wasn't happy with it, of course."

"Why are you whispering together?" Calista appeared at the steps leading onto the terrace. She wore a thin pink nightgown that fluttered around her as she walked towards them. "Isn't it a beautiful night? It should have been a full moon, then it would have been perfect."

"Perfect?" Raoul echoed. "Someone died here today."

Calista pulled up a deck chair and sat down in it, folding her legs underneath her. With her hair down, and without makeup, she looked like a girl. A very pretty, innocent girl. She frowned hard, as she eyed Raoul. "Paula died of heat exhaustion, Victoria told me. It's sad, but people who aren't used to the hot Greek sun often underestimate its power." She smiled to herself, a short, satisfied smile.

"You didn't like Paula, did you?" Raoul asked.

Calista looked at the sea before she replied. "I heard from Luca that she was often brusque with him and pinched his arm when she didn't like what he did. I believe little children should be treated with compassion. Luca can be wild but he doesn't need punishment to make him better."

"Paula hardly seemed like a demanding nanny," Atalanta observed quietly. "In fact, she seemed more interested in flirting with handsome men and finding ways to get away from the burg, than in disciplining Luca."

Calista laughed softly. "Paula was the second to fall for Andreas's fanciful stories."

"What fanciful stories?" Raoul asked, leaning back in a leisurely way as if he was chatting at a party.

Atalanta hoped he recalled he was sitting on a stone ledge with a steep drop behind him.

Calista played with a lock of her long loose hair. "Andreas has this story he found in a book about Santorini. Or perhaps a local told him? But it claims that many years ago, there were pirates in these waters and they raided ships and stole their valuable cargo. Because no one could know who the pirates were, they hid the cargo in grottoes on this island. Andreas believes that it can still be found. Gold goblets, coins. He engaged Letitia, that foolish girl who was companion before *she* came," Calista nodded in Atalanta's direction, "to help him look for it. That was why she wanted to scour the cliffs, even though she had vertigo. She wanted to be rich. Then she could travel for her photography. She believed she would one day have an exhibition in New York." She shook her head with a disbelieving laugh. "I think Andreas only uses this tale to get gullible girls to spend time with him. He's rather flirtatious."

"So you don't think there is actual pirates' gold to be found?" Atalanta asked. Was that the lucrative business Paula had referred to? Not blackmail, not dark secrets, but legendary treasure hidden on this island?

But if Andreas had an idea where it was, why not look for it himself? Why engage Letitia? Had she been out on the cliffs to take photos, and had she seen Andreas busy with some mysterious activity? Had he then persuaded her to keep her mouth shut about it, in exchange for a share of the proceeds? Letitia had indeed wanted to travel – her mother had confirmed that during the conversation on Murano.

But if Letitia had agreed to this proposition, why had she died? Because they had found the treasure and Andreas didn't want to share? Had he pushed the girl to her death to have the legendary gold all to himself?

But if he knew where it was, why later involve Paula? Or had Paula followed the pair to spy on them, thinking there was a romance going on, and had she somehow witnessed the murder? Had she blackmailed Andreas into giving her Letitia's share? Paula had been quite outspoken about her interest in money to buy herself beautiful things such as jewels and perfume.

But why trust a man capable of murder? Wouldn't Paula have told someone the truth? The police, her employers?

Or had she simply not believed that Andreas would dare kill her, another death so soon after the previous one? Had she felt completely safe?

Paula had been rather self-confident.

Calista turned her eyes on Atalanta. "Has Andreas already asked you to walk with him, Mademoiselle Renard? Or isn't he interested in you?" Her voice was sharper, as if the mere idea that he might not be interested aroused her suspicion.

"The prig tried to kiss Mademoiselle Renard earlier today,"

Raoul said. "But she told him in no uncertain terms she didn't want him to."

"I see. Because you're already taken?" Calista batted her eyelashes at Atalanta. "Is there a man somewhere you write letters to? Do you save money to go and visit him? Or to have him come over here?" She glanced quickly at Raoul. "I dare say that if people didn't know better, they'd think the two of you were too close for mere acquaintances."

"We share a common interest," Raoul said casually.

"Oh." Calista seemed piqued. "And what can that be?"

"Why did you tell me that you saw Paula half an hour before I came looking for her?" Atalanta cut in, hoping to shake Calista with the unexpected question. "Paula was already dead when you allegedly saw her."

"I must have mistaken some other girl in white for her." Calista shrugged. "With those flower garlands, everyone looks alike."

Atalanta had to admit that was probably true.

There was a cry nearby. "Calista? Where are you?"

Calista rose to her feet and called, "I'm here, Victoria." She smiled down on Raoul. "I still think a full moon would have made the view even more enticing."

Mrs Bucardi came onto the terrace. She had exchanged her festival garment for a dark dress and had pulled her hair away from her face in a stern bun on the neck. She looked like a disgruntled nanny who had come to tell an unruly pupil it was way past her bedtime. She said to Calista, "The police are here. They want to talk to you."

"Me?" Calista raised an eyebrow. "What on earth for?"

"They found the pills in your room." Mrs Bucardi's tone was brusque, her voice brittle as if she were close to tears.

"What pills?" Raoul asked with alarm.

Atalanta glanced from him to Calista and back. But Calista wasn't looking at Raoul. She stared at her friend, without understanding.

Victoria spread her hands as if she were sorry but couldn't help it either. "The barbiturates. The police think Paula ingested wine laced with barbiturates, and that caused a heart attack. They searched the house and…"

"But I thought Paula died of heat exhaustion?" Calista looked bewildered. "What does it have to do with some pills I take to sleep better?"

"You said you wouldn't take pills anymore," Raoul said sharply, and Mrs Bucardi added, "You promised all of your friends."

Atalanta sensed the tension brewing as the three stood looking at each other. Calista sighed. "It's just an innocent sedative to help me sleep. I'm a grown woman, not a baby. You should stop fussing over me."

"I did everything to help you," Mrs Bucardi said, her face pale with rage. "Everything. I even risked my marriage. And now you've started with the pills again?"

Calista raised her hands. The sleeves of her nightgown fell away from her bare arms. She had a touch of sunburn. "I don't have to defend my choices to you."

"Of course not. It has always been like that. You use me when you see the advantage and afterwards you do as you please." Mrs Bucardi's voice shivered with tears. "But I can't help you now. The police want to talk to you and … take you for questioning because of Paula's death."

Calista walked up to her. Her eyes glowed with defiance. "I don't need your help. That's your problem. I once asked you for a favour and now you think I owe you, for the rest of my life. But I don't. I'll solve this by myself." She hurried away from the terrace, the pink gown fluttering around her on the wind.

"Raoul, do something," Mrs Bucardi said. She took two steps to Raoul and reached out both hands in a pleading gesture. "She'll destroy herself. She doesn't understand…"

Raoul grabbed her hands and squeezed them. "Don't worry, Victoria. I won't let anything happen to her. You know that."

For a moment they stood looking into each other's eyes, reinforcing some earlier promise without words. Then Raoul let go of her and went after Calista.

Mrs Bucardi stood and drew a deep breath.

Atalanta's heart was racing. The emotion between these people couldn't be mistaken. The underlying implications couldn't be ignored. Was Luca Raoul's son? Did some deep bond connect these two former lovers? Had Raoul promised Mrs Bucardi, the love of his life, the mother of his child, that he would help and protect her poor wild friend? Had the two of them feared that Calista had killed Letitia? Had Raoul come here to supposedly help Atalanta, but in reality to lead her astray?

She wanted to believe he wouldn't go that far, but having sensed the emotion thick in the air, she wasn't so certain anymore. People weren't themselves when emotional pressure was applied. Even people who claimed to be perfectly rational…

Mrs Bucardi seemed to remember Atalanta was there and said with difficulty, "Mademoiselle Renard, I must ask you urgently not to say a word to anyone about what you just heard. Calista is a very dear friend of mine and … she had some trouble, but I believe it is all in the past. She must have a chance to start over, you understand?"

"Sometimes you want to help someone, but they don't want to be helped." Atalanta waited and added, "Some people live to destroy themselves." Her own father had been such a man: kind and generous, full of brilliant ideas, but always throwing himself into the wrong business ventures and losing money. But he kept believing he could win it back and had stacked mistake on mistake, plunging himself and Atalanta into misery.

As a child she had known times of affluence and joy, but more often poverty and embarrassment when the debt collectors called. Even after her father's untimely death, it had taken her years of hard work at the Swiss boarding school to repay his creditors. Still, she had loved him, and she knew what it was like to hurt for someone who should change his ways, but simply couldn't.

"You have no idea what you're talking about," Mrs Bucardi said in a low voice. "And if you speak of this to anyone, you'll be very sorry."

The haughty threat on top of the other emotions of the day triggered Atalanta to respond. "Did you also threaten Paula like that?" she asked. "Was she going to talk about this burg's secrets? Or Letitia?" Atalanta held her employer's gaze. "Both girls died while working for you."

"Letitia had an unfortunate accident." Mrs Bucardi stepped back. "We won't mention it again."

As she walked away, seemingly in command of herself, Atalanta could kick herself for her unprofessional response.

Why ask such direct questions? she chided herself. *Had you expected a confession?*

She formed her hands into fists by her side. *Stupid, stupid, stupid.* Now she had only alerted the woman to her interest in both deaths. Or at least, the fact that she thought them suspicious.

Was that enough to put her in danger?

Chapter Twelve

A soft but insistent knock on her door woke Atalanta. She blinked her eyes a moment to remember where she was and what had happened. Paula's lifeless face drifted through her memories, the moment Raoul had clasped Mrs Bucardi's hands in his and promised to help her save Calista. The way in which she had let herself down by putting those confrontational questions to Mrs Bucardi.

She groaned as she slipped out of bed. She was losing her self-control, and that could ruin the entire case. She had to be more careful and keep her emotions in check.

But hadn't Paula said there was a curse on the burg? Not in the sense of some evil stalking people, but inside the people themselves, because of their feelings? Was Atalanta herself falling victim to this curse, being pulled along by the strong tide of rising emotions? An undertow of malevolence that would suck her under and drown her before she could achieve anything meaningful here?

The knock sounded again. *Yes, I'm coming.* She put on her

dark-red dressing-gown and went to the door. Her heart beat fast. Who would knock on her door in the dead of night? Had something happened? More complications in a case that was going over her head already?

She leaned her hand against the door and asked, "Who is there?"

"Raoul. I need to talk to you."

She hesitated a moment. It was hardly appropriate for a member of the staff to invite a guest into her bedroom at night. If it got out, there would be trouble.

But why would it get out? The others were probably fast asleep. She could reason with herself that it was safe enough.

Or did she already know that despite her better judgement, she would let Raoul in, if only to learn what he had to say that couldn't wait until morning?

With a sigh she opened the door. Raoul was still fully dressed in his white festival clothes and looked infinitely weary. A strange sense of protectiveness overwhelmed Atalanta and she invited him in with a simple hand gesture. She offered him the chair in front of her dressing table to sit on, and he fell onto it with a sigh. He stared a moment at his hands resting on his knees, and then said, "My worst fears are confirmed. There are traces of barbiturates in Paula's blood. The police think Calista tried to harm her because she was angry with her."

Atalanta let these words sink in for a moment. She wanted to say something, ask a dozen questions, but Raoul lifted his hand. "Wait. There is more. And it gets worse."

Atalanta sat on the edge of her bed, pulling her gown closer around her. "Tell me." She knew that Raoul's involvement in the case made everything harder, and still it meant the world to her that he had come to her. Perhaps he only wanted her to know of the latest developments before they became widely known. But still, she hoped that he knew he could trust her with whatever bad news there was, and that she would do anything in her power to help him.

As long as it is within the limits of the law, of course, she told herself.

Raoul took a deep breath before saying, "Victoria told me that Paula drank wine from her cup. She thinks the barbiturates were meant for her. To kill her."

"But…" Atalanta's head swam with the implications of this revelation. "That makes no sense at all. Calista would never harm her. They are the best of friends."

Raoul shook his head. He released his breath in a huff before he said, "It's far more complicated than that. Yes, they are the best of friends, but you heard Calista tonight. She feels like Victoria is stifling her. That because she saved her earlier in life when she was down and disillusioned, she thinks she now has a right to interfere in how she lives, what she does, who she sees. Victoria doesn't like her friends, the men she dates, the travelling lifestyle… As soon as they are together, they argue about it."

Yes, that was true. Atalanta listened intently, trying to connect the dots and reach the horrible conclusion that murder had been the only way out. "Does Mrs Bucardi genuinely think that Calista feels so restrained by her well-meaning advice that she would resort to something as brutal and drastic as murder to be rid of her?"

"Murder disguised as accidental death. Too much wine, heat, dancing during the festival… A heart attack, and everyone calls it a tragedy, not asking any questions about it."

Raoul rubbed his forehead. "Victoria thinks that Letitia's accident gave Calista the idea."

"Calista was here when Letitia died?"

"Yes. She stays here often." Raoul looked at her. "Please don't tell me that you now also think Calista killed Letitia. Why would she? The two of them had nothing to do with one another. Letitia didn't take care of Luca. They can't have argued about that."

Atalanta waved a hand. "Let's not complicate things too much, and let's focus on Paula's death for the moment. On the assumption that the barbiturates in the wine weren't meant for her but for Mrs Bucardi. How well do you know both her and Calista?" As she asked the question, her hands trembled for fear of what the answer might reveal.

He looked up at her. "Does that matter?"

She hoped the light in the room was too dim for him to see her flush. "I just wonder if you can assess their state of mind and how far they would go to…" She bit her lip before adding, "Also, when Mrs Bucardi asked you to help Calista, as she was under suspicion, the two of you looked rather close."

Raoul sat and stared at the carpet. It seemed he was considering how much he could tell her. She hoped he would feel he could trust her with the truth.

Then again, he might be bound by some promise he had made to conceal the truth?

The moments dragged on in silence, and she worried he would fob her off with some contrived story.

But at last, he spoke: "Five years ago, when Calista broke down at a party, fainted and was carried off, I was there. I informed Victoria that her friend wasn't well. She came over at once and cared for Calista. She had her removed to a remote

162

villa because … she was addicted to pills she was taking, and it took some persuasion to wean her off them. In fact…"

Raoul took another deep breath. "Calista was quite violent during those times. She even struck Victoria on several occasions because she refused to give her the pills she craved. Victoria didn't allow anyone to come there because she didn't want them to see the frantic state Calista was in. It was something close to madness at times and wouldn't have painted her in a favourable light. Calista depends on her beautiful wild-girl image to sell the dresses she makes, and Victoria wanted to protect her from a scandal and lasting damage to her career. Bucardi didn't like the situation because his wife was pregnant with their son, Luca, at the time. He was afraid she would be hurt and lose the baby. His heir to everything."

He gestured around him. "Victoria cared for the baby, of course, but she also felt she should try and save her friend. I've always thought that the months she spent at that remote villa changed her. She was more outgoing and softer before. Now she is aloof and … I think she hides behind a cool façade so as not to be hurt again."

"You sound as if you feel sorry for her," Atalanta said softly.

"Yes, of course. She only wanted to help someone. Calista is…" Raoul looked for words. "She can be marvellous company. Witty, daring. Everyone loves her when she is in a good mood. But don't you catch her on a bad day. Then she can come tearing at you and say the most horrible things. She even accused Victoria, to her face, of not being a good mother to Luca because she doesn't indulge in every wild game and asks him to sit at the table during dinner and go to bed on time. If Calista could have her way, Luca would be raised without any rules. Giving a child boundaries is damaging, in her view. Victoria was understandably hurt."

Atalanta nodded and then put the question that seemed so logical. "Why does she keep seeing Calista if their relationship is getting more and more difficult?"

Raoul laughed softly. "Because she can't let go of her project. She saved her friend and she feels she must keep saving her. I wish I could tell you it's out of the goodness of her heart and because she loves her. And perhaps that was once part of it. But now it has become much more. Victoria won't let go of what she started." He shook his head with a frustrated huff. "I told Victoria several times that it can only end badly, but she won't listen to me. Or to anyone else for that matter."

Atalanta stared at her hands. Would she dare ask him if Luca was his son? But it made no sense in the context of this conversation, and if she was wrong... The mere idea that Raoul would hate her for her suggestion clawed at her heart. How could she risk it?

Raoul said, "I don't believe for a moment that Calista tried to kill Victoria."

"But you just said it could only end badly."

"Yes, I meant that someday Calista would tell Victoria that she hated her for being so uptight and worried all the time and ... that they would have a huge fight, full of reproaches, and Victoria would be heartbroken. She risked her marriage, her pregnancy, everything for Calista, and Calista just doesn't seem to appreciate it."

"She does appreciate it, perhaps, but she doesn't want to repay the debt forever. Can't you see?"

Raoul rubbed his forehead again. "Oh, I can see it. Clearly. But they can't. They are tied together in this … painful friendship where they're both loyal and loving, but are also both suffocating in the ties they created. It must end."

"And Calista can't have wanted to end it with a handful of pills in Mrs Bucardi's wine?" Atalanta asked softly. "You said yourself that Letitia's accident might have given her the idea for it. If Mrs Bucardi had felt unwell during the party, and died of a heart attack, there would probably not have been a police investigation at all."

Raoul sat with his head down. He didn't reply.

"You think Calista is capable of it." Atalanta's heart squeezed for him. "You wouldn't have come to me to discuss this if you thought the police's allegation was pointless and would come to nothing."

Raoul looked up with a jerk. "How can they investigate the truth? There were dozens of cups used and they were washed clean. There's no way to prove in whose cup the pills were introduced. I convinced the police for now not to arrest Calista, but they're worried she will leave the island and escape justice. I'm afraid that come morning, they will be back here to arrest her anyway. What argument can we come up with to stop them?"

Atalanta considered this question. Had someone consciously put a large dose of barbiturates in Mrs Bucardi's cup to have her die? Or could there be another explanation for the traces of pills in Paula's blood? "Can Paula have taken the pills by mistake? Perhaps she had a headache and wanted to take a painkiller and ingested the wrong pill?" Atalanta sat up. "What if Paula complained to someone about a headache and they gave her pills to take? Allegedly to help against the pain."

"Interesting, but we can never prove that unless the person who gave them to her comes forward. But now that Paula is dead, they won't. If they intended to kill her, they won't speak out, of course. And even if it was accidental, too large a dose taken by Paula because she had a terrible headache from all that alcohol she imbibed, the person will fear being accused of her death and keep silent." Raoul looked at her with weary eyes. "It would have been hard if we knew for certain that Paula was the intended victim, but with Victoria's confession to me that Paula drank from her cup... If *she* should have died, we're looking at a completely different field of suspects."

"Such as?" Atalanta asked.

"Her husband? He doesn't seem to love her at all. Perhaps, now that he has his son, he would rather marry someone else?" Raoul counted on his fingers. "Calista, unfortunately. And then there's Andreas. You said he threatened Victoria earlier."

"Yes, and that didn't seem to make sense then, but now that Calista has told us about the pirates' gold... If Andreas wanted to look for it and Mrs Bucardi somehow stood in the way... Those caves where you saw evidence that someone had been there are really close to the burg. What if they are part of the Bucardi property? If Andreas located treasure there, it would belong to the Bucardis, not to him."

Atalanta thought for a few moments and added, "We shouldn't forget Delilah. She never liked Paula and she even said to me that she stole from her. Paula told me that Delilah had given her a golden necklace, but what if that wasn't true? What if Paula took it from among Delilah's things, thinking that if she missed it, people would simply assume she had misplaced it, because of her alleged forgetfulness? If Paula did steal from Delilah and Delilah's complaints about missing items weren't believed, that would certainly make Delilah very angry. She also uses pills, to sleep. That is, she told me that she doesn't take them but saves them. For what?"

"Good question. You should ask her."

"I doubt I will get a clear answer from her."

"Is she that confused?"

"No, not really. I have a feeling she's extremely clever and plays people against each other. Her weakness at times can be a ruse to make people feel sorry for her. In the meantime, she gets away with all her orders and complaints and nasty remarks."

"So she is the pitiful old lady who doesn't remember everything anymore, but..."

"Paula made fun of her." Atalanta knotted her fingers. "Wouldn't it be ironic if it turns out that this little old lady she joked about killed her?"

Chapter Thirteen

The next morning when Atalanta went into Delilah's room, the old lady was sitting at the window overlooking the sunny view, just as she had done on the first day when Atalanta arrived. She didn't turn her head to look at her when Atalanta came to stand beside her. Her expression was impossible to read. Was she worried about the death at the burg? Another death so soon after Letitia had fallen off the cliffs?

Or was she secretly satisfied?

She had called Paula wicked.

Were those calm, placid features Atalanta was looking at the features of a cold-blooded killer?

"I've been thinking about it all night," Delilah said.

Atalanta watched her carefully. "About Paula's death?"

"No. About what I saw."

Atalanta's heart skipped a beat. Had Delilah witnessed something? Pills given to Paula? Pills dropped into a goblet? An empty cup hastily removed or even broken, conveniently shattered on the cobbles? Something that had meant nothing to her at the time but took on a gruesome meaning now?

"I don't know if I should tell anyone." Delilah sounded almost lost. "Whether I must create trouble or be silent. In my youth nothing was as important as honour. As protecting the family name. But is it still like that today?" She knotted her thin, breakable fingers. "Must I be silent or speak out and stir things up?"

"I've felt from the start you are a woman who speaks her mind." Atalanta tried to feel her way around the situation. Delilah's mention of protecting the family name suggested she had seen a family member do something. Bucardi? His wife? Had Mrs Bucardi given Paula the pills, then later claimed they had been meant for her, to divert suspicion? Did Delilah know?

But it had seemed she didn't like Mrs Bucardi. She had struggled with her for the upper hand as mistress of this *castello*. Would Delilah really hesitate to incriminate the hated in-law?

Wouldn't she sooner protect her nephew? Mr Bucardi ... killing Paula for what reason? To hide an affair? Delilah had said to Bucardi's face that he had played on the girl's vanity, making her believe she could be mistress of the burg.

Or had he killed Paula because she knew something and had blackmailed him? What had been her lucrative business?

"What do you think I should do?" Delilah asked. "Is honesty always the best policy, Mademoiselle Renard?"

"If you saw something that can help clarify how Paula died, you must tell the police. Lying to them, or withholding information, won't help anyone."

"Saw something that..." Delilah laughed softly. "I wouldn't

lift my little finger to help solve the death of that irresponsible, wicked girl. She deserved to die."

"How can you say such a thing?" Atalanta didn't ask it in a sharp, condemning tone; instead, she inserted a touch of surprise and confusion to invite further explanation.

Delilah looked up at her. "Paula neglected her duties and put the child at risk. She wasn't worthy of her position here."

"That may all be true, but does that mean she deserved to die?"

Delilah considered the question. "Perhaps it doesn't mean she deserved to die in the sense that her behaviour called for the death penalty." She said it earnestly, as if she were on a jury judging a case brought before her. "But if you act like she did, you make enemies. And then one of them might lash out at you."

Atalanta thought that this was probably true. Looking at it that way, Paula, with her forward behaviour, must have made a few enemies. Which one of them had decided to act?

"But we weren't discussing Paula, Mademoiselle Renard. We were discussing the broader question of whether one should act on one's knowledge or remain silent. What do you think?"

"That depends on the situation. Sometimes sharing things you know can only hurt people and won't bring anything good. Sometimes it's the other way around and keeping silent is harmful." Atalanta leaned down closer. "Can you tell me something about your dilemma, so I may help you?"

"I think that would be difficult."

"Because it is so delicate?"

Delilah took her time replying, and Atalanta almost

thought her mind was wandering off, when the old lady suddenly said, "Because *you* are one of the parties involved."

Atalanta widened her eyes. "Me?"

Delilah looked up at her. "Why did you come here?"

"To work as your companion." Atalanta gave the answer instinctively, quickly, without thinking. She hoped it looked like the truth, although her heart was pounding and she felt sweat break out on her brow.

Delilah laughed. "Yes, on the face of it. But what were your deeper reasons? You've always worked in France. You needn't have come to this Greek island."

"I wanted a change of scenery."

"What is it worth to you, Mademoiselle Renard?"

Atalanta straightened up. Blood droned in her ears but her voice was steady when she said, "I don't know what you mean."

"My silence. About what I know. What I saw."

"I have no idea what you mean." Atalanta's thoughts raced to understand what the elderly lady could be driving at. Delilah had accused others in the household of snooping and theft. Would she also accuse her of some made-up crime? Would she even implicate her in Paula's murder? Claim she had seen something, witnessed an argument?

If the police found out Atalanta had come here under a false name, it could put her in a spot.

"If I tell Mr Bucardi, he wouldn't care. But Mrs Bucardi..." Delilah waited a moment. "I should hope that she would be shocked." She waited a moment and added in a strange tone, "For more than one reason."

"I don't understand what you are referring to."

"The man who visited your room during the night. The race car driver."

Raoul coming to her room ... Delilah had seen it. It was possible, as the elderly lady had earlier been called a light sleeper, and afraid of prowlers. If she had heard someone in the corridor, she might have gone to see who it was and what he was up to. That way she had also seen Letitia return from Mr Bucardi's workroom, she had claimed.

Now she wanted to tell Mrs Bucardi about Raoul visiting Atalanta's bedroom in the dead of night. Would her employer be shocked because it was improper, going on under her roof? Or because Raoul had once been her lover? Was the father of her child? Did Delilah also know that, or at least suspect as much?

Atalanta said hurriedly, "Mr Lemont did come to my room, but it was merely to tell me what the police had discovered about Paula's death. We know each other only superficially."

"I wouldn't have guessed, from the way you're always separating yourselves from the others and whispering." Delilah sat up straighter. "I might not go out much, but I can see from my window." She gestured at the view. "I saw you walking with that man while you had sent a maid to my room instead of doing your duties. I think it's shameful how young people behave these days."

"I asked Mr Lemont to help me look for Paula. She was already missing then. I assure you, we were merely concerned for Paula's safety. Nothing untoward happened. So there is no need to bother Mrs Bucardi with this. Paula's death caused enough damage."

"Damage? That's an interesting word." Delilah gave her a probing look. "What damage would it do?"

"Another death so soon after Letitia fell from the rocks." Atalanta took a deep breath before adding, "You told me that was murder."

"I believed so. But now I doubt it."

"*Now* you doubt it?" Atalanta was genuinely confused. "A second girl gets murdered, and you doubt that the first death was murder?"

"Yes, because Letitia and Paula were poles apart. They had nothing in common. Why would anyone want to kill both of them? Paula, yes, she was manipulative, devious and cruel. But Letitia was a darling girl. She might have been stubborn in wanting to go out on the cliffs while she had vertigo, but she never hurt anyone with intrigues or lies."

"But you told me that Letitia snooped in your nephew's study."

"I only saw the figure of a tall slender girl sneaking through the corridor. It could have been Paula. And even if it was Letitia, somebody put her up to it. She wouldn't have thought to do something forbidden."

Atalanta frowned. This assessment of Letitia's character matched what Paula had said, about Letitia being afraid to criticize her employers. Had someone put her up to snooping in Bucardi's things? The man she was in love with? Someone she had been willing to break rules for?

Delilah said, "You're very clever, Mademoiselle Renard, appealing to my family duty in telling me not to burden Mrs Bucardi with my knowledge of your shameful behaviour with the race car driver. But I know you only have your own interests at heart. You wish to conceal your clandestine affair. But it cannot be hidden."

"I assure you nothing—"

174

"I don't care what you assure me. I will speak of this, and you can't stop me." Delilah waited a moment and added, "Or will you also put barbiturates in my wine, like you did with Paula?"

"Me?" Atalanta echoed. It didn't sound fully disbelieving to her own mind, as she had already anticipated that Delilah might try to implicate her in something.

"Paula followed that race car driver around all day. She saw you two" – Delilah looked for a word that she dared pronounce – "together, and then she pressed you to give her money to keep silent. Instead, you killed her. You put her in her room on her bed and then pretended to find her dead body. But you were behind it all."

"I looked for Paula, because I was concerned for her. Mr Lemont was with me most of the time. I won't listen to any of this nonsense." Atalanta retreated to the door, her back straight, her head held high. But her madly pounding heart told her the same as her panicked thoughts: this reasoning might just make sense to the police. Paula could have been killed because she was a risk to someone.

"I know where you got the barbiturates," Delilah shouted after her. "You used *my* saved pills. They're no longer in their place."

"I didn't know where you kept them."

"Of course you did. I showed you."

"No, you didn't." Atalanta's palms were slick with sweat. Delilah had welcomed her as the new companion with prosecco. Now she accused her of monstrous things. Why?

Delilah called out to her to come back to her, but Atalanta opened the door and fled from the room. How could she protect herself against this woman's outright lies?

Rushing down the stairs, she came into the hallway where two uniformed policemen stood on either side of Calista. She wore a simple dark dress and with her loose hair she looked like a schoolgirl caught sneaking back into boarding school late at night. Mr Bucardi, crisp in a light suit, spoke to the policemen in Greek. Raoul stood a few paces away, watching the scene with frustration written across his features. He had predicted last night that the police would feel obliged to arrest Calista to keep her from leaving the island, and apparently, his assessment had been correct.At last the policemen took Calista by the arms and tugged to get her to the door.

"No, no!" Luca came running down the stairs, his wooden sword in his hand. He attacked the policeman on the right, hacking at him with the sword. The policeman tried to shield himself against the blows by turning away while still holding onto Calista's arm.

Bucardi barked, "Luca, stop this. Stop it, now!" He reached out to grab his son's arm, but Luca turned on him and beat him with the sword as well.

Bucardi raised a hand to strike the little boy in the face.

Calista gasped and Raoul jumped forward and pulled the boy away before Bucardi's hand could hit home. Raoul lifted Luca on his arm and said something to him. Luca was crying now, tears rushing down his cheeks. As Atalanta saw the two faces together, Luca's and Raoul's, she was again struck by the resemblance in the brown eyes and dark hair.

Calista held her head down and spoke softly to the policemen. They led her away. Raoul restrained Luca, who squirmed to be released and go after Calista to protect her.

Bucardi spat, "You needn't have interfered, Lemont. He should learn his lesson."

"At this moment? While his heart is broken?" With a disgusted expression, Raoul turned away, carrying Luca back up the stairs.

Bucardi cursed.

Atalanta asked, "What happened to make the police arrest Calista?"

"They found a pestle in her room used to crush barbiturate pills into powder. They think she put them in Paula's wine. Or in wine meant for someone else." He rubbed his forehead. "They say it could have been meant for another person and Paula drank it by chance."

Atalanta tried to maintain a calm expression. "Why on earth would they think that?" Had Mrs Bucardi shared her suspicions with the police? *So soon?*

"There was an altercation at the party yesterday about mixed-up cups or something. I don't know. I haven't personally seen it." Bucardi pressed his hands to his face and breathed deep. "What a way to begin a new day. Calista arrested and…"

Mrs Bucardi came racing down the stairs. "What happened?" Her voice was shrill. "Where is Calista?"

Bucardi said curtly, "They took her away. They think she killed Paula."

"Nonsense, why would she?" Mrs Bucardi wanted to hurry outside after the policemen but her husband caught her arm. "It's over now," he said with a hint of satisfaction.

"What?"

She pulled to be released but he held on tightly as he said, "You trying to help her and her not appreciating it. She only used you. She took advantage of your good intentions. Now she's killed someone in our home. I'll never forgive her, and I don't want her to ever set foot here again." He waited a moment before adding, "If she is indeed guilty, she will be locked up and will never have another chance to influence our child."

Mrs Bucardi wanted to say something, but Bucardi said, "No good could have come of it, Victoria. Try to see that. You wanted to help her, but she never wanted to be helped." He let go of his wife and walked away.

Mrs Bucardi seemed torn. Stay put or run outside anyway?

Atalanta acknowledged that Mr Bucardi's assessment might contain some truth. Had Calista really meant to change her ways when her best friend Victoria had spent months trying to help her recover? Perhaps she had meant it at the time, but had fallen back into her addiction to pills. Could Calista even help herself, or was her need for the sedatives stronger than anything else? Even stronger than the friendship that bound her to Victoria Bucardi?

It was sad how people struggled and came up short.

Softly Atalanta said, "Is there anything I can do to help?"

Mrs Bucardi looked at her and blinked, as if she had only just become aware that a stranger had watched this painful scene. "No. Oh, yes, perhaps. Now that Paula is no longer with us, can you take care of Luca? Until we've found someone new. I don't think Delilah will require much attention today. I knocked on her door a few minutes ago and she told me she had a terrible headache and was in bed."

"Oh." Atalanta blinked. Apparently, Delilah hadn't jumped at the opportunity to incriminate her. That was good news. Or was it?

"I'll go and see where Luca is," she said quietly and went upstairs.

Chapter Fourteen

She found Raoul in the nursery. He sat in a wicker chair by the window with Luca in his arms. The little boy had hidden his face against Raoul's shoulder and was still sobbing. Raoul patted him on the back and spoke Italian with him. He looked up as she entered. "Is it over?" he asked in English.

Atalanta nodded. "The police have taken her away. Mrs Bucardi asked me to look after Luca for the time being. It seems Delilah doesn't need me right now."

Raoul didn't make a move to get up. The protective way in which he cradled the sad little boy against him clogged Atalanta's throat. Even if Raoul had decided that he wouldn't openly acknowledge the child he had fathered, that didn't mean he could not love the boy and want to care for him. Especially as all this misery unfolded. And Luca so needed someone to love him and make him feel safe. He obviously didn't get this comfort and security from Mr or Mrs Bucardi.

Raoul said, "Can you get him some breakfast? There is food

and other supplies in the cupboard there." He gestured to a door in the far wall.

Atalanta nodded and went over. It was a nice diversion to prepare some crackers with cherry preserves and serve fresh milk from the pitcher a servant brought in. Behind her back she heard Raoul's melodious Italian continue. She had no idea what it was about, a story perhaps, for distraction?

"There you are." She put the food and milk beside Raoul on the small table and took a chair opposite. She said in French, "Can we discuss the murder without him understanding?"

"Yes. He knows a few words of English, but no French. Especially if we speak fast."

Atalanta smiled at him. "Thank you for intervening and saving him from that blow from his father."

Raoul held out a cracker to Luca who turned his face away. He said something to him and tried again. Now Luca accepted the cracker. Crumbs rained on Raoul's neat suit as he ate. Raoul said to Atalanta, "When Bucardi is violent to him, I could break his jaw. But he is master of the house, and he feels entitled to exert his power on his family, the servants."

Atalanta noticed that Raoul had not called Bucardi Luca's father. Wouldn't it have been more natural to say, "He is the lad's father, he thinks he's entitled to discipline him"?

She said, "I know from my pupils at boarding school that physical punishment is normal in well-to-do families, especially if the children are smaller. Even teachers apply it, slapping hands with rulers and the like. I've always felt that such force was the wrong way to get a child to obey you, but I don't have children myself."

Raoul's expression didn't change as she said it. But he didn't meet her eyes either as he fussed with the milk glass to get Luca to drink. Luca turned his face away and refused to take any, but when Raoul persisted, he relented and did drink.

Atalanta wished for a moment that Raoul could stay at the *castello* longer and give Luca a carefree time. The little boy had been through a lot lately.

She said, "The police found something in Calista's room."

Luca looked at her with a jerk. "Calista?" he asked in a high-pitched tone, and his face contorted again. Raoul spoke some comforting words and offered him the glass of milk. He said to Atalanta, "Avoid her name. He does recognize it, and every time we mention it, he gets upset."

She nodded and started anew. "Something was found in her room. I heard from Mr Bucardi it was a pestle used to grind the pills to powder, to easily slip them into the wine."

"Apparently. Assuming that she's not the murderer, that pestle must have been put there to incriminate her. It shows me that our killer is nervous. Afraid to be accused. If this crime was so brilliantly conceived that the police can never lead it back to the perpetrator, why lay a false track to someone else?"

"Extra security? Besides, if the killer was familiar with Calista's addiction to pills, it would be a very logical thing to do." She studied her hands. "Do you know anything about an altercation at the party concerning switched cups?"

"No. But we were away from the party for quite some time."

Atalanta flushed at the mention. "It seems our absence was noticed. Delilah told me this morning, quite brusquely, that she feels she has to inform Mrs Bucardi of our affair."

"Affair? Elderly ladies can't think of anything else." Raoul sounded half amused.

"I can't see it as an innocent fabrication. She saw us leave the burg and walk together. We were looking for Paula, of course, but she doesn't believe that. I feel that if she revealed what she saw, to Mrs Bucardi specifically, it would cause major trouble."

Raoul looked up at her. His brown eyes were questioning, but not alarmed. "Why? Victoria is the first to say her husband's aunt is often confused and can be quite fanciful in her stories. She wouldn't believe her."

"You don't think so?"

Raoul held her gaze as he added, "You and me having an affair is not very probable, is it?"

Atalanta felt a flush creep up.

"In fact," Raoul continued, "it's quite unlikely. You are but a companion for a rich family. People expect me to go after heiresses, to say the least. Money, titles, anything to further my career and ensure I have unlimited access to money."

Atalanta's cheeks were now on fire. She recalled that during the first case in Provence, a guest at the wedding feast had told her quite snidely that Raoul had flirted with a German princess and that he had to marry well to have the money he needed for his adventurous lifestyle. It seemed Raoul himself was aware of these stories about him. Or did he perhaps even admit to himself that they were right? "So you think no one would believe it? Not even if Delilah said she saw you come from my bedroom in the dead of night?"

"Not even then. If she told Victoria and Victoria came to me, I would simply tell her the real reason I was with you."

Atalanta's jaw dropped. "And that reason is?"

"You are a poor relative of mine whom I'm supporting discreetly. We are keeping our family connection hidden because it is painful to me. Your father was the black sheep of the family. Or something like that. We can make up a plausible story. In fact, we should have before we came here. We should have realized that our exchanges could be noticed and interpreted in the wrong light. But it's too late for that now."

"I said earlier that I know you because you came to the house of my employers for dinner."

"Yes, you made that up because I encouraged you to hide the family connection." He waved a hand. "I'll make a good story out of it and Victoria will believe me. She is very socially conscious. She won't readily think I'd go after a servant."

He held her gaze a moment and then laughed. "Oh, Mademoiselle Renard, your expression is priceless. Are you considering slapping me in the face for what I just said?"

Atalanta fought for composure. Him calling her fictional father the black sheep of the family had hit home in a very painful way. Her real father had shamed his aristocratic family and had been alienated from his father for most of his adult life. It was the main reason why Atalanta had never had a chance to get to know her grandfather, Clarence Ashford. That he had nevertheless left her his fortune and vocation had come as a major surprise, and a happy one at that. But she still felt sharply she would have liked to know him on a more personal level. Especially as she was following in his footsteps, she wanted to know how he had talked, reasoned, acted.

Raoul said, "You may feel offended by this reasoning. But it's true, you know. A man in my position has so many women to choose from that he doesn't need to go after a companion in a place where he's staying for a few days. Besides, my reputation as Casanova is hardly warranted. At parties I may dance and chat like everyone does, but outside of that I'm far too busy with my racing to get serious with anyone. I don't have the time or the inclination."

"You needn't get serious if you're having a mere affair."

"Women tend to see that very differently. For a man an affair might be brief, for a woman there is always the expectation of more. Even if she knows the rules from the start."

He sounded rueful, as if he couldn't quite understand it, or understand his own past belief that it was possible to simply have an affair without having true feelings and hopes.

Atalanta wondered if Victoria Bucardi had ever expected more of Raoul. If she had looked for affection outside of her loveless marriage and had believed Raoul would become her new husband once she was divorced. Perhaps she had even fallen pregnant to persuade him to do so? Perhaps Raoul had at first been offended by her scheming, but had later realized how she had genuinely ached for him to love her and provide her with a happy home. Also for the child's sake.

Raoul made a hand gesture. "Never mind. You needn't worry that Delilah will cause problems for you. I'll disarm her stories. That's all you need to know."

The idea that he was sitting there, holding his son in his arms, and not telling her the truth about it, hurt. But then they weren't that close. He needn't confide in her, certainly not about an intensely personal matter. Perhaps she would do well to remember that?

She should, for her part, also keep a bit of distance and not allow herself to be swept away by the feeling that she had, for once in her life, made a meaningful connection with someone. She had always managed to survive on her own, so why would she need to rely on someone else now?

The door opened and Mrs Bucardi came in. She looked at Raoul holding Luca, then at Atalanta opposite them in a chair, and snapped, "Why are you not taking care of Luca, Mademoiselle Renard? I asked you to, not Raoul."

"I offered to do it," Raoul said hurriedly. "Luca was upset. I tried to calm him down." He added something in rapid Italian. Atalanta thought it was about Bucardi having tried to hit the boy. Mrs Bucardi answered and it seemed she said something about not attracting further attention.

Atalanta frowned. *What is going on here?*

Mrs Bucardi said, "You can now leave us, Mademoiselle Renard. Go and see if Delilah wants breakfast."

"You previously said she had a headache and was in bed."

"Don't talk back to me." Mrs Bucardi's eyes flashed. "You also shirked your duties yesterday. Now go and do as you're told. Leave us." She barked the order, as if speaking to a dog.

Without looking at Raoul, Atalanta came to her feet and made for the door. She could imagine that this kind of belittling tone wasn't welcome to Calista. What if her best friend Victoria, who had once been a dear help to her, had gradually become a choking force in her life? What if Calista had thought that the only way to get rid of her was to kill her?

Not in a violent manner but softly, without causing pain or fear, with a powder that would make her fall asleep and die without having any idea what had struck her?

Chapter Fifteen

F earing that Delilah wouldn't welcome her company after
   their earlier brush about Raoul's night-time visit to her
bedroom, Atalanta retreated into the courtyard. She needed a
few moments to regain her calm and decide how to proceed
from here.

In the wide-open space, with the clear blue skies above, she
found Andreas Papoudopolis putting away the last wooden
tables from yesterday's festivities. A few feet away from him
two crows pecked between the cobbles, apparently having
found some leftovers from the feast. With their glossy black
feathers these scavengers seemed a symbol of the sudden
change that had come over the burg: just a short while ago
people had danced and sung here, celebrating life and joy, but
now death had struck this house once more and the
inhabitants were eyeing each other with suspicion.

Hearing her approach, Andreas looked at her and asked if
she had slept well.

Normally, she would have thought he was rather brazen to

address her at all after his ill-fated attempted kiss, but right now she wanted to talk to him and gather his ideas on the nanny's sudden death. Paula had seemed close with Andreas. Had she even spent time with him yesterday? And what was this pirates' gold he was allegedly after, looking for it in grottoes that belonged to the Bucardi family?

"Not at all," Atalanta answered his question. She shook her head sadly. "I kept seeing Paula's dead face."

"She died in her sleep, did she not? It must have been peaceful. She wasn't hurt like the other girl was, battered against the rocks by the sea."

Atalanta shivered under his unfeeling description of Letitia's fate. "Still, death is death. It is so … final."

Andreas shrugged. "We Greeks embrace death as part of life. In our old tragedy plays, death is often a catalyst to transform people's lives. It can bring about change and good things."

"And what good things do you think Paula's death can bring?" Atalanta asked softly. She kept her eyes on Andreas's expression. Did he know that the nanny's death had removed a threat of exposure of his activities?

He turned his back on her however, fussing over a table. The clatter of its legs on the stone made the crows fly up, only to descend again a few feet down the courtyard. "I was speaking in general," he said, in a dismissive tone. "I don't know about this girl. She wasn't Greek."

"So then, it doesn't work that way?" Atalanta felt impatience rush through her at Andreas's philosophical outlook on life. He was a man of flesh and blood who acted in the here and now. And he should own up to his actions. "You took her on walks. Perhaps you were friends?"

"Friends?" Andreas laughed. "Paula felt herself far too good for the likes of me. She had set her eyes on something better. Someone higher."

"Mr Bucardi." Atalanta made it sound like a statement rather than a question. After all, he was the first person who was "higher" to come to mind in this context of the *castello*.

Andreas turned to her. "He cannot have killed her. He was here all the time, overseeing the festivities."

His defence of the employer he allegedly loathed took her by surprise. Why would Andreas not allow her to think Bucardi had been involved in Paula's death? Why was he so quick to alibi him?

Andreas continued, "And Paula died on the beach."

Atalanta blinked. For a moment she thought she must have misunderstood him. "She died in her bed," she corrected.

"No. The doctor said so. He speaks Greek. I can understand him very well. The talk is all over the island." He gestured around him as if the rumours buzzed like bees in the air. "She died on the beach."

"Why does the doctor think so?" Atalanta asked with a puzzled frown.

"Because her body was sunburned. Her arms, her neck and part of her legs." Andreas waved his arms. "Everywhere. The doctor said that he believed she had lain in the sand sunbathing for hours."

Atalanta didn't know quite what to make of this information. "Paula lay in the sun for hours?" She repeated it to ensure she did understand correctly.

"Yes. The doctor says that if he had not found the medicine in her blood, he would have thought she had died of exposure to too much sun. Sometimes that happens to tourists. They sit or lie in the sun and fall asleep, and then they get badly burnt, and because of dehydration and heat stroke they die."

Atalanta nodded slowly. That did make sense. "So Paula lay in the sun for hours, and then she came back to the burg and drank wine with barbiturates in it, and she felt unwell and lay down on her bed and died." Had she imbibed the barbiturates by accident? Had they indeed been meant for someone else, as Victoria Bucardi had suggested?

Suddenly she blinked. "But you said she *died* on the beach?"

"Well, the doctor says she died lying face down. He can tell from marks on the body. But she lay on her bed face up. Now, you explain that."

Atalanta considered this. Had someone been in the room before she had entered it with Lemusier? Had he or she turned the body over and, upon seeing Paula was dead, left the room, locking the door again to let someone else find the unfortunate girl?

But who had a key to the room?

Andreas came over to her, rubbing his hands. He stopped in front of her and held her gaze. "Why, Mademoiselle Renard, would you even want anyone to explain that? In a household where you accepted a job, someone dies. You should be shocked and keep yourself out of it. But you're asking everyone questions." He leaned closer and added, "That isn't the behaviour I'd have expected from a discreet companion."

Atalanta tried not to flinch under his probing look. Of course he had questions about her behaviour and she should play along, inventing a plausible reason for her curiosity.

She said with a quick smile, "Well, perhaps I'm not *that*

discreet. I … was dismissed in my earlier position because I was too inquisitive. Too free, as my mistress called it."

Andreas nodded. "And instead of learning your lesson and keeping your head down here, you start again?"

"Who could resist it?" Atalanta enthused. "I mean, other households might have minor secrets, a few debts, or an uncle with a fondness of booze, but here there is something major going on. I mean…" She held her breath a moment, as if she was too excited to go on. "Delilah mentioned to me that Letitia was murdered as well. She didn't fall into the sea. No, she was killed by someone. Shoved off the rocks." She widened her eyes at the latter words, as if it was hugely exhilarating. "I can't believe I landed in such a situation. It's just like a movie."

"And you accuse us Greeks of being inconsiderate about death?" He laughed softly. "We're all alike, it seems. Death fascinates us. Sudden death, with a mysterious air to it, puzzles us, and the brain must find answers." He hesitated a moment. "To be honest, I never believed that Letitia's death was an accident."

"You didn't?" Atalanta looked about her to ascertain they weren't overheard and asked, "What do you think happened?"

"Well, at first I did think she simply fell. And I felt guilty because I had told her stories about the island myths and the grottoes by the sea, and she might have clambered down to see them and fallen and died. She wanted to take photographs that would make her famous."

"Yes, I heard she was a photographer. Is her camera still here?"

"It was around her neck when she plunged down the cliffs. The camera fell in the sea with her and got washed away from her body. It was never recovered."

How convenient, if she had been photographing something forbidden.

Andreas continued, "I should have warned her it was dangerous. I did, actually, but you know how it goes when someone is eager to explore."

He pulled up his shoulders and let them fall again with a sigh as he continued, "I felt guilty until I realized that she had probably been pushed off the rocks. You see, Letitia was a kind girl and she loved Luca like a little brother. She spoiled him and she couldn't stand it that Mr Bucardi was so harsh to him. She even commented on him striking Luca once. That wasn't to his liking. He would glare at her as if … he could just kill her. I think he pushed her into the sea."

"But surely a man like Mr Bucardi has nothing to fear from a simple comment one of his staff members made about his behaviour towards his son?" Atalanta was confused as to why Andreas would latch onto Mr Bucardi as a possible suspect for Letitia's murder, while he had been so quick to deny that his employer could be involved in Paula's death. She had to find out if Andreas knew something pertinent that suggested Bucardi's guilt in the matter.

Andreas pursed his lips. "Letitia was very close to Mrs Bucardi. She impressed upon her that her husband was cruel to the child. I wonder if Mrs Bucardi secretly contemplated leaving her husband. Now, I don't think it would have gone down very well with a proud man like Bucardi, to be humiliated by a public divorce."

Atalanta had to admit he was probably correct in that assessment. Still, his description of Letitia's role threw up more questions than answers. "But why would Mrs Bucardi be close to a servant? Her aunt's companion, not hers?"

"Her husband's aunt's companion, to be precise," Andreas corrected with a pedantic smile. "I don't know. It seems Mrs Bucardi liked the girl because she was educated, young, ambitious. They often sat together on the terrace at night, talking about books and Venice. Letitia had many beautiful photographs of the city, which she showed her."

So the photo of Venice in Paula's bedroom could indeed have been Letitia's. *Interesting.*

Andreas continued, "Mrs Bucardi misses her hometown. I think it was another reason for her to consider divorce. She wanted to take Luca and raise him in Venice."

And allow for the real father to play a part in the child's life? Atalanta wondered. The longer she thought about it, the more sense it made. The arrival of Letitia as companion for Delilah had put things in motion. Mrs Bucardi had longed for Venice. Had abhorred the brutality of her husband against the child. The child that was not his. Did he suspect? Would his behaviour worsen? Would it not be better to remove the child from his presence? Leave this place, go back to the city she loved, be happy again?

Andreas said, "Mrs Bucardi was shocked when Letitia died. She supported the accident story and even wrote the letter to the girl's family herself. But I doubt that she believes it in her heart. She can look at her husband in a way that makes me wonder if she knows the truth. Bucardi shoved Letitia into the sea to keep his wife here on the island."

"If he did, he took a chance. Someone could have witnessed it."

"He knows this island like the back of his hand. He was raised here. He could have found the perfect spot for it. He could even have used Letitia's interest in the grottoes to lure her to some spot. I'm certain that…" Andreas fell silent as a servant emerged and walked past them, sending the crows into flight. Their cries echoed against the stone walls as they flew away towards the village.

Andreas lowered his voice, continuing, "I suspected him from the start."

"Why did you not tell the police of your suspicions?"

"It was an accident. Everyone said so. I couldn't go and shout murder." Andreas rubbed his hands again. "It would certainly have meant the end of my work here. And I love my work."

"More than you loved Letitia?" Atalanta held his gaze. "You were together, weren't you? Delilah told me Letitia was in love."

"She might have been, but not with me. I only showed her around the island. We never even held hands, let alone anything else." He tilted his head. "Did you think I seduced her? Is that why you refused to let me kiss you?" He moved closer in a heartbeat, lowering his face to hers.

Atalanta ducked away. "That is the second time you've behaved like this. If I tell Mr Bucardi, he'll dismiss you. Did you not mention moments ago how you love your work here?"

Andreas's eyes sparked fire. "Are you threatening me? That's not a good idea." He seemed to want to say more but then he turned abruptly and left the courtyard through the small wooden door leading onto the cliff path.

Atalanta drew breath slowly. That Andreas wanted to stay working at the burg, despite his dislike of Venetians in general and Mr Bucardi in particular, was suggestive. Why did he want to remain? Because it explained his presence while he was looking around for the pirates' gold? Was he certain that it could be found around the burg?

Could that even explain why Letitia had been seen leaving Mr Bucardi's workroom? Had she been pressured by Andreas to look for documents among Bucardi's things? Ownership papers, perhaps, or a map or drawings that clarified which parts of the cliffs surrounding the burg were part of the property, so Andreas could be certain that the gold found there was Bucardi's or his?

Also, the mention of Paula having lain in the sun for hours was most interesting. Where could she have been exposed, why had she been there, and had someone been with her? Andreas came to mind, but would he have shared the doctor's conclusions so readily if he had indeed been with Paula? Besides, his remark that Bucardi had been at the burg all the time suggested he himself had also been there, helping out with the games and food.

Yes, her conversation with Andreas has been most fruitful.

Atalanta didn't want to think about the animosity she had evoked in him by ducking his attentions, again. But she could certainly not allow him to kiss her. Better to have an enemy in Andreas Papoudopolis than to endure his attempts at wooing her.

Chapter Sixteen

L ater that day Delilah sent Atalanta on an errand in the village. She suddenly had such a craving for almond cake and would Atalanta get some for her? They were sold in a small shop on the village square. She had probably seen it when she walked up to the burg on her arrival.

Although it was phrased like a request, Atalanta knew it was truly an order and she set out right away. It was nice to leave the burg and the oppressive atmosphere there and enjoy the summery brightness of the island. She hadn't seen the bakery before and could use that as an excuse to explain taking a long time to return from her errand.

While she walked down, she didn't see anyone in the street. It was the hottest hour of the day and people were probably hiding in the coolness of their houses. Even the chickens she saw in the village square had lain down in the shade of a structure that looked like an outside oven. Atalanta walked up to it to study it more closely. Wood could be put into an opening, heating the stone slab over it. Bread and other items were then probably placed directly on the slab to bake. There was still a vague scent in the air, of fire, ashes and something sweet.

A voice sounded at her shoulder, and turning, she saw a short woman in her seventies looking up at her with bright, bird-like eyes. She smiled widely, holding out a flat bread such as Atalanta had seen at the feast the previous day. She shook her head and tried to explain she wanted almond cake. The woman gestured her along, into an open doorway, through a living-room-like space with pillows on the earthen floor, into an area for cooking. Here several low tables held baked goods. Atalanta pointed out the almond cakes and held up three fingers to indicate the number. The woman wrapped them in a piece of cloth and handed them over. Atalanta gave her the Greek coins Delilah had provided her with. Atalanta then gestured to indicate she wanted to look around. "What is there to see?" she asked. The woman eyed her with apparent confusion, then suddenly smiled and nodded. She waved her along and led her down another steep street to the open door of a bright-blue domed building. It was a church. There was no one inside. Atalanta thanked her impromptu guide, who scurried away, her head down against the strong sun. She stayed in the back, choosing the last pew, to sit for a while and soak up the silence and coolness. It helped to clear her mind and rearrange all the information about the murders.

It seemed highly likely now that Letitia had indeed been murdered. In that case, the fact that her camera had disappeared into the ocean could be highly significant. Had the killer caught her taking photographs of something incriminating and believed that shoving her over the edge would solve all the problems? Letitia would never be able to tell what she saw and the proof of it – the photographs – would be lost. Even if the camera had miraculously resurfaced, exposure to water, and salt water at that, would certainly have ruined the film.

Had Paula gone after the same thing as Letitia? Using the festival at the burg and all the people being occupied there as the perfect cover to do a little exploring on the cliffs. Had she been sunburned there? But why on the back of her legs? The doctor had said she had died face down. In the sun? But she had been found dead on her bed. That didn't make any sense.

And Delilah had raised an interesting point: what connected the two girls? Letitia had been wilful, but friendly, universally liked, even a close confidante of the lady of the house. Paula, on the other hand, had played people, made enemies by her forward behaviour. Still, the two girls must have had something in common which provoked the murderer to silence them. Letitia had written to her mother about a sensational discovery. Had Paula found out what it was after her death and tried to make money out of it?

Or had she not even known anything solid, but had suggested knowledge which had spooked the killer? The cryptic remark to Mrs Bucardi. Mrs Bucardi's winded state as she had stood on the terrace. Her suggestion that the barbiturates in the wine had been meant for her, not for Paula at all. By suggesting that Paula had never been supposed to die, she removed interest in the girl. If Paula hadn't been the intended victim, no one would look for people who had wanted her dead. Everyone was now focused on Mrs Bucardi as the target. Perhaps the police had even arrested Calista to prevent another attempt on Mrs Bucardi's life?

What a perfect move, if she herself was Paula's murderer.

Atalanta looked up sharply as a shadow fell over her. Someone slipped into the pew beside her. It was Raoul. He said, "This is the second time we discuss murder in a church, Mademoiselle Ashford. Is it quite appropriate?"

"Mademoiselle Renard, please. And I like to think that justice is a good thing." Atalanta looked at him. "So it must be appropriate. And with the heat of day, there is no one here at prayer whom we might disturb."

Raoul smiled as he nodded to the saints' statues at the front. Small earthenware vases at their feet held white flowers, probably put there for the festival of saints. "My mother always says that I shouldn't taunt the saints. That I risk my life and still expect them to protect me. But I expect no one to protect me. I make my choices and I deal with the consequences, by myself."

His words were in a way familiar. So often in her life Atalanta had felt like there was no one to fend for her and she had to do it all by herself. That it was even better to rely on yourself and not need others who might disappoint you and let you down.

Still, it was a life in isolation, away from true human connection.

"Are you never lonely?" Atalanta asked softly. "When I saw you sitting with Luca in your arms, I thought … you could have been a father by now."

"You could have been a mother," he parried, "and still you travel and see the world. Wild blood cannot be tamed." He put his hands on his knees.

"But you must long for connection sometimes, a feeling that you belong."

"Perhaps it is the other way around." He glanced at her. "Perhaps being here, in a household, fussing with a child, shows me that belonging isn't for me. That I get irritated and restless. That I only ... want to run away."

"From closeness?" she asked.

"Or obligation, if you want to put it bluntly." Raoul stared into the distance. "I can fend for myself. I get beaten in a race sometimes, or am quite literally beaten by a man who doesn't like me having dinner with his wife, but that doesn't hurt quite as much as seeing a little boy struck by his father, ignored by his mother..." The anger in his voice reverberated in the air. "It makes me livid, but I can do nothing about it. That is why I'd rather go. Only you keep me here."

"I?" Atalanta queried, confused.

"The case and my promise to help you. Or else I'd be long gone."

Then they had to discuss the case, she supposed. There were numerous things she wondered about, and he might provide answers. "Did Victoria Bucardi ever mention to you that she wants to leave her husband and return to Venice, to raise Luca there?"

A cynical smile pulled at Raoul's lips. "She might want to, but he'll never give her the chance."

"Letitia seems to have enticed her to try. With her collection of photos of Venice, her loving stories of the place, she kindled Mrs Bucardi's longing for her hometown. She seems to have made concrete plans. To return to Venice, with Luca, to raise him there, in the city she loves, and close to her family." She glanced at Raoul. "Did you know? Did she discuss it with you?"

"Why would she discuss it with me?"

"I thought that…" Atalanta took a deep breath. She just couldn't make herself say it. "Letitia might have been murdered because she tried to wean Mrs Bucardi away from here." She told him everything Andreas had just told her.

Raoul listened intently and then considered it for a while.

It was so silent inside this building, as if there was no world outside. No evil events, no death. It was a refuge for a weary heart.

At last Raoul asked, "But why was Andreas so forthcoming with all of this information? He should be angry with you for your response to that attempted kiss."

"Perhaps he never meant anything by it. It was just … his Greek way, I guess."

"Nonsense. He should have felt piqued at your rejection and instead he tells you all this freely, as if you are the best of friends? I don't believe it. Can't he have killed Letitia? Because they had an affair and she wanted more of him? Or because she knew of the pirates' gold and he was worried Bucardi would claim it, and he would be left empty-handed? Regardless of who owns the grottoes exactly, Bucardi could always claim Andreas found the gold in his employ, so he was entitled to it. With his name and status on the island, he would easily have arranged things his way." Raoul sounded certain.

Atalanta wasn't so sure. Weren't they attaching too much value to the story about the pirates' gold? A story, she recalled with a sharp sense of awareness, revealed by Calista. Perhaps it was a fabrication, to lead them astray? "Perhaps. I'm not excluding Andreas, but I'm pointing out that Bucardi had a powerful motive for killing Letitia. To keep his wife and son here instead of losing them as they returned to Venice. It would have been a factual divorce even if they didn't file for one officially. Bucardi would have been publicly humiliated. And according to Andreas, Letitia and Mrs Bucardi talked about the possibility of leaving all the time. Letitia actively fed her longing for Venice with her photographs."

"Which explains why Bucardi so readily accepted you as the new companion. Someone French would not remind Victoria of her hometown and the prospect of losing her would be removed."

"Exactly." Atalanta looked at him. So far their reasoning seemed to make sense and Letitia's murder seemed to have a plausible motive. "But Paula's death... She wasn't close with Mrs Bucardi at all. On the contrary, there seemed to be constant tension between them. Bucardi needn't have killed her to get her away from his wife."

"If she was the intended victim. If, however, we assume the wine with the barbiturates was meant for Mrs Bucardi, the killer could still have been her husband. Perhaps he was so angry at her for wanting to leave him that he wanted to kill her, but in a way that would not lead back to him. However, Paula's move to drink the wine instead made a perfect plan go massively awry."

Atalanta considered this. Mrs Bucardi did seem a more likely target than the nanny, but something about Paula's death nagged at her. "What do you think of the idea that she died on the beach? If she did, then how did her body get back in her bedroom?"

Raoul said, "If she did die on the beach, someone carried her to the burg and put her in her room. Rather daring. There were plenty of people around to see it."

"Not if you hide the body inside something. There were some large barrels around for the festivities." Atalanta frowned. "Still, it would have taken time and effort, and would have brought some level of risk. Why not leave her on the beach? Andreas said that tourists sometimes die of exposure to too much sun. If she had been found on the beach, the cause of death would have been obvious and no one would have even thought of looking in her blood for barbiturates. If the murderer wanted it to look like a natural death, moving the body was a giant mistake. It got everyone suspicious and revealed the presence of the barbiturates."

"True. But the killer might have had another priority. What if attention had to be diverted from the beach, and the pirates' gold? That points at Andreas Papoudopolis again."

Atalanta nodded pensively. "But it's possible that Andreas merely moved the body and didn't actually kill Paula. What interest would he have had in her death?"

"She could have been blackmailing him. If she knew Letitia had checked paperwork for him and threatened to reveal this to Mr Bucardi ... it could have got Andreas dismissed, or even worse, suspected of involvement in Letitia's fall off the cliffs."

Atalanta nodded. "True. That reminds me: the pestle they took from Calista's room, have they checked it for fingerprints? If there are other prints on it than Calista's, it could prove it was planted."

"I'll ask about that. I was to contact the police anyway for more information on Calista. If they're holding her, for how long, and all that." Raoul drummed his fingers on the edge of the next pew. "I can't believe she's guilty. But Victoria suggested the pills were meant for her and..." He shook his head. "When you asked me to help you..."

"When you offered to help me," Atalanta corrected quickly.

"Whatever. At that time, I had no idea this would be such a ... complicated thing."

Touching him personally? Because the woman he had once been in love with was involved? She assumed he must have some feeling left for Mrs Bucardi, if Luca was indeed his child. Had he avoided telling her that he knew the Bucardis more personally because he had been worried she would draw a conclusion once she had come here and learned more about the bad marriage? But he knew she was a good detective. He would have realized that she would find out, sooner or later. She wanted him to tell her of his own accord. To prove to her that they were indeed friends and that she could still trust him. The possibility that she couldn't depend on him was so painful she shied away from even thinking about it, but with her safety at stake, she couldn't be too careful.

"You can tell me the truth, Raoul." She said it very softly, smiling to encourage him. "I won't judge. I just need to know how the personal relations play out, or I can't do a proper investigation. I realize it must be handled delicately but we must speak of it."

Raoul hitched a brow. "I don't quite understand what you mean."

"Luca." She swallowed hard before adding, "He looks so much like you. And I can see you genuinely love him and want to protect him from Bucardi's cruelty. I realize the danger if Bucardi finds out. But if you tell me, I won't ever share it with anyone else. I promise."

Raoul stared into her eyes. For a moment she was certain he would confess the whole thing to her, open his heart. Tell her how he felt when he saw Bucardi lift a hand to strike his son, the child he couldn't help but love, even if he didn't want to take responsibility for him. She hoped she would see a side to him she hadn't seen before.

Then he rose abruptly and looked down on her. "My offer to help you was a mistake. You can no doubt solve this matter on your own." And with those curt words he left the church.

Chapter Seventeen

With heavy steps, Atalanta came back to the burg, carrying her package of almond cakes for Delilah. Her head was so full of thoughts, she didn't see much of the gorgeous landscape around her, the contrast between the rich scarlet bougainvillaea and the blue sky overhead, the large flocks of white seabirds diving and rising on the wind. She was just angry at herself for having handled it this way and having lost Raoul. Ever since she had seen the likeness between him and Luca, it had itched at her that she needed to address the topic. But now she realized how foolish that had been. She wasn't certain about it and to suggest something like that was rude.

Besides, whether it was true or not, that didn't even matter. She couldn't claim any confidentiality between them. It was presumptuous to think Raoul would share anything personal with her. He was a fiercely independent man who kept his feelings closely to himself. She could even understand that.

Her lonely upbringing had also made her guarded and determined to do things by herself as much as she could.

Why had she let herself be tempted by the quiet in the church to ask? It had ruined everything.

"I told you so many times!" a voice boomed. It was an explosion of anger in the quiet air. Atalanta stepped through the gate and saw Bucardi standing in front of Luca, who held a mangy brown-and-white puppy in his arms.

"Those dogs are filthy," Bucardi roared. "They can bite. Put it down."

"No. I love him." Luca buried his face in the fur of the dog.

Bucardi reached out to pull the puppy away from him. Luca cried, "No, no, he's mine. Calista said I could have him."

"Put him down!" Bucardi struggled to get a grip on the puppy and then yelped. "The wretched beast bit me." He studied his left hand a moment. A bit of blood showed on the skin. He broke into a stream of crude curses. "Give him to me. I'll drown him in the well."

"No!" Luca cried and ran away with the puppy in his arms.

"If I catch you, I'll break both your legs!" Bucardi fumed as he moved to chase his son.

Atalanta placed herself in his path. "Mr Bucardi, can we please discuss this?"

Without as much as a glance, he pushed past her and in doing so gave her such a shove she landed on the cobbles. Pain stung her hip and elbow. The thud echoed in her head.

Bucardi cornered Luca against the wall. "I'll drown the dog in the well," he growled.

Not while I am around! Biting down the pain, Atalanta scrambled to her feet and rushed over. She grabbed Bucardi's arm. "Mr Bucardi, please, we can discuss this. If the dog isn't allowed to live in the house, we can find a place for him in the storerooms. Luca can brush him and…"

"It has to die. It bit me and now it has to die." Bucardi's eyes rolled in his head. "Look at the filthy beast. He could have given me rabies."

"You don't need a dog bite to get rabid. You already are." With these words Mrs Bucardi appeared by their side. Her eyes shot sparks at her husband. "If you hurt that dog, or Luca for that matter, I'll leave you. I'll go back to Venice and tell everyone what kind of a man you really are. A beast, a monster who solves everything with violence."

Bucardi's eyes narrowed. For a moment Atalanta was certain he would grab his wife and try to strangle her. But then a voice called, "Luca! I'm back!"

Luca's pale face lit up and he ran to meet Calista, who lifted him and the puppy into her arms. Raoul stood beside her.

With wide-open eyes Mrs Bucardi said, "They released you." It sounded as if this wasn't exactly what she had expected.

Mr Bucardi merely straightened his clothes and went inside.

Luca said, "Papa wanted to kill my puppy."

"You must have misunderstood." Calista sounded cheerful. "No one is going to hurt the puppy. I gave him to you, remember? We must think of a name for him. How do you like Achilles?" She put her arm around his shoulders and ushered him into the storerooms.

Mrs Bucardi hesitated a moment and then went after the pair. Perhaps to ask how Calista was? Or why she had been released so soon? Or to keep an eye on the woman she suspected of having tried to kill her who was now playing with her son...

Raoul came to Atalanta. He pointed at her arm. "You're bleeding." It sounded gruff.

Atalanta looked and saw her elbow had been chafed from contact with the yard's cobbles. Blood trickled down. "I'll go and wash," she said softly.

Now that the charged situation was over, she felt light-headed and swayed on her legs. She almost stumbled on her way to the door.

"Take it easy." Raoul appeared beside her to support her. "I can't leave you alone for an hour, can I?" he asked in a cynical tone.

"I only wanted to defuse the situation. The puppy bit Mr Bucardi and he wanted to hurt him. I thought if I tried to reason with him... But he shoved me aside so violently, I fell."

Raoul said in a whisper, "Perhaps Letitia also argued with him about his treatment of Luca. He shoved her and she fell into the sea. He might not have intended to kill her, but still... After she had plunged to her death, he had to hope it would be taken for an accident. He couldn't tell anyone the truth."

Inside the house it was very quiet. Raoul took her into the drawing room and rang for a servant, ordering hot water and tea to be brought. He placed Atalanta in a chair and stood leaning over her. "You must be careful with him. He doesn't accept anyone standing in his way."

"I only wanted to protect the puppy. And Luca's feelings. If his father threw the dog he loves into the well, it would be the end of their relationship. Which is already fragile. But I feel Luca still wants his father to love him. He seemed very upset at the idea of his father leaving them and never coming back."

"When did that idea come up?"

She told him about Andreas's threat to the young boy.

A servant brought steaming water and Raoul drenched his handkerchief in it, letting it cool a bit before applying it. Then he washed her elbow. There was a quiet concentration in his features as if he was completely engaged in this task.

Atalanta bit her lip. The sting of cleaning the chafe drove tears to her eyes, but the real urge to cry was prompted by his kindness to her after he had left her so abruptly.

"I'm sorry," she said. "I thought we were friends and I could afford to ask such an intimate question, but I guess I was wrong."

Raoul took his time wetting the handkerchief again and washing the wound. Then he said, "My response was too fierce. You mustn't think of what I said. Obviously you can't handle this alone. I'll help you again. You made a promise to the lady in black who is grieving her deceased daughter. We must find out what happened to put that mother's mind at ease, and get justice for Paula. Whether she was the intended victim, or not, her life was brutally cut short."

Those were all good reasons, and convenient excuses, to explain his renewed commitment to the case. But by listing those, he has skilfully avoided confirming or denying that Luca is his son, Atalanta thought. But she didn't say anything to point that out. Not now. She was just glad she had received a second chance with Raoul. To do better and lay a foundation for trust before she asked him about intimate matters of his personal life.

Her arm hurt, her hip hurt, her head spun and she was happy to let Raoul take care of her. Happy to know that she need not do this all by herself.

"How did you persuade the police to let Calista go?" she

asked curiously while Raoul bandaged her elbow with some clean linen the servant had brought.

He met her eyes a moment. "Who says they needed persuading?"

"Well, it seemed the evidence against her was quite strong. Her fingerprints were on the pestle and she had a reason, even if it was a reason only valid in her own mind, to harm Mrs Bucardi. Paula drank the wine meant for Mrs Bucardi by mistake and died. But perhaps..." She hesitated, searching her mind for an argument that might have induced the police to let go of the suspect they had so readily arrested. "Perhaps they feel there isn't enough of a connection between the barbiturates Paula imbibed and her death? She died because of the combination of alcohol, heat exhaustion and sunburn."

Raoul smiled. "You should have become a lawyer. You argue exactly along the same lines as one of them would. Paula died of a combination of things. Her death might have been prevented if she had received help as soon as she came back to the burg, after having been on the beach too long."

"Do the police think Paula came back to the burg by herself? She did *not* die on the beach?"

"Admittedly, the doctor told them she died lying face down and she was found on her bed, face up, but still they seem to think she returned to the burg by herself. They don't think it is likely someone else would have carried her inside without being seen. There were so many people around."

"In the courtyard, yes. But aren't there other ways into the *castello*?"

Raoul gestured with both hands. "I'm merely covering what they told me. To them it's not easy to prove Calista's guilt in Paula's death. You'd need to be quite certain that she was the one putting the barbiturates in the wine and that the cup was intended for Paula. In the hustle and bustle of a large party this can be hard to prove. So for the moment they let her go on the condition she stays on the island. I think it was also because she is quite a celebrity in Greece, and they feel it's not a good idea to go after a famous person without solid proof."

"It's never right to persecute someone when the evidence is lacking," Atalanta said primly.

Raoul laughed out loud. "See? You should have become a lawyer." Then he grew serious and said in a low voice, "But you became a detective. And how do you like it? It was difficult in France but it's even harder here, I'd say. Or perhaps I'm prejudiced?"

Atalanta thought a few moments and then nodded. "Yes, it is harder. And yes, you're prejudiced."

Raoul straightened up and stepped back from her. "I think we should have a look in Paula's room. Perhaps something there can help us."

"Can we do that? Shouldn't the police have a look there first? What if they accuse us of disturbing evidence?"

"They won't. They're not interested in the room at all. They found the key in Paula's pocket and are certain she locked herself in because she wasn't feeling well and wanted to rest."

"But the butler had a spare key. And there might be more."

"We can safely have a look. Come on." Raoul went ahead of her.

It was so quiet in the house, almost as if it were abandoned. Atalanta wondered where the others were. Mr Bucardi had probably rushed off to cool down. His wife was with Luca and Calista. How would she receive her friend after the accusation she had made against her? Did Calista even know about this accusation?

She caught up with Raoul and asked softly, "Is Calista aware that Mrs Bucardi declared that the cup with the barbiturates in it was meant for her?"

"Yes. Calista knows that and she sees it as an act of friendship. She reasons that everyone knows they are the best of friends and she would never harm her. So, the testimony that Paula drank the wine meant for Victoria is, to Calista's mind, proof that it wasn't her putting the barbiturates in the cup but someone who disliked Victoria." Raoul shook his head with a rueful smile. "Calista has a far-too-rosy idea of the world."

They came to Paula's bedroom and Raoul tried the door. It was unlocked. They looked at each other a moment before he opened the door and went in. Everything was as it had been when Atalanta had found Paula dead on her bed. The covers were still rumpled where her body had lain. It was odd, invading her room and going through her things while her presence still lingered.

Raoul was already at the dressing table and pulled open drawers. He rummaged through makeup and jewellery, handkerchiefs and stockings. He didn't seem to find much, judging by his dissatisfied grunts.

"If you see photos, take a good look at them," Atalanta said. "They could be Letitia's and something in them might have caused her death."

"Then Paula learned of it by way of the photos and decided to use her knowledge for a spot of blackmail?"

"Possibly." Atalanta knelt and looked under the bed.

Nothing. Not even a suitcase. She got back up and straightened the loose carpet in front of the bed.

Raoul closed the last drawer. It seemed to stick a little. He suddenly pulled it out of the dressing table and stared into the black cavity where it had been. He inserted his hand and felt around. Then with a "Eureka!" he pulled something out. It was an envelope which came away with a tearing sound from the place where it had been hidden.

Atalanta came to stand beside him as he opened it and peered inside. It contained a single sheet of paper that was folded once. Raoul opened it. The white paper was blackened, as if someone had rubbed ashes over it. A few white indentations were visible.

Atalanta whistled. "This paper was originally under another sheet someone wrote on. Paula must have taken it and used something like charcoal to bring out the imprint of what was written. What does it say?" She frowned hard to make it out.

"Such bad handwriting. The first word has three letters. The second also three. Or is it four?" Raoul tilted his head. He put the note on the windowsill and they stood side by side, trying to make sense of it.

"The first word looks like *red*," Atalanta said. "And the second like *rod* ... or..."

"*Rock*," Raoul suggested.

"Red rock!" Atalanta exclaimed. "The night I arrived here, Paula asked about the red rocks. Mrs Bucardi said there was a red beach, but it was on the other side of the island. Paula said she might ask Andreas about it, as he knew the island like the back of his hand."

"I thought he wasn't a local?" Raoul commented.

"So said Mrs Bucardi. But apparently Paula thought he would still be helpful. Or she was a little in love with him and thought the story of the red rocks could get him interested in her."

"I doubt that she was interested in him. She flirted with me."

"Perhaps she tried to make Andreas jealous?"

"She kept this hidden," Raoul said. "So she took it from someone who shouldn't know she had taken it."

"Red rock what?" Atalanta asked. "There is another word. That's a *t*, for sure. Then I can't make it out, but that is a *u, t* …"

"*H. Truth*. Red rock truth. The truth about the red rocks." Raoul sounded excited.

"Can they be the hiding place of the pirates' gold?" Atalanta asked. "Did Paula share her find with Andreas, and did he kill her to keep the secret to himself?"

"But who wrote the words? It's logical to think someone in this household did."

"Perhaps Letitia?" Atalanta wondered. "Was she after the red rocks? Did she find a reference to them in Bucardi's things? She looked through his papers, remember? Delilah caught her coming from his workroom. Did Letitia make some discovery that could enlighten Andreas as to where the treasure was hidden? Did Paula discover this after Letitia's death? She must have searched her things. She also has that photo of Venice." She pointed at the mirror.

Raoul said, "Letitia might have given it to her."

"Hmmm. I don't think Letitia and Paula were the best of friends. Paula mentioned to me that Letitia was always worried about being accused of gossiping. She seems to have wanted to please her employers."

"And still she searched Bucardi's desk at night?"

"Yes, that doesn't quite fit. Unless we assume that Letitia pretended to be meek and dutiful and was something else altogether." With a sigh Atalanta folded the note and put it back in the envelope. "I'll hide this in my luggage with my notes."

Raoul nodded. "To determine who wrote the original note, we have to see samples of everyone's handwriting. Have you found anything else of interest?"

"Not really. That photograph of Venice under the edge of the mirror seems to be the only one here. I wonder where Letitia's other photographs are. Would Mrs Bucardi have them? She did love the reminders of her old hometown." Atalanta checked the waste-paper basket. She emptied it on the floor and went through the contents.

"Is that routine or do you expect to find something there?" Raoul asked.

Atalanta said, "You never know. But I'm especially interested in the missing fingernail."

"Missing fingernail?" Raoul echoed.

"Yes, Paula was very proud of her fingernails. They were pristine on the morning of the festival, painted a fiery red that wasn't quite a match for her white dress and flower garland. But when I saw her here on the bed, dead…" Atalanta swallowed a moment. "The nail of the ring finger on her left hand was really short. It had been cut or torn off, perhaps? There were also abrasions on the wrist of the same hand. I assumed Paula might have hurt her hand scampering across the rocks. But…" she searched through the waste before her on the floor, "… now I wonder if Paula cut the nail herself and threw it in here. If I find it in the basket, I can dismiss my theory that the nail got torn when she was exploring caves. But I don't see it."

"So she could indeed have torn it outside the house."

"Yes. I wonder where and how." Atalanta gathered the rubbish and put it back in the basket. "It could tell us something about the way in which she died. Did she argue with someone?"

"Did she threaten to expose some secret and did the other party feel so cornered, they put the barbiturates in her wine?" Raoul tilted his head.

"Remember we found the grotto and speculated about who met there? It could have been Andreas and Paula. If he knew that she would go away from the house when she felt drowsy to sleep it off, somewhere, he might have followed her. And he was moving around those big barrels, he could have hidden her body in one of them."

Raoul nodded. "We have enough options other than Calista. But we can't exclude her. She was away from the party too." He sighed. "Anyway, we need to see the handwriting of multiple persons to get a better idea of who wrote the reference to the red rocks. Then we might clear up why Paula had this piece of paper and what she intended to do with it."

Atalanta looked around the room. "One thing I do wonder about. I mean, there are a hundred things I need to look into, but one thing comes to mind that we haven't discussed yet." She turned to Raoul. "Is Paula's death connected to Letitia's? Or is it a coincidence that both girls died?"

"The writer of the note about the sea taking Venetian

sacrifices would certainly not think it a coincidence," Raoul said cynically.

"But Paula wasn't dragged from the sea." Atalanta frowned. "Should she have been? Did the killer put her on the beach in the hope that the tide would cover her body, and she'd be found later?"

"If so, why did they change their plan and move the body to the house to put it on the bed where there is no connection with the sea at all?"

Atalanta stared at him. "That could be it."

"What?"

"Perhaps the killer left her on the beach, and someone else moved the body to the house and put her on the bed, to make it look like she had locked herself in her room, feeling unwell, and died in her sleep."

"To make it look like a natural death?" Raoul looked doubtful. "With that sunburn all over her? And the barbiturates in her blood?"

"It might have been argued that she took them herself. A painkiller, a sedative ... She could have overdosed by mistake. Besides, I don't say that it had to look like a natural death. Only that someone might have been eager to avoid the connection with the beach and the sea."

"Because of that silly note sent about sacrifices?"

"Or because of the pirates' gold." Atalanta made a hand gesture. "Andreas would certainly have been shocked if he found a dead girl on the beach near where he looks for treasure. He might have decided to move her, although he wasn't involved in her actual death."

"But in such a scenario we have a killer and someone who

moved the body for other reasons." Raoul rubbed her forehead. "This is getting rather complicated."

"Murder usually is." With a jerk Atalanta turned her head towards the door. "Was that a scream?"

Raoul had already opened the door. Indeed, in the distance they heard someone cry over and over, "No, don't do it. No!"

Raoul cursed under his breath and raced down the corridor. Atalanta followed.

In the courtyard they found Mrs Bucardi looking up at the burg's tower with its merlons. She had a hand clasped to her chest and cried, "No, please no!"

Atalanta looked up to see what shocked her so. Calista was on top of the tower, scrambling to climb onto the merlons. She had a wild, exultant expression on her face and was singing in a strange high-pitched voice, as if she were a siren.

Mrs Bucardi shouted, "Move away from the edge. You will hurt yourself."

Chapter Eighteen

R aoul raced back into the house. Atalanta assumed he wanted to stop Calista. Her heart beat fast. If Calista stood on the edge as Raoul reached her, and he tried to latch onto her, and she still lost balance or even jumped, she might pull him along too. They'd both fall and die.

I can't just stand here and await what is going to happen. I have to do something.

Atalanta raced after Raoul. He was pulling at the metal ring on the door leading into the tower, but the door didn't move. "Locked somehow," Raoul huffed. He ran up the stairs, turned left, and reached the first-floor entrance into the tower. That opened easily and he sped up the narrow, worn stone steps. Atalanta followed, pushing a hand to her side where it stung with the exertion.

When she reached the tower's roof, Calista was still trying to climb up the merlons. She had one foot on the wall and pulled with both her arms to stand upright. But her coordination was so poor, she couldn't quite make it work. She wasn't singing anymore but humming in a low voice, punctuated by frustrated groans, as she couldn't drag herself up onto the wall.

Raoul grabbed her arm. "Are you mad? You'll fall."

"The sea is calling me," Calista said. "Can't you hear it? A nice cool dive is all I need to wash myself clean. Clean of the blood."

Raoul pulled at her. "You're not close to the sea. It's hard, unforgiving stone down there. Step back. This is dangerous."

"I can hear the waves. They're calling me. *Come to us, become clean.*" Calista's eyes shone with a strange fervour. "Let me go. I need to forget. Forget it all."

Atalanta grabbed Calista's other arm. She looked at Raoul. "We have to get her into a lying position. On the count of three. One, two, three!" They both threw their weight to the tower's tiled floor, dragging the woman with them.

Calista hit the tiles with a thud and cried out in pain. "Let me go!" she cried angrily. "Let me go! Why can't I decide anything for myself?" Then she began to sob uncontrollably. Raoul secured her to the tiles. He looked at Atalanta with a tight expression. "She mentioned blood she had to wash away. Did she kill Paula after all?"

Atalanta shrugged. She kept her eyes on the woman who was now shivering from head to toe. She looked very ill. "Perhaps she's running a fever? We have to move her away from here. Put her in bed."

Raoul nodded. "Help me lift her."

Between the two of them they dragged Calista away and down the steps. They had to stop every few paces to readjust her weight and they were both panting by the time they reached her bedroom door. Raoul kicked it open and carried her inside. Then he froze. He inhaled the air for a moment and barked to Atalanta, "Away from here! There is…"

Atalanta noticed it herself. A strange, sharp odour in the air. It invaded her nostrils and immediately changed her view of the world. As if everything started to sway.

She backed to the door. Her head swam. In the corridor she tried to draw clean air deep into her lungs. She had to concentrate and not allow her brain to wander; to imagine colours and sounds that overwhelmed her like she was on a roundabout.

Raoul coughed. "We must carry her…" He staggered.

Mrs Bucardi appeared. "You have her. Thank you! Oh, but what is the matter?" She stared at Raoul, who had collapsed on his knees and was pushing his hands against his face.

Atalanta said, "There's something amiss in Calista's room. The air seems to be poisoned. Raoul inhaled a lot of it…" Past Mrs Bucardi she saw the butler staring at them with worried eyes. "Help us," she cried. "You and Mrs Bucardi carry Calista into a room in the other corridor. I'll help Raoul."

Mrs Bucardi supported Calista and with the help of the startled butler they managed to move away.

Atalanta put her arm around Raoul. He was breathing deeply. "How are you feeling?"

"The race is not safe." His voice was strained. "The car… Have a look at the car."

"Come with me. Away from here." Atalanta pulled at him. She had to play along with his imaginings to get him into action. "The car's engine is going to explode. Lean on me."

Raoul struggled to his feet and leaned heavily on her as they moved away. His eyes were bloodshot, and his lips moved without producing a sound. Atalanta herself just felt a bit light-headed and incoherent. She had inhaled but little of the air in the room and the effects were already wearing off. She was clear enough to realize they had both escaped from a terrible danger in that room. Calista's room. Had something in there influenced her mind and driven her to the tower to take a fatal jump?

Mrs Bucardi and the butler had put Calista on the bed in a guestroom. Mrs Bucardi sat on the edge patting her friend's arm. "You could have been killed," she repeated. "You could have been killed."

Atalanta led Raoul to a chair and pushed him onto it. "We're safe here," she said. "The car is far away now."

Raoul seemed to relax. He stared at the room's ceiling, muttering, "Far away. Far away." Then his eyes became clearer and he focused on Atalanta. "Why are you here? You're not in the race."

Relief washed through her that he recognized her. "The race is over," she said quietly. "You're safe now and with friends."

Raoul blinked. "The tower," he said. "Calista…"

"She's well. Just sit for a moment." She squeezed his shoulder. Things could have taken a nasty turn if Raoul had been influenced as Calista had been and had tried to do something dangerous. He was so strong that she doubted she'd have been able to stop him. But he was safe now. The realization of that drove tears to her eyes. But she wouldn't let him see that.

She moved to the bed and asked Mrs Bucardi, "How is Calista?"

"Unconscious. I sent Lemusier to fetch the doctor. I can't believe she risked her life that way."

"She might have been under the influence of some—"

"Hallucinatory medicine?"

"Yes, there was a strange odour in her room."

"She burns powders and inhales the fumes." Mrs Bucardi looked bitter. "I don't know what it is exactly or how she obtains it. She tried it before. She says those medicines make her more creative. Under their influence she designs her dresses. And they help her to cope with everyday life. But she can't see how dangerous they are." She bit her lip. "If she had fallen down... How could she do this to us, her friends? And with Luca around."

Atalanta studied Calista's still face. Despite the trouble this woman had caused at the burg, she felt sorry for her. "She must be very troubled. Very unhappy. She seeks freedom, but she can't find it."

Mrs Bucardi stared at her friend. Tears formed in her eyes and dripped down her pale cheeks. "Perhaps I made a mistake," she said softly. "All those years ago. I thought I was acting in her best interests, but..."

"You tried to help her, to wean her away from the pills. But people who have a weakness often fall back." Atalanta thought of her own father, his promises that he would do better. He had always meant it. He had honestly loved her. But he had been weak.

She forced a smile. "You mustn't blame yourself for her lapse."

"I don't want to have her around Luca." Mrs Bucardi rose. Her voice trembled and she clasped her hands together. "It must end. Now. Here." She left the room with a sob.

Raoul sat up, shaking his head as if to clear it of fog. "What did she say?"

"She wants Calista removed from the burg, for Luca's sake." Atalanta kept her eyes on Raoul. "She thinks that … Calista's behaviour…"

"She's unstable." Raoul wanted to stand up, but Atalanta rushed over and pushed him back in the chair.

"You can tell me whatever you want to say from a sitting position."

Raoul grimaced but obeyed. "Calista is the type of woman who will always be in trouble. With men, with money. It's her way. But I thought, honestly, that she had learned her lesson about the addictive powers of those pills and powders." He pushed his hands against his temples. "I believe that whatever I inhaled in her room was some drug she burned, to escape reality."

"The bitter reality of being involved in a murder case?" Atalanta suggested.

Raoul nodded as he continued sadly, "When I collected her from the police station and heard that they doubted their ability to build a solid case against her in connection with Paula's death, I was relieved. I thought the danger came from the outside, from accusations and charges. But it comes from the inside. From inside Calista's own head, her ache for wild experiences, for feeling grand emotions. Normal life is never enough for Calista. She must always reach for something higher, without thinking of the consequences. We wanted her released so we can prove her innocence, and then she goes and does something like that. Showing the world how unreliable she truly is." He sighed. "How can we save her if she doesn't want to be saved?"

"I think that she does want to be saved. I mean, Calista loves life. Freedom. The idea of being locked up in a small cell, or worse, must be horrendous to her. Why would she not want us to help her prove her innocence and give her a chance to start over?"

"If she does want that, she has an odd way of showing it to us." Raoul rubbed his forehead as he stared at the motionless figure on the bed. "We'll ask her when she comes to. But will she tell us the truth?"

Chapter Nineteen

The doctor came and looked at Calista, proclaiming she needed rest and she would recover. He didn't want to go into the room to establish what the drug was that she had burnt and inhaled. He declared that the windows had to be opened to get the smell out, and it would be fine after that. He seemed in a hurry to leave.

"He must think we're all mad in this place," Delilah declared with a look of disgust on her face. "Our family name is smeared by that irresponsible woman's behaviour. She must leave. As soon as possible."

As Mrs Bucardi had said much the same thing, Atalanta expected that Calista would have to depart the burg as soon as she was physically able to.

Delilah continued, "I heard you rushed to her rescue, Mademoiselle Renard. That was foolish. Such insane people are terribly strong. She could have dragged you down with her to your death."

Atalanta said, "I wasn't alone. Mr Lemont helped me."

"Oh, Mr Lemont." Delilah focused on her across her knitting. "Do you fancy him? He is very handsome, I admit. The type of man one can never have for oneself. You're not the sort of woman who would accept infidelity. Some women do accept it…" Her knitting needles clacked viciously.

"Do you mean Mrs Bucardi?"

Delilah huffed. "You're a servant. You have no business snooping in our affairs." After a short silence she said, "I despise weak women who have no backbone and no morals."

Atalanta looked at the frail elderly lady. Had Delilah intended to kill Mrs Bucardi at the party? Had she crushed her saved pills and inserted them in Mrs Bucardi's wine cup, waiting with secret glee until she got news of her collapse, not knowing the wrong person had drunk the wine?

But Delilah had been in her room most of the time. When would she have had the opportunity to insert the barbiturates in the cup?

Or had Paula been the intended victim all along? Had she discovered something Delilah was up to?

Was it even possible … that Delilah had also killed Letitia? Her companion who had discovered some shocking secret about her? The woman with the veil had mentioned something sensational her daughter was about to uncover.

But could a frail old woman push a healthy young woman off the rocks? Delilah rarely left the burg.

Or had she drugged Letitia too with something in her drink? Had she offered her a glass of prosecco, laced with barbiturates, so later when she went for a walk, she would feel unbalanced and fall?

It seemed like such an uncertain murder method. What if Letitia had felt drowsy before she set out on her walk and had decided not to go at all? Wasn't it more likely that Letitia had fallen into the sea after an altercation with a person present at the scene? Not someone who plotted her demise from afar, having to count on the workings of pills without certainty that they would actually have the desired result?

Then again, if they didn't, no one would have been the wiser. Letitia would have slept off her fatigue, not knowing what had caused it, and Delilah could have safely tried again.

Delilah looked at her. "Dear Mademoiselle Renard, you look as if you disapprove. But surely you must also despise weak women who have no morals. Or are you yourself not as prim and proper as you appear to be?" She raised an eyebrow. "What is going on with you and Mr Lemont? He came from your bedroom."

"I may be your companion," Atalanta said, "but I'm employed by Mr Bucardi. If he feels I have done something wrong, he should tell me."

Delilah's eyes sparked with anger. "This is my home. I have a say too." She dropped her knitting in her lap. "Bring me a book. And some tea. Hurry."

Atalanta left the room. In the corridor she saw Andreas walking away. Had he listened at the door? Why would he be interested in what Delilah had to say to her?

Downstairs she found Mr Bucardi about to leave. He was carrying a briefcase and said, "I thought you wanted her gone? I'll never understand women." Without a greeting he left the house.

Mrs Bucardi seemed about to rush after him but when she saw Atalanta, she forced a smile. "Good morning. I hope you're well, after yesterday's strange events?"

"Yes. I've slept well and feel much better. How are you?"

Mrs Bucardi seemed to hesitate between appreciating this interest in her and considering it forward. "I've come to the conclusion," she said in a forced tone, "that it is better for Calista to stay here and recover."

Atalanta blinked in surprise. Was that what Mr Bucardi was angry about? Understandably. "But ... yesterday you seemed concerned about the bad influence she may have on Luca."

"Yes. That's why I want to ask you to look after him. Delilah doesn't need a companion, as she's indoors most of the time. If she needs anything, she can ring for a servant. I want you to accompany Luca at all times. Never let him out of your sight."

Atalanta felt the weight of this sudden responsibility pressing upon her. "Why would you..."

"Paula is dead. I can't find a new nanny at short notice. You seem to handle Luca well. And he likes you. When I told him that Paula is no longer here to take care of him, he said that he wanted you to do it instead." She grimaced for a moment, as if she realized he hadn't asked whether his mother could spend more time with him. "He has endured a few shocks in a short time and I think he should have someone he likes around to comfort him."

Atalanta opened her mouth to ask more, but Mrs Bucardi said, "You work for me, and as such I can allot you new tasks."

"But I have no experience with young children."

"If you keep him safe, I'm satisfied." Mrs Bucardi turned away, adding, "We can't have anything happening to him while my husband is away on business. He would be very angry."

Atalanta released her breath. And with that, she had become responsible for the safety of a little boy in a household where very strange things were happening. How could she possibly keep him safe?

She asked a maid to bring Delilah a cup of tea and a book, and then she went up to the nursery. As she came to the door, she heard a voice say, "And then the knight looked into the room and there was the treasure chest, brimming with gold..."

She opened the door a crack and saw Raoul sitting on the ground with Luca, the little boy looking up at him with wide eyes. Raoul said, "Finally, he could get his reward for all his hard work. He walked over and looked at all the gold goblets and..."

"Crowns!" Luca called.

"Crowns and gems. He was rich now and he would never have to do hard chores again. He could live in his castle and be happy ever after."

Without a princess, Atalanta thought. *Fairy tales usually end with a happy couple walking into wedded bliss. But not for Raoul.*

Luca looked up and saw her at the door. "Atalanta!" He ran to her. "Mama says you will take care of me now that Paula is gone. I don't know where she went. Is she cross with me?"

"Why would she be cross with you?" Atalanta asked, lifting him on her arm. He was a bit heavy to be carried around, but after all the commotion, he needed to feel sheltered, she supposed.

"Because I saw her kissing Andreas and I said I would tell." Luca held her gaze honestly. "She said that if I told, she'd be sent away and she'd be very sad, and I shouldn't make her sad. I told no one, honestly, and still she is gone." He hung his head.

"I don't think you had anything to do with that," Raoul said. He came over to Atalanta and put his hand under Luca's chin, lifting the little boy's face to him. "I thought you didn't like Paula, anyway."

"She was always busy with other things. She did play with me but she wasn't really there. She was thinking of another place. I know. Like when I have to learn words and I want to be outside catching crabs."

"You're only four." Raoul brushed his cheek. "Why would you have to learn words?"

"Papa says I have to be clever and become a banker or a lawyer." Luca shrugged. "I'd rather become a fisherman. Then I can be on a boat all day and see the sea creatures." He pushed Raoul's hand away. "Where's Calista? Can we play on the beach?"

"Calista doesn't feel well," Atalanta said. "She must sleep a little longer."

"Can I see her and give her a kiss? Kisses make you feel better." Luca wriggled to be released. "I want to go and see her now."

"Let her sleep," Raoul said. "You can see her later. You know what? I'll ask the butler to pack a picnic basket and we'll go to the beach now. The three of us."

Luca cheered up and ran to the other room to get his little metal shovel and bucket and whatever else he needed to build sandcastles.

Raoul said, "Has Victoria already given you the news? Calista is staying and you are to watch Luca so he doesn't go near her." He shook his head. "I don't understand. Why can't she see that her covering for Calista is only allowing Calista to make the same mistakes over and over again? One day this is going to go dramatically wrong…" He clenched his hands into fists. "I feel I should do something about it, but I don't know what."

Atalanta wet her lips. His helplessness touched her deep inside. She wanted to be there for him, support him, give him good advice. Or perhaps just put her hand on his arm and squeeze to let him know she sympathized.

But she didn't dare reach out. She felt so uncertain how to handle this whole situation. She couldn't understand the full extent of it, all the emotions involved, unless he was honest with her. But that was his choice to make.

"Luca is probably packing all of his toys," she said with a forced smile. She went to the door of his bedroom and peeked in, fully expecting to see him gathering heaps of toys in a bag. But the room was empty. Her gaze rushed past the bed, the chair in the corner with his stuffed bear, the jars on the windowsill. Her cheeks paled. "He's not there." She turned to Raoul. "He escaped without us noticing."

Raoul exhaled in frustration. "Little brat. Where can he be?"

Atalanta thought a moment. "I think he went to Calista anyway."

"But she isn't in her own bedroom. Her bedroom is locked up. At least I think so." He frowned worriedly. "Luca mustn't get in there."

"Surely the odour will have evaporated by now?" Still, her heart raced. "Let's have a look." Atalanta hurried to Calista's original bedroom. To her relief, the door was indeed locked and the little boy was nowhere in sight. She went to the new room allotted to the troublesome house guest. There voices resounded.

"I'm going to kiss you better," Luca said.

Atalanta peeked in and saw that the boy had crawled onto

the bed and was showering Calista's pale face with wet kisses. Atalanta smiled in spite of herself. The little boy's liveliness might have a favourable effect on Calista's low spirits.

Atalanta knocked briefly and entered. "Luca, come with me. I told you not to bother Calista. She must rest."

"He's no bother at all," Calista assured her at once. "I want him with me." She said to Luca, "Will you stay with me and tell me stories so I get better soon?"

"Of course. Raoul just told me a story about a knight and a treasure. Do you want to hear it?" Luca nestled himself against Calista and began, "Once upon a time…"

"Luca," Atalanta said, "you really must come with me. Your mother asked me to take care of you. And Raoul is waiting with the picnic."

"But Calista needs a story to feel better."

Calista looked at Atalanta. There was something challenging in her eyes. As if she wanted to ask, "Do you even want me to get better?" Did she suspect everyone of resenting her recovery because she had caused her own problems by experimenting with the dangerous powder?

Atalanta said, holding that gaze, "Calista, you know you must rest. Tell Luca to come with me. We want to take him to the beach. He loves it there."

"If he wants to stay with me, he can. There's no need to keep him away from me." Calista's voice was brittle.

Raoul pushed past Atalanta and lifted Luca in his arms. He tickled him. "You promised me a picnic. Now you must give me one. Or I won't stop tickling you. Ever."

Luca gasped for air. "Stop! Please stop."

"Are you coming on the picnic then?"

"Please stop." Luca laughed so hard he'd turned red in the face. "I'm coming!"

"Good." Raoul carried him to the door. "We're getting your things now." He left with the boy.

Calista's expression was pained. "Has Victoria ordered this?" she asked sharply. "That he can't be with me for a single minute? Because I'm a danger to him? Because I'm not sound in the mind? It's all a ruse, a lie to make me look bad. I did nothing. I took nothing. I did experiment in the past, but those days are over. Honestly."

Atalanta turned away. The lies were familiar, the assertions it was over and it wouldn't happen again. Her father had promised her so many times he would do better and they wouldn't get into debt again. But he had never kept his word. He hadn't been able to.

Calista said behind her back, "You must believe me. I did nothing to cause my collapse. I was so relieved to be out of the prison cell. When I arrived back here, I went to my room and the curtains were closed. I thought it was just as well, as I was very tired and wanted to sleep. I lit the lamp beside my bed and sat down on the bed to take my stockings off. I noticed the air was getting heavy with some sharp scent. I went to the window to open it, but it was stuck. I couldn't get it open. While I was at it, I inhaled that heavy air and ... I can't remember much after that. I don't recall what I did or what..." She fell silent, then added in a sob, "How I almost died. You saved me. I know that. I know that ... you think I did it on purpose. But it wasn't true. I don't know what happened. But I didn't take any hallucinatory drug. I swear."

Atalanta said, "You need your rest." She left the room and

closed the door. Still, what Calista had said echoed in her mind. *I didn't do it…*

Could someone else have introduced something into the room before her return from the police station? Had that person jammed the windows so she couldn't get to fresh air and would be overpowered by the effects of the substance?

She went down with Raoul and Luca to the kitchens to get the picnic ready. She asked the maid there who had been in Calista's room after the incident. "Who opened the windows to clean the polluted air out of the room?"

"The butler did, Mademoiselle Renard."

"Did he mention that the window was stuck?"

"Not to us. But you can ask him yourself. He should be back in here any minute."

Lemusier came in with a tray and said to her question, "The window was easy to open, Mademoiselle. I didn't notice anything amiss with it. How come?"

Atalanta thanked him. She walked beside Raoul who carried the picnic basket, while Luca ran ahead after a butterfly. She told him what Calista had said and how she had checked on it. "When she talked to me in the guestroom, I almost believed her. That it wasn't her doing. But then Lemusier said the window wasn't stuck at all and…" She grimaced. "I guess that … she is such a vibrant personality, I want to like her, think well of her. I can't help but feel sorry for her, for her unhappiness and how she tries to solve it. But perhaps the sad fact is that Calista is manipulative in her core and a compulsive liar who constantly twists the truth to suit her own purposes."

"Not necessarily." Raoul looked at her with a frown of concentration. "Let's accept that the window was truly jammed to prevent her from opening it. And that something burned in her room."

"How?" Atalanta asked. "There was no fire in the hearth."

"So it must have come from another source." Raoul thought hard. "She said to you that the curtains in her room were closed and she lit the lamp beside her bed, didn't she?"

"Yes."

"So there was a flame in the room. In the lamp."

"Yes, but how can that release a hallucinatory drug into the air?"

Raoul pursed his lips. "What if a powder was put in the rim of the lamp so that it evaporated on the air when it got hot? That made her hallucinate. She tried to open the window, but because she was already under the influence of the drug, it didn't work. Or the window was truly jammed. After she left the room in her delirium to go to the tower, someone could have sneaked back into her bedroom to un-jam the window. If they were aware of the dangerous drug in the air, they could have covered their face to avoid being influenced."

"It's possible, but it does seem a bit far fetched," Atalanta said with a sigh. "Perhaps we are so eager to remove blame from her that we'll go to any length to make up a story. Why would anyone put a drug in Calista's room which she had to inhale before noticing what was happening to her?"

"To make her look mad? To actually induce her to take a leap off the tower and kill herself?" Raoul gestured. "It could have been taken as an admittance of guilt in Paula's death. You heard what she said about having to wash blood away. No doubt it was a figment of her frantic mind, just as I imagined my race car was going to explode." He grimaced. "But it would have sounded to many as a confession of sorts. The

239

police let her go because they weren't certain they could build an airtight case against her, but had she died tragically, under these circumstances, they needn't have. The case would have been officially closed, and Calista would have been seen as the murderer, despite never having confessed. How convenient for the real killer."

"And how terrible for Luca." She looked at the little boy playing ahead of them. He threw a bit of rock on the path and then jumped towards it as if he were doing hopscotch. "He loves her so very much."

"While his own mother is so cold and distant to him?" Raoul asked softly. "I've known Victoria for a very long time. She's a level-headed woman who looks at life with a practical approach. She accepts that her husband doesn't love her and even betrays her from time to time. She runs her household efficiently, dealing with a difficult old aunt and servants who aren't loyal. She does care for Luca, I think, but… Put yourself in her position. For years she waited for a baby, perhaps believing that once she had given him a son, her husband would love her. But Luca's birth hardly changed anything. Bucardi didn't change his ways. On the contrary. He's more arrogant than ever. And he doesn't seem to love the child either. In any case, he's far too strict with him. He wants to bully him into obedience."

He was silent a moment, a grim expression on his face. Was he thinking back to the moment where Bucardi had wanted to strike Luca, and he had only just been able to prevent this? He had to realize that this had been just one occasion where he could save the little boy from a beating and normally, when there were no visitors in the burg, Bucardi could do what he wanted without anyone stopping him.

Raoul sighed. "I assume that Victoria doesn't allow herself to love her child because she feels it can only lead to heartbreak. Like her marriage did."

"That's so sad," Atalanta said.

Raoul shrugged. "Lots of people lead sad lives. They don't experience that fantasy of meeting the love of their lives and being happy. They make do." It sounded as if he knew many such couples among his acquaintances. Had that made him reluctant to even contemplate marriage for himself?

Raoul added, "I suppose that considering her circumstances, Victoria is making do in a good way."

"But I do wish she could love Luca and he would love her back. All children need love."

"But not all children get it."

They continued in a heavy silence, watching the playing boy. He had now spread his arms and was imitating the gulls soaring overhead. On the surface it didn't seem as though the tragic events had influenced him at all. He might not understand the full extent of what was happening, having been told Paula had left and Calista was merely ill, but he had experienced, first hand, how brutal his father could be. How much damage was such violent behaviour inflicting on a young child?

"What happened to the puppy?" she asked Raoul.

"Andreas took him along to give him to a local. That little dog wouldn't be safe at the burg. Once Bucardi has put his mind to something, he doesn't rest until it's exactly as he wants it. They say this is a trait that runs in his family. His father and grandfather seem to have been like it. Ruthless businessmen."

"Denying a child a dog has nothing to do with business." Atalanta studied the colours on the wings of the butterfly that had sat down on a rock for a moment, sunbathing. The atmosphere was confidential, there was no one around who could overhear a mention of the explosive secret. She took a deep breath before asking softly, "Can't you confide in me, Raoul? I know we are hardly intimate friends but … I'm losing control of this case. I must have some solid facts to work from." She looked at him, trying to read his emotions as she asked, "Is Luca your son? Is it possible that Paula found out and blackmailed Mrs Bucardi? Was that why she had to die?"

Raoul held her gaze. "Do you want to know for the case or for some other reason?"

Atalanta felt a flush creep up and looked away to the path ahead and the playing child. "For the case, of course. If I'm merely making assumptions, I'm building my theories on quicksand. I need facts to build a solid case. Just look at me. I'm not making any progress. On the contrary. I was asked to come here by a grieving mother and now another young woman is dead. Mrs Bucardi asked me to take care of Luca, to ensure his safety, but how can I, when I don't see the full picture? What if something happens to him while he is in my care?" She swallowed hard. "I must uncover the dark undercurrents in this house or … I'm afraid we will have another victim soon."

Raoul nodded. "I do agree with you there, and I can tell you this. I never had an affair with Victoria Bucardi." His brown eyes were honest. "I even resent that you thought that I had. I don't involve myself with married women. It goes against my conscience, even if some find it hard to believe I have one." He laughed softly. "But perhaps you think better of me?"

Atalanta suppressed the wide smile that relief threatened to bring to her face. It would be odd under the circumstances. "Thank you for confiding in me. I'll of course never say a word about—"

"Something that never happened," he supplied ironically. "Now shall we try and enjoy the picnic?"

"I wish I could enjoy it but how could I with all these thoughts racing through my head? This place is so idyllic and beautiful, and yet there seems to be so much evil brewing below the surface."

Raoul said, "I've seen a sample of Victoria's handwriting in the kitchen when we waited for the picnic. There were instructions about dinner on the table and the cook confirmed it was written by Mrs Bucardi. She didn't write that cryptic reference to the 'red rock truth'."

"Unless she disguised her handwriting."

"But why, if she didn't think anyone would ever read it?" Raoul shook his head. "We need to make progress here, so I hope you approve of my action."

"What action?"

"I called the villa where Letitia's parents live and asked to speak to her mother."

"The veiled lady?" Atalanta asked, surprised by this move on Raoul's part. Why hadn't he asked her opinion beforehand? She was now confronted with a fait accompli.

"Yes. She wasn't home but the butler said he would give her the message that I had asked her to send me some letters written by her daughter, so I could see the handwriting. I told him that I was staying on Santorini, but I didn't mention the Bucardi burg, of course. I gave him an address in the village. He said he would ask her to send them this very day. They should arrive soon enough." He looked at her. "Should I have asked for your permission first?"

He looked so tired that she didn't want to argue. "You don't need my permission for anything, but if the veiled lady wanted to keep her inquiries into her daughter's death a secret, this will be hard to explain. The butler might mention it—"

"I impressed on him that he mustn't mention it to anyone but her. He assured me that he would follow my instructions to the letter. Servants are usually extremely conscientious and loyal, and will do exactly what is expected of them."

"I see." Atalanta frowned. "You think the 'red rock truth' note was written by Letitia?"

"That makes the most sense to me."

"Look!" Luca came running back to them and showed them a rock. "Everything is volcanic here. That means it can explode. There's fire under the earth and it can come to the surface. Andreas told me. He says I can't go near the holes because the fire will pop out and grab me and burn me alive."

"What holes?" Raoul asked.

"The holes in the rocks. There are steps leading down. I wanted to look once." He shuffled his feet as if he was caught out. "Andreas saw me and told me about the fire. It's very dangerous. I do want to have a look but … I think it would hurt if you got burned by fire."

"You'd better believe it would." Raoul brushed his hair. "And your mother wouldn't like you clambering down those steep steps. You could fall."

"But Calista can do it. She's like a mountain goat." Luca grinned. "She's not afraid of anything." He ran away again to look for more bits of rock.

"Not afraid of anything," Raoul repeated in a strange tone. "It sounds as if it's a recommendation, in his book."

"And in yours." Atalanta glanced at him. "You race cars at high speed, and you don't fear death." As she spoke the words, she recalled the moments in which he, half dazed by what he had inhaled in Calista's room, had said it wasn't safe – the race, the car. Did he know fear anyway? Was he less self-assured than he feigned to be?

"At least," she added, "you make it look like you don't."

Raoul laughed softly. "That is all part of the game we play. How we make ourselves believe we are untouchable. Death is something for old people. Not for us. We still have so much to do, to see." He looked at the playing child. "But at times I wonder. Is life really all about racing from one place to the next, eager for yet another new experience, yet another booze-filled evening of dancing and flirting and fun? Or is it quieter than that? Can it be about taking a little boy on a picnic and just enjoying the sun and the sea," he glanced at her, "and the company?"

Atalanta felt her heart skip a beat. She looked straight ahead. "Only you can answer that question."

There was silence for a few breathtaking moments. Would he say something? That he would like to get to know her better? Part of her wanted to hear those words more than anything in the world.

But fear also trickled through her – fear of what it might entail. How she herself would be expected to open up and how she knew she didn't really want to.

I can't. Raoul probably thinks I had a wonderful relationship with Grandfather because he made me his heir. I don't want him to know about Father's bad behaviour, our poverty and… No. Let the past be the past. Better not speak of it ever, to anyone. Especially not someone I like.

"Luca! Don't stray!" Raoul dropped the basket on the path and ran to overtake the boy, who was clambering on a few stones beside the path. He lifted him into his arms and shook him playfully, calling him Italian names that probably meant something like "little rascal", or "bandit".

They're so sweet together.

Atalanta sighed and picked up the discarded picnic basket. Raoul always knew how to snap from a charged, personal conversation that drew them closer, to everyday reality. They might be connected by a case they were working on, but were poles apart in character and outlook on life. Perhaps that was even part of his attraction? That he was a mystery to her and would forever stay one.

Chapter Twenty

When they came back from their picnic, Raoul heard there had been a phone call for him in his absence. "A lady from Venice," the butler said. Mrs Bucardi, who stood in the hallway refreshing flowers in a large vase seemed to perk up and listen attentively to every word said.

Raoul handed Atalanta the empty picnic basket. "You take this to the kitchen. I'll go up into the workroom to return the call. It must be about the race I'm planning. Her husband is very rich and wants to invest money in it." He smiled at Mrs Bucardi. "I must use all my charm to make this work." He whistled energetically as he started up the stairs.

Atalanta had to admit he was playing this very nicely. By looking straight at Mrs Bucardi and involving her in the conversation about the phone call, he defused any suspicion she might have about it. No one would have guessed that this seemingly innocent phone call in reality concerned a murder investigation.

Two murders, she reminded herself, assuming poor Letitia was also pushed to her death.

"Mama, look what I found." Luca showed his mother the volcanic rock he had picked up on the way.

"Better leave that outside, Luca," Mrs Bucardi said. "I don't want dirt in the house."

"It's not dirty. I want to keep it in my room."

"I'll see that the rock gets a nice place in a box or something," Atalanta rushed to say. "It won't make stains anywhere."

Mrs Bucardi huffed. "Next moment he'll be throwing it at someone he doesn't like and we'll get a charge filed against us."

Luca ran upstairs with his rock. Atalanta wanted to go after him, but Mrs Bucardi stopped her by asking, "Do you think Luca is normal for his age?" Surprised by the sudden question, Atalanta frowned. "How do you mean, 'normal'?"

"Well, I've been told he has quite a temper. I'm afraid it comes from his father's side." Mrs Bucardi smiled apologetically.

Having seen Mr Bucardi's temper, Atalanta could understand she was worried about this. "All small children can be forceful when they want something or don't get their way. I assume it's quite normal as long as they don't actively hurt other people."

Mrs Bucardi kept smiling but her eyes showed a flash of insecurity. Or perhaps even fear?

A cold feeling skittered across Atalanta's back. Mrs Bucardi had asked her, the companion, to look after Luca in the absence of the nanny. Had she also asked Letitia to do that at some time? Had Letitia taken Luca walking and … had she then fallen off the cliffs? Did Mrs Bucardi fear that Luca knew more about this?

If he had been around when Letitia fell, it had to have been an accident. Perhaps he had run up to her with a live creature in his hands – a lizard, perhaps – and she had stepped back and fallen? Atalanta herself had taken the lizard she had seen at the cyclops rock for a snake and had jumped in fear. Suppose Letitia had done the same thing, taken an unfortunate tumble. Something the little boy couldn't have foreseen. Just an unlucky set of circumstances. No intention to harm anyone.

It would be too terrible to assume that Luca had done something to *wilfully* push Letitia to her death.

Then again, when a child was young and impressionable, could you be certain what he thought, how he reasoned? Perhaps he had been naughty, and Letitia had threatened to tell his parents about it? Luca might have believed he would be punished and in anger lashed out at Letitia to push her away. Then she had stumbled and fallen and …

Atalanta's heart raced at the idea. Luca had the example of his father who solved everything by violence, lashing out at people, even chasing someone with a knife, if Paula were to be believed. Luca had hacked at the policemen with his wooden sword when they had wanted to take Calista away. The actions of a frustrated little boy, or proof of what Luca was capable of when his temper was provoked?

Did Mrs Bucardi know more about the exact circumstances of Letitia's plunge off the cliffs? Had she helped to cover up what her son had done? To protect him, of course, thinking he was too young to understand the consequences of his actions?

Mrs Bucardi put the last flower in place and studied the bouquet. "Just perfect," she sighed.

Yes, for her life had to be perfect. At least it had to look perfect from the outside. But what was brewing beneath the surface? How much did she know?

Atalanta bit her lip, thinking that upstairs Raoul was speaking to Letitia's grieving mother while here in front of her another mother stood, perhaps the mother of the child who had caused the fatal fall. But surely, even if Luca was to blame, the bereft mother in Venice couldn't demand that a child of his tender age must be accused, charged, prosecuted?

Mrs Bucardi said, "You'd better go and see where Luca is, Mademoiselle Renard. He could very well be at a window this moment, throwing his rock on somebody's head." It sounded resigned, even slightly amused, but Atalanta sensed the undercurrent of worry and tension in the woman's stance. Was one of her reasons for staying aloof that she feared her child had his father's violent temper and couldn't be trusted to grow up into a responsible human being?

"Mademoiselle Renard?" Raoul stood at the top of the stairs, gesturing at her. The look on his face suggested urgency.

Atalanta gripped the railing and rushed up to meet him. "What did she say?" she whispered. "Is she angry that you approached her household?"

"On the contrary. She was totally surprised." Raoul drew her into a niche and looked about them to ascertain they weren't being overheard. "She says she never went to Murano last month. She didn't meet you or me and she didn't ask for an inquiry to be made into her daughter's death. In fact, she's quite convinced it was indeed accidental, as Letitia's vertigo was well-known. She also assured me her daughter was very stubborn and never listened to good advice. That they hadn't understood at all why she'd want to stay on an isolated island while she could have had a full social calendar in Venice. Letitia also never wrote home about any sensational discovery to be made here. Although in one of her letters she did mention pirates' gold. A legend that a local man had told her about."

"Andreas..." Atalanta spoke the name automatically. But her mind was elsewhere, recalling the meeting with the veiled lady in the little church on Murano. Knowing it hadn't been Letitia's mother put everything in a new light. She went over the entire conversation, reflected on every word said, every gesture made. Those tears, the evident heartache ...

How could anyone who wasn't Letitia's mother have acted the part so well?

"Did Letitia have a sister?" she asked Raoul. "Can she have posed as her mother to ask for our help?"

"I immediately thought the same thing, so I asked, but Letitia only has brothers. It's a mystery who engaged us, or why. What is more," Raoul grimaced, "the lady told me, in no uncertain terms, that she doesn't want a scandal. The Bucardis are distant relatives and she fears upsetting them with speculations. We can't suggest to anyone that Letitia's death wasn't an accident. She told me that you should resign your post as companion immediately, under some pretence – a family emergency, for instance – and leave the burg. She won't expose you, as obviously that would raise questions she would rather avoid, but she doesn't want you to stay here any longer. Her good name or the Bucardis' shouldn't suffer in any way."

"But Paula died." Atalanta held his gaze. "Even if we assume that Letitia's death was an accident, I still have to find out how and why Paula died. It's a matter of honour, of having to end a case properly. I can't just walk away. And Luca—"

"Mustn't be left alone. I agree." Raoul ushered her towards the nursery. "You stay with him. I'll try and find some other proof of Letitia's handwriting. Her mother obviously won't co-operate by sending us anything. She won't expect you to leave today, so we might have a few more days left to solve the case. We must find a major lead."

Atalanta nodded and hurried to get to the nursery, where she found Luca on his knees on the floor. He had put his rock in the centre of a ring made of smaller stones he had apparently collected before and had put a knight figure on top of the rock. He was proclaiming that he was now lord of the entire country.

Atalanta smiled as she watched his concentration on this game of make-believe. He was a sweet child. It was unfortunate that his parents spent so little time with him and left him in the care of girls who didn't seem to care much for him either. Because he felt neglected, he could be wild.

Luca looked up and said, "Are you in love with Raoul?"

Atalanta almost choked at the unexpected question.

"Paula said she was in love with Raoul." Luca eyed her earnestly. "She said he was so handsome and she wanted to kiss him. That she wanted to see the view of the sea with him, from the tower. I can't go up there so I said she couldn't either. But she just laughed at me." He hung his head. Then he looked up again, eyes ablaze. "I can too. I will, now that Papa is gone. He can't beat me now that he's gone."

"You stay here and play a little." Atalanta rang the bell and when the maid showed up, she asked her to take care of Luca for a few minutes. "Stay with him. Don't let him out of your sight."

The maid nodded and hovered at the door.

Atalanta left the room and went to the tower. She walked up the steps, recalling how she had run up here with Raoul to save Calista. Her heart rate shot up at the memory. It had been a close call. But they had made it, together.

Up on the tower she stopped and looked closely at the tiles. Her gaze went past every inch of them, searching for a clue that Paula had been here on the day she died. If she had wanted to savour the view…

With Raoul? Or with another man?

Suddenly her eye fell to something small but fiery red. She leaned down over it and gasped. It was a torn-off fingernail. The fingernail she had looked for in Paula's bedroom, thinking she might have cut it off and thrown it in her waste basket.

But Paula had lost it *here*.

Had there been a struggle? When Paula realised that the wine she had been drinking had been drugged, had she tried to claw at the person with her? Did that also explain the abrasions on her wrist?

But how had the leather on her shoes been damaged?

With a deep frown Atalanta collected the fingernail and put it in her pocket. She tried to envision the scene: the man putting his hand over Paula's mouth to keep her from crying out and alerting the people in the courtyard below. Her body going limp for lack of oxygen, or the sedative in the wine taking full effect. Had he dragged her for a bit, chafing her shoes?

She pictured him lifting Paula's body in his arms, carrying

her away and putting her on her bed, locking the door as he went out so it would seem she had locked herself in.

But if the same person who had sedated Paula had left her on her bed, thinking she was alive, they had taken a huge chance. If Paula survived, she would identify the person who had been with her on the tower. Besides, when had Paula been on the beach where she had got sunburned? Before she met the man here? But why go to the beach at all?

How did it all fit?

Puzzled, Atalanta shook her head and went back down. As she navigated the narrow steps with care, her hand on the thin metal railing attached along the wall, her heart beat faster, and with each passing moment her unease increased. She thought of her grandfather's advice to her, to always assess facts with an objective mind and be suspicious of everyone, even her client. Now she knew her client didn't exist, in the sense that Letitia's mother had never engaged her. Who was the person hiding under the dark robes of the woman in black? What had been the objective in hiring her?

And if she did look at the facts with an open mind, as her grandfather had instructed her to do, she had to count Raoul among the suspects. He was an attractive man. Paula had claimed to be interested in him, wanting an autograph and possibly more from him. She had mentioned the view from the tower to Luca. The lost nail betrayed that she had indeed been up there before she died. Wasn't it logical to assume she had been sightseeing from the tower with Raoul? He had admitted that Paula had approached him and he had rejected her, to Paula's frustration. Had the altercation taken place on the tower?

But Raoul had suggested Paula had rushed off after their

conversation. That meant she had left the tower alive and well. How had her fingernail been broken off?

Or had she walked away first and then, thinking it over and becoming angry, returned to tell Raoul what she thought of him, only to find he had left and someone else was waiting for her instead? Had someone followed her up and used the opportunity to harm her?

Atalanta bit her lower lip. Any detective worth a penny would investigate what Raoul's role in events could be. She couldn't exclude him because she liked him, and because they worked together. Right from the start of the investigation he had kept things from her and he was still not being totally forward, she felt. He knew more than he had revealed to her.

Had he been looking at the view with Paula when she had collapsed because of the drugged wine? Had Raoul thought she had fainted and brought Paula to her bedroom, believing she only needed to rest a little and would be fine afterwards? But when she had died, he had thought it better not to mention the fact, so as not to be suspected. After all, Raoul was quite a celebrity. He had a name to protect, a reputation to uphold with his investors who would be quick to withdraw their financial support of his racing if he was mentioned in the same breath as the sudden death of a young woman.

She wasn't certain it could have happened like that. If Paula had lost consciousness, would Raoul simply have put her on her bed and left her? Would he not have asked a servant to look after her?

And why lock the door?

She sighed. She didn't look forward to asking him a few questions about his encounter with Paula, but with the nail burning a hole in her pocket and the logical conclusion that the tower was a location where Paula had been shortly before she died, it might be inevitable. She had to handle it tactfully, though. Her suggestion that Luca might be his son had already almost caused a breach between them. She couldn't afford to make any mistakes that would further endanger their bond.

Chapter Twenty-One

With a heavy heart she closed the door leading into the tower. In the corridor Delilah stood looking at her. "I thought you had to watch Luca," she said with a suspicious frown. "Victoria told me she is afraid for him and he must be watched all day long. Now I see you snooping and the child is nowhere in sight."

"I'm not snooping," Atalanta said, irritated at being caught, again. "Luca is with a maid. He mentioned to me that Paula had left some toy of his on the tower and he is not allowed to go there on his own, so I went to look for it. But it is not there."

"A toy of his?" Delilah snorted. "Paula went up on the tower, yes, but not with Luca or any toys. She carried binoculars. She wanted to watch the entire surroundings. She lied to me that it was for some rare bird that nested here on this island, but I never believed her. She wanted to keep an eye on that man, Andreas Papoudopolis."

Atalanta blinked. This information put the nail she had just discovered in a totally new light. Paula might not have been on the tower with a love interest during the feast, she had been there to actively spy on what was happening below. What had she seen? Had that caused her death? "Why would Paula want to keep an eye on a man who works at the burg?" she asked.

Delilah gave her a shrewd look. "You might think she was in love with him and worried he would be flirting with another. But I think she was after something else altogether."

The pirates' gold? Letitia had written to her mother about it. That suggested it was more than just local lore. Had Paula believed Andreas was about to find it? Had she watched from the tower where he went? Had she followed him? Had she died on the beach because of a struggle with the man who wanted to protect his secret of hidden gold? But if she had died on the beach and Andreas had brought her back to the house in a barrel, as Atalanta had speculated before, how had Paula's fingernail ended up on the tower? Had she first watched Andreas and then followed him?

But why would her nail have broken if she had been alone on the tower, keeping a lookout over the land?

Delilah said, "Two young women came here to work and stuck their noses where they didn't belong. They're both dead. You'd better not follow in their footsteps." Her tone was neutral, but the intensity in her eyes suggested malicious glee rather than concern for Atalanta's safety.

Again, Atalanta wondered if the elderly lady had anything to do with the deaths. But if Letitia and Paula had both been involved with Andreas and after his gold, why would Delilah have felt the need to kill them? Out of propriety? Spite? A need to punish them for being so forward?

"I really liked you when I first met you, Mademoiselle Renard. I thought you were different from the others. More sensible and conscious of your position. But you're all the same. You lust after things that are not meant for you. And in the end it destroys you." Delilah shook her head slowly. "It's sad but it can't be changed."

She turned around and shuffled away to her room. Atalanta followed the stooped figure with her eyes. Someone fragile, seemingly harmless. But in reality, a double murderer?

A cry down the corridor pulled her attention away. Luca came running towards her, a thick red tablecloth around his shoulders. "I'm king," he cried. "You all have to bend down for me. Bend down."

Atalanta made a bow. "Your majesty." She looked down the corridor to see where the maid was who was supposed to keep an eye on Luca.

"Bend down," Luca demanded. "On your knees." He eyed her with expectancy.

Raoul came sauntering up. "I sent the maid to do her duties," he said to Atalanta and continued to Luca in a conspiratorial tone, "I don't think Mademoiselle Renard wants to do your bidding."

"Then we must lock her in the cellar," the self-professed king proclaimed. "There are cells there. And skeletons."

"Skeletons?" Atalanta asked, unsettled.

Luca nodded. "Papa says I shouldn't go there, but I peeked in once. The door was open. I didn't go in far. Andreas found me. But he never told Papa. He said if I didn't tell I saw him there, he wouldn't tell on me either." Luca stood motionless and then looked up at Raoul. "Now I've told you. But you will keep it to yourselves, won't you?"

Raoul gave him a pat on the shoulder. "Certainly, your majesty. We are your council; we can be trusted."

Atalanta's throat constricted at these simple words. Raoul was her council, her partner in sleuthing, even – as she saw it – her friend. How could she suspect him of keeping things from her? He had probably told her the truth about his encounter with Paula. It had nothing to do with the tower.

Had it?

Luca ran off to ask the servants to kneel for him. Raoul gestured to Atalanta that they should follow him from a distance. "You look very serious," he said.

"Two people have been murdered."

"Letitia's real mother seems convinced her daughter's death was an accident. If she says so… Don't mothers always know best?"

"The veiled lady claimed that her maternal instinct told her the death wasn't accidental. That as a mother she knew…" Atalanta stared ahead with concentration. "That must mean something." How was the veiled lady connected to Letitia? If she wasn't her mother or sister, then who could she be?

"Or someone wanted to play a prank on you," Raoul suggested.

"Such an elaborate one? Meeting me on Murano, getting me a job here and… No. There must be another reason." She glanced at him. "Do you have any idea who that lady might have been? You seem to know so many people."

"She was dressed in dark clothes, her features hidden behind a veil. She perhaps even disguised her voice. I don't see how I could have recognized her." Raoul stopped and clasped his hands behind his back as he watched Luca talk to some of the paintings in the corridor. Bucardi ancestors, Atalanta assumed. Stern men with deep-set dark eyes, black beards and moustaches, sitting at tables full of merchandise. None of them had a woman with them or a family.

Atalanta swallowed before she asked, "I think Paula was on the tower shortly before she died. She mentioned that she wanted to enjoy the view from up there with you. Have you been there with her?"

"No." The answer came fast and assured. "I told you, she tried to flirt with me but it was embarrassing for both of us. She must have decided to try her luck with someone else."

"The tower offers a great view of the countryside," Atalanta said pensively, "but also of the courtyard where the festivities were going on. What if Paula was up there and saw something she shouldn't have?"

"Like what? A kiss?" Raoul sounded as if he thought such a minor thing would hardly have been worth mentioning, let alone being a motive for murder.

"An exchange? Something that didn't even make sense to her. But whoever was conducting it looked up and saw her, and realized that sooner or later, she would make the connection and would be a risk. So they drugged the wine, sedating her, and then put her in the sun to die."

"I still feel it's a lot of bother, taking her to the beach and everything. There are always boats on the water. They could have been seen."

"Most fishermen fish in the early hours of the day, even before dawn. Why would they be around and able to see things on the beach?"

"Still, it seems complicated," Raoul insisted.

"Yes, well, he couldn't have put Paula anywhere where she could be easily found. There were so many people around..." Atalanta stared into the distance. "I have a feeling that I have enough puzzle pieces now to make sense of them. Or at least, connect a few to show me which information I'm still missing."

"Ask Andreas if he was with Paula on the tower. You just heard from Luca that Andreas warned him not to go near the cellars. I wonder what he wants here at the burg. Perhaps he found gold and is hiding it in the cellars?"

"Why hide it? He could take it away and no one would be the wiser. No, he must still be looking for it. Letitia could have searched Mr Bucardi's workroom for maps of the burg. To aid Andreas in his search?"

"Ask him. Act as if you know more than you do and press him for answers."

"As if he would tell me the truth!"

"I'm pleased to hear that you think *I* would tell you the truth. After all, you did ask me." He sounded piqued.

Atalanta sighed. She was almost sorry she had even wanted to know. But her grandfather had been right that she should take nothing at face value. "Look, I'm trying to be thorough. I need all the information I can get about people's whereabouts, events, altercations that might have contributed to the murder. Besides, if you had been up there with Paula, you might have seen something interesting."

"I would have told you, if I had."

Really? There are other things you haven't told me. She couldn't shed the feeling that it was somehow relevant that Raoul had claimed to know the Bucardis only superficially, but she had now discovered that he knew a lot more about their personal relationships and had even informed Mrs Bucardi of Calista's collapse at the party, which had led to Mrs Bucardi's decision to care for her friend at a remote villa, much to her husband's dismay. Besides, as soon as Calista had been in trouble, Mrs

Bucardi had asked Raoul to help her solve it and he had made her a solemn promise to do so. He had gone to the police station to get Calista out and he had saved her life at the risk of his own.

She shook her head briskly as if to dispel all unsettling thoughts raging through her head. "No matter what, I'll solve this somehow. I have to."

Chapter Twenty-Two

When they came in to dinner, Calista was already seated at the table, smoking a cigarette. Mrs Bucardi, who entered shortly after Raoul, Atalanta and Luca, grimaced when she saw the smoke curling up towards her pristine white stuccoed ceiling. "Would you mind putting that out? I do hate the smell before eating."

"Of course." Calista held her gaze a moment, then reached out her hand and extinguished the cigarette by pushing it against the marble foot of a flower vase.

"Calista!" Mrs Bucardi's voice was sharp, as if she was rebuking a child. "Should you even be out of bed? A servant could have served you dinner upstairs."

"I feel fine." Calista leaned back and laughed. "I even thought that with your bothersome husband away we could have some fun. He's the straight-laced one, not you." The daring look in her eyes suggested she was thinking of some prior occasion where Mrs Bucardi and she had indulged in behaviour that wasn't exactly acceptable in society.

Atalanta wondered if Calista knew things about Mrs Bucardi that could damage her reputation as a perfect wife. Was Calista somehow a danger to Mrs Bucardi, more than just by her reckless acts?

"There's a child present," Mrs Bucardi warned. She sat down at the head of the table, in her husband's place, and gestured for the butler to serve the soup.

Calista sat quietly until the man had left the room. Then she looked up and said, "Shall we play games after dinner?"

"What kind of games?" Raoul asked.

Calista smiled as she held his gaze. "Truth or dare."

"We've had enough dare when you almost toppled off the tower," Mrs Bucardi said sharply. "If you want to play games, we can choose something else."

"Charades?" Calista asked. "They're boring. I want to shake things up."

"Have you been drinking?" Mrs Bucardi asked. "You really shouldn't drink before dinner. It goes to your head."

"You can't always blame everything on alcohol or pills."

"Apparently with you I can."

Calista raised an eyebrow. "You just reminded me that there's a child present. Do you want to discuss this in front of him?"

Mrs Bucardi's eyes flashed but she didn't speak.

Atalanta held her breath. What secret hung between these women? Was it explosive enough to kill for? And who had the biggest interest in protecting it?

Raoul said, "Have you been in Athens lately, Calista? I heard that the Krakitoi family have built a new villa that is even more spectacular than the previous one."

"I went to a party with them the day before I came here."

Calista started to tell them about the party which had included fancy dress, fountains spouting coloured water, three-tier cakes built of fruit and acrobatics in the open courtyard. "The woman balancing on the cord almost lost her footing and we all gasped, but it turned out to be part of the act. It was exhilarating."

"Risk of death is not a thrill." Mrs Bucardi's voice sounded unsettled.

Calista didn't look at her and continued her tale to Raoul. The main course was served, and conversation went on about other parties and boat trips on yachts. Atalanta admired how Raoul skilfully steered Calista to be the star of the stories, keeping her engaged and unable to annoy Mrs Bucardi.

As soon as dessert had been served, however, Calista seemed to remember the earlier situation. She sat up and pushed her plate of chocolate mousse away. "I'm suffocating in here. I'm going to the terrace. Are you coming with me, Luca?"

Luca nodded and shoved the entire meringue that had topped the mousse into his mouth. He wanted to slip off his chair but Mrs Bucardi said, "He's finishing the meal in a proper manner."

"Give him some freedom," Calista chided.

"You've never raised a child. You don't understand that he needs structure."

"Come, Luca." Calista offered her hand and Luca put his in it.

Mrs Bucardi said, "Mademoiselle Renard, you go with them."

"I don't need a nursemaid," Calista snapped.

"But Luca does. He's only four. Mademoiselle Renard…"

Atalanta put her damask napkin on the table and rose to her feet. Calista glared at her. "I don't want you near me."

Luca put on wide eyes, not understanding what the fuss was about. Raoul said quickly, "Because you're a king, you need a bodyguard. Mademoiselle Renard is your bodyguard."

Luca's expression brightened. "You have to protect me. Come with me."

Calista seemed pained at the use of the words "protect me". She cast Mrs Bucardi a scorching look, grabbed Luca and pulled him out of the room. Atalanta followed quickly. She said to Calista, "I'm glad to see you're feeling better and could get out of bed."

"Don't patronize me. Just because Raoul and you saved me, I don't owe you anything."

"And you feel you don't owe Mrs Bucardi either? I thought you were friends."

"Yes, but I'm not constantly thinking about her petty demands. Don't smoke, don't drink, don't make jokes, don't play games. If it was up to her, I would have no life left." Calista sounded quite dramatic and almost like a spoiled schoolgirl such as Atalanta had often seen in her Swiss boarding school. But Calista was older and should be wiser.

"*En garde!*" Luca pulled his hand from Calista's grasp and went ahead to conquer the terrace. He made sweeping gestures with his arm as if to mow down invisible enemies in his path. A dove that had been peacefully pecking at something flew away with an indignant coo. The flapping of its wings sounded loud in the evening quiet.

"I love Luca," Calista said softly to Atalanta. "And Victoria is just breaking his spirit. She doesn't want him to be a little boy. He must be responsible all of the time and speak as though he is an adult. He always has to be ahead of his age, learning new words and knowing it all. But he is a child. He should play."

"Then discuss that with her when you sit down together. But don't make it into a competition. She is trying."

"Trying?" Calista scoffed. "To do what? Be a good mother? Please her husband? Be mistress of this burg? I see her failing on all counts." She fell silent for a few moments and added in a softer tone, "You probably think I sound quite mean and self-centred. And that I judge a situation I know nothing about. But I've been coming here for years now and it's just pitiful to see how Victoria wants to please her husband while he doesn't love her. Pietro has affairs, even under her nose. I wish…" Her lips pinched a moment. "That she knew what he truly is."

"Perhaps she does and still she chooses to stay with him. I've seen it before in families where I worked. Not everyone is cut out for rebellion."

Calista's shoulders suddenly slumped, and she sighed. "I know. I guess I wish Victoria had more of my spirit. She is a dear friend and I love her, but … we're just so different. That's hard to bear."

"Still, you mustn't hurt her feelings." Atalanta spoke rapidly, as these moments to themselves might be brief. "She's trying to do everything right. Especially for Luca. To you it may not seem like she loves him, but I'm certain that the idea that something could happen to him does prey on her mind."

"Oh, I believe it does." Calista's voice had a strange tone.

Atalanta studied her expression from aside. Was Calista also worried that Luca wasn't safe here? Or did she think Mrs Bucardi knew who had killed Letitia and Paula and was shielding that person, putting Luca at risk?

Or was it something else still, not connected with the murders? Something Atalanta was still searching for, the last missing element that would make everything else logical? She felt she was so close to the answer, if she could just see the connection. The one thing that would explain it all, like a blinding ray of light piercing the darkness in a cellar.

Mrs Bucardi came after them, with Raoul by her side. He stopped her by putting a hand on her arm and pointing out something in the distance, and they laughed. That careless laughter changed Mrs Bucardi's face in an instant, making her younger, more approachable and attractive.

Seeing that intimacy gave Atalanta a little stab inside. Raoul had said he had never had an affair with Mrs Bucardi, and she wanted to believe him, but still there was something that connected those two people, some unspoken bond, and it unsettled her. Because she wasn't certain how far Raoul would go to protect it.

If things came to a head, if in the end Raoul had to choose between supporting Atalanta in solving the case and keeping promises of old, what would he choose?

Chapter Twenty-Three

When they had all arrived on the terrace, Atalanta noticed that the view across the sea was tinged orange but with grey clouds hanging low over the water. Their colour darkened while they were gathering, as if invisible hands had piled them together. There seemed to be a thunderstorm brewing.

"I want lemonade," Luca said with a winning smile.

"Not before bed," Mrs Bucardi responded.

"But you all drink coffee and I have nothing."

"Some other time."

Calista said to the butler who served the coffee, "Fetch Luca some lemonade."

Mrs Bucardi said, "This isn't your house, Calista." Her tone was friendly, but firm. She said to the butler, "That is all, thank you."

Lemusier bowed his head and wanted to leave. But Calista placed herself in the butler's path and said, tilting her chin up, "I want a glass of lemonade. Now fetch it for me. Right away."

"Don't listen to her, Lemusier," Mrs Bucardi warned. "You can go."

Lemusier was fiery red and he didn't seem to know what to do. Atalanta felt sorry for him. Servants shouldn't become a pawn in a struggle for power between a guest and the hostess.

Lemusier tried to skirt Calista with his head down. He muttered something suspiciously like an apology.

Mrs Bucardi said, "You need *not* explain to Calista that you follow my orders. That's self-evident, as this is my house."

"*My* house, *my* house." Calista stamped her foot and turned around to Mrs Bucardi in a flash. "You treat me like a baby."

"That's because you behave like a baby," Raoul said, coming up to Calista and putting an arm around her. His tone was light and persuasive. "I know you like to spoil Luca, but he has had enough for the day. Let's play games, as you suggested over dinner."

"Fine." Calista's expression changed in a heartbeat from petulant to triumphant. "Truth or dare. I want to ask Raoul first." She looked into his eyes. "When you race, are you ever afraid to die?"

Raoul laughed softly. "Of course I am. Fear is healthy. I take every precaution not to die. Now that I have told the truth, I can ask someone a question." He let his gaze roam past Mrs Bucardi to rest on Atalanta. She held her breath at what he might ask. "You seem so efficient, Mademoiselle Renard. Do you ever allow yourself to be silly?"

"If so, we want an example," Calista added. Her eyes glittered as if she had a fever.

Atalanta smiled and said, "I can be very silly. When I was still working in Paris, I would go to see the Eiffel Tower, and I imagined that I would scale it from the outside like a mountaineer. I would use ropes and climb all the way to the top."

Luca cheered and Raoul's eyes were amused, but Calista said, "I don't believe you. You're making this up. You didn't tell the truth, so you have to do the dare. Walk on that edge." She pointed at the edge of the terrace. About a palm wide, it was broad enough to walk on but there was a steep drop right beside it.

Raoul said, "It was my question, so I can think of a dare." He added after a short silence, "But I believe Mademoiselle Renard's story. So, a dare isn't necessary."

"I can't see her having a vivid imagination like that. And who says she ever worked in Paris? Have you checked her credentials, Victoria? Or did you let your husband's family shove a companion on you, like they did with that insipid girl Letitia? Did you ever check on why she came to work here?"

Atalanta narrowed her eyes. How well had Calista known Letitia? She had stayed here some times while Letitia was working here, but her strong opinion about the deceased girl opened an interesting perspective. Had Calista not liked Letitia? Had she pushed her into a dare, for instance asking her to climb down the steep steps to the water and navigate the narrow ledge to the caves? Had the girl been hit by a bout of vertigo and fallen to her death because of that?

Was Calista guilty, in a sense?

But if she had caused someone's death by pushing them to their limits – and beyond – why do the same again now with Atalanta? Couldn't she help herself? Or was she under the influence of stimulants that made her reckless? There was something unnatural about her appearance.

"We can try another game," Raoul said. "How about charades? If we keep it simple, Luca can also play."

Luca gave a shout of delight but Calista sighed and threw herself on a deck chair. "You always want to play boring games. I want to have some fun." She pointed at the storm clouds in the distance. "Soon lightning will be whooshing across the water. It's so impressive to see the forces of nature on display. I'm going to sit here and watch it. I'm going to let myself get soaked to the skin."

"If you want to..." Mrs Bucardi said in an indifferent tone. "Come, Luca, I'll take you to bed."

"Already? Can't I stay up a little longer? I want to see the storm too."

"No, it's past your bedtime already. Say goodnight."

Calista spread her arms wide, and Luca ran to hug her. She held him against her, whispering in his ear.

"Really?" he asked. His eyes were wide.

She nodded. "Honestly."

Mrs Bucardi looked troubled that she didn't know what was being said. Perhaps Calista had made promises she wouldn't be able to keep, and Mrs Bucardi feared the tantrum that would follow when Luca discovered that.

Luca hugged Raoul and waved a hand at Atalanta. Then he went with his mother, ignoring her outstretched hand and running ahead of her, holding his arms up in the air.

Calista laughed, a short derisive sound.

Raoul turned his head towards her, as if stung, and said, "You needn't make it so utterly difficult for her, Calista. She's trying."

"She's trying so hard, it's painful to see. The boy doesn't love her. He senses how insincere she is."

"And you're much better?" Raoul's eyes flashed with anger. "You enjoy playing people against each other. That's cruel. You don't care one bit about how Luca feels, just as long as his affection for you can hurt Victoria." He took a deep breath and then continued in a quieter tone, "Change your ways, Calista. No good can come of this hostility. I want Luca to grow up in a safe environment."

"Safe?" Calista's voice was shrill. "How naïve can you be? He's *not* safe here. That is the whole point." She glanced at Atalanta before adding, "And that is why I'm taking him away with me. The sooner the better."

What? Atalanta blinked. "You cannot take him away from his parents. That would be child abduction. You could be prosecuted."

"Will they really make trouble for me?" Calista sounded challenging. "That wouldn't be wise. Considering what I know about them."

Atalanta's heart skipped a beat. Letitia could have known something explosive. She was dead. Paula had mentioned a lucrative business. Possibly blackmail. She was dead. Would Calista be next?

Raoul said, "Why would you want to create a rift? Victoria tried to help you. She cared when nobody else did. Remember that and have some mercy on her."

Calista shook her head. She was deadly pale. "She didn't help me, she used me for her own purposes. She made use of my weakness to..." She bit back what she wanted to say and ran off the terrace, down the path to the cliffs.

Raoul called after her, "Don't be silly. Come back. The storm is about to break."

But Calista didn't listen.

Raoul turned to Atalanta with anger in his eyes. "She can be so childish. Doesn't she know storms are dangerous? We've had enough deaths here. She has to come back to the burg before the bad weather breaks." He hesitated a moment and then said, "I'm going after her. You tell Mrs Bucardi." Without waiting for a reply, he hurried off after Calista's disappearing form.

The rising wind tore at Calista's hair and dress, making her figure look like a creature from Greek mythology storming towards its destruction. Could Raoul stop her? Or was he overestimating his own powers?

Atalanta sat down on the deck chair Calista had vacated and looked at the dark clouds pulling closer. It was as if this storm had been brewing from the first moment she had set foot here at the burg. All these people, so conflicted, so complicated in their personalities. Trying to outdo each other.

Now the moment of confrontation was near. The big clash. A shiver went down her spine and gooseflesh crawled over her arms. She was powerless to stop it. She was here, but she was only a bystander. She could do nothing to influence the outcome.

The lethal outcome?

Mrs Bucardi came to her and asked, "Have the others gone to bed as well? How strange. It's still early."

"Calista ran off in anger and Raoul thought it was dangerous, with the weather being so unstable. He went after her to talk sense into her."

"I wish him good luck." Mrs Bucardi went to stand at the edge of the terrace. She stared at the dark skies where the hostile clouds only allowed a trickle of sunlight to set their edges on fire.

It took Atalanta a while to deduce from the way Mrs Bucardi's hand moved up to her face occasionally that she was wiping away tears. She didn't know quite what to do. Go over and offer support? She was just an employee here. Not a friend of the family. Mrs Bucardi had made it clear from the start that she ought to know her place.

Still … to let someone be smothered by pain and frustration without lending a hand seemed like an inhuman thing to do. Something going against Atalanta's character and inclination.

Raoul came back to the terrace, his breathing heavy. He brushed hair away from his sweaty face. There was a red rash on his left cheek. "She's dead set on roaming the beach in the storm. I can't talk sense into her. She even struck me in the face." He laughed softly. "What a fool I was to think she'd listen to me."

Mrs Bucardi turned to him and said, "I thought she would listen. She loves you. At least that's what she told me."

"When?" Raoul asked cynically.

But Mrs Bucardi seemed to think it was a genuine question because she replied in a rush, "When she was so troubled five years ago. She told me that she loved you and that she had believed you loved her too. That you would marry her. Certainly because…"

She fell silent.

In Atalanta's mind, suddenly the pieces clicked into place. Raoul had had an affair with Calista. And…

"Luca is your son." Mrs Bucardi said it softly, new tears dripping down her cheeks. "You must save him. You must ensure no harm comes to him. I never thought that I would actually say it out loud, but I can't do it. I can't protect him." She raised her hands to her face and sobbed.

Raoul had turned pale under his tan. He looked at Atalanta and then back to Mrs Bucardi. "Did Calista tell you…" his forehead furrowed, "Luca is my son? But I don't understand. How…"

Mrs Bucardi drew down her hands and stared at Raoul. Her face was mottled. "The truth must get out now. It must." She drew a deep breath. "When I went to care for Calista five years ago, she was with child. She couldn't keep it. I wanted a child. We lied to everyone. My husband believes that…" She bit her lip. "He cannot know the truth. Ever."

Raoul said, "I don't think that…"

But Mrs Bucardi cut him off. "If he finds out Luca isn't his, he will kill him. He'll never tolerate…"

"A boy not of his blood taking his inheritance?" Atalanta suggested.

Mrs Bucardi looked at her as if surprised that a third party was present. Her nostrils flared.

Raoul said, "You can be certain, Victoria, that Atalanta will be very discreet. She's not a companion. She was sent here on purpose. To look into matters."

Mrs Bucardi whispered, "Does anyone suspect, then, that Luca…"

"Not that. Letitia's death. It wasn't an accident." Raoul gestured to Atalanta. "She's a very good detective. I've seen a sample of her work before, when I attended a wedding in Provence. I can't tell you much about it, but you can trust her with your life."

Atalanta's heart filled with warmth that Raoul vouched for her in that way. So readily, without a second thought.

Mrs Bucardi's features contorted. "I may need that kind of support. You see, my husband has more than a violent temper.

That's exactly why I agreed to the arrangement with Calista in the first place." She took a deep breath. "I'll tell you everything. Then you can tell me what to do."

After a short silence she began: "I married my husband because my family wanted me to. It was a good alliance from a property point of view. But I soon discovered he was unfaithful, fickle, violent. I also ... heard that in his family several male members had become mad. Over time I saw the beginnings of that madness in him. When something went wrong, when someone didn't do what he wanted, he completely lost control. He destroyed things. He harmed animals. Without remorse. In fact, I think part of him enjoyed it. And the more he allowed these feelings to take over, the worse he became."

She swallowed hard before continuing, "I couldn't bear the idea that a child of mine would carry those same traits and would suffer that fate. So I wondered if I would dare have an affair and ensure that the child I bore was from another man. Then Calista told me she was with child. This was even before her collapse at the party. She told me and I saw the perfect solution. I explained to her what my reasoning was and together we decided on the plan. I would tell my husband I was with child. After a while, Calista would have a public breakdown. Exhaustion, alcohol, pills. I would take her to a remote villa to care for her. There she would bear her child and I would come back with a baby. *My* baby. It all worked perfectly. No one had any doubts or asked any questions. But..."

"Calista wants a part in his life," Raoul said.

"A bigger part than I'll allow her to play." Mrs Bucardi

knotted her fingers. "Then she also asked you to come here. The father."

Atalanta now understood why Mrs Bucardi had become so unnerved at Raoul's arrival. She had believed that the two lovers were reuniting to take her son away from her.

Raoul shook his head. "I'm not Luca's father. And I didn't come here at Calista's request."

"No?" Mrs Bucardi swallowed hard. "I was certain she had asked you to help her put pressure on me to allow her a bigger role in Luca's life. I even thought perhaps you ... still love her and wanted to form a family with her."

Raoul made an incredulous sound. "Why?"

"You're so protective of her."

"So are you. Friends must stick together."

Mrs Bucardi wetted her lips. "I have no rest when she's here. I worry, day and night, that my husband will suddenly understand the truth and he'll vent his blind anger on Luca. It may seem strange to you but ... I do love that boy."

"But you can't fully love him because of this shadow hanging over you," Atalanta supplied.

Mrs Bucardi nodded. "I wish I had never suggested it to Calista. But on the other hand, it was so perfect. She could never raise a child, living as she does. Which is why it's nonsense that she wants to spend more time with him now. She's so ... unpredictable. I fear she will expose our secret and..."

Raoul said, "And at the time, Calista told you explicitly that Luca was my child?"

"Yes. She spoke often of you, of the great times you had."

Atalanta's heart was heavy. When she had asked Raoul about Luca, he had said he had never had an affair with Mrs

Bucardi. He hadn't said he had never been with Calista. Wild, beautiful Calista. Was Raoul even certain it wasn't his child?

Raoul said, "Have you tried to reason with her? Explain how your husband will hurt the boy, once he knows he isn't his child? Calista can be cruel, but I'm certain she does love Luca with all of her heart. She can't be willing to risk harm coming to him."

"Of course I told her. I explained over and over that my husband can't be trusted, that Pietro is violent and that the madness running in his family is slowly taking over his character."

Had Calista grown to believe it only after Letitia had died? Had she therefore hired Atalanta, disguised as the veiled lady, to find out if what Mrs Bucardi had told her was indeed the truth?

Atalanta said urgently, "You must reason with her again. Luca's safety is most important. And you're agreed on that point."

"She wants to take him away from here. I don't know where to. I don't even know if she'll let me near him again. She blames me because of Pietro's violence. But I can't help that. I've been sorry I married him for years now." She sobbed again.

Raoul looked at Atalanta. The frustration in his features touched her heart. She had seen him with Luca and felt how much he cared for that little boy. If anything happened to him, Raoul would blame himself, she knew that.

She said, "If Calista loves you, Raoul, you might be able to talk sense into her."

Raoul laughed gruffly, touching his burnished cheek where

Calista had slapped him. "I don't think so. I don't believe she loves anyone but herself."

"Don't judge her so harshly." Mrs Bucardi swallowed hard. "I took away her baby. I do understand why she feels hurt. She believes I took advantage of her when she was desperate, and she only agreed because she had no choice."

"Nonsense." Raoul sounded sharp. "I know Calista well enough to state plainly that a child is the last thing she wants in her life. Oh, when she's here, it's easy enough to spend time with Luca and look for crabs and spoil him, but Calista wouldn't want to care for him on a day-to-day basis. Giving up freedom to provide a structured day? I can't see her do it." He added after a few moments, "I can't see her do it, because I myself am the same. Freedom means everything to me. Nothing and no one can tie me down."

Atalanta didn't look at him but at Mrs Bucardi and asked, "Do you think Calista really means it about playing a bigger role in Luca's life?"

"I tend to think, like Raoul, that it doesn't fit with her lifestyle, but … she is his mother. She must have some feeling for him. If he were mine, I would also fight for him." Mrs Bucardi's mouth pinched in pain as she added softly, "I often wish he were mine…"

Atalanta's heart hurt for this conflicted woman, who had tried to solve several problems in a single stroke, believing she herself would have no emotional difficulty dealing with the complex situation she had created. Now it all turned out to be much harder than she'd imagined.

"Have you told Calista how much Luca means to you? That you do wish he was yours?"

"Calista thinks I don't love him. She calls me cold-hearted

and distant and cruel. She thinks I..." Mrs Bucardi gasped for breath. "She thinks I'm a bad mother and she herself could do much better. But Luca was raised in our home and ... I may not be as sensitive as Calista as to what he wants and needs, but..."

"Who says Calista is sensitive to that?" Raoul asked sharply. "Yes, she plays with him and allows him everything and he loves her for that, but raising a child also means setting boundaries and providing certainty, and Calista is a destabilizing factor more than anything else. She must realize that."

Mrs Bucardi folded her hands. "I made a terrible mistake thinking I was doing her a favour by taking her baby away from her. I honestly believed I was doing what was best for her and the child. Also for me, so I would know that my husband's madness could not be passed on. But now I ... feel like I ruined everything for everyone. Luca most of all. He may not have Pietro's violence in him, but he can be just as wild and reckless as Calista. Left in her care, he will be completely spoiled and become a danger to others and himself."

Atalanta now understood why Mrs Bucardi had asked her if she thought Luca was different from other children. Because she feared that Calista's wildness and propensity to addiction and destructive behaviour was inside Luca too, waiting to grab hold of him and ruin his prospects for a good life.

Raoul said, "We must think about the situation and come to some kind of solution before your husband returns from his business trip. We must ask Calista what she truly wants. There are moments when she sees sense, and we can reason with her. She must also understand that she can't take away what you've built for Luca, if she doesn't intend to offer him a stable home instead."

"But what if she says she will? What if Calista genuinely wants to sacrifice her freedom and her wild ways to have Luca with her? Do we have to agree then? Will I lose him?" Mrs Bucardi's eyes were wide with fear.

Raoul squeezed her arm. "I can't tell, Victoria. I don't know what Calista wants. But we must all sit down and speak about it. She can't go on threatening you. And you can't go on living in anxiety every day, thinking your secret will be exposed."

"Did Letitia know about it?" Atalanta asked. "Did she suspect? Can her death have anything to do with the secret?"

Mrs Bucardi looked at her, bewildered. "No, of course not."

"But I was told you spent a lot of time with her, looking at photographs of Venice and speaking about your hometown. That her enthusiasm about it fed your feelings of being misplaced here, and you wanted to return and live near your family."

"Yes, I did think about returning. Letitia assured me it would be better for everyone involved. Delilah wanted to stay here, of course, and Letitia had said she'd stay with her because she had fallen in love with the island."

Mrs Bucardi thought for a few moments and then added, "I never considered her death anything other than an accident, but even if you claim it was deliberate, I can't see it had anything to do with us here at the burg. It must have been an outsider. I heard rumours, after her death, that she was in love with a local. If I had known before, I would have warned her against it, as her family would surely have objected to an alliance with some fisherman."

Atalanta recalled that Delilah had told her it wasn't a fisherman but "someone better". Andreas?

Mrs Bucardi said, "Perhaps she wanted to break if off and he pushed her over in anger? Or it was a local who didn't like her snooping around the grottoes. The locals are very protective of their heritage. They consider us intruders. Especially the Venetians who came here to rule the island from their imposing burgs."

She smiled sadly as she continued, "They may act friendly when we offer them a party, but they don't really like us. I know that. In fact…" She shivered, wrapping her arms around her narrow shoulders. "I never feel at ease here. And then that odd note about the sea wanting a sacrifice. I told Pietro we should go back to Italy to live there. But my husband loves this *castello* and his decisions are always final."

"When you told your husband you wanted to return to Venice, can he have felt Letitia had put you up to it?" Atalanta asked, and Raoul added, "Could he have argued with Letitia about her influence on you, and she fell into the sea because she was afraid of him, stumbled backwards, something like that?"

Mrs Bucardi's expression changed briefly. It was so short that Atalanta barely noticed it. But it was there, a flash of relief? Joy, even, that a solution was handed to her, so easily?

She said, "Yes, it's possible, of course."

"Possible," Raoul said with disgust. "We don't know anything for certain. And now Paula is dead as well."

"Do you think the same person killed Letitia and Paula?" Mrs Bucardi held a hand to her throat. "But why? Even if Pietro had a reason to dislike Letitia, he needn't have hurt Paula."

"Delilah claimed she was stealing from her," Atalanta pointed out softly.

She expected Mrs Bucardi to say that Delilah couldn't be trusted, but Mrs Bucardi fidgeted with her necklace as she said, "Yes, of course. Delilah told Pietro and he got angry about it. He easily flares up about a minor thing. Not that stealing is a minor thing. And from a helpless old woman too. So wicked."

The word echoed Delilah's assessment of Paula. For a moment Atalanta wondered if Mrs Bucardi had been aware of Paula's thievery. Had she devised a plan to get rid of Paula and divert attention by claiming the drugged wine had been meant for her?

A cold wind came whooshing across the water and the first errant drops of rain began to fall. Raoul lifted his collar and said, "We'd better go inside and have our coffee there. We must make a plan to convince Calista to do what is best for Luca."

"But what *is* best for Luca?" Mrs Bucardi said with a sigh. "I believe he should have a stable home, not be dragged along on Calista's endless travels. She still takes pills, you know, and she occasionally drinks too much. She isn't capable of providing him with the certainty he needs."

"Still," Atalanta felt compelled to add, "if your husband is so unreliable, is Luca truly safe here?"

Mrs Bucardi straightened up. "I could take him to my family in Venice. My mother loves Luca and we could hire a new nanny. Someone much more suitable than Paula."

Curious, Atalanta thought, *how Mrs Bucardi will then get everything she wanted: she will be back in her beloved Venice, she'll have her child by her side, but she'll be away from the loathed husband who wants to stay here or who travels for his business.*

She'll embed Luca firmly in her family and Calista will have even less of a chance of ever being near him.

Such a perfect solution for Mrs Bucardi.

Had she suddenly confided in them to reach this result? Wasn't it odd that a proud and independent woman would break down and confess a major secret so easily? Perhaps to a trusted friend like Raoul, but in the presence of an employee? She hadn't known that Atalanta was, in reality, a detective.

Unless...

Mrs Bucardi had been the veiled lady hiring her.

Calista or Mrs Bucardi. Which one of them? And why?

The rain intensified and Mrs Bucardi rushed away, holding her head down. Raoul pointed at the tray with the coffee cups. "The butler will have to come and get this. You can tell him when you come inside."

Atalanta held his gaze. "Are you not coming with us, back to the house?"

She knew what his answer was going to be before he gave it. "No, I'm going to look for Calista. She shouldn't be out in a storm. She could hurt herself. And if she gets soaked and wanders all night in her wet clothes, with that chilly wind from the sea, she'll catch pneumonia."

Atalanta looked in his eyes. She wanted to ask why he was so concerned for Calista. If he had once loved her.

If he still did.

But did she really want to know the truth?

Chapter Twenty-Four

Raoul came back to the house late that night, soaked and bitter. Shaking his head, raindrops splattering around him, he reported that he hadn't found Calista. It was as if the earth had swallowed her. "Silly girl," he fumed. "She could catch her death out there."

"Perhaps she took a fatal fall, just like Letitia," Mrs Bucardi said worriedly.

Raoul looked at her, standing there, dripping, his feet planted apart. "Wouldn't that be convenient?"

Mrs Bucardi winced as if struck. Her face was pale in the meagre light of the few lit lamps. "I don't wish Calista dead, honestly not."

"Why did you then accuse her of having put the barbiturates in your wine?" Raoul's eyes flashed. "Was that the behaviour of a true friend?"

"I was afraid. That Calista would go so far as to kill me to get Luca back. She was making more demands by the day and … I may be getting hysterical, but I don't feel safe here." Mrs

VIVIAN CONROY

Bucardi retreated to the stairs. "If you'll excuse me, I must get some sleep."

Raoul stood staring after her with a brooding expression. Atalanta said softly, "Charging at her like that isn't helping much."

"Then you do better." He glared at her. Raindrops rolled across his face and dripped from his chin. "You think of a way to solve this whole mess. Do you realize what we're dealing with here?"

"Hush." Atalanta put her hand on his arm. "Go upstairs and put on dry clothes. Then we can talk. I'll wait for you in the drawing room." Her throat was tight with the tenderness she felt for him, while at the same time anger pulsed through her at the way in which he always tried to provoke her. "If you don't change out of those soaked clothes, you'll catch a cold."

Raoul huffed at this lame excuse to dismiss him, but he trudged up the stairs anyway.

Atalanta went into the drawing room and stood at the fireplace staring at the blackened stone of the hearth's back wall. It wasn't really cold but she wished she had asked Lemusier to light a fire so she could look at the happily dancing flames instead of the charred wood and ashes. It was similarly pitch black inside her brain. She felt around for answers that would explain everything, but came up empty. How could she fit all the elements into a meaningful whole?

Letitia's death, then Paula's. Did it have to do with the secret of Luca's birth? Or was it totally unrelated? How could she ever find out? Both girls were dead and would never speak again.

The only things they had left were traces. A white flower on the steps leading down to the grotto. Had Paula been there?

290

Had she died there and had someone taken her back to the house? But how had she been severely sunburned in a grotto? That would only happen on an open surface. An exposed stretch of beach...

Atalanta tried to envision Paula's last hours but came up short. It didn't seem to make sense either way. What had she been doing? With whom had she been? Why had no one seen her go back to her bedroom? Why had no one seen anyone taking her to her bedroom? If the person moving her had come from the beach to the house ... There had been so many people about. It would have made much more sense if Paula had died inside the house. But the sunburn couldn't have happened inside.

Atalanta paced the room, looking for the moment of enlightenment that would forge everything together. Who had slipped the barbiturates in Paula's wine? Who had access to those pills? Delilah? Had she crushed and applied the pills and then later put the pestle in Calista's room to let her take the blame? But Calista's fingerprints had been on the pestle. She crushed pills for her own use.

And how does a frail old woman move a tall girl?

She stopped and huffed in frustration. She needed another angle, a break in the case. But no new information was forthcoming. She only had Paula's fingernail in her pocket. Such a tiny trace left on the tiles of the tower...

The tower!

Atalanta gasped for breath as she considered it. Was that the answer? A place at the burg, but still open and exposed to sunshine... Paula had come up to look at the view. She had felt drowsy because of the drugged wine and fallen onto the tiles. The sun had burned down on her mercilessly, dehydrating her and changing her skin into the fiery redness of a lobster. Then someone had come and moved her from the tower into her bedroom. That was fairly easy to do and the risk of being seen was almost non-existent. During the party there had been no one on the floor where the bedrooms were.

But that meant that people she had formerly excluded as killers were once again viable suspects. Andreas. Mr Bucardi. They were both sturdily built, strong enough to lift a young woman into their arms and carry her off. It wouldn't take a lot of time. They needn't have left the festivities for long.

Hadn't someone mentioned to her that Mr Bucardi had gone into the house a few times?

But why had Calista said she had seen Paula drinking wine shortly before she had been found dead? If Paula had died on the tower and had been moved to her bedroom as a diversion, she could certainly not have been walking about alive shortly before Atalanta had found her. Had Calista been mistaken, taking one young woman in white for another? It seemed plausible enough. Or had she lied deliberately? To mix up the timeline? To suggest Paula had been alive longer while in reality she had already been dead. Had Calista been with her when she died on the tower?

If Paula had guessed the secret surrounding Luca and had tried to blackmail Calista, she might have misjudged her opponent…

But if Calista was so eager to keep the truth hidden that she even wanted to kill for it, why now be suggestive, brazen, threatening to throw it all open? That made no sense.

Atalanta turned her head to the door when it opened. Raoul stood on the threshold, in dry clothes, his face furrowed into a frown. "Is Victoria here with you?"

"No. She went upstairs, you saw that yourself."

"She's not in her bedroom. I knocked but there was no answer."

"She might not want to talk to you now. Sit by the fire and we can discuss a strategy to help."

Raoul seemed reluctant to follow her suggestion. He put his hands in his pockets and sauntered to the window. He lifted the curtain and looked out. Lightning illuminated the view with its blinding white light and the thunder made everything tremble. "Nice idyllic island," he commented. "Those forces of nature have threatened to devour it for as long as it has existed. Not just the thunderstorms but also the volcanic eruptions. Actually, men should probably not have settled here. But we always want to own everything."

Atalanta came to stand by his side. She looked at his face lit by the glare of the lightning. Cut out of marble and still strangely alive. "Can you talk sense into Calista and persuade her to let it go?"

"For a while, perhaps. But she'll always be back. She's like that, changing her mind over and over. One moment she's reasonable and tender, wanting what is best for another, the next she's utterly selfish and out of control." He laughed softly. "I'm surprised that Victoria was so afraid of a child with Bucardi's personality, but not afraid of one with Calista's traits. She may foster more sympathy because she looks so pretty and fragile at times, but underneath she can be as cold as ice. Like Bucardi. They may have more in common than Victoria thought."

"I guess at the time she just wanted to help, and it seemed to solve her own problem too. Both she and Calista had selfish reasons to agree to the scheme. Only later did she realize what the consequences were. Then she began to worry about Calista's demands to see Luca, and about her personality shining through in his."

"I suppose so." Raoul dropped the curtain. "Can I have a stiff drink?"

"There's no drinks cabinet in here. But there's one upstairs in Mr Bucardi's workroom."

"Good." Without another word Raoul picked up a lamp and left the room. Atalanta followed. Upstairs he opened the door of the workroom carefully and immediately headed for the desk. Atalanta closed the door and pointed at an array of bottles on a side table. "The drinks are..." Her jaw sagged when Raoul put the lamp on the desk and began to open drawers and search through papers inside. "What are you doing?"

"Looking for proof that Bucardi is in financial trouble, wanting to sell this burg, or whatever else Paula might have discovered that got her killed. You pour me a drink. That's our excuse for being here, should anyone come in."

Atalanta thought this was all rather risky but it was late and their host was away from the island. She poured brandy into a glass and asked, "Do you suspect Bucardi of having killed Paula?"

"I can't tell. I wonder what part the old lady plays in all of it." Raoul looked up at her across the desk. "You see, if there is one person in this household who is fiercely proud of the Bucardi name, it's Delilah. She can't stand the idea of any kind of stain being attached to the name. If Bucardi made a mess of his finances..."

"What if she found out that the adored son and heir to it all is not a true Bucardi?" Atalanta asked.

Raoul's jaw set. "I fear she might try and kill the child. Then everyone would sympathize and call it tragic, and no one would be the wiser about the truth."

"So Luca could be in direct danger?" Atalanta wasn't certain Raoul was drawing the right conclusion. Delilah did have strong opinions and had acted with remarkable coldness when Paula had died, calling her wicked, but ... killing a child?

Raoul said, "*If* Delilah knows. But why would she? She lives in seclusion and doesn't really speak to Calista much."

"But she's a clever woman. She can sense the tensions and draw her own conclusions." Atalanta looked at Raoul, who overturned items in the drawer he was searching. His expression was grim and she felt the urgency, the need to achieve some kind of break in the case, pulsing through her own veins.

"I'll be right back," she said and went to her bedroom to fetch the note they had found hidden behind the drawer in the dressing table in Paula's room.

Back in Bucardi's workroom, she unfolded the note and held it over the lamp. The light shining through the imprint made the letters a little clearer. "*Red rock...*" she muttered. "Not *truth*. But ... *thrush*?"

"Thrush?" Raoul looked up at her. "That's a bird. Why would anyone write down the name of a bird?"

Atalanta pursed her lips. "I have to ask my butler Renard if he knows an ornithologist who can tell us what the significance of this bird might be. It could be very rare. Perhaps Letitia was looking for it?"

"Pirates' gold, rare birds. It's all so distracting," Raoul grumbled.

Ignoring him, Atalanta picked up the receiver and called Renard. He was probably in bed but this could be important. When he answered, however, his voice didn't sound groggy at all. "I'm so glad you called," he said. "I was somewhat concerned about the case. Of course Mr Lemont is helping you, but still…"

Helping? Yes, in a way he was and she was glad he was here, but trying to find out how he fitted into the puzzle was also a major distraction to her. It occupied more of her thinking than she should allow, perhaps. "I need to know something about a bird. The red rock thrush. Can you find out from an expert whether it lives on Santorini? Where it lives, if it is in any way special? For instance, if a photograph of it would be valuable. And I need the answer as soon as possible."

"Can you stay by the telephone?"

"Yes. Mr Bucardi is away on business and everyone else is in bed."

"I'll hurry." Renard disconnected.

Atalanta lowered the receiver with a sigh. Did she really think that the red rock thrush could help crack the case? Perhaps she was so desperate for a break that she was clutching at straws?

Still, the note had been hidden. The red rocks were mentioned on the night before Paula had died. She had referred to the tower and watching across the island with binoculars. She had mentioned a lucrative business. Blackmail over something she had seen?

Renard called within half an hour. He sounded very self-satisfied. "I managed to get through to Antoine Bachalier. He is one of the greatest bird experts in France and a specialist on Mediterranean bird life. I asked about the red rock thrush. He only knows a blue rock thrush which is fairly common, also on Santorini. He has never heard of this red rock variety and even teased me that I had probably been duped. But he did add that species are still being discovered and that it would be possible that a variety existed that had not yet been listed. After all, they're still discovering even large mammals, like the okapi thirty years ago, so why not find new birds these days?"

"And such finds would be important?"

"Oh yes, hugely exciting."

"And photographs of a new bird would be worth money."

"Undoubtedly. Does this help?"

"Yes, well, I'm not sure. But thank you for looking into it for me."

"Take care, Mademoiselle. *Bonne nuit.*"

"Good night, Renard." Atalanta put the receiver down and told Raoul what she had just learned. "Letitia might have been looking for a rare new bird to establish her position as a photographer. She could have fallen down the cliffs because she took risks for a photo."

"An accident anyway?"

"But then, why would Paula think the reference to the red rock thrush was important? She kept the note, she asked about the rocks. I can't see her being interested in a new bird species. She must have wanted something else."

"Perhaps someone pulled Letitia's leg with the mention of a supposedly rare bird to send her on a wild goose chase? But when it led to her death, Paula thought she could put pressure on that person by referring to the red rocks, hoping she'd get something out of it."

"Hmmm. It feels a bit weak to lead to murder." Atalanta suppressed a yawn. "I'm not going to find out any more tonight. But I can do something." She walked to the door. "I'll go and sleep with Luca tonight. I want to ensure no one harms him. In the morning, in the light of a new day, we can hopefully think with a clear head and come to decisions. By then Calista will have returned to the burg and can also be part of the conversation."

Raoul nodded. "Good idea. Leave that drink with me. I have a feeling I may need it."

Chapter Twenty-Five

Atalanta awoke with difficulty, her body still floating on the remnants of sleep, her mind slowly clearing to her present situation. Her bed felt awfully hard and her shoulder hurt. Her neck, her head… *Why is this mattress stiff as a stone slab?*

She felt around her with half-numb fingers and realized she was lying on the unforgiving floor, huddled under a blanket. During the night she hadn't been able to relax and sink into a nice mattress, and all her muscles had tensed. Now she felt as sore as if she had been beaten. *What happened? Where am I?*

Panic surged and for a moment she feared she was in the cellar. Had Bucardi unmasked her as a detective out to prove he was a killer? Had he locked her in?

But she didn't recall an altercation with him and the ceiling above her was high. Turning her head slowly, as it hurt, she discerned the shape of a bed.

Oh, yes, she had wanted to sleep in Luca's bedroom to watch over him. She had sneaked in and lain down on the floor beside his bed, without waking him. Her head full of thoughts, she had struggled to fall asleep and lain awake at first, listening to the thunder outside the window. Thinking of Raoul and how she might help him, even though he didn't want to confide in her.

Bleak morning light was visible over the curtain and she came to her feet quietly to open the curtain a crack. The view was washed clean, the sky clear of clouds. In the courtyard someone was chopping wood, for the kitchen stove probably, to make breakfast. He whistled as he was at it. Everything seemed so normal that Atalanta's tight throat relaxed a little. She turned back to the room with a smile.

The morning light fell on the bed where the little boy rested, breathing peacefully.

Atalanta's smile widened when she looked at him. All the hurting muscles were worth it when she saw this innocent child, at peace with the world. He lay with his wooden sword clutched against him. She studied his relaxed features, searching for the resemblance to Raoul she had earlier detected. But so many Mediterranean men had black hair and brown eyes. Luca had to be the son of ... some other lover Calista had had. Someone she had never told Mrs Bucardi about.

Certainly, if Luca was his, Raoul would have slept here tonight to protect his boy against potential danger.

Atalanta's smile died away when she noticed something dark moving across the sword. It used the wood to navigate, to move its long and slender body upwards. Its front was now near the little boy's soft neck. It was ... a snake.

No! Atalanta stared in horror as the animal's tongue tasted the air while it slithered across Luca's chest. A snake in the child's bedroom! One wrong move and the beast would bite, insert its venom in the child's soft flesh. Luca would die, here in his own bed. And there was nothing she could do about it. If she moved in and tried to remove the snake, she might incite it to bite.

Where had it come from? She had been in here all night with the door locked on the inside…

She walked over to the bed, careful not to send tremors through the floorboards. The snake was now resting on Luca's right shoulder and seemed undecided whether it would move down the blanket or onto his head.

Let it be the blanket, Atalanta willed.

But the snake's tongue flitted against the boy's cheek. If Luca felt something, flicked a hand up, struck out at the animal, he could provoke the fatal bite.

There was a knock at the door. Atalanta shot upright. *No, not now. Go away.*

Luca stirred. Atalanta called out, "Get away from the door!" She hoped her voice wouldn't anger the snake and Luca wouldn't move again.

But the person outside kept knocking and Luca did move. Atalanta had to act. She reached out, grabbed the sword and used it in a single swift movement to shove the snake off the bed. The sword's tip grazed Luca's jaw and he cried out in pain.

Outside the door a female voice called, "Luca? Luca, open the door."

Atalanta scooted around the bed and saw the snake disappear into a crack between the floorboards and the wall. *Gone.*

For now.

She pulled Luca out of bed and carried him to the door. Confused, he asked her what was happening. She unlocked the door with one hand. It flew open instantly.

Mrs Bucardi looked at her with wide, suspicious eyes. "What were you doing in there? Why had you locked the door?"

"She hurt me," Luca wailed. "Look, I'm bleeding." He showed his hand to Mrs Bucardi. It didn't have blood on it, but the graze on his jaw was fiery red.

Mrs Bucardi pulled the child from Atalanta's arms and said, "I want you to stay away from him. Go to your room and stay there. I'll decide what to do next."

"There was a snake in the room. On the bed. It wanted to bite and kill Luca. I moved it away with the wooden sword, grazing his cheek in the process. I saved him."

"Nonsense, there are no snakes in this house."

"It vanished into the wall. It probably crawls through empty spaces between the stones. It wasn't that big."

Mrs Bucardi said, "There are snakes on this island, I know that." She shivered as if she recalled having first been acquainted with the fact. "But I was told, repeatedly, that they are harmless. That they don't attack people and that they're not venomous."

"I didn't know that. Besides, who says this is a snake native to this island? It could have been introduced."

Mrs Bucardi paled. "To..." She looked at Luca and held him closer. "You go to your room, like I ordered. I want to think this over." She pushed a hand to her face.

Atalanta said, "Your son may be in grave danger. Why don't you leave the island with him this morning?" Luca had to be saved, at all costs. Then she could solve the murders without having to worry for his safety all the time. "Your husband is away at the moment, he can't stop you."

"I don't know. Perhaps you made it up about the snake? How do I know I can trust you? Or anyone?" Cradling the boy against her, Mrs Bucardi rushed off.

Atalanta closed the door of the bedroom. She felt like barricading it to keep the horrible creature inside but knew there would be little point to that action. The snake was small enough to fit through cracks and slits and could appear again in any other room. She hadn't had a good look at its appearance, as it had been dim in the room. So it would be hard to determine whether it had indeed been a harmless snake such as the locals knew, or a dangerous one which a mysterious hand had released here.

Who would want to kill Luca?

Delilah? But how had she acquired a venomous snake? She never left the burg.

Atalanta pressed her fingertips against her temples and took a deep breath. This case was going over her head in a major way. She had no idea how to stop the clever killer at work here. And with the life of a young child at stake, she couldn't afford to make a single mistake.

Chapter Twenty-Six

Atalanta had gone to her bedroom, as Mrs Bucardi had asked her to. Not just to heed her employer's wishes but also to freshen up and change her clothes. She felt like the painfully long night should be washed away, and with a fresh dress on and her hair done, her courage returned. She did have enough information to crack the case. She had to go through every bit of it and connect the dots.

Atalanta sat down on her bed and read her notes carefully, against the background of her new knowledge that Luca was Calista's son. How many people had known about that, or at least suspected it? Was it the motive for murder? Or was it totally unrelated?

Had Letitia died when Luca struggled with her? Or because Delilah had drugged her wine, and she had wandered along the cliffs with her precious camera, half sedated? Had Letitia been in love with Andreas and had she discovered something about the pirates' gold he coveted? Had she tried to flirt with Mr Bucardi, and had she died when he pushed her away from him? Accident? Intentional? Or even cold-blooded, pre-calculated murder?

Then Paula. Had she known how Letitia had died? Had she watched from the tower through her binoculars to keep an eye on Andreas, and then seen something she shouldn't have? Someone returning to the burg in haste? Had she tried to blackmail them with her knowledge, thinking she could acquire a lot of money and leave, to start the kind of exciting life she had always dreamt of? She had mimed looking through binoculars on the terrace that night, right after her mention of the red rocks. The red rocks were also mentioned on the sheet she had hidden in her room.

Had she died on the tower?

If Atalanta was correct in assuming this, the murder had been committed by someone who had access to the barbiturates, could move Paula from the tower into her bedroom and lock the door with a spare key... A member of the household. Mrs Bucardi? Mr Bucardi? Delilah seemed too fragile to move the body. Andreas might not have had access to a spare key.

Calista... Had Paula blackmailed her with knowledge or alleged knowledge of her secret? Calista was strong when she put her mind to something; she could certainly have moved the body.

But the snake in Luca's room... If it was the same person doing all these malicious things, it couldn't be Calista, because in spite of all her weaknesses, she would never hurt Luca.

Or would she? Was she angry enough at everyone who thwarted her to want to hurt them via the child?

Atalanta rubbed her forehead. This was very complicated. There were too many assumptions or speculations and no solid facts. In the previous case she had been able to ascertain facts, to build a framework of things she knew for sure, without constantly having to doubt everything. But here she couldn't. She often only had one person's word for it that something had happened. That Letitia had snooped in Bucardi's papers, for instance. Or that Paula had stolen a necklace. Had Letitia loved swimming, or had she been afraid of water? Did the red rock thrush even exist? Did the pirates' gold?

Grandfather, how would you have handled this?

She stood up and went to her suitcase to consult the letters hidden in the lining. They were letters her grandfather had written and left to her upon his death. They all bore a few words to indicate what their contents were. What kind of helpful hint or kind advice they contained.

There was one marked: *When you are at a loss.*

Atalanta had meant to save it for as long as possible, for some extreme situation much later in her detective career. It felt rather disappointing to already have to open it during her second case, but Luca's life could be at stake. Her pride shouldn't stand in the way.

She tore the letter open and extracted a sheet. The mere sight of her grandfather's strong handwriting was comforting:

Dearest Atalanta, when you've opened this envelope, something (or someone?) has you stumped. But you mustn't let yourself be fooled by smoke screens. Think of what magicians do: they distract their audience by focusing their attention on one thing (their left hand) while they are performing the trick out of sight (with the other hand). Ask yourself: am I looking at the wrong hand?
Your devoted grandfather, Clarence Ashford.

Atalanta re-read the few lines. Was this all? Did she have to solve two murders with this meagre advice?

Disappointment rippled through her and she dropped the letter on the floor, staring ahead with a sinking feeling that she could never get to the bottom of all this. Her grandfather had believed she could be a detective, but she couldn't. She simply didn't have the skills for it. She had been led astray by her earlier success. But perhaps it had been a fortunate coincidence then, everything coming together to lead her to the right outcome. Here she was wandering as if caught in the Minoan maze. There were too many distracting details leading her away from the main picture. She had accepted a task too big for her.

From a client who isn't even Letitia's mother!
You let yourself be fooled and now you're at your wits' end.
All is lost.

But despite the dejection trickling through her with an insidious cold feeling, a will to fight ignited. She wasn't about to give up and walk away. Yes, she had made mistakes, but that didn't mean she couldn't solve the case. She had all the information in hand.

Her grandfather had done this work for many years, decades even, and he knew exactly what mattered. His advice might look sparse, but it had to be hugely significant.

She could open up her mind to a whole new perspective. If only she allowed herself to see.

She picked up the letter, smoothed it on her knee and re-read this sentence: "*Ask yourself: am I looking at the wrong hand?*"

What had she been looking for when she came here? Reasons to assume Letitia's death had been murder.

Why had she been doing that? Because the veiled lady on Murano had told her that her daughter's death couldn't be an accident.

But now she knew that the woman in black hadn't been Letitia's mother. Who had it been? Why had she hired her?

Atalanta leaned her fingertips against each other and stared into space with utter concentration. Without immediately speculating about the true identity of the woman in black, she had to establish some general facts first. Someone had wanted her to come here. Someone who … wanted her present when Paula was murdered? Someone who had believed she would connect Paula's murder to Letitia's?

A chill went down her spine. Had Paula's killer hired her before the act? To ensure that Paula's death wouldn't be investigated on its own but in connection with another death? That way, the killer could have wanted to complicate the investigation so attention would be diverted from the real reason why Paula had to die.

She went back over every little detail of the meeting with the veiled lady. It had been a woman under those robes, she was certain of that. Delilah was too short and besides, she never even left the burg, let alone the island.

It could have been Mrs Bucardi. Had she wanted to have her husband suspected of murder? She knew of his violent temper, of the madness in his family. She was afraid of him and what he might do if he discovered the truth about Luca. Had she killed Paula to blame it on her husband and get rid of him? To be free to return to Venice with Luca and start over, in a life that would never again involve the violent man she hated?

But if the objective had been to get Pietro Bucardi behind

bars, then why kill Paula in such a way that Calista's pills were involved, laying a false trail to her?

This same argument also excluded the veiled lady being Calista, planning to kill Paula. She would not have incriminated herself in the crime. She would have used other means to point at other members of the household.

Still, if Atalanta let go of the idea that the veiled lady had planned Paula's murder and merely assumed she had suspected Letitia's death to have been murder, and had wanted a detective at the burg in case another death occurred, then it could have been Mrs Bucardi or Calista. Either of them could have acted out of fear for Luca, a need to find out if a murderer lived with the child and could strike again. Calista had even said explicitly that Luca wasn't safe at the burg. That she wanted to take him away.

Letitia had been murdered. But why?

The *wrong* hand. What had Atalanta assumed about Letitia? That she was ambitious and wanted to travel. Why? Because the veiled lady had told her so. Atalanta had later wondered if Letitia had wanted to acquire money via the pirates' gold, to leave Santorini again for her photography. Why? Because Calista had told her about the pirates' gold and Letitia's alleged interest in it. But if Calista had been the veiled lady on Murano, her tale of the ambitious girl who wanted to travel might have been made up. How well had Calista actually known Letitia? Had she read her right? Or had she projected her own love of travel and foreign places on the girl, believing all young people were like that? Had her information unintentionally led Atalanta astray?

What if Letitia hadn't wanted to leave Santorini at all? What if her behaviour should be interpreted in another light?

Her mother had said to Raoul during the telephone call that it had been odd that Letitia had wanted to leave Venice, and a full social calendar, for the isolation of an island. She had never been here before, so she couldn't have fallen for a local man. But she could have known Bucardi from his visits to Venice. She could have wanted the position as companion because she was in love with him and wanted to be near him.

Atalanta frowned as she stared ahead. Letitia had hummed all day long, Delilah had told her. So Letitia had been satisfied that things were going well. What had she been doing? Getting closer to Mrs Bucardi, feeding her love of Venice, her desire to go back home. What would have happened if Mrs Bucardi had left? She would have taken Luca with her, and therefore also Paula, the nanny. But Delilah would have stayed. Letitia would have stayed. And Mr Bucardi. He loved the *castello* and wanted to spend as much time here as possible. Letitia would have been virtually alone with Mr Bucardi, an excellent opportunity to try to start an affair with him.

Delilah had tried so hard to impress on Atalanta that Letitia's love interest had been a local. Because she feared, deep inside, it had been her nephew?

Atalanta turned her head with a snap to the window. On the windowsill stood the glass jar containing rock fragments. On top of a book. A book she had noticed on her arrival, but attached no special meaning to.

Jane Eyre.

The tale of a girl coming into a sinister household and falling in love with the master of the house. If Letitia loved such dramatic, romantic stories, she might have fantasized about a future for herself as Bucardi's ... second wife once the undesirable first wife had been removed?

But how had Bucardi responded to these overtures? Had he at first flirted with the companion, not realizing what fire he was igniting inside of her, until Letitia had almost succeeded in driving Mrs Bucardi away? Something Bucardi didn't want.

Here on this isolated island he could much better control his wife than in Venice, where she had her family and friends near. Here she had to put up with behaviour which she might not tolerate back home. So Letitia's antics to get Bucardi to herself had caused domestic problems that Bucardi wanted to solve.

Atalanta rose quickly and walked to the window. Setting the jar of rock fragments aside, she picked up the book and opened it. It had an *Ex Libris* note on the title page, with a name:

Letitia.

There it is. A sample of Letitia's handwriting. Holding her breath, Atalanta rushed to her suitcase and extracted the note Raoul had found behind the drawer of Paula's dressing table. She compared the handwriting of the words *red rock thrush* to *Letitia*. The two samples were definitely the same. Without a doubt, Letitia had written down the name of the non-existent bird species.

Atalanta stared at the lettering with a deep frown. Bucardi was a flirtatious man. But he would never truly have an affair with a servant. He disliked Letitia because she weaned his wife away from him and was upset when he hit Luca. Had he wanted to dispose of her, but in such a way that it would look like an accident?

He knew the island well because he had spent summers on the burg ever since he had been a little boy. He could convincingly talk about bird life there, about the best spots to see something special. He could have fed Letitia's infatuation with him by suggesting he wanted to help her to make a spectacular photograph and show her parents what she could do. He might even have said that once her fame was established, she could travel with him to his other homes – Monaco, the Riviera – to take photos there. Caught up in her own romantic fantasy, Letitia had readily believed him. She had written down the name of the allegedly rare bird and torn off the sheet to keep it. Paula had then found the sheet and tried to make Letitia's last written words visible. She had mentioned the red rocks on the terrace on the eve of the festival, to see who took the bait?

Atalanta recalled how Bucardi had sat on the deck chair after Paula had walked away to follow Calista and Luca. He had paid no attention to the derogatory treatment of his wife by his aunt. He had been deep in thought. Because he had realized what Paula's words meant?

Had he felt threatened by the idea that Paula had been on the tower watching everything from on high, able to see for miles around if it was clear? Had she seen Letitia wander, looking for something? Getting too close to the edge and falling in? By herself? Or with someone present to administer the fatal shove?

If Bucardi had indeed perked up at Paula's mention of the red rocks and her binocular act the night before the festival, he had had the entire night to plan his murder of her. To take Delilah's pills and crush them, put the powder in his pocket to put in the wine when the time came. He could have waited until Paula had already drunk a few cups of wine, dejected that Raoul had rejected her, and then handed her the fatal cup. He would have known the sedatives would start working soon and kept an eye on her to see when she started to sway on her legs. When she had gone inside to lie down, he had gone after her and taken her to the tower, where he had left her unconscious body in the sun to achieve the sunburn that would suggest she had been on the beach. He could play host in the courtyard, in plain sight, while Paula lay dying on the tower.

He only needed a brief interval inside later to move the body away from the tower, through the first-floor door and into Paula's bedroom. He was strong enough for it, he had a key to lock her door from the outside. And during the feast people might go inside on the ground floor, to the kitchens or lavatories, but no one went up to the bedrooms allotted to the staff. He ran no risk of being seen.

He had even locked the ground-floor door into the tower, so no one would suddenly come up and catch him in the act. It all fitted.

The wrong hand. She almost had to laugh because it was so ironic. She had believed that the secret of Luca's birth had something to do with it. That that had been Letitia's shocking revelation. That Paula had somehow learned of it or suspected. But it had nothing to do with it.

Nothing?

Atalanta froze. She had been focusing on all the wrong questions in the case, so was it possible that she had also been looking at Luca's origin from a skewed perspective? Because she had been so worried that Raoul was somehow involved. That he was the father. But he wasn't. Some stranger was.

A stranger, really?

Or someone she knew?

Her mind suddenly saw a possibility that took her breath away.

Surely, it wouldn't be.

It couldn't.

But snippets of conversation flashed through her mind. Calista telling her that Victoria had never stood up to her husband and that she should see him for what he truly was. What did Calista know about that, unless...?

Raoul saying about Bucardi and Calista, "They may have more in common than Victoria thought."

And why had Calista blatantly lied that Luca was Raoul's child? Why had she never revealed who the real father was? Because it was too scandalous to speak of? An inexcusable betrayal? What if was not Bucardi who should remain in the dark about the truth, but Victoria.

Her door was thrown open so violently, it banged against the wall. Raoul stormed into the room, waving something white in his hand. "Quickly. Come with me."

Atalanta eyed his grim expression. "What's the matter?"

He held out the white item to her. It was a note. "I found this in Victoria's bedroom. I looked for her in the nursery, but a maid said she had asked her to care for Luca. I thought she was resting after the shock of the snake in Luca's bedroom and knocked on the door. When there was no answer, I peeked in and spied the note. Read it."

Atalanta cast her eye across the few words: *Must speak with you, urgent. Come to the ruins of the old monastery. Calista.*

Raoul gestured wildly with his free hand. "Calista outsmarted us. She lured Victoria away from the burg. By now she could have pushed her into the sea, like she did with

Letitia. Another Venetian sacrifice... She must also have sent that note ahead of the festival celebrations to create tension."

"But I was just thinking in a completely different direction." Atalanta was almost certain she had finally aligned the elements and seen the full picture. It would come as a shock to Raoul too.

"Tell me later. We have to go to the monastery now." Raoul raced away and Atalanta had little choice but to follow. Her thoughts raced just as fast. Was he right that Calista was the culprit? She seemed to have enjoyed the eerie suggestion of a "Venetian sacrifice" and had talked to Luca about the vengeful goddess of the sea. Had those superstitions aided her in her plan to kill Mrs Bucardi during the festival, and have Luca to herself? Had the barbiturates been meant for Mrs Bucardi anyway, and had Paula drunk the laced wine by mistake?

Had Calista planned the whole thing? Even her own alleged drugging? Had she herself released the substance in her bedroom, leaving quickly, untouched by it, but acting as if she were severely intoxicated by it? She had made attempts to climb on the tower's merlons but not very successfully. Had she never intended to be in danger, only to gain sympathy and lead everyone astray?

Raoul had danced to her tune perfectly, saving her, feeling sorry for her, looking for ways to clear her name. Even last night he had followed her into the storm and been so dejected when he had come back.

The idea that Calista had abused him without mercy lit Atalanta's blood. That woman really had no conscience and was willing to do anything to get what she wanted. Even kill her best friend?

The anger gave her energy to keep up with Raoul as they

navigated steep steps down and up again to reach the ruins of the old monastery. If Calista intended to hurt Mrs Bucardi, they had to stop her.

But still something nagged at the back of Atalanta's mind. The possibility that what she had figured in her bedroom was the truth, and Calista too was a victim of the situation. A woman desperate to remove Luca from the island, not because she wanted to take him away from his mother, but from his father. Something she could never explain to Victoria, because doing so would mean having to reveal the terrible thing she had done.

The one thing Victoria could never forgive her for?

But she had no breath to explain it all and Raoul would probably not even want to hear it. He seemed fully convinced that he knew all the answers now and the case was just about solved. Calista was the murderer and all they had to do was prevent Victoria Bucardi from becoming the next victim.

Raoul panted as he managed to squeeze out a few words to her. "Should I have ... taken Bucardi's pistol? He keeps one ... in his workroom. I came across it last night ... looking for clues amongst his things."

"What do you ... want to do with a pistol?" Atalanta drew breath with difficulty. "Shoot Calista?"

"Might be our only chance. But too late now." Raoul looked grim and Atalanta knew he wouldn't let any harm come to Victoria Bucardi. If Calista was armed, Raoul would instead be hurt himself. If there was a struggle, Raoul might be seriously injured. Or killed.

If Calista was dead set on dealing with her rival for Luca's affection, she might stop at nothing.

What can I do to help? I can't watch idly while Raoul risks his life.

"There." Raoul pointed ahead to the ruins of the monastery. Part of the tall grey wall was still standing, with an old open archway in the centre that formed a gate. Raoul reduced speed and pressed his shoulder to the wall, creeping along it carefully until he was at the gate. He peeked in. Then he quickly walked past the opening and took up position on the other side. He gestured to her to look, but carefully.

Atalanta lowered herself onto her haunches and looked inside.

This entrance had probably previously led into a corridor about fifteen feet wide. It was now wide open and on the other side was just a crumbling low wall. Beyond it was nothing but air and the sound of waves breaking from below. Two women stood at that rickety wall, their backs towards them, faces turned to the sea view.

At first glance, they could have been mistaken for tourists simply enjoying the beautiful morning at this historic site. But Calista's appearance was rumpled after her night out in the storm and across the distance their strident voices could be heard.

Mrs Bucardi barked, "Did you allow Luca to keep a snake in his room? I told you before, I abhor all those creatures he drags in. Crabs, lizards. But a snake…"

"They're quite harmless."

"Mademoiselle Renard didn't think so. She almost drove a hole in Luca's cheek with his own sword in her attempt to rescue him from the snake's venomous bite."

Calista burst out laughing. "That wasn't necessary at all. She must be as highly strung as you are. It's merely a new pet.

318

Because your dear husband didn't allow him to keep the puppy."

"So you did give it to him." Mrs Bucardi was fuming. "You heartless woman."

"It's a harmless snake. It isn't poisonous or anything. You make every little thing into a big drama. As if I'm a danger to Luca."

"You are."

The two women now faced each other, their gazes locked. Calista's clothes were torn, her hair hung loose. Compared to her, Mrs Bucardi looked impeccable. But her contorted features betrayed that she was beside herself with anger.

Ready to do something drastic?

"You've done nothing but cause misery ever since you came here," Mrs Bucardi screeched. "I want you out of my life. Go away and never come back."

"Luca is *my* son. I want to spend time with him. I'm entitled to it. More than you."

"You agreed to let us raise him."

"Us? Your husband is hardly fit to raise a child. You told me so yourself. It was your excuse to steal my baby. That tale of how mad your husband was... How his insanity was taking over, and he was becoming more inhuman by the year. But you yourself are the one without a heart or conscience. You never kiss Luca, you don't show him love. You're breaking his spirit. All I want to do is rescue him. Take him to a place where he can be happy. He never will be at that accursed burg."

"Rescue him?" Mrs Bucardi's voice was sharp. "What can you give him? You claim to love him, but your love is fickle. One moment you play with him and smile at him, the next you're writing to a lover and have no time for him. You drink and take pills. You burn powders to 'open the mind', as you call it, but it's truly madness. You're unreliable and dangerous. How can you ever care for a child?"

Raoul gestured to Atalanta. His lips moved slowly as he mouthed, "Go over to them and intervene?"

Atalanta shook her head. The altercation was painful, but neither woman seemed physically violent and they should at last speak their minds. Luca's future was at stake.

Calista said, "If you despise me so much…" Her voice was hoarse. "And you don't want me back at the burg, then why did you come out here to look for me? Is it that idea of yours that you are somehow responsible, that you must save me? You hate me and yet you want to save me?"

"You wrote me a note asking me to come here."

"I didn't."

"Oh Calista, please stop lying. It's so tiresome. You wrote me a note to drag me out here. Because you knew I would come to see if you were well. Yes, at times I hate you, for what you've become. But I remember who you were before the pills took over." Mrs Bucardi's features softened. "And in spite of my better judgement, I do want to save you."

Calista laughed. "You're trying to make me look mad, telling me I burned the powder in the room myself. But I did not. Someone else put it there. And now I sent you a note I never wrote? I've spent the night in one of the grottoes, cursing this isolated island and everyone on it. I've made plans to abduct Luca and take him where you can never find him. I certainly didn't write you a note to ask you to come here. What for? I have nothing more to say to you."

Mrs Bucardi said, "If you didn't send it to me, then who would?"

A voice said, "I did."

Atalanta jerked back as a man appeared over the edge of the outcrop the women stood on. Within seconds he had pulled himself up and over the crumbling monastery wall as if it was the most normal thing to do. He was dressed in dark-blue simple clothes like an islander but his face was familiar.

"Pietro…" Mrs Bucardi gasped.

Atalanta clenched her jaws. *I was right. Why didn't I convince Raoul to listen to me before we set out? Why did I let myself be dragged down here in a rush? Now it's too late. Neither of us is armed.*

Raoul had inched back the moment the new arrival appeared. He threw Atalanta a bewildered look. She gestured to him to stay low and keep watching. She held her breath as she carefully peeked around the rough stone.

Mrs Bucardi stared at her husband. "I thought you were away on business."

"Yes. Of course you did. That was the plan. But I never left. I watched you. I know you're betraying me. With that smug race car driver, or Papoudopolis – but that doesn't matter. I wanted to see with my own eyes what you're doing. You're a wicked, wanton woman who goes after every man she lays eyes on."

"I'm not. How can you say that?"

Mr Bucardi leaned over to his wife. "If you're so loyal, then tell me here and now: is Luca my son?"

Mrs Bucardi took a deep, shivering breath.

"You know what they did in the old days with women who were unfaithful? They killed them. Death by stoning, or other very unpleasant means." Bucardi spoke in a quiet tone. "Today we are more civilized. We simply ask for a divorce. But in such a case the woman lives on, free to do as she pleases. I've always felt it's not quite what she deserves."

Raoul glanced at Atalanta. She thought he was thinking the same thing. That he should have had the gun. In the mood Bucardi was in, he might do something drastic in front of their eyes.

Mrs Bucardi said, "I never betrayed you. I swear."

"Stop this." Calista's voice was brittle. "Why do you do this? You accuse her, but you yourself are at fault."

Yes. If what Atalanta had seen in one luminous moment in her bedroom was true, Bucardi had indeed betrayed his wife in a monstrous way.

"Be silent." Bucardi moved his hand up as if to strike at Calista. "You play no part in this."

"Don't I?" Calista was pale. Standing there with her wild hair around her face and her frantic eyes, she looked like a vengeful Medea. "I play a huge part in it. I agreed to an unspeakable lie. But I'll no longer continue."

"Calista, please …" Mrs Bucardi said. Her lips trembled.

Atalanta held her breath. Before she had understood, she had feared what Bucardi would do the moment he knew Luca wasn't his. But right now she realized it was even worse. The moment Calista revealed the truth to her friend, everything they had formerly relied on would be blown apart, as if by a volcanic eruption.

How could they stop the tragedy that was unfolding before their eyes?

Calista said, "I'm so sorry, Victoria, I should have believed you. I should have … but I …" She fought against tears.

Bucardi said, "She might as well know now. Luca is *not*

your son, Victoria, but he is mine. I fathered him. *I* was Calista's secret lover."

Atalanta looked at Raoul. His mouth fell open.

Bucardi continued to talk. "When she told you about the pregnancy, of course keeping my name out of it, and you offered to accept the child and pass him off as yours, that was exactly what I had hoped for. I wanted an heir who was *my* child, who has *my* blood running in his veins. But you feared me and you didn't want a child that would be like me. So I gave you what you wanted. A son who wasn't tainted with the shadow of madness hanging over him. Oh, I knew it all. What you looked into, my grandfather, father… How you abhorred me more with every discovery… But you felt safe once Luca was there. He was the perfect child, in your eyes. And I was satisfied too."

"No!" Mrs Bucardi cried. "No! You're lying. He's not yours. He's not." She looked at Calista. "Please tell me he's lying."

Tears dripped down Calista's face. "He's not lying, Victoria. I'm so sorry. I—"

"You knew how afraid I was, and you betrayed me? You lied to me that it was Raoul's baby? You played along with *him*?" She pointed to her husband with a look of utter revulsion and hatred on her face. "All that time?"

"I made a terrible mistake. I realized soon enough. I wanted to save Luca. I … hired Mademoiselle Renard after Letitia died. I wanted her to find out that Pietro had killed Letitia. So he would be locked up for life and you and Luca would be safe. But then Paula died and…"

"Did you kill Paula so Pietro would be suspected?" Mrs Bucardi asked in a breathless voice.

"No! Paula should never have died. Your husband tried to

323

murder you. He had this insane idea that if you were dead, I would marry him and we could be a little family. He had no idea how I despised him. You must believe me."

Mrs Bucardi stared at her friend, her eyes wide with horror.

Atalanta frowned hard. She could hardly believe Bucardi had wanted to kill his wife and had murdered Paula by mistake. Paula had been blackmailing someone.

Mr Bucardi tutted, "No, no, Calista, as usual you're wrong. I don't want to marry you. You're far too wild and unpredictable for my liking. I need a decent wife."

"Because you're such a decent man?" Mrs Bucardi's eyes narrowed. "I knew what you were capable of. You killed Paula and wanted to let Calista take the blame for it."

"*You* thought Calista wanted to kill you. That the drugged wine was meant for you. Is that a way to treat an old friend who gave up her baby to you? A child not tainted with a dark family history? Someone perfect? Everything has to be perfect with you, Victoria. Admit it. You no longer love him now that you know he's mine. Now that he doesn't fit into your dream life. You had it all figured out so beautifully. Leave me here, take Luca to Venice. You said you sent the photos of Venice to the family with the girl's other belongings, but you haven't. You kept them to pine over."

"You're despicable. You never liked Letitia."

"Logically." Bucardi shrugged. "You had instructed her to go through my things."

"No, I hadn't."

"Yes, you did. You were as thick as thieves. You put her up to it. Delilah knew all about it. She caught her at it, in the dead of night."

"Delilah? Is she your confidante? Do you actually believe a

word of what she says? An old woman who is often confused? Who thinks everyone is stealing from her?"

"Paula was stealing from her. She claimed Delilah had given her a necklace, but she lied." Bucardi straightened up. "That 'old woman', as you call my aunt, at least has a sense of honour and a love of the Bucardi name. She keeps me meticulously informed of everything that happens at the burg. How Letitia snooped for you and had already decided that you could return to Venice and she would stay here, allegedly for Delilah and to take photos, because she was so in love with the island. With the island? Phah! I knew what she was after. But her photography hobby was ideal for my plan. It was easy to mention a special place on the island to Letitia, to lure her there with the promise of that one special photograph."

"*Red rock thrush*," Atalanta muttered to herself.

"I didn't tell her, of course, that the rock is very unstable there and if you get too close to the edge, your weight can cause it to collapse. She did fall in, all by herself. I was too far away to help her." His voice had a forced hint of pity, but his eyes were full of malicious delight. "It really was an accident."

"You killed her for nothing," Mrs Bucardi whispered. "I never ordered her to go through your things."

No, Atalanta thought, *Letitia had spent time in the workroom at night because she had wanted to be close to the man she loved.* Perhaps she had sat in his chair, leaned her head where he leaned his. Touched the desk he sat at when he worked. Perhaps she had even drunk out of a glass he'd drunk out of. Infatuated, dreaming of the time when Mrs Bucardi had returned to Venice with Luca and Paula, and Mr Bucardi would be left with Letitia, so she could care for him.

But when Delilah had mentioned to Bucardi that Letitia

had been in his workroom, he had drawn the wrong conclusion that she was going through his things under orders from his wife, and it had only fed his anger against the girl he already disliked because she kept talking to his wife about the city she missed so much.

"I don't believe a word you say, Victoria," Bucardi scoffed. "You did put her up to it. You also forced her to tell me I should be nicer to Luca. You always need others to fight your battles."

"Letitia herself thought that you should be kinder to him. He's only four years old."

"It doesn't matter now. Order is restored. Letitia is gone and you're staying. You promised me 'until death do us part', and that's exactly what I want to get."

Atalanta looked at Raoul. He was staring intently at the scene, all his muscles tense. She was certain he was calculating how he could jump Bucardi without risking the man realizing they weren't alone, before he got to him. He need only give his wife a firm shove to send her over the wall.

"So here we are," Bucardi said. "And you know what they say. Two is company, but three is a crowd." In a flash he pulled something from under his wide, dark shirt. It was a pistol. He pointed it at the women, alternating between them. "You decide. One of you lives, the other one dies."

"What do you mean?" Mrs Bucardi gasped, tears in her eyes.

"Well, my suggestion is this: You push Calista into the sea. She dies. You tell everyone she attacked you in a fit of madness induced by her pills. You struggled with her and she fell to her death. You already told the police that the wine Paula drank was meant for you. That was Calista's first attempt on your

326

life, which failed. She unfortunately killed an innocent bystander, so she had to try again. And don't you think that after that scene last night, they will believe you that she was unstable and couldn't be trusted?"

"You know what happened last night?" Calista asked sharply.

"I was never far away. I was lurking and I know everything." Bucardi glared at his wife. "You confided in Lemont because you're in love with him. You want to leave me and be with him. But I won't let you. You'll kill Calista and she'll take the blame for Paula's murder. Not even you could save her after she had killed a girl in your household. The police will officially declare her the murderer, but as she is herself dead, there will be no trial. No damage to our good name. No reason for you to leave. We'll continue our lives as before."

Atalanta's arms were full of gooseflesh at the idea that Bucardi had listened in on the scene at the terrace, had heard his wife's confession that Luca was not a Bucardi. How angry it must have made him that she gave her secret away, especially as he had believed she did so to a man she was in love with and wanted to be with. How he must have rejoiced in Calista's wild behaviour and her subsequent flight, spending the night away from the burg. It had all fitted perfectly into his plan to solve the situation while he was allegedly away from the island on business. People would believe that the power struggle between the former friends had finally come to a head and had ended tragically for one of them.

It would never lead back to Bucardi.

Mrs Bucardi swallowed hard. She kept her arms pushed against her body. "I won't hurt Calista."

"Fine. You never wanted to do what I asked. That's stupid, as you'll now experience firsthand. Because ..." Mr Bucardi looked at Calista, "I have an offer for you. You push Victoria into the sea. You tell everyone she came at you like a mad woman, accusing you of having put a poisonous snake in her son's room. It's widely known you're the animal friend and Victoria hated you for the introduction of all those creatures. You tried to explain it was a harmless snake, but she didn't want to listen. You struggled and she had an unfortunate fall into the sea. That will be believed too. There was a snake. Mademoiselle Renard saw it. Her impartial testimony will support your story."

Atalanta stood as if frozen. Bucardi had a gun and he was mad enough to fire it. If he noticed they weren't alone, he could easily shoot both women before Raoul and she had a chance to disarm him. He would never allow them to live on if he got caught and had to pay for his actions. Would he be able, in his last act of fury, to destroy them all?

Bucardi continued to Calista, "I know how you hate Victoria for being so prim and proper, for trying to change you. And if she's dead, you can take care of Luca. You can come and live at the burg with us. He needs so much more than a careless nanny. He needs his mother. His *real* mother."

Mrs Bucardi cringed.

Bucardi was still talking to Calista: "You can play on the beach with him, take him to bed at night, tell him stories. You can be a part of his life. Victoria will no longer be there to stand in your way. All you have to do is push her over the edge. Then you can have everything you wanted. Think of how much you want it. How you dreamt about it, in your bed at night. Wishing you could have what you gave up on. Wishing you could turn back time and do it all differently. Now you can."

Calista looked at her former friend. Insecurity raged in her features.

Atalanta bit her lip to keep herself from crying out. *Don't do it, don't listen to him, he's lying, he'll never let you near Luca.*

Mrs Bucardi said in an insistent tone, "He'll never keep his word."

Calista shook her head with a pained expression as if she couldn't stand listening anymore. "Stop telling me what I have to believe, what I have to do."

Mrs Bucardi continued, louder, "After you push me in, he'll push you after me. I guarantee you."

"Calista…" Mr Bucardi's voice was warm and persuasive. "You never liked Victoria. You only needed her to solve a problem. But now she has become a problem. Deal with her. Push her off the outcrop and it's all over. It's a steep drop and if the impact on the waves doesn't kill her, she'll surely drown. It's fool proof. You can have your son and be happy." His tone was sweet like honey, almost intoxicating. And Calista had proven before that she was capable of making bad decisions on the spur of the moment.

"No, Calista, please…" Mrs Bucardi begged.

Calista didn't stir or speak. She stared at Bucardi with wide-open eyes, as if she was in shock. How rational was she after her night out, lacking sleep, food? How befuddled was her brain, clinging to the beautiful picture he had painted for her? What if she listened to that insidious voice telling her that a single push was all it took to have her son?

Atalanta's hand closed round a loose rock at her feet. It felt reassuringly solid under her touch. If only she could get close enough to bring it down on the back of Bucardi's head.

But the moment she sprinted forward he would hear her. He could fire at least one shot before she'd manage to hit him. One woman would die and the other one would have to live on, plagued by nightmares of this horrible scene.

Bucardi said, "We can't stand here all day long. Someone has to make a choice. Someone has to do the deed and accept the consequences. I can tell you it's easy enough to live with the knowledge you killed someone. If the motivation is right. If they were a danger to you, you had to remove them. That's simple self-preservation. In the end we're no different from all other creatures in this world. We have to survive. Your life, or hers. It's so simple."

Calista whimpered.

Bucardi said, "Or else I'll be forced to make the decision." He came one step closer.

Mrs Bucardi backed away. Her calves touched the wall and she gasped as she almost lost her balance and toppled.

"You can make it easy on all of us," Bucardi said. "Let yourself fall backwards, Victoria. Calista need not push you. You fell. You don't want to live anyway. Consider it. Your worst fear has come true. Luca is mine. The violence you hate so much, it's in him too. The madness you fear, waiting to break out into the open. You no longer love that little boy." His voice rose in strength. "You hate him as much as you hate me. Your life has become worthless. End it, now."

Mrs Bucardi stood motionless, blinking hard as if she was trying to take in everything and come to a decision.

A fatal decision?

"Don't believe him," Calista said. "We can only defeat him together."

"Together?" Bucardi smirked. "You knew Victoria was afraid of me and you handed her my baby, my son, to raise. Who is evil here?"

Atalanta saw the pain ripple across Mrs Bucardi's features and for a horrible moment she was certain that the tormented woman would reach out and push Calista to her death.

But Mrs Bucardi didn't move. Her lips were trembling, but she still held her arms tightly against her body.

Bucardi pointed the pistol at Calista. "You push her into the ocean, or you die. I know how you love life. More than you care for this so-called friendship. It wasn't worth much to begin with if I could come between you so easily. Kill her!"

Raoul sat crouched like a runner at the start of a race, ready to propel himself upwards and forwards. But the tension in his features told Atalanta that he feared that in jumping Bucardi, he would induce him to fire and hit one of the women.

Calista shook her head. "I will do no such thing." Her voice trembled and she shook as if she was close to exhaustion. "You can never get me to harm Victoria. Not with anything you say."

Mr Bucardi inhaled sharply. The hiss of something venomous. He shifted his hand a fraction, turning the pistol from Calista to Mrs Bucardi. "Then I decide."

"Noooo!"

The moment he pulled the trigger to drive a bullet straight into Mrs Bucardi's heart, Calista dived in front of her friend. The bullet struck her and she cried out in pain.

"Calista!" Mrs Bucardi grabbed her and the weight of her friend threw her off balance. She toppled backwards.

As fast as a cougar, Raoul bolted across the distance and managed to grab Mrs Bucardi by an arm and a leg. "Hold on," he cried. "Hold on."

Bucardi had been frozen a few moments by Calista's sudden move, too baffled to fire again. But now that he realized that they hadn't been alone, he roared with rage, pointing the gun at the three forms crumpled against and half over the wall. While he was focused in that direction, Atalanta stormed forward and brought the rock in her hand down on his head with all the force she could muster. Bucardi cried out and his hand squeezed the trigger. A shot rang in the air, the bullet whizzing away without striking anything.

Mr Bucardi fell at her feet, the pistol slipping from his limp hand. Atalanta kicked it away and ran to help Raoul pull the two women away from the wall onto the rocky floor. Then she returned to Bucardi at once to tie his hands behind his back. While doing so, she noticed the dirty bandage around his left hand. Did it cover the wound Luca's puppy had inflicted?

She looked at Raoul who was asking Mrs Bucardi how she was. Mrs Bucardi clutched Calista against her. Blood spread across Calista's dress and her eyes were closed.

"Calista, no," Mrs Bucardi whispered, tears streaming down her face. "No. Don't leave me now. Please … don't die."

Raoul grabbed her shoulder and said urgently, "Press down hard on the wound to stop the bleeding. I'll run and get a doctor." He said to Atalanta, "Is he tied up securely?"

"Yes." Relief made her hands tremble but still she managed to act. "I'll also tie his legs. You go and fetch that doctor as fast as you can."

Chapter Twenty-Seven

A talanta paced the drawing room waiting for news of what transpired upstairs. The doctor had come with a few locals and they had moved Calista to the burg. Mrs Bucardi hadn't wanted to let go of her and Raoul had to prise her blood-stained hands away from her wounded friend. He had supported her as they walked back slowly. The police had taken Bucardi to lock him up and one policeman had remained to take statements about events at the ruins of the old monastery.

Atalanta's mind was still reeling. It had gone so quickly, and the revelations seemed unreal. Although she had seen the truth before Raoul had stormed into her room, part of her refused to accept that Luca was Bucardi's son anyway. Heir to all the Bucardi property, but also to the temper that had made Bucardi such an evil man? What prospects did the little boy have? Could he ever lead a normal life? A happy life?

The door opened, and Raoul came in. His features were tight with worry.

"And?" Atalanta asked.

He sighed. "Calista lost a lot of blood. The doctor can't tell if she will recover. She could develop a fever or other complications. We won't know for a few days. Victoria is with her." He looked at Atalanta. "Victoria keeps telling me that Calista saved her life. And she can't die now. But I..." He bit his lip. "I don't know if there's any fighting spirit left in Calista. She hid a terrible secret for all these years. She didn't believe what Victoria told her about Bucardi's madness. She had always thought Victoria was too prim and proper, someone who couldn't understand a need for freedom or silliness. But after Luca was born, as she visited here and saw his behaviour, how he could lash out at people, abuse animals, she must have realized the truth. After Letitia's fall off the cliffs, she hired you to prove he killed Letitia, so he would be locked up and her best friend and beloved child would be safe. But it all went awry."

Atalanta nodded. "She must have thought during those moments at the monastery that whatever happened, Victoria mustn't die. That it was better if she herself died, to pay for her mistakes."

"No. I think Calista wanted Bucardi to be the one to die there. But she had no way of forcing him over the cliff. She would have tried, had she seen a chance." Raoul sighed. "I can't blame her. That man is insane. The way in which he played them against each other ... merely for the pleasure of seeing one of them crack and kill the other to save herself. Which would have been pointless, as he would also have forced the survivor into the sea. He couldn't let a witness of his crimes live."

Raoul exhaled in a huff and continued, "How he enjoys

himself at the expense of others is revolting. I wager he was smiling when he watched Letitia fall to her death, merely because she wanted to take a photograph that could propel her to fame."

"Because she wanted to impress him, the man she loved," Atalanta corrected. She shook her head. "That's so sad. But Bucardi pulled it off perfectly. A tragic accident. Everyone accepted it as such. And he also set it up like that with Paula. He wanted to kill her with the drugged wine and have it pass as a tragic natural death. A combination of heat exhaustion and too much alcohol. She may have drunk from Mrs Bucardi's cup at some point during the festivities, but the barbiturates weren't in there. Bucardi gave them directly to her before taking her to the tower. He probably saw it as poetic justice that she died there, because she had threatened him with her knowledge of Letitia's death, allegedly acquired by watching from that very tower. She had mentioned the red rocks, said she'd talk about them to Andreas. Bucardi didn't want a clever man like Andreas doubting the accident story or pressuring him for money. He had to close the leak as fast as he could."

"During a festival," Raoul scoffed.

"Of course. The perfect cover. So many people who could declare he had been in the courtyard for most of the day. And when the doctor found traces of barbiturates and the natural-death scenario became unfeasible, he led everyone to believe that Calista had wanted to kill Mrs Bucardi. The altercation about switched cups worked to his advantage, as did the pestle in her room with her fingerprints on it. It was actually hers, used to grind her own pills. But Bucardi killed Paula with the barbiturates stolen from Delilah. He knew no one believed what she said anyway. If she reported her pills missing, it wouldn't be connected with Paula's death, as everyone already suspected Calista. A suspicion further fed by her outrageous behaviour when she climbed the tower after Bucardi had put the powder in her room and jammed her window shut."

"He did that too?"

"Yes. Remember how this happened right after Calista had returned to the burg to find him arguing with Luca about the puppy she gave him? Bucardi was livid that his authority was being questioned, and the dog had bitten him. It must have goaded him to put the powder in her room while she was in the storeroom with Luca, finding a place for the puppy. He didn't care whether Calista would really manage to kill herself or not, as she would look guilty of Paula's murder either way."

"Ironic how he tried to frame her, while she hired you to expose him." Raoul shook his head sadly. "She must have been desperate for a solution to remove Bucardi from Luca's presence. She hoped that you would find evidence against him that he had murdered Letitia."

"With multiple testimonies of what he said at the monastery, he will be tried and condemned for certain."

In the end I did do what my client wanted of me. Despite all the subterfuge, I managed to complete the case.

I just hope Calista will survive…

"And we needn't fear he'll ever be back here." Raoul gestured around him. "He'll never raise a hand to strike Luca again." He looked at her. "I know you wondered why I care so much for Luca if he's not my son. In that little boy I see myself. Child of a distant mother, and a father who believed that physical violence makes a real man. He wanted me to fear him, even hate him, rather than ever having me cry in his presence or tell him I loved him." Raoul clenched his hands into fists by his sides. "That was just weakness."

Atalanta's throat was tight, realizing how lonely Raoul must have been as a child. And how it had formed him into the man he was today: always taking risks and laughing at the danger, going through life skirting true connections because they made him uncomfortable, because he didn't know how to handle them.

Wasn't that very familiar, in a way? For different reasons, her childhood had also been lonely and her ability to connect with people underdeveloped.

A knock resounded on the door and a policeman entered. He looked grave. "The prisoner wasn't feeling well and we called the doctor to look at him."

Raoul spat, "Did he manage to use the occasion to escape?"

Atalanta could feel the tension in his stance resonate in her own body. Bucardi was so clever, it was frightening. But he mustn't get away.

The policeman shook his head. "The doctor found a wound on his hand that was festering. He asked some questions and it turns out the prisoner was bitten by a dog. The doctor thinks this wound caused blood poisoning. The prisoner is running a high fever and his condition is deteriorating rapidly. They don't know if he'll survive the day."

Relaxing his tight shoulders a little, Raoul said, "Both Calista and Bucardi fighting for their lives ... I know who I want to survive."

The policeman said, "The prisoner in his delirium is asking for his wife. Should we bring her to him?"

Raoul snapped, "How can you even propose this? He tried to kill her."

The policeman said, "He could be dying. This could be her only chance to see him and hear what he has to say."

Raoul looked at Atalanta. She said, "We can't keep this information from Mrs Bucardi. She has to make a choice whether she wants to see her husband or not. If he's dead by morning, she might feel cheated out of a last chance to hear him out or speak her own mind."

Raoul sighed and then nodded. "You could be right. But you go and tell her."

With a leaden feeling in her chest Atalanta went upstairs and knocked at the door of Calista's bedroom. She opened it and peeked in. Mrs Bucardi sat beside her friend's bed, looking worn. She gestured for Atalanta to come closer. But Atalanta shook her head and waved her to the door. She didn't want the unconscious Calista to overhear anything about the man who had almost killed her.

Mrs Bucardi asked sharply, "Why take me away from looking after Calista?"

"Your husband is in the cell. He's unwell and a doctor established that the dog bite, from the puppy Luca was playing with, might have infected him with blood poisoning. He's very ill and might die soon. He's been asking for you."

Mrs Bucardi stared at her. "Asking for me? Now? After all he did?"

Atalanta said, "I thought you should know about it. So you can decide what you want to do. If you want to see him one last time."

Mrs Bucardi stood and thought it over. Her expression was serious and her voice calm when she finally spoke, "I knew who Pietro was and what he was capable of, even before this morning. But at the monastery he said enough to confirm my darkest thoughts. He can say no more to make it worse, or better. I also don't have anything to say to him. No comfort. No ... empty words that I don't blame him. I do. And if he dies and can't be judged here in this life, I hope he will be in the next." She turned her back on Atalanta and went back into the bedroom.

Atalanta returned down the corridor and passed Delilah's door. The elderly lady was sitting in her chair knitting and called out for her. "How is my nephew? It must all be a misunderstanding. He's no murderer. He'll be released soon."

"No, he's gravely ill. He might die."

Delilah rose to her feet, the knitting falling on the floor. "Die?" Her voice was shrill. "I must see him, speak with him. He can't die before I speak to him." She walked over to Atalanta and demanded, "Take me to him."

"He's in a cell. It won't be pleasant."

"I've done many things in my life that weren't pleasant. Take me to him."

Atalanta saw the determination in the old woman's eyes and sighed. "Come along with me."

Chapter Twenty-Eight

In the small damp cell Bucardi was lying on a simple wooden cot. Someone had put a blanket over him but he had thrown it off. He was sweating profusely and at the same time shivering, his teeth chattering. He tossed and turned as they came in, repeating, "Victoria, Victoria…"

Delilah walked over and looked at him. She clicked her tongue. "You were always pathetic, Pietro. When you kicked that dog to death because he didn't want to fetch a stick for you. You were only ten. Perhaps it's fitting a dog bit you and now you're dying. Even animals want vengeance."

She stood up straight, her eyes blazing as she studied the writhing figure. "You thought that violence solved everything. That making people afraid of you would get what you wanted. And perhaps it did, for a while. But you always had to go a step beyond. You had to push further, risk more. It had to end badly."

Delilah's features softened and her shoulders slumped. "Pietro…" Tears came to her eyes. "You were our family's only hope. You were going to continue the line. You and your son, Luca. Everything was going to be his, whether those stupid Greeks wanted it or not. We are Venetians. We rule the world." Her voice grew stronger as she continued, "You fought to keep what was yours. And I helped you. But it wasn't enough. I should have known that before." She bit her lip. She was now swaying on her legs.

Atalanta said, "You helped him by telling him everything that happened at the house. You told him Letitia was snooping in his things, that Paula stole from you, and that Mrs Bucardi was betraying him with other men."

"I saw it with my own eyes." Delilah gave a prim little nod. "That Greek and her standing together closely, whispering."

"Andreas was making advances but Mrs Bucardi rejected him. And Letitia didn't go to the workroom to snoop. Your so-called help only fed Mr Bucardi's paranoia. Why did you do it? You knew what he was capable of, even from a young age. You just said so."

"It takes a strong man to rule a household and prevent his wife and children from going astray. He was away too often on business."

"He wasn't away. He stayed on the island to spy on his wife. Because he believed she was unfaithful."

"And she was. I never liked her."

"I know. You wanted her to be blamed for Letitia's death. Why else tell me it was murder the day I arrived? You certainly didn't want me to think it had been Mr Bucardi, did you?" Atalanta held the old woman's gaze. "Or did you want yet another to be blamed? Andreas Papoudopolis? You emphasized Letitia was in love. That it was a local man but not a fisherman. You wanted to start a rumour that it had been Andreas, to remove him from the burg. Because he was a threat to the Bucardis' marriage, in your mind. You never liked Mrs Bucardi but she had to stay here with her husband, to avoid a scandal at all costs. Avoid damage to the Bucardi name that means everything to you."

"I don't have to talk to you." Delilah tilted her chin up.

Behind her back Bucardi turned his head to them. His eyes gained a moment's clarity and he said, "Aunt Delilah, is that you? Come sit with me. I don't want to be alone." He sounded like a little boy again, pleading.

Delilah snorted. "I'm not going to sit with you in this filthy cell. I wish I had never known you. You're a disgrace to our family." She went to the cot and said in a low voice, "At least it will end with you. Luca isn't a Bucardi. I've known that all along. He's a child of infidelity. I despised your wife for it. But there's one advantage. He doesn't carry that evil blood which destroyed my father, my brother and now you. Luca will be good to the property, good for the family name. It must be done, to have our line continue. To keep Bucardis here at the burg for centuries to come."

Bucardi stared up at her. His dry lips whispered, "Luca is mine. Calista bore my child. I may die here but the Bucardi blood will live on."

Delilah stared at him in horror. "No. That cannot be true. No. You're lying. Our family must continue to rule the burg and the island, but with dignity. With control. You never had that. People didn't respect you. They must respect Luca. He must be different to you." She hissed, "You want to poison my mind before you die. Turn me against that boy by telling me he'll be just like you. But it won't work. It won't work!" She put her hands over her ears and ran to the door. "Open it. Let me leave."

Bucardi looked at Atalanta. "Ask Calista." His voice was hoarse. "She knows the truth. The boy is mine. He will…" His eyes turned glassy again and he shivered.

Atalanta leaned down and put the blanket back over him. Bucardi had done terrible things, but he was still a human being and judging by his condition, someone near to death.

Outside Delilah waited for her, her shawl pulled tightly around her shoulders. "Don't you believe a word he says. Luca isn't his. I was willing to overlook his origins to have our lineage continue. The Bucardis have conquered land and created silk for centuries. It can't end. There must come someone who will turn things around. But now he tells me that I must believe that… No." She shook her head violently. "It cannot be true."

Atalanta sensed the old lady was close to collapse, and they still had to walk back to the burg. She had to be gentle with her. She said evasively, "Calista knows, but she's very weak. If the gunshot wound proves fatal…"

Delilah stared ahead. Her expression was sad but also resigned, as if the idea of the secret being taken to the grave was actually the best solution, for everyone. She muttered, "A little boy without parents who will never know the truth…"

Chapter Twenty-Nine

A talanta sat on the terrace and looked out across the sea. The sun was setting, turning the waves orange and red. The sky hovering over it was a deep blue with hints of lilac and purple. Sparrows chirped, bees buzzed along the potted yellow flowers and all was so peaceful and perfect. All but the feelings inside her. What had this case shown her? That family loyalty went too far? That people were always selfish and intent on choosing the easiest way for themselves?

Or rather that, in the end, friendship conquered all? Calista had risked her life to save Victoria.

Raoul came to sit beside her. He stared at the view for a few minutes with a morose expression and then said, "I don't think Santorini will ever be quite the same to me."

"The island isn't to blame. The people who live here are kind and friendly. And the sights are spectacular. Perhaps..." Atalanta smiled ruefully. "The Venetians should never have come here."

"So it's all because they wanted to rule this island that we had the deaths?" Raoul shook his head. "That's too easy for me. I have lots of Venetian friends." He waited a moment and said, "I came to share news."

Atalanta's heart skipped a beat. "What news?"

"Calista will recover. The doctor says she's showing signs of improvement. He advised that as soon as she's fit to travel, she should move away from here to forget the traumatic events. Victoria said she will go with her. She also wants to leave this place behind."

"And Luca?"

Raoul sighed. "Calista wants to talk to you. She asked for you specifically. I think she has something to say."

Atalanta stood up. "Then I'll go and see what it is."

The atmosphere in the house felt oppressive after the freshness of the evening outside. She met Lemusier in the hallway. He greeted her with a nod. She asked him, "Why did you drop the suitcase when I mentioned Letitia that first day I came here?"

"I suspected the Greek of having killed her, but I had no proof. You came in after walking up to the burg with him, and you mentioned her death." Lemusier wet his lips. "I wondered if you were immediately suspicious of him. For your sake, I hoped it was so. But later he sought your company and you even seemed to like him, so I felt I had to warn you." He lowered his head. "I feel rather silly now."

"No, you meant it kindly. Thank you."

Lemusier smiled at her. "The French must look out for each other. Even when on foreign soil." He turned away to see to another household matter.

Atalanta knew she could never tell him she wasn't French at all. Mrs Bucardi had emphasised she didn't want the staff to know details of what had happened. They had only been told that Mr Bucardi had died of blood poisoning brought on by the dog bite he had sustained before leaving on business. Not feeling well, he had tried to return home but had collapsed before he could reach the burg. The police had apparently agreed to keep the truth under wraps, now that the murderer was himself dead. It made sense, as there was no point in burdening the living, but to Atalanta it also proved that the influence of the Venetians was still strong on this island. When they demanded that dark secrets were discreetly covered, they were.

But perhaps there was no injustice in it, as the murderer could no longer stand trial. And Letitia's mother, who had never doubted the accident story, would not be any better off by knowing her daughter had been lured to her death because of a forbidden love for a married man. She could better remember her daughter as a life-hungry girl who had wanted to forge a path in life, fulfil her dreams, and who had died taking too much of a risk for it.

In a way that was the truth.

Atalanta walked up and noticed how the sound of her footfalls was drowned out by the carpet. Everything seemed to be muffled in here, deprived of life.

In Calista's bedroom Victoria rose from the chair beside the bed. "You mustn't tire yourself," she said to Calista and then to Atalanta, "Just a few minutes."

Atalanta nodded and sat down. But as soon as Victoria had left the room, Calista gestured for her to come and sit on the edge of the bed. She spoke softly. "I was the one hiring you on Murano. I meant to tell you once I had arrived here, but I feared that ... As you had agreed because of my convincing act of motherly grief I wasn't certain you would still want to help if you knew the truth, so I left it at that."

"Why did you hire me?" Atalanta asked. "Did you know Letitia's death was murder?"

"I didn't know for certain. I had no proof of it. It seemed to me she admired Bucardi and would do anything he said. Another victim of his charm. He could be so utterly ... engaging when he wanted to." Calista smiled ruefully as if remembering the times she herself had been under his influence. "Someone had to see him for what he was and stop him. Having known your grandfather, I thought you could. I didn't think that in the end I'd have to stop him myself, by catching his bullet."

Atalanta wanted to apologize but Calista made a dismissive gesture. "It's for the better. If you had unmasked him as a murderer and shared the truth about Luca, Victoria would have forever hated me. Now she knows that I never meant to hurt her. It was just ... a very bad idea. I could have given birth somewhere privately and let the nuns care for Luca. But I wanted to stay in touch with him. I wanted Victoria to have him for selfish reasons, so I could always come and see him grow up. But I honestly didn't know that Pietro was so ... evil. It wasn't until Letitia died that I became too uneasy to leave things be. If Luca wasn't safe here, I had to engage a skilled investigator to sort matters out." She stared into the distance. "I wonder what kind of child Luca is. Just wild and irresponsible or ... with two parents who aren't exactly..." She looked Atalanta in the eye. "I hope we can keep him from becoming too much like his father."

"I think that with Mrs Bucardi's rational approach and your love of him, it will be possible. You must never fight each

348

other, but stand united to help him. Save him from carrying on the Bucardi—"

"Curse?" Calista asked. "I don't know if love is an antidote against that. But I'll certainly try. And I agreed with Victoria that I won't bring in snakes or other terrible pets."

She smiled a moment, then added earnestly, "I keep thinking about those moments when Pietro put us to the choice. He suggested that after either one of us had killed the other, life could actually go on. Perhaps, in his mind, it was possible? He had no conscience."

"No," Atalanta said quietly. "He knew very well that it couldn't. That the survivor would know too much and would always be a risk to him. He only wanted to put you to an impossible choice and see who was hurt enough to act on the pain he inflicted. That was what fed him: seeing pain in others, making them suffer. But neither of you did what he wanted. You were stronger than all of his madness and hatred."

Atalanta put her hand on Calista's hand and continued urgently, "On that outcrop I saw that you have the inner strength to turn your life around. Don't worry about the past. Forget that you made mistakes and don't feed your self-pity when you're down. Look ahead. Take care of your son together with Mrs Bucardi. She's a strong woman who does care for Luca, even if she shows it in different ways."

"I know. We finally sat down and discussed everything. I never knew how much the guilt and shame about my betrayal was eating at me. Propelling me to do reckless things, just to feel I was alive. But that's different now. Everything is out in the open and we know that we can rely on each other. We've already decided Victoria will take care of his upbringing, supported by her family. I'll travel and drop by and spoil him, and she must always tell him it's time for bed and not to talk with his mouth full … I get the better end of things." She turned her hand over and squeezed Atalanta's. "Thank you for your help. I never wanted Pietro to die like he did, but … it's a relief to know he won't be coming back somehow. That it's truly over."

"It is." Atalanta nodded. "I wish you and Mrs Bucardi well. I'll miss Luca."

"We'll send you the occasional letter to let you know how we are doing. After all, we have a mutual acquaintance. Raoul Lemont." Calista's eyes twinkled. "Raoul told me that you suspected Luca was his son. It was merely a lie to Victoria at the time, but apparently, you had your own reasons to think it was the truth?"

Atalanta felt her cheeks flush. "In the interest of the investigation, I had to establish…" she faltered.

Calista said, "I could never get Raoul to see more in me than a friend. I think Victoria had the same experience, even before she was married. It drove me mad that he was apparently close to you, and I even had you two followed."

"So the man in black clothes watching us during the festival was…"

"I gave him money to keep an eye on the two of you. I feel rather ashamed of it now, but at the time I even told myself it was also for your safety because I wasn't sure what Bucardi would do." Calista shrugged, with a flush on her cheeks. "I guess I misunderstood your relationship because I myself could never quite get a grip on Raoul's feelings. He's … a difficult man to understand. There's much more to him than the careless race-car-driver persona he shows to the world."

Because of his childhood. I saw a little of that here. I can now understand at least some of his behaviour.

Calista continued, earnestly, "I have the impression he might let his guard down with you sometimes, Mademoiselle Ashford. You must treasure that. It's not his way."

Atalanta didn't know quite what to say in response but Calista didn't seem to expect a reply. She continued thoughtfully, "When I stood opposite you in that church in Murano, I wondered if you were special enough to accomplish anything here. I knew that your grandfather was resourceful because he had saved me from an embarrassing situation many years ago. But he was a man of the world and you seemed to be a woman with little experience of navigating difficult situations. I even felt a bit guilty about what I was exposing you to. But I see now I was wrong. You *are* special. You have a talent for being in the right place at the right time. Thank you for all you did."

"No thanks are necessary. I wish you the very best." Atalanta smiled warmly at her and then left the room. She hoped that life could start over for Mrs Bucardi and Calista and that they could rebuild their friendship of old, before the devious Pietro Bucardi had come between them. Together they could be strong enough to steer Luca in the right direction.

Mrs Bucardi came towards her, carrying the little boy. He wriggled to be released and told Atalanta with a pout, "They caught my snake. They lured it with prey and took it away in a cage. It can't live here, they say." His expression brightened when he added, "Perhaps they're taking it to the zoo? I want to visit a zoo soon."

Mrs Bucardi promised him that they would do just that. "You go and see Calista. But don't jump on the bed. She's still weak."

When Luca had vanished, Mrs Bucardi said, "Snake or no snake, I don't feel comfortable here at the *castello*. I'm leaving as soon as Calista is able to. I asked Delilah to come with us, but she won't travel. She wants to stay here. I don't know what she sees in the place."

"She's a Venetian," Atalanta echoed the woman's own words. "And they like to be in places they conquered. It may be better to … put some distance between you and her. She was very close to her nephew and might blame you for his death."

"Is that a warning?" Mrs Bucardi asked with a hitched brow.

"Some friendly advice. When she went to see your husband in the cell, he told her that Luca is his."

Mrs Bucardi stared at her, blinking hard as if trying to process the meaning of these simple words. "If he told her that, there's no…" Suddenly, understanding dawned on her face. "She knows about the violent streak running in the family. She hoped that Luca would not…"

Atalanta nodded. "To hear he is a Bucardi anyway came as a shock to her. I think you had better avoid her company." Not to mention that Delilah herself had a manipulative streak and would always cause dissension.

Mrs Bucardi nodded. "I understand. I don't mind not seeing her again. I'll even stop calling myself Bucardi and resume my maiden name. People will be surprised at first, because they'll merely take me for a bereft widow, but … let them be. Even though there will be no trial and publicity, I want to remove any connection."

"That's understandable. Good luck and goodbye."

Atalanta returned to the terrace where Raoul was still

sitting on a deck chair overlooking the sea and the quiet village below. With the sun setting, even the ever-present gulls became quieter, circling away to find their roosts for the night.

Raoul looked up at her and asked, "And?"

She said slowly, "Calista shared her plans for the future with me. Mrs Bucardi will provide Luca with a stable home in Venice, close to her family, and Calista will come and visit. She laughed when she said that she was getting the better end of the deal, but I could sense her mixed feelings. They're both concerned about Luca, how he'll grow up, being the son of a man who solved everything by violence, even murder. No matter how hard they try to feel positive about the future, that fact won't change."

Raoul gestured around him. "The entire island is a giant volcano. People have been living on top of this volcano for centuries. It can erupt and wipe away their homes, their livelihoods, their entire existence. But it can also stay dormant for decades. Centuries, even. They don't waste their days worrying about an eruption that may never come."

Atalanta let those words sink in. The people she had seen here – the old woman kneading dough, the friendly seller of the almond cakes, the village elders playing *tavli* – they didn't live in fear, but enjoyed every single moment.

Peace spread inside her and she soaked up the view and the company of the man who had proven himself a loyal ally once more. A hard man to understand perhaps, but someone she could rely on when she had to. Apparently, if she could believe Calista, they shared a special bond.

Right now, as she stood here, with the last warmth of the Mediterranean sun on her face, she wanted to believe that, with all her heart.

Acknowledgments

As always, I'm grateful to all agents, editors and authors who share online about the writing and publishing process. Special thanks to my fabulous editor Charlotte Ledger, whose insightful feedback always inspires me; to the entire One More Chapter team for their work on the series; and to Lucy Bennett and Gary Redford for the gorgeous cover illustration which captures the island's atmosphere brilliantly.

When I proposed the Miss Ashford Investigates series to my editor, I envisioned taking Atalanta to Athens on an exciting adventure amongst the temple ruins. But Charlotte suggested Santorini as a setting, and when I started brainstorming a plot that would be firmly connected with the location, I realized that so many elements of island history lend themselves perfectly to a mystery: the grand Venetian *castelli* that were still standing in the 1930s (they were mostly destroyed by earthquakes later); the summer festivals celebrating saints; superstitions connected with the sea, and much more. I fictionalized it, of course, but still I hope it gave you, the reader, an escapist experience exploring the island alongside Atalanta and being enchanted by its many authentic elements and wonderful cuisine (although I'd pass on the octopus!).

As with the previous instalment, I couldn't resist working little nods to Sherlock Holmes into this story, and if you're familiar with the great detective's adventures, you will certainly have spotted them. My greatest indebtedness as a writer is to Agatha Christie, the queen of crime, whose books fed my youthful dreams of being published to take readers on adventures of my own. As I fondly recall long summer afternoons sleuthing on the Nile with Poirot, I hope that likewise you enjoyed this armchair travel adventure, and will check out other instalments in the series that will have Atalanta visiting gorgeous locations where baffling mysteries await her. Happy reading!

ONE MORE CHAPTER

YOUR NUMBER ONE STOP

FOR PAGETURNING BOOKS

One More Chapter is an
award-winning global
division of HarperCollins.

Sign up to our newsletter to get our
latest eBook deals and stay up to date
with our weekly Book Club!
<u>Subscribe here.</u>

Meet the team at
<u>www.onemorechapter.com</u>

Follow us!

 <u>@OneMoreChapter_</u>

 <u>@OneMoreChapter</u>

 <u>@onemorechapterhc</u>

Do you write unputdownable fiction?
We love to hear from new voices.
Find out how to submit your novel at
<u>www.onemorechapter.com/submissions</u>